A Christmas Carol

The 21st Century Tale

Jacqueline Maylor

Copyright © Jacqueline Maylor, 2020
Published: 2020 by
The Book Reality Experience
Western Australia

*

ISBN: 978-0-6489496-3-3 - Paperback Edition
ISBN: 978-0-6489496-4-0 - E-Book Edition
*

Typeset in 11.5pt Garamond

Cover Design by Luke Buxton | www.lukebuxton.com

For Charles Dickens
Who wrote such a wonderful book it changed
and guided the thinking of generations for over a
hundred and fifty years.

And for my daughters Rosie and Kat
Who turned my black and white world
into one of many colours.

Are we just responsible for our own place in the world, or do we have a wider obligation, not only to our friends and neighbours, but to strangers, near and far, and even people in other countries we'll never know?

Our "civilisation" is presently established on a consumable, expendable economy, which leaves devastation behind and avoids the responsibility for renewal.

Instead, we need to nurture an economy that drives only positive expansion, especially in developing countries.

Don't we all have the ethical responsibility to stop, change our ways, and instead invest in culture, community, and sustainability, whatever the cost?

And isn't it time to stop talking around these issues and make these changes now, before it becomes too late to fix the damage we've done?

Your answer will shape the future of the world
your grandchildren will live in..

An Introduction

I was once told by my mother that when she was a child, there was no such thing as daytime TV.

Honestly, no daytime TV!

No breakfast television, no morning shows, no midday movies, no soap operas, no afternoon comedies, in fact, no schedule of daily broadcasting at all.

What was shown was a hodgepodge of shows that were broken up by the "test-pattern" which featured a little girl sitting next to a weird manic-looking clown doll, playing noughts and crosses on a blackboard. The girl, not the clown.

While there were some programs shown during the day, in what can only be referred to as the audio-visual dark ages, the TV came on and went off with no regard for dead airtime.

In the morning there were some brief children's shows, all of which was done with puppets; including pigs, talking flowerpots (what's that about?), and a puppet who lived in a picnic basket and couldn't talk.

This was followed by Sesame Street when it eventually hit our shores and the educational sanity of Play School. Never knock Play School because without them I would have never learned how rubber gloves were made.

Following that there may have been something informative and patronising for the *little woman*, a cooking show perhaps (not that much changes), and at three-ish in the afternoon they showed some slightly more informative children's shows, mostly science-based, and what I can only describe as a sort of current affairs/craft show for kids. It touched on everything; from taking care of pets, to demonstrating how to make dolls furniture from yogurt containers, even showing one poor bloke trying to stop an elephant sniffing his crotch on live TV. After this, there were more cartoons that entertained young minds with cut out animations and double entendres.

Lastly, before the six o'clock news, there was a fifteen-minute puppet cartoon which featured a hyperactive sugar-addicted dog, an exuberant vegan snail, a highly sprung magician with a handlebar moustache and a mattress fixation, a sweet little girl with appalling dress sense, and a stoner rabbit.

But between all this was the little girl and her clown leering out at you. Quite freaky really.

Now I have enough difficulties trying to imagine today's media leaving such huge gaps of TV advertising time empty, not to mention all those poor infomercial actors out of work, but then my mother stunned me by saying the highlight of every child's day was a story broadcast on radio.

When I quipped, "the radio?, Really!" She put me in my place saying, "Yes darling, that talky, music-y thing with no pictures that you listen to in your car."

My mother can be very sarcastic sometimes.

Apparently, in the old days of black and white TV, they used to listen to it in the house as well! The radio that is, not her sarcasm.

This story time was apparently when mother and child supposedly settled down to share some quiet moments together, (as opposed to today when mums can't wait until Play School comes on the TV so they can plop the kids in front of the telly while they have a quiet cup of coffee, brush their hair and look out of the window to check what season it is.)

At 1.45pm every day, *Listen with Mother* presented 15 minutes of suitable children's entertainment for mother and child to enjoy, full of stories, nursery rhymes and songs from Mother Goose, Brothers Grimm, or Hans Christian Anderson fairy tales.

It was popular for kindergartens too and, according to my sources, the threat of missing *Listen with Mother* could quell even the most rambunctious child.

How times have changed.

When my kids were in kindergarten even the threat of thumbscrews couldn't shut some of the little… darlings up.

Every day *Listen with Mother* began the same way. Just as the Star Wars™ movies begin with their trademark "A long time ago in a galaxy far far away"

Listen with Mother would always begin with the words "Are you sitting comfortably? Well, I'll begin."

With those seven magical words, children everywhere would be coaxed into silence to listen to the wonderful stories, songs, or rhymes.

Later, as TV grew up, *Watch with Mother* became the new medium. Now mums could sit in front of the television, sharing the experience with their child, and the never-ending debate about "too much television" was born.

Anyway…It seems fitting somehow, that I borrow those fairy-tale words, which belong to a generation of adults who've endeavoured to explain to their children and grandchildren what it's like to grow up in a world without 24-hour TV.

So now, I will start my story which is one of Mystery, Spirits, Love, Christmas, Joy and Redemption.

Oh, by the way, I'll be dropping in here and there as our story unfolds as a sort of aide-memoire. You can identify me by my wit, savoir-faire and the bold font I'm using now.

Are you sitting comfortably?
Well, I'll begin…

Part One

Chapter 1: Marley's Death

Seven Years Ago

Okay, it's important you know right from the start that Jacob Marley is dead.

If anyone tells you otherwise, don't listen to them.

He's definitely dead.

Kicked the bucket. Dropped off his perch. Cashed in his chips...

Indubitably dead.

Not the most cheerful way of starting a story. Nevertheless, you need to remember it because it's important. Without knowing that piece of information nothing in the story I'm about to tell is going to make any sense, or sound as wonderful as it really is.

Why we choose different methods to disclose somebody's passing I'm not sure. Certainly very few people would just turn up and blurt out the news of someone's death.

Instead, because we are considerate, we try to explain it in terms that are more suitable for those who need to believe it. However, can the way we choose to describe it make the reality better or worse?

Take, for example, describing someone as being, "as dead as a Dodo." Does that make the death more or less confronting? I only mention this as we can never know for certain how dead a Dodo can be. We are told that the Dodo is extinct; but can we be sure of that? Just because no one has seen one since 1662, it doesn't mean they're not out there, somewhere, hiding from human civilization, cannily protecting the last small pocket of birds that are still alive. Therefore, would describing someone as being "as dead as a Dodo" imply that some hope may still be present, thus offering a little comfort to the bereaved?

Conversely, the same expression, "as dead as a Dodo" could be used to categorically confirm that life is 100% extinct. Those individuals who insist there may be a small colony of Dodos somewhere beyond our reach are blatantly grasping at straws in ridiculous anticipation, as all scientific and extinctuary data tells us otherwise. Accordingly, using "as dead as a Dodo" would still be the correct terminology when describing someone who is most definitely deceased, with no believable chance of post-mortem revival. And, given the nature of a deceased individual, saying they're "as dead as a Dodo" could, in certain circumstances, be very reassuring.

All that said, however, I have never seen a Dodo, so I have no idea how they behaved, alive or dead. Therefore, the difference between the two states could either be very animated or so negligible that one doesn't know if it's still living until you poke it with a stick.

Anyway, this is where we begin. With Marley. Who is still dead.

His death was first witnessed by his housekeeper, Mrs Edna Green, a widow, age 62 from Hackney. Mrs Green lived in for both their convenience, but by mutual understanding she and Marley ignored each other as much as possible, mostly communicating by handwritten notes. Regretfully however, Mr Marley had unexpectedly taken to his bed in recent weeks, and Mrs Green had been forced by necessity to speak to him more often than she preferred.

On this particular night, Christmas Eve, she'd tried several times to wake her employer, and having no success, finally steeled herself to reach out and give him a bit of a shove. Finding him cold to the touch, she shrieked in horror and ran down the hall, and into the sitting room where the telephone was.

Knowing that time was of the essence and it was imperative she call Mr Marley's doctor and an ambulance immediately, she rushed straight to the locked drinks cabinet, where she clicked the lock with a hairpin and helped herself to an exceptionally large brandy.

Two more glasses followed in rapid succession until she was calm enough to make the necessary telephone calls that set our story in motion.

Doctor Bryant was the first person she called and the second person who witnessed Marley's death. He hauled himself up several quite punishing flights of stairs to Marley's apartment, and, after catching his breath and accepting a glass of water, examined the patient, opining that Marley, based on his rigidity, his coldness to the touch and his staring, unresponsive eyes, was in all probability, dead. You may ask if Dr Bryant checked for a heart-beat, to which the answer would be, yes...but as the doctor had experienced before, being unable to find a glimmer of a beat within Marley's chest, or a pulse on his wrist was no guarantee of anything. It could have been, as it had in the past, a simple effect of the patient's physical encumbrances.

Dr Bryant, although secure in his diagnosis, said categorically he wasn't putting his signature to anything in connection to Jacob Marley, so he telephoned Marley's cardiac specialist for a second opinion.

Mr Chakrabarti, a bariatric heart surgeon who had his rooms in Harley Street, was unused to making late-night house calls in the dead of winter but arrived at the front door within forty-five minutes of Dr Bryant's' summons; cold, cranky, and breathless. Thereby followed several minutes of conversation about his difficulty in finding a parking space, then he too examined the patient, concurring that Marley was indeed, dead.

A brief discussion between the two medical men concluded that Marley's death was caused by a sudden cardiac arrest and Mr Chakrabarti said he would be more than happy for Dr Bryant to issue the death certificate. Dr Bryant thanked his colleague but said he would be even happier if Mr Chakrabarti would take care of that last piece of medical bureaucracy as he preferred not to get involved in anything to do with Jacob Marley if he could possibly avoid it. This struck the specialist as quite strange and he questioned Bryant on his standpoint. The doctor replied succinctly that he'd known the deceased far too long and wouldn't put it past him to rise from his deathbed and sue him for malpractice the moment the death certificate was signed.

The second person Mrs Green telephoned was the undertaker and he arrived just as she was making a pot of strong coffee. While it may seem precipitous for him to be present at the apartment less than two hours after her shocking discovery, the housekeeper had called to ask how soon Marley could be removed from his residence as she was adamant she wasn't going to spend one night under the same roof as her dearly departed utterly dead employer.

If for one moment that was likely, she said, she was going to pack an overnight bag and go to her sister's, because although they hadn't spoken to each other for ten years, she preferred to go there, rather than staying in a house where she knew she'd never get a wink of sleep.

Much to her relief, the undertaker assured her that once certain formalities had been completed by the doctors, they would remove Marley as soon as possible. Mrs Green, sitting in the kitchen amid floods of tears, sobbed with dramatic relief into her handkerchief and patted the funeral director's hand, saying how kind and understanding he was whilst she gulped cup after cup of coffee, liberally laced with her employers' finest brandy.

The last man to arrive, and the most important to our story, had been unwillingly summoned by the housekeeper after she'd phoned for the doctor and undertaker. I say unwillingly because she didn't like his company, nor he hers, but he was her employer's business partner and she had strict instructions to contact him should Mr Marley's condition take a turn for the worse. As his death was most definitely applicable under those parameters , she had, reluctantly, called.

Ebenezer Scrooge was his name, and he was the one person in the world who knew Marley's nature well enough to witness his life was most definitely expired, rather than him being immersed in some deep state of catalepsy. Marley and Scrooge had been business partners for decades, working together in the same establishment, two like-minded individuals with the same ideas; making money and then holding on to it. Even so, Scrooge's main emotion wasn't sadness at the passing of his old partner, but relief that Marley, having always been an excellent businessman, had thoughtfully arranged for his exit to land late on Christmas Eve, which meant Scrooge wasn't forced to shut the office during working hours to come and observe this last goodbye. In fact, once he'd arrived at his partner's bedside that cold winter's night, it was all he could do to stop himself from giving everyone a high five in gleeful appreciation of Marley's timing.

Scrooge had in fact previously visited his partner's bedside earlier that afternoon, to offer Jacob a few token words of solace and pretence about his recovery. He had stayed for a quarter of an hour trying to think of what was proper in the circumstances, but finally ran out of words and moved to extricate himself as neatly and quickly as possible from the dying man's presence. As he made for the door Marley instead beckoned for him to come towards the bed and Scrooge, thinking to clasp his hand in brotherhood then leave, approached. To his shock, his old friend grabbed hold of his shirtfront and pulled him down so his ear was close to Marley's mouth. He was trying to tell Scrooge something, but his voice was so weak Scrooge couldn't make out what he was saying. On top of that, he was extremely

4

uncomfortable bent over Marley's bed, discomfort caused by his proximity to the dying man's terrible breath, and his awful body odour. Standing up abruptly he said, "Well now Jacob, lots of rest, that's all you need. You'll be back on your toes in no time," and with a final nod, he took his leave.

It wasn't until later when he was sitting on the tube heading home, that Scrooge worked out what his partner had been mumbling. Straining to speak, he'd whispered, "ghosts Ebenezer, see... see... There! Behind you... ghosts..."

Scrooge, having no idea what he'd meant, dismissed it as the ravings of a deluded man. "Rubbish and nonsense," he huffed to himself. "Rubbish and nonsense."

Four hours after he arrived home, Scrooge was summoned back to the apartment by the housekeeper. Marley was dead.

***

Scrooge was the sole mourner for his late partner; a role he performed in the theoretical, not in the actual. Oh, he accepted what few condolences were offered, wore black and looked suitably mournful, but he didn't care a jot.

In fact, when Scrooge looked upon Marley's face for the last time, before watching the undertaker close and screw down the lid of the coffin, Jacob's body and its disposal ceased to be his concern and he quickly dismissed any further thoughts of it from his mind. From then on, his contemplations switched from Marley's body to the more interesting details of Marley's estate.

Scrooge was Marley's executor, his main beneficiary and sole residuary legatee, which meant, in plain English, if there was anything left after the will was distributed, he copped to that as well. Bunce on top of bunce as it were. After settling death duties which, much to his irritation he couldn't avoid paying, and dispensing the £100 gift Marley left to Bob Cratchit in appreciation for his 15 years of loyal service, Scrooge rubbed his hands together with glee as he savoured his legacy.

He'd inherited the other half of the business and all of Marley's money, a delightful endowment of some forty-two million pounds, amassed by his deceased partner over the last thirty years because Marley, like Scrooge, avoided spending anything all his life.

Well, nearly.

5

Marley did spend generously on one thing whilst he was living, and on that, he never ceased to indulge himself.

Jacob Marley had been a glutton of the first order.

While most of us eat to live, Jacob Marley was one of those men who lived to eat and he regularly filled his stomach at some of the most expensive restaurants in the country: From John o' Groats to Lands' End, wherever his business took him, he would find the most celebrated restaurants and stuff himself with as many local delicacies and gastronomic delights as he could.

In private dining rooms, he would always begin with the same aperitif of one or two glasses of single malt whisky, produced by the best distilleries in the land, to sharpen his immense appetite. Entrees were followed by several large, rich courses of the finest food, cooked by Michelin starred chefs. Every course was accompanied by bottles of international award-winning wines, specifically chosen by the sommelier to complement the dining experience.

To round out each meal there was a myriad of pâtissier crafted desserts, all served with sticky wines for maximum flavour, and to finish, Marley would indulge in coffee made from luxury beans imported from around the world. Beans so expensive, a single cup would cost more than a day's wage paid to the waiters who'd served his gargantuan meal.

With a snap of his fingers he would command the finest French cognac to go with luxurious hand-rolled cigars and he would disappear behind a cloud of expensive smoke. By the time he was presented with the bill, he could hardly get up from his chair. And if those who had cooked and served him his colossal meal were expecting an equally large tip, they were sadly disappointed. It was here that his extravagance ended for Jacob Marley had never left anyone more than a 10p tip in his entire life.

The result of this indulgence was not unexpected. Following the onset of chest pains, Marley had been referred by Dr Bryant to a Harley Street Specialist. A double diagnosis of congestive heart failure and coronary artery disease was the verdict and Mr Chakrabarti advised that an immediate change in diet, increased exercise and quitting smoking were the only ways Marley could avoid an early grave. However, claiming abstinence from his way of life was itself a death sentence, Marley ignored Mr Chakrabarti's orders and continued to stuff and smoke himself into the aforementioned early grave. By the time he died, aged fifty-four, Marley tipped the scales at four hundred pounds and was as fat as a hippo.

If it hadn't been unethical, one could have proposed that, due to the incredible amount of weight on his four-foot ten-inch frame, which had consequently changed his body into a near-perfect round shape, it would have been easier for the undertaker to bounce him down the stairs like a beach ball, in order to get him out to the hearse.

Failing that, another case could have been made to position the body at the top of the staircase, give it a good shove, and let gravity take over from there. However, as neither were within the funeral director's code of ethics, he instead had to plan the removal of Marley's mortal remains with all the strategy of a prison break. Eight men, with several pieces of equipment, winched Marley from his oversized bed, and onto a heavy-duty trolley. Several other assistants busied themselves with shifting furniture and unscrewing interior doors to make his egress easier, but it still took over an hour to finagle him through these tight spaces and out of his front door.

The second stage was to manoeuvre him into the service lift, where he would make the short drop to the basement. Once he and two minders were squashed inside, the elevator groaned its way down, until they landed again on terra-firma in the underground parking area, where the apartment bins were kept, tenants parked and where the undertaker had backed in the hearse, ready to receive the body.

In this third and penultimate stage, the men carefully manoeuvred Marley out of the lift, rolled the trolley to the special high-top hearse with reinforced chassis and, with one last effort, shoved him into the back, shutting the door with relief.

Finally, upon his arrival at the other end, several new personnel saw to his removal from the hearse and his transfer to the funeral home's preparation facilities. This second crew assuming management at this point because those who had shouldered the burden so far were, by now, completely knackered.

It's interesting to note that the difficulties that arose from Marley lying flat, would have mostly disappeared had they strapped him upright to a two-wheel trolley and rolled him out that way, much like one does when moving a wardrobe or fridge. However, like the previously mooted beach ball idea, this too was dismissed as folly and not just because they would have to deal with some of the same difficulties posed by excess fat. No moving Marley this way would be a disaster waiting to happen because, in the standing position, any unforeseen interference to his smooth passage could have resulted in an unfortunate shift in gravity, causing him to fall forward and splat face-first on the ground. Besides, there was the perennial dramatis personae of Hannibal Lecter, complete with face mask and immortal line, "*I ate his liver with some fava beans and a nice Chianti*" none of which, the undertaker said, would have preserved the dignity of the occasion.

It was only by good luck, and certainly not by good management, that at the time of Marley's death, there was on hand an extra-large coffin perfect for his mortal remains, even if it was a tight fit. Had one not been available, Marley would have made a short detour to spend a few days in the morgue of the local hospital, it having enough space in their freezer to hold his considerable bulk, while the funeral director hit the phones to see if anyone else in the business had a suitable casket available, or if not, to place an order.

However, one was in stock and the undertaker and his assistant obstinately pulled, pushed, wiggled, tucked, and stuffed for over forty minutes until they finally managed to wedge Marley inside and close the lid. One or two discrete screws were placed here and there to ensure the coffin held together and, as Scrooge watched, at last Marley was ready for his final journey.

Meanwhile, the previous buyer of the casket, who'd had the good sense to prearrange his funeral, was happy to sell it on at a discounted price, as he'd had the good fortune to make an excellent recovery and was now on a strict diet.

Scrooge, to get back to his inheritance, also now owned, free and clear, the entire building that housed the office, plus all the business assets therein. He received Marley's apartment, including his furniture, personal items, and clothing. Not that the clothes were of any benefit to Scrooge, who was tall and thin, while Marley, as you already know, was short and very fat. Side by side, they reminded one of Laurel and Hardy, without the comedy and bowler hats (If you don't know who Laurel and Hardy were, ask your parents. If your parents are under forty, ask your grandparents instead.)

In the end, it took less than four months for the estate to be settled because there was no one else to leave it to but Ebenezer Scrooge. No family or friends to dispute his will. No one else was even remotely interested.

Mentioning Marley's will reminds me again of my opening statement. Jacob Marley was dead.

Consider the plays of Shakespeare. The personification of English literature who wrote such long, long, long plays we all studied at school. If, for example, we didn't know at the start that Hamlet's father was dead, then Hamlet taking a moonlight stroll around the castle walls and meeting his Dad would be of no mind to us and the play would end. Short, sweet and everyone back to the pub before closing. Our interest is only piqued because, as we all know from the beginning of the play, his father has, to quote his son a few pages further in, shuffled off his mortal coil, and we want to see what happens after the Spirit informs Hamlet of his murder. The fact that it takes over four hours to get to the point is testimony to Shakespeare's brilliance as a writer and the audience's ability to sit still and stay awake that long.

Thus, it is with my story. You know now, from the start, that Marley is dead. Now you must stay a while and see why that's so important, and what adventures lie in the pages ahead.

Chapter 2: Ebenezer Scrooge

Present Day

I once knew of a man who had black coffee and half a grapefruit for his breakfast every morning of his adult life. That's not strange, monotonous, but not strange, and I still can't help thinking bacon and eggs or a nice English muffin would have made a welcome change. However, he never changed his breakfast in over twenty years and developed the curious habit of using the same little square piece of cling wrap to preserve the uneaten half until the following day.

He would cut his grapefruit, then place his small square of cling wrap over the uneaten segment and pop that into the fridge for tomorrow's breakfast. The following day he would remove it and stick the piece of wrap to his fridge door until it was needed again. How he never got Ptomaine poisoning I'll never know, except perhaps he was too mean to pay for a doctor, but I once calculated he kept a single square of cling film going for seven weeks and six days before it was finally so tatty and tangled he had to, begrudgingly, throw it away. By the time he had used up the whole 120-meter roll and needed to buy another, the packaging design had completely changed and the price and gone up by 26%.

One of the greatest joys of his life came with the production of those elasticised plastic bowl cover things that resemble shower caps. As these came in several sizes he found one that was a perfect fit for grapefruit, and thereafter the cling wrap was forever banished to the bottom drawer of his kitchen units, while the plastic cap was used every day, for years, until it too, finally fell apart.

Ebenezer Scrooge admired thrifty practices. He was a collector of them. Some people collect stamps, some recipes, but Scrooge collected all ways, from the practical to the downright ridiculous, of saving money. Thrift was his watchword or at least one of them, but thrift is not an adequate word that describes Scrooge or his attitude to money, for thrift implies savings rather than the greed and avarice that made up his existence. To explain him better, one must employ the thesaurus, to describe his nature and outlook:

CUPIDITY-Greed for money or possessions

MISERLINESS-Excessive desire to save money, extreme meanness.

PARSIMONY-An extreme unwillingness to spend one's money or use one's resources

Nonetheless, it should be remembered that Scrooge had no problems using other people's money or resources, just not his own, which he protected as well as Cerberus guarded the gates of the underworld and with as much subtlety.

Oh, he was a merciless, stingy, horrible tightwad Ebenezer Scrooge! He had the shortest arms and deepest pockets of anyone ever known. He lived and breathed greed. He squeezed the last penny out of his customers, wrenched the last drop of work from his clerk, coveted the riches and possessions of others, grasped at any and all money that came his way! He rationed rubber bands, stockpiled staples, saved safety pins, collected paper clips, and watered down witeout. He offered no refreshments to his clients, no waiting area for them to sit comfortably, not even a miserly water fountain for refreshment. He never paid a bonus, a commission, or a compliment to anyone.

He employed every penny-pinching idea he could think of, from saving soap scraps that he pressed into a new bar, to how many times he flushed his loo per day.

Scrooge employed a little ditty by which he governed the frequency of his flushes.

"If it's yellow, it's okay - if it's brown, flush it away."

I know disgusting right? You didn't want to eat that anyway, did you?

Each one of his little niggling habits contributed to saving pennies, to his never-ending financial satisfaction.

In addition to his delightful character was his monumental rudeness. The one thing he wasn't, was politically correct. He referred to clients in objectionable, disrespectful ways behind their backs, while straining to remain, at best, agreeable in their company. His best behaviour he saved for new customers. At these times he could be polite, feign interest, make small talk and chit chat like a normal person. However, once a client was committed to business with Ebenezer Scrooge, all this went out of the window and he became downright rude. Once he had them on the hook, nothing else mattered. The way he spoke to whomsoever he spoke with, was irrelevant. It had absolutely no effect on the outcome of any business transaction. Good manners, according to Scrooge, had no cash value.

He could not claim to have any friends. Under the dictionary definition that friends were "a person whom one knows and with whom one has a bond of mutual affection" those who he would deem as a friend each fell far short of this characterisation. His satellite of acquaintances included all of those who thought as he did: money first, profit second, business third, reputation fourth and customer welfare a very unimportant fifth. Creatures he would naturally gravitate to at a free conference or seminar would be telling stories to each other, not about accomplishments, but about the insignificant and unfortunate clients who'd fallen foul of their heartlessness and suffered the consequences.

Scrooge had no associates, no colleagues and, since the death of Marley, no partners. He was as isolated as an oyster and sovereign of his own domain. No acquaintance ever called to invite him to lunch. No business affiliate asked him to have dinner at the club. No one invited him for drinks to unwind at the end of a stressful day. Any business luncheons he attended were exceedingly rare, limited only to those that were free, with an open bar. Anyone else who shared a meal with Scrooge usually did so at their invitation, probably because they needed his help and they always, without exception, paid the bill.

No lady love ever asked him to escort her to a play, or a party, a movie, or a wedding. Indeed, no lover ever asked him anywhere because he didn't have one. That emotion that fires up within us all and speaks to others, which starts friendships, romances, or lifelong companionships, that little spark of feeling had long ago been washed away by the waves of coldness that flowed from Scrooge like arctic waters, always keeping the rest of humanity at bay.

Any associate who saw him in the street would prefer to duck into a side alley or nip into a shop, rather than stop to make idle chit chat with him.

No happy tourists ever asked him to take a picture for them.

No strangers ever asked for directions this way or that. One glance at his emaciated face, pugnacious attitude and general appearance was enough to make them say to one another, "I wonder if they might know over there," and cross the street to ask.

In fact, it was as if the entire human race had, by silent agreement, elected to dissociate themselves from Ebenezer Scrooge.

Physically Scrooge wasn't attractive. It wasn't that he was a bad looking man. He could have been called pleasant looking, distinguished even, for his age. He COULD, but sadly he never was. He was thin as a rail and constantly had a bitter, ugly expression on his face as if he had just swallowed a mouthful of sour milk. His face was never touched by the glow of a healthy sun. His eyes were continually bloodshot and watery from squinting under dim, cheap office lights. His lips were always blue from lack of heat, and thin from always being pressed together in annoyance. His voice sounded harsh, and went through you like nails on a chalkboard, setting teeth on edge and eyes twitching. And for some strange reason, probably because he thought it was impressive, which it wasn't, he had adopted certain mannerisms, as though he'd stepped out from the 19th century and into the modern age. His absurd Victorian idiosyncratic behaviours would pop up at the oddest moments, leaving those around him nonplussed and searching around for a conversational non sequitur.

His clothes were too awful to describe, but I'll try. If, as they say, "fashion maketh the man" then what fashion made of Ebenezer Scrooge was anyone's guess. To be fair, he did have one good suit, which he wore for important business meetings and "discussions" conducted in restaurants. Beyond that though, he wore an eclectic mix of trousers, shirts, jackets, and shoes bought from second-hand charity shops, not because he wanted to do his bit for the needy, but because they were cheap. Not one matched the other, some still had a faint aroma of mothballs, most were 1990s style, and all were either too large or too small. Even the redeeming quality of suggesting he dressed in vintage clothes can't be applied to Scrooge. Vintage implies style, and believe me, he didn't have any. But he didn't care. They were cheap, they did the job. Up to date smart city fashions were a waste of money. Fashion, according to Ebenezer Scrooge, had no cash value.

He never smiled a genuine smile or never laughed a fulsome laugh. He never said a generous or thoughtful word. His manner was standoffish and sulky. He abhorred kindness, compassion, sympathy or understanding, considering all to be detrimental to the workings of commerce. He was, without doubt, a mean, miserly, cantankerous, thoughtless, sinful old man.

To quote an associate of his, Scrooge always had "a miserable gob on him." But true to form, , he didn't care. He cultivated a unique profile to get the most out of every business deal he made and from every person he dealt with. Ebenezer Scrooge was a shrewd, intelligent, razor-sharp financier, who came across as a reasonable, straightforward, and ingenuous sexagenarian, but had the killer instinct, ruthlessness, and brutal disregard of a forty-year-old corporate raider.

Cash was his cause and profit were his bottom line.

Everything else was secondary and not important. Distraction from the main goal had no cash value. And the main goal was money. Making it and keeping it.

He liked the look of money, the feel of it, the smell of it, and he especially liked seeing it accumulate in his bank account.

Money was his merchandise. He put investors who had money together with people who needed it, and he seldom, if ever, risked his own cash on anything.

He called his clients either investors or investees and functioned as an intermediary between them, so neither ever met the other. Two such clients could be sitting next to each other during a business lunch or convention and have no idea one was lending money to the other. Each party courted him because both needed him. Investors never lost money with Ebenezer Scrooge. In today's flat market of low bank returns or dicey stock market investments with its peaks and troughs, an investment with Ebenezer Scrooge gave a healthy return. Money was paid on the dot, and profit was guaranteed. Everyone was happy. Those borrowing got their loans easily not like the banks with all their snooping, collateral, and guarantors. Well, yes okay, they paid above the market rate, but that's because their loan was unsecured and clients knew the terms, some would say harsh terms, before signing on the dotted line. Still, as Scrooge would say, pulling his thin rubbery lips into his version of a smile, banks too laid down some tough terms these days, even with all their checks and business plans and forward estimates.

As for the terms at Scrooge and Marley's, they were simple. A first missed payment meant a twenty per cent levy was added to the total value of the loan. Miss a second and credit was cut off. Clients could never do business with Scrooge and Marley's again. A significant blow for those who needed money and traded outside the bank's lending algorithm.

Miss the third and Scrooge moved in to foreclose on the client and seize all their assets. No argument, no second chances. If they couldn't pay the whole sum back in full, Wham Bam, in came the bailiffs. Illness, family crises, natural disasters, a downturn in sales were no excuse. It was useless appealing to his better nature because he didn't have one. That human trait was an anathema to Scrooge and not good business practice. No one ever got rich being kind. Sympathy had no cash value.

While the term of the loans may sound a bit excessive, Scrooge considered his conditions justified. He still hadn't recovered from that one occasion in thirty-five years of trading when a client, and the money he'd borrowed, disappeared without a trace. Although it was many years ago, Scrooge still felt a sharp sting in his wallet when he remembered having to cover all the losses on the investment, interest included, rather than risk the loss of any future business by admitting a client had done a runner. The direct result of that one and only instance was the hastily added clause to the contract of investors saying Scrooge and Marley's Financial Services would not be held liable for any losses incurred by the investee. In other words, if they don't pay up, don't come crying to us.

Like a mother watching over her precious child, celebrating each milestone of its development, Scrooge watched his bank account grow. From fifty to a hundred thousand to a million and beyond. He knew that money was his, earned by the sweat of someone else's brow, through some tough economic times.

His thoughts and ideas went beyond normal satisfaction after each business transaction. Undoubtedly, he was well pleased with his accomplishments, but his vainglorious attitude to every success justified to him not only the tough terms of doing business with Ebenezer Scrooge but also the appalling way he treated everyone at the same time. In fact, so bad was his reputation for greedy money-grubbing habits, it was a common joke amongst the business community that if Ebenezer Scrooge shook your hand, you should probably count your fingers.

While he could never technically be called a loan shark, he did cruise some financially muddy waters waiting for those who needed money fast and were desperate enough to agree to his conditions. This gave him a splendid opportunity to make a profit from their desperation, and each time he did, he would be glad he lived in a society where money talked, and morality kept its mouth shut.

He didn't struggle with the guilt that would fill so many others with remorse. Neither was he the kind of man who wrestled with contrition over a proneness towards normal human vices. Nor could his many sins be dismissed merely as venial, for they were not the result of everyday human weaknesses. No, he sinned willingly and sinned often, with his meanness, his avarice, his hardness of heart in the face of human tragedy, and his willingness to turn his back on the pain and desperation of others. That he carried these mortal sins on his soul meant nothing to Scrooge. You had to believe first, and Scrooge didn't. As far as he could see, religion insisted you stick to a set of principles and a code of propriety that couldn't exist alongside modern business practices. The churches took your money and made you feel guilty for making a profit and God definitely had no cash value.

Scrooge's assistant was a man by the name of Bob Cratchit. When Scrooge had inherited all Marley's possessions, I suppose you could make an argument that he also inherited sole propriety over Bob Cratchit. Bob had, at the time of Marley's death, worked for both men for more than fifteen years, and Marley had rewarded his loyalty with a £100 legacy from his will. As Marley had been a millionaire the sum had not exactly dazzled Bob or his wife with its munificence, and, after much discussion, they had used the money to pay for a truckload of cow manure for the back garden, something Bobs wife though was both hilariously funny and an absolutely fitting way to spend the cash. She was quoted at the time as saying that as the bequest was nothing more than a pile of shit, they may as well spread it on the garden.

Bob's was the voice of moderation in Scrooge's office. His right-hand man, his investigator, his computer operator, and general secretary. He worked long hours for no appreciation, little encouragement and certainly no recognition. "Never praise your staff," was Marley's dictum, "if you do, they'll think they're too important and ask for more money."

Bob knew everything about the business, everything about each client, about each transaction they had with the company, the balance owing on

16

every transaction, even the details of their credit score. He could answer any question Scrooge had faster than a computer. Lots of people said Bob should move on, work somewhere else rather than put up with his employer. However, Bob stuck to his job and he stuck to Scrooge. He'd long ago secured an automatic 7.9% wage rise every January 1st, and as he was the one that put the direct transfer order through, made sure it was paid. Each January Scrooge would complain long and loudly that he had to be crazy paying Bob a wage increase almost twice the national average, but at the same time, he was smart enough to realise that if he lost Bob it would cripple his business. That didn't stop him scratching around looking for ways to wiggle out of his end of the bargain, but no matter how Scrooge looked at it, any other alternative would cost him a lot more than 7.9%. So, although it meant he spent weeks burning with suppressed impotence, Scrooge paid Bob's wage rise while gritting his teeth so hard they were in danger of cracking.

Can we talk about Bob Cratchit for a moment?

Bob is a small little man, timid, toadying and very scared of Scrooge. A wimpy individual, he has never stood up to him, lets Scrooge walk all over him and takes all manner of nonsense, insults and put-downs, simply saying, "Yes, Mr Scrooge, Sir" whenever called upon to reply, too afraid to say a word in his own defence...

Well, let's face it, that's what you expected, wasn't it?

Bob's always been talked about as an obsequious little man who, if I may say it delicately, has no balls and sucks around Scrooge like a worried little rabbit too scared to put a foot wrong.

Well, I'm here to correct that image because Bob Cratchit's nothing like that in real life. Its true Bob is a gentle man. I say gentle man rather than gentleman because he is a gentle, kind person, and he is a real man. That's not saying however, that he's an effeminate, man-bag carrying, flower arranging metrosexual. Neither does it mean he's covered with tattoos, can drink his body weight in beer and can piss further up the wall than anyone else. It does mean he's patient and calm, pleasant and friendly. He's like you and me. He gives people the benefit of the doubt and protects and cares for his family, just as we do. He helps the vulnerable, digs deep in his pocket to help anyone affected by a natural disaster, can't pass anyone shaking a charity tin without dropping in a pound or two and stands up for what he believes in. He has a similar set of values to most of us and tries to bring up his kids accordingly. He believes in a socialist democracy, votes Labour, supports the Monarchy, and believes everyone should have the same chance to succeed no matter who they are, where they were born or how much education they've received.

He's a man of faith, but not a bible bashing God-botherer. Likes football, isn't too keen on cricket, drinks Guinness or lager occasionally and dislikes spicy food. He's an animal lover but is also fond of a bacon butty or a good lamb roast. Bob is not perfect, he occasionally rows with his wife, sometimes shouts at his kids and leaves the running of the house to the Mrs whilst he watches the football on TV.

But what he isn't and never has been is a frightened little man. What he has been is quiet, industrious, respectful, dependable, and hopeful. Furthermore, we must remember, he has now worked for Scrooge for over 20 years so knows him better than anyone alive.

While he finds Scrooge tiring, irritating, and frustrating he doesn't, and never has, found him intimidating or threatening regardless of Scrooge's blustering and blathering, most of which he ignores.

Scrooge's rudeness annoys him because it's so unnecessary, and his ascetic behaviour irritates him because it sharpens Scrooges temper and erodes his humanity.

Bob indeed puts up with a lot from Scrooge, more than most, but you will find out why further on. In the end though, more than anything else, Bob's an incurable optimist. Maybe he's just waiting for the day when Scrooge sees the light...

Knowing what you now know about Ebenezer Scrooge it may surprise you to learn that he embraced modern technology in his office. Well, sort of. Having once been shown that a computer could work out the numbers faster and more accurately than a person could, and with no errors, he and Marley had taken the bull by the horns and invested in a second-hand PC. It was a pre-millennium tower with CD and 3¼ disk drives which was still running Windows98. Attached to this was a large square monitor and an ancient daisy wheel printer that was probably first used by Noah to print out an A-Z list of animals for the ark. Now it banged out contracts in a noisy, tired fashion, protesting its age and begging for a power surge to finish it off.

Its sole function was to print out documents detailing the terms of those investing monies with, and those borrowing monies from, Scrooge and Marley's Financial Services. With heroic effort it produced the contracts for each client to sign. Two variations of the same documents, one for the investor and one for the investee, were printed. Neither detailed the exact commission charged by Scrooge and Marley's Financial Services in a simple, straightforward way, but rather explained in that deliberately confusing accounting jargon that makes no sense to the average person. Such was the legalese jargon of the contract it may as well have read, "based on 0.045% of the quarterly balance, calculated on the daily repayment rate before the half-yearly balance that was taken at the height of the full moon by a pink unicorn during the spring equinox" or some equally ridiculous nonsense that no normal person understood.

However, each contract being signed and witnessed, business could begin and everyone, theoretically, was happy. Certainly, Scrooge and Marley were happy and never short of customers.

Neither had understood the actual workings of the computer, not thinking it necessary to take any kind of instruction in its operation. The completion of each contract was down to Bob, who did understand. Both Scrooge and Marley would jovially advise their clients that they needed to return to their office on the morrow to sign the contracts when "the computer had done its jiggery-pokery" and all the paperwork was printed, bound and ready to go.

The computer itself had no problems with accessing the internet because it had no modem. It sat in splendid isolation, ignorant of its kin that inhabited the information superhighway, somewhere out there, beyond the four walls. It never upgraded and was as isolated as its owners from the rest of the world, kept in the locked "computer room" like a tiger in its cage, away from the clients it served.

It was also the bane of Bob Cratchit's existence. It was always freezing halfway through printing and Bob would vent his frustration by giving it a good wallop. Furthermore, it was Bob's job to re-ink the printer ribbons by dipping them in bottled ink and then dry and iron them between two pieces of brown paper, before re-spooling them back onto the cassette, a job that left his fingers black for days as Scrooge considered rubber gloves unnecessary.

It may be argued that Bob could have bought his own gloves, as a box of one hundred was not that expensive, and while that is true, he refused to do so because if history has shown him anything, it was that buying something that Scrooge should be paying for set a very dangerous precedent. Scrooge would conveniently forget that Bob had supplied whatever it was as a courtesy, and a long, drawn-out dispute would follow with Scrooge continually bellyaching about who should pay for the next box. Bob still shuddered when he remembered the great Hobnob Dispute of 2008.

While he constantly had daydreams of new, up to date office equipment Bob also knew he had as much chance of Scrooge spending money on that as him taking a trip to the moon. But everyone must have a dream, it's what keeps us from going mad sometimes.

My personal dream is that people stop leaving their cars running for ages outside their houses at the crack of dawn...Hello! Some of us are still sleeping you know!

For other paperwork work, Scrooge had Bob use a better, more modern computer to run certain credit checks, background reports on would-be clients, research assets, uncover the financial trends of different companies, and the details of commercial properties. He also sent and received daily emails and other business correspondence, arranged business appointments, scheduled property viewings and so forth. Scrooge was not a fool. He knew he needed all the conveniences of the computer age. He just didn't see why he should pay for it. Consequently, each day at 11 am Bob would take dictation of his emails, notes to research into someone's financial or business history, any referrals for proposed financial investments, appointments to accept or refuse and any additional instructions, then leave his small outer office to walk half a mile down the road to the public library, where he had a daily booking for one of their computers. Bob didn't mind this daily ritual, it got him out from under Scrooge's eye for a couple of hours. And Scrooge didn't mind it either. The computer in the library was free.

No matter how much Bob could run certain aspects of the business online, Ebenezer Scrooge stuck to his habit of personally checking his bank balance each day. A short constitutional would bring him to the main doors of the bank, which he would throw open and enter like the conquering Claudius, who'd just left his elephant parked at a meter outside.

Unfortunately, whenever Scrooge entered the bank, it emptied of staff like cockroaches running when the lights are switched on. Tellers suddenly began making terribly important phone calls, checking customer queries, dusting backroom shelves, answering sudden calls of nature, searching under their desks for missing contact lenses or restocking the ATM receipt rolls. Those already serving clients stretched out business with friendly chats and helpful tips, before surrendering to the inevitable gloom of having to serve Mr Scrooge, who, it was generally agreed by anyone who had ever served him, had never yet returned a polite or friendly greeting.

On 14th March 2006, at the Corporate and Mutual Fidelity Bank of England, a staff member accepted a bet that he could get some kind of positive response, or even a smile from Ebenezer Scrooge, just by making conversation with him. This daring young man therefore asked him how his day had been today and gave Scrooge his best corporate grin, teeth included. In reply, Scrooge fixed him with a basilisk stare and demanded to know why the quality of his day was significant to an utterly apathetic and demonstrably vacuous stranger. The young man, not sure what vacuous meant, but certain he'd just been insulted, folded immediately under this verbal strike and accompanying death-stare, and conducted the rest of business in a sullen and offended attitude. Needless to say, he lost the bet.

Every day Scrooge would present at the counter, dressed in his mismatched ensemble, smelling of mothballs and impatience and snarl in a rude and demanding way, "A printout of my statement, now! Don't keep me waiting!" And the unlucky teller would grit their teeth into a corporate smile, trying to remember that the customer is always right.

Next Scrooge would scrutinise the document, line by line, regardless of how many others were in the queue behind him. Checking it against a book of notations he always carried with him, he would question why certain amounts had not been credited to his account.

This was the tricky part of serving Scrooge. Each day the teller would politely explain that the funds would indeed be credited to his account when they were deposited by his clients. "If monies were not yet credited Sir, perhaps your customer hasn't deposited the funds when they said they had?"

21

His reaction to this was always negative, rude, and argumentative. He scribbled notations in his book or even phoned his clients right there and then, to catch the bank out withholding monies.

It was frustrating and annoying, but not yet dangerous for the teller behind the window. The danger started to slowly bubble up when he would run his finger down the statement and compare it to his book asking the same question over and over for each client whose payment was not showing.

One query after another, as if the answer would change for each tardy client. The poor teller, now stuck like a fly in amber, was forced to answer the question repeatedly while hanging onto their corporate politeness by a thread.

"No, Mr Scrooge, Mr Williams's payment has not been credited yet, perhaps he hasn't deposited to your account when he said he did. You may need to check that with him.

"No, Mr Scrooge, Mr Allan's payment has not been credited yet, perhaps he hasn't deposited to your account when he said he did. You may need to check that with him.

"NO MR SCROOGE, MR PETERS PAYMENT HAS NOT BEEN CREDITED...!!"

By the time the teller had done this seven or eight times, they were trembling with a stress-based anxiety attack as they struggled with the overwhelming urge to shout,

"OH FOR GOODNESS SAKE! WHAT ARE YOU, DEAF? THE MONEY'S NOT IN YET. I DON'T KNOW WHY IT'S NOT IN, IT'S JUST NOT IN. GO AWAY YOU IRRITATING OLD FART BEFORE I COME AROUND THERE AND THUMP YOU."

Of course, the teller did resist this urge, because to give in would've had two instantly negative results. Firstly, it would upset the other customers, and secondly, they would be fired on the spot, even if the manager did sympathise with them.

Every day Scrooge came into the bank. Every single day...

Every day he was thoroughly unpleasant and obnoxious.

Politeness, said Scrooge, has no cash value.

All the staff hated serving Scrooge because he was rude and obtuse. While most of us have that cut off switch in our head that says, "Okay, I'd better stop now, I've gone too far" Scrooge either didn't have one or ignored it. Certainly, if the two angels of our nature were upon his shoulders, the bad one was kept terribly busy, while the good one was nowhere to be seen, probably just leaving a sign in its place that read "Gone fishing"

At the bank, there had been more than a few grumbles about Scrooge and once or twice the staff had been heard to mutter the word "strike" when talking about him. Everyone knew however they couldn't strike over an awkward customer, so they continued to hope that one day he would move to a different establishment. Nevertheless, it was true that teller service slowed right down and finally ground to a halt between three and four pm and finally, the bank manager had to step in. With staff nearly causing themselves an injury racing to answer the phone, elbowing and shoving each other in the pursuit of serving the "nice customers" and loudly arguing over who'd already done the post office run this week, it had become such a nightmare to keep tellers on the desks that he finally instigated a "Scrooge service roster" which stopped all the nonsense and allowed other customers to get served, rather than standing in a bank that resembled the deck of the Marie Celeste.

You may find it interesting to learn that a man who insisted on living and working so frugally owned a mobile phone. This was in fact the second mobile he'd owned and it had come into his possession at just the right time by way of a foreclosure of one of his clients and seizure of their business assets. Scrooge was no idiot when it came to saving a quid. When he calculated that using a mobile with a phone/text package would be cheaper than paying the rental on one landline including calls, never mind two, he had his office and home phones ripped out tout suite and the mobile moved in. Now, for the lowest phone deal he could get, he could make unlimited free calls and send unlimited free text messages. He was also entitled to 5 gigabytes of data a month, but as he never used the internet, he never exceeded his allowance. Scrooge made hundreds of calls and sent hundreds of texts for less than the cost of what he used to pay just in line rental. He also had the added advantage of being able to contact his clients from anywhere and at any time of the day or night, which was something he found especially useful if they were behind in payments. Nothing like a 3 am phone call to remind you to pay your bills.

Scrooge's mobile was not flashy, but it suited him. He didn't care that it took photos, downloaded music, TV shows or movies. All this cost money, which he dismissed as "fripperies" that chewed up time that should be spent doing business. His phone was a tool for commerce. Nothing more. How old it was, or what it looked like being irrelevant. He saw no need to update it simply because of its age.

Several years ago, when the mobile network switched from analogue to digital, Scrooge has sent long letters to everyone from parliament to British Telecom, complaining about the expense of having to purchase a new phone to replace a perfectly good one he'd had for years. No one replied, but the previously mentioned seizure of property had resolved his need for a replacement and stopped his whining.

Ebenezer Scrooge did have one redeeming quality. He abhorred smoking in any form and refused to allow it anywhere near him, his office, or his home. He had tolerated Marley's habit only because he kept to his own office, but he hated the ever-present smell of cigarillos and cigars Marley brought with him whenever he entered a room. Marley dealt with all the clients who smoked until his death, and thereafter, any clients who wanted a cigarette were informed to smoke it before the entered or after they left Scrooge's building. Any client recklessly lighting up in his presence received a heavy burst of cheap air freshener sprayed so close to their face, it made them cough, splutter, and fight for breath. It also made their eyes itchy and nose run. On top of that, they would smell like stale carnations for weeks on end because that stuff, once sprayed, clung like hell on earth to their clothes and hair no matter how many times they washed them.

This then is your brief introduction to Ebenezer Scrooge. What are we to do with such a man? A man with no warmth of spirit or joy of heart. A mean, miserable, objectionable, cantankerous old sinner.

And what DOES have cash value...?

I'll get back to you...

24

Chapter 3: Scrooge's Nephew, Fred

The sign etched on the glass front door of the business read:

Scrooge & Marley's
FINANCIAL SERVICES

Scrooge never changed it, never removed Marley's name. This regularly caused confusion with his clients, with some calling him Scrooge and some calling him Marley. He really didn't care either way and answered to both names. In the seven years since Marley's death, Scrooge had conducted entire business transactions in both names and never contradicted his clients one way or another. When customers who called him Mr Marley found out he was really Mr Scrooge, he didn't give a single thought to their confusion or embarrassment. That was their problem. Emotions had no cash value.

Such was the layout of the premises, that upon entering and to the immediate right, was an office with a floor to ceiling glassed in-wall, looking for all the world like a large fish tank. This was the office of Scrooge's clerk, and poor Bob Cratchit was the sole occupier, swimming alone in its cold, cheerless waters.

The offices were unfriendly, severe and nothing to soften that image survived long within its walls. Scrooge discouraged Bob from hanging pictures drawn by his kids, referring to them as "childish daubs of colour" and sneered at them as vulgar. No colourful calendars adorned the walls, no framed prints hung pride of place to create a relaxing environment. No water cooler offering "designer water" stood within, no plants sprung from the corners, colouring the edges with soft, inviting greenery, breathing freshness and life. The one and only plant that had ever occupied Scrooge's offices eventually committed suicide rather than continue to live within the toxic environment.

Bob's office was a walk-through entry, but as you entered his fish tank, almost immediately to the left, were the double doors which connected to Scrooge's office. These doors were kept open, except when Scrooge was seeing clients, so he could keep a constant eye on Bob and make sure he was never slacking on the job.

Right now, Bob was trying to encourage the ageing copier to print some letters. The copier was perfectly sound in Scrooges opinion, after all, it was a mere 10 years old, he said, and had become part of his office equipment due to the aforementioned business foreclosure.

The room was very cold, but Scrooge, being Scrooge, had removed the tap wheel that allowed Bob to turn up the heat on the small wall radiator in the room. Bob had fleetingly thought of asking his employer for the wheel to turn the heat up a notch, but the last time he did that Scrooge's face had deepened to a florid red as he denied permission and followed up with a prediction that he could easily get someone else to do Bob's job if he didn't like the working conditions. They both knew that was a hollow threat, but occasionally Bob let his employer think he had the upper hand.

As it was near closing time and having no other way to keep warm, Bob tucked his scarf around his neck and pulled his desk closer to the copier. It may be old and cranky, but it did give off some heat.

Although the office was cold and the company dismal, the day itself was one of happiness and delight. Outside Scrooge's office, the streets shone with lights and decorations and burst with happy, friendly people all joining in one of the most wonderful and joyous days in the year because it was the last day before that most special and sacred celebration, Christmas Day.

Scrooge was sitting hunched at his desk when suddenly, with great enthusiasm and joy, the front door banged open and a happy faced young man burst in off the street, bringing a swirl of cold afternoon air and the gravid scent of rain on pavement. Rubbing his hands together and blowing into the palms to warm them, he was tall and pleasant looking, with a passing resemblance to Scrooge, but on him, the features were friendly and agreeable. The green eyes he'd inherited from his mother looked out under a tousled mop of dark hair; he was solid but not fat.

With a huge smile he cried, "Happy Christmas Uncle Ebenezer. Happy Christmas Bob. Happy Christmas both, may God bless you and yours!"

That's a wonderful greeting don't you think? You and I would answer enthusiastically, "A Happy Christmas to you too Fred (for that was his name). Happy Christmas to all of your family," or some such like it. Not Scrooge. No. Whilst Bob immediately answered with a similar Christmas wish for Fred and his loved ones, Scrooge, with a mean eye and a sour mouth, looked at his nephew, muttering, "Absolute crap!"

"Absolute crap, Christmas? Come on Uncle, that's a bit harsh isn't it? You don't mean that, do you?" Appealed Fred sitting on the edge of Scrooge's desk and swinging one foot.

"Oh yes I do!" said Scrooge, "and what makes you such a cheerful little ray of sunshine today anyway? You have no money," he continued, ticking off his fingers, "no assets, no savings, no investments, you're up to your armpits in debt! And will you get your bottom off my desk!" He gave Fred an ineffectual shove and tried to arrange his papers back in order.

"Well, why are you so bad-tempered then?" Fred asked, jumping to his feet and striding around the office, throwing his arms out in a theatrical manner, "you've got money, savings, assets, investments, no debts and your rich!" And coming full circle, he put both palms on Scrooge's desk, smiling down at him, "Plus, you can even sit on your desk," he laughed.

Scrooge looked at him and didn't answer.

"Oh, come on Uncle, don't get grumpy... It's C H R I S T M A S. !" boomed Fred in a happy sing-song voice. Throwing himself into the client's chair opposite Scrooge he opened his coat in a "what's hidden in here" gesture and produced a large Christmas cracker from his inside pocket. Holding one end and waggling it in front of Scrooge he said, "Go on Uncle...Pull."

Scrooge ignored the cracker, complaining, "Don't get grumpy? This world is so full of imbeciles and half-wits who spend the whole of December parroting "Happy Christmas, Happy Christmas" like they're some magic words that set the world to rights. Spending money buying useless gifts and toys, while not even thinking that they're one year closer to death but no better along in life. The bills mount up, but there's no money to pay them and still they spend more and more money for *Christ-mas*," he sing-songed. "If I was in charge for just one day, one day mind you..." he added, "every stupid fool who wished a "Merry Christmas" or sung one Christmas carol, or produced one sprig of mistletoe would be stuffed like his turkey, right up his..."

"Thank you!" said Scrooge's nephew, holding up a "STOP" hand and cutting him off. "I get the gist"

Scrooge made no answer, and went back to his books, scribbling away for a few minutes until he realised Fred wasn't moving. He looked up at his nephew who had placed both elbows on the desk, folded one hand over another, rested his head on his hands, and, puppy style, was watching his Uncle with kind, green eyes.

Scrooge scowled back at him saying, "Was there anything else?"

Fred smiled cheekily and waggled the cracker again. "Come on," he said coaxingly, "you can keep the toy."

"Frederick," said Scrooge, "will you kindly go away. Have your Christmas celebrations however you want to and leave me alone to have mine."

"But you don't do anything for Christmas!" exclaimed Fred throwing his hands up.

"Yes, well, that's how I celebrate Christmas, by doing nothing. It doesn't do anything for anyone. It costs too much, and you get no profit back. It's bad business and it's bad for business." He paused the said grandly, "Christmas festivities have no cash value."

Fred looked at his Uncle sardonically, "Well, I'm sure the retail sector would disagree with you there…"

He trailed off, then went on quietly, "But you're right of course. Christmas doesn't make sense if you just count its value in money. But it's not about money Uncle. Christmas is when the world stops looking at each other as foreigners and enemies and realises that we're all part of God's human family and that's how we should treat each other. It's a time when we need to stop talking about keeping out refugees and asylum seekers and remember Jesus himself was once a refugee from Bethlehem when the Holy Family fled to Egypt." Fred rose again and walked around behind his Uncle's desk, continuing in his monologue, "People sing carols, attend services, and, as at other special times of the year, we learn from the words of peace and love and fellowship. So, you know, even though it can be costly, and I must admit I've never actually tried to make any money from it, I love it and will go on celebrating it and remember the child who was born that day."

Bob, listening to Fred's speech, broke into applause, only stopping when Scrooge shouted, "Thank you! This isn't the Royal Variety, enough of that. Your opinion wasn't sought on this matter. You can enjoy Christmas in a dole queue if you don't knock that off."

Fred pulled a face behind his Uncles back, causing Bob to smile and wink in return. Luckily, Scrooge missed both gestures nevertheless he turned to his nephew and clapped his hands in admiration saying, "Bravo, bravo. You should get yourself nominated by those Lefties and Greenies and run for parliament. You'd make a good politician with all your fine, "let's all hold hands and hug and the world will be ok" rhetoric. Very..." he finished sarcastically, "convincing."

"Oh, come on Uncle, don't be like that. Come to lunch tomorrow. We would love to have you there."

"No," said Scrooge, flatly.

"Why not?" challenged his nephew. "You always say no but never tell me why."

Scrooge leaned back in his chair again and looked up at his nephew.

"Why? Why? What matters is why? Why this, why that. Why did you get married?" Said Scrooge as an answer to the question.

"Why did I get...? Because I fell head over heels in love with the most wonderful woman in the world that's why!" said Fred.

"How sweet," mocked Scrooge. "I can hear bluebirds twittering in the trees and squirrels dancing in the snow! *Head over heels in love*," he spat derisively throwing his pen down on the desk and saying, "There's a statement that makes just as much sense as a Happy Christmas! The idea of a grown, intelligent, man being so affected by "love" that he just throws all common sense out of the window, is so ridiculous... What is love anyway? It's just a four-letter word used to make you go to places you don't want to go, see things you don't want to see, meet people you don't want to meet and, spend money you don't want to spend....." Scrooge grumbled.

"You could put that to music," said Fred, "it's sure to be a hit." He grabbed the pen off Scrooges desk and, using it as a microphone, sang badly, to the tune of Tina Turner's *What's love got to do with it*:

"What's love anyway, anyway-anyway,
What's love but a four-letter word,
Making to see things you don't want to see
Making you spend cash you don't want to spend..."

"HA – HA!" said Scrooge with studied sarcasm.

"Not a Tina Turner fan then?" Fred asked, as he eased back into the chair opposite his Uncle and waggled the cracker again, "Come on, you can keep the toy even if you don't pull the big half." Fred tempted his Uncle.

Scrooge snatched it out of Fred's hand and slammed it down on his side of the desk, not amused.

"Look Fred," he said standing up, trying to hustle his nephew up and out of the chair, "I have work to do even if you don't. Out... Out... You go."

Fred got to his feet saying, "Uncle you're not seriously suggesting my getting married is the reason you won't come to dinner. You never came around before, so you can hardly use that as an excuse now. I don't understand it. When did we ever have a falling out that's made you like this? I wish you would tell me because for the life of me, I can't remember it."

"I'm very busy. Cheerio, off you go, on your way, goodbye," said Scrooge, ineffectually shoving him towards the door.

"Don't you understand Uncle!" cried his nephew, "I don't want anything! What do you think is going to happen there? I don't want to borrow money or want you to guarantee a loan. All I'm asking is to invite you to lunch to meet my wife, my friends, eat turkey and drink champagne that's all!"

"Goodbye," said Scrooge again.

His nephew sighed heavily, "Well, it's a shame you feel like this, but you're not going to ruin my Christmas Spirit. The offer still stands. Lunch is at 1 pm. I hope you change that stubborn old mind of yours and we'll see you there!" Fred grinned, and leaning over he retrieved the Christmas cracker, placing it gently on top of the page where Scrooge was working. "And... Let's face it, a miracle on Christmas Day is bound to make the news!"

Fred laughed a great laugh, turned, and left Scrooge's office. He stopped briefly to chat with Bob and ask about his family and Christmas plans. They talked for a few minutes, shared a hug and Fred reminded Bob to, "Send my best to your wife and kids."

One last time Fred leaned back through Scrooge's door, waggled his fingers in a cheeky "tootle-oo" wave, and then stepped out into the cold, busy streets.

Ebenezer returned to his chair and saw the Christmas cracker lying on his desk where Fred had gently placed it. He picked it up, shook it briefly, muttered, "Crap, total crap," and dropped it into the top drawer of his desk.

As Fred had left, he had opened the door to a blast of ice-cold wind that blustered through the already chilly office, and with it came two serious looking gentlemen, both warmly bundled against the cold, but with tell-tale red noses and ears where the biting wind had pecked at them, chilling them as they went about their business.

Both men entered Bobs fish tank and extending their hands, they introduced themselves as Mr Smyth and Mr Huffam. Mr Smyth was carrying a clipboard and writing pad, thick with notes and different coloured post-its while Mr Huffam seemed to be the spokesman of the duo. With a wide smile, he asked if it was possible to see the boss. Scrooge however, was already on his feet. Expecting new business he threw open the doors of his office and asked the gentleman in.

Both gentleman offered their hands for Scrooge to shake, as Mr Smyth asked, "Scrooge and Marley's financial services?"

Scrooge nodded, a professional smile stuck to his face. "That is what the sign says on the door gentlemen, yes," he replied to their statement of the obvious.

"Are you Scrooge or Marley?" Mr Huffam asked in a jolly fashion.

"I am Mr Scrooge," Scrooge replied, emphasising the "mister" in his reply. "Mr Marley is dead. He died, er...Seven years ago. Seven years today in fact."

This sobering answer stopped the men long enough for Mr Smyth to say, "Oh dear, what a shame," and "Sorry for your loss." But Scrooge's indifferent expression forced Mr Huffam, in a desperate attempt to lighten the mood in the room, to blurt out "Well I'm sure you share his spirit of charity and compassion, Mr Scrooge!"

Scrooge did share Marley's views on charity and compassion. Avoid it like the plague. Charity took your money and compassion made you feel guilty until you gave hard earned profits away. Scrooge and Marley had agreed that both of these dangerous socialist ideas had no place in their office, and they had, over some twenty-five years sent hundreds of collectors, flag sellers, tin shakers, raffle ticket sellers and sponsor seekers back through the door with nothing but a stinging rebuke for wasting valuable time and a diatribe on pecuniary economics. So well-known were they for this attitude that no one had so much as left an information leaflet in over ten years. Scrooges golden rule was simple, charity had no cash value.

However, once Scrooge heard the sentence, "Well, I'm sure you share his spirit of charity and compassion, Mr Scrooge!" his welcoming expression switched off and the habitual scowl that his face was more comfortable with took its place. "Oh I do," he said.

"Capital, Mr Scrooge! Mr Huffam said enthusiastically, and went on in aloud and merry voice, "We represent all the shops and offices in this area and were trying to raise some extra funds so that people who need it can have a better Christmas and celebrate a little more."

"Oh?" said Scrooge.

"You see I'm sorry to say even in this day and age, so many people don't have anything to give their families. Too many will go without this Christmas. Children will have no gifts; families will have no food. Many are living in their cars or on the streets. We try to spread a little Christmas cheer by providing for these people and helping as much as we can."

"Oh?" said Scrooge again.

Presuming that Scrooge was simply a man of few words, the Mr Smyth now smiled a happy, Christmassy smile and opened his book. He turned over page upon page, filled with his big bold handwriting, where he'd jotted down the names of the people, and businesses in the area who'd already pledged contributions, and the amounts they'd promised to give.
Finding a place at the bottom of the list, he clicked his pen and looking directly at Scrooge asked expectantly, "How much can I put you down for?"

Scrooge never had any aspirations to become an actor, but the pause he left before drawing himself up and delivering his one-word reply would have done Olivier proud. "Nothing!"

"Nothing?" Said the men in unison. Then understanding dawned. Mr Smyth nodded and said, "Oh I see, you want to make an anonymous donation then? Of course, Mr Scrooge, that's no problem, we can do that easily."

"I mean gentleman, that I'm not making any donation." said Scrooge cutting him off mid-sentence. "I don't celebrate Christmas myself; I consider it an utter waste of time and money and I'm certainly not going to pay for other, shiftless layabouts to celebrate it. Not with a single penny of mine."

"But Mr Scrooge," blustered Mr Huffam, "Too many people are living hand to mouth. Some cannot afford to feed their children or pay their bills; some people sleep on benches and in shop doorways! Surely at this time of year, you can give a little to help those less fortunate than yourself?"

Scrooge regarded his visitors with a sceptical eye. "It is my opinion, gentlemen that the number of "unfortunates" increases each year at this time, simply because the lazy and indolent have come to expect that others will provide everything for them. As for your request, I say again, No. No, Sir! It's none of my business gentlemen. I have enough problems trying to understand my own affairs without involving myself in the lives of others. My life occupies me constantly. Thank you for calling. Good afternoon."

The two men, however, were made of sturdier stuff and pressed on, "Surely a small endowment is not beyond your pocket at this time Mr Scrooge, even if you don't celebrate? Fifty pounds would hardly break the bank. There is so little available to the poor, and those living on the streets, that those of us who have something to spare have a moral obligation to assist them, don't you agree?"

Scrooge had moved around his desk and was about to sit down when the gentleman mentioned the figure of fifty pounds. Caught off guard by the audacity of this suggestion, he tripped over his feet and landed with an undignified thump on his chair, shocked that the man dare suggest such an outrageous amount in so casual a manner.

"Fifty…," Scrooge stammered in astonishment, "Fifty pounds! You want ME to give you FIFTY POUNDS so some idle layabout can eat turkey and do nothing all day!"

"It is a modest sum, Sir," said the man, "for a business. You must agree there are so many needing help and too few places they can go."

"No, I don't agree! Furthermore gentlemen, I suggest that with fifty pounds in their pocket they could probably take tea at the Ritz hotel!" stormed Scrooge.

The two men made no reply but looked at Scrooge with suitably saddened and imploring expressions.

Scrooge had endured all he would of this invasion into his workplace, and the ridiculous flights of fancy proposed by the two strangers. Seeking to end all this nonsense once and for all he leaned forward in his chair and said, "I see by your expressions gentlemen, that you're not intending to leave until you've somehow persuaded me to part with my money. I can assure you both that won't be happening.

"Let's see, these people have nowhere to go, you say, no one to help. Uh-huh, well, what about welfare? Free money provided by the state and, to match, there's also free health care. There are council houses or flats let at cheap rent, benefits to pay rents, free school dinners, help with council tax, help I don't get by the way, medical centres where anyone can walk in and receive free treatment and dozens of more schemes, loans, credits, and assistances that are available. I pay enough in taxes to support these institutions, why don't you send your people there?"

Scrooge paused momentarily, as if giving time for the gentlemen to answer but, as one began to speak he continued bombastically, "And of course, there are always an abundant number of so-called charities and organisations for the bone idle and professional unfortunates of this city. Any one of whom can make a very comfortable living skiving from one charity to another. Why even some "charities" themselves make a pretty good income from their "charitable deeds." I can't walk down the road sometimes without one or more of the little buggers shaking a tin at me or trying to sell me a ribbon for something. And if they don't fancy those, how about one of the residential homes that provide free bed and board? Sounds like a good deal to me. Failing that, I suggest orphanages, correction centres or remand homes? And of course, prisons. Are there no prisons anymore? I know of many a thief, beggar or tramp that should be given a good home in any one of those places!" Scrooge paused again, but this time the men remained silent.

"Maybe you could find your way to some of the organisations I've mentioned and ask them for money because you definitely aren't getting a penny of mine. Now, if you turn around, you'll find the exit is located behind you, feel free to use it with my compliments. Good afternoon."

The two men looked at him, then Mr Smyth closed his book saying, "Mr Scrooge, of course there is welfare but it's not enough. People going there are made to feel worthless and a failure..."

Scrooge interrupted the man by snorting in agreement.

"...Every part of their life is picked apart by strangers before they are given an insufficient amount, so they still live well below the poverty line, often having to decide between heat or food for their family. And yes Sir, there are charities, good, hard-working people, but they're buckling under the weight of trying to help so many who need it, now THEY need help. As well, there are houses for the homeless, but there are not enough to stop hundreds, even thousands of people living on the streets."

Mr Huffam broke hurriedly into the conversation, "And Mr Scrooge, abuses in some of those 'residential homes' are so bad that in exchange for

34

basic food and a bed and a few pounds a week, residents have to work up to forty hours! They're little better than glorified workhouses!" he said indignantly. "And whoever you think you know who needs to be in prison, Mr Scrooge, you would change your mind if you had, for just one day, been inside one. People steal for a reason Mr Scrooge, it is up to the rest of us to find out why and help, not condemn these people."

Scrooge smiled and leaned back in his chair. "Ah yes, the famous, "we punish the sin not the sinner" approach. Rubbish and nonsense. Prison is what they need, prison I say!" he exclaimed, doing his best Mr Bumble impression and rapping the table with his knuckles. "Now, you'll excuse me, gentlemen, I don't know these people, therefore they are not my problem. The door is still in the same place, Goodbye!"

The men looked grave as Mr Huffam continued to speak quietly but earnestly, "All these places, these institutions exist. Some are good, like the ones we're trying to help here today. But even so, some people would rather not go through the embarrassment of applying for those services. Some people cannot because they are too old or sick, and many would rather die first!"

"Ah well," said Scrooge, clapping his hands and rubbing the palms together as he rose from his chair and steered the men towards his door, "problem solved then. Cheerio to both of you, *don't call again will you.*"

"Wait a minute, what do you mean, problem solved?" they chorused indignantly, stopping at the office door. "What does that mean, problem solved, Mr Scrooge?"

"Simple," Scrooge replied, a satisfied smile on his face. "If they would rather die then they should get on and get it over with. Quit this world, cut short their life, stop cluttering up the streets, sucking up my taxes, and reduce the surplus population. It would be the only act of civic virtue they've done in their whole worthless existence. *Now, for the last time, good afternoon gentlemen. DON'T EVER call again, will you!*" And with that Scrooge pushed both men out of his office, through Bobs fish tank and back onto the street, firmly shutting the front door in their unhappy faces and yanking down the small half window blind. Returning through the fish tank he barked, "Get on with your work" to Bob, who was shaking his head at him with a mixture of sorrow and shame.

Nevertheless, Scrooge returned to his desk feeling quite well, as a short, sharp argument with left-wing do-gooders always resulted in him feeling refreshed and satisfied. Especially when he won.

Despite that though, it was not one of Scrooges better days because today was December 24th. That most special time of the year, Christmas Eve, when many of us gather with family and friends, so that tomorrow, we can celebrate together, if not part of the Christian family, at least participating in the message of Christmas giving, goodwill and peace on earth.

Scrooge thought not of these. Life, for him, was money. That was his bottom line. His raison d'être, and those parts of our nature we call the humanities were not important. For Scrooge, sentimentality had no cash value.

For the past two months, Scrooge's temper had increasingly become shorter and more unpleasant. As the Christmas trees appeared in shops and stores, when the bunting and bells were strung across the streets, and particularly since the Christmas lights were switched on in Oxford Street and shone every night with the message of a Happy Christmas and Peace on Earth, Scrooge had been hurting. Every bell, every star, every carol, every twinkle. Each angel, each shepherd, each candle, and all the tinsel. Every symbol of Christmas struck Scrooge like a dagger in the one area of his anatomy that pained him the most.

His wallet.

In an interesting little piece of gossip, I must tell you Scrooge was a great admirer of Americans, their sense of business and marketing, in which, he said, they were second to none. Indeed, he was sure they showed their intense pride in their fiscal achievements when they stood for their national anthem, placing their hands on their chest in reverence and tribute.

However, unlike the Americans themselves, who knew they were putting their hands on their hearts in homage to flag and country, Scrooge was convinced they were, in fact, placing their hands on their wallets, as a glorification of commerce and profit, and no amount of explanation, including the twenty-minute conversation he'd recently had with the American Ambassador, would shift him from this ridiculous opinion.

Now, several things caused Scrooge immense irritation, taxation being the main one. Income tax, property tax, VAT, wealth tax, death duties you name it and Scrooge could talk long and loudly 'that it was simply the government's way of legally stealing money off hard-working people like himself, who could hardly keep body and soul together.'

Recycling was another. Why he had to split his rubbish into categories constantly irritated him. 'Rubbish was rubbish' he said, and all this namby-pamby sorting out had absolutely no cash value whatsoever.

Bicycle couriers were up there too. They were constantly getting in the way, cutting him off on the footpath, causing him to trip and stumble. Bicycles should stay on the road and out of his way.

But the greatest of his pet peeves, and the one that really got his goat, was from October 1st he couldn't get away from the constant and ever-increasing reminders of the holiday he hated the most.

As if the decorations in the windows, bells and buntings in the streets and the Christmas lights were not enough, now carol singers were appearing more frequently, corporate greetings cards mixed in with his mail, flyers advertising Christmas concerts pushed under his front door and an unreasonable increase of foot traffic as Christmas shoppers came out in greater numbers, bringing their sticky-fingered offspring with them. Children who squealed, whined, or cried, driving him nuts, as they, and their unwelcome parents, constantly got in his way during his walk home!

But even these he could just about cope with. His real bone of contention and the one that had him grinding his teeth right down to the gums was this; Not only was he required to give his clerk, Bob Cratchit, time off on Christmas Day, but he was also forced to pay him a full day's wage for the privilege! Bad enough Bob had other days off with so called *holiday pay*, but this time of year was the WORST! Holiday pay? It was nothing more than legalised robbery!

A full day's pay, and no work! **Cheat!** And the prospect of once more seeing Cratchit walk away on December 24th with money in his pocket he hadn't even earned, ignited in Scrooge a slow, steady burn that increased his bad temper right up to Christmas Eve.

Scrooge sat watching Bob with snake eyes as the clock ticked down to the end of the working day. Eventually it came with darkened streets, the last of the sunlight having gone by 4 pm. Bright lights and people bustling about on last minute Christmas business filled the streets and shops. Everywhere there were shouted greetings with nearby churches ringing out their merry carillon.

Everyone was joyful and happy.

Mostly everyone, apart from those stuck in traffic, trying to get home through hordes of shoppers, busses, taxis, ubers, mini cabs, delivery vans and hundreds of other drivers.

Some of whom are again relishing the delights of that annual winters event, How to drive home safely, even though the headlights of either a Range Rover, four wheel drive, Land Cruiser or any comparable vehicle (which, by the way, is totally unsuitable for city driving, and we all know you only bought it as a status symbol anyway,) is far too close to my sedan in front. And the driver of said poncy vehicle fails to realise, or care, that their headlights are now higher up than usual, which means they shine right through my back window, dazzling my drivers' rear view mirror! Dip your lights or back off Buster, you're blinding me!

Oh sorry.... Where was I....

Carollers were keeping the old traditions alive, going from shops to offices and were generally well received, sometimes workers came out to watch them sing, take selfies with them, and push a few coins into their charity tins.

Unfortunately, when they reached Scrooge's door, they had no sooner piped a note and started to harmonise, "Deck the halls with boughs of holly..," When he leapt out of his chair, dashed to the entrance, threw open the front door, colloquially requested they went on their way and slammed it shut again with such a bang it sounded like a rifle shot.

In this instance, retreat was considered one of the better parts of valour, so they decided it would be best to move on, and at least Bob waved to them as they passed the window.

It was freezing outside, really *brass monkeys*, and not much warmer inside. The photocopier had retired, defeated for the day, taking its small amount of heat with it and Bob had shut off the ancient computer and printer after the last contract had been pulled from its cartridge. All this was done under Scrooge's steady stare as he continually checked the office clock against his second-hand digital watch to see if there were not still a few minutes he could pinch back from his clerk. When at last he finally declared it was time to close. Bob, being ready with everything filed, put away, covered and locked, pulled on his gloves and stood up.

"Am I to expect you'll still be wanting all day off tomorrow … Again?" asked Scrooge, fixing Bob with a fisheye stare.

"Yes, thank you, Sir," said Bob jovially.

"And.....the following day off as well, I suppose? What's it called?"

"Boxing Day Sir," said Bob knowing that Scrooge was fully aware what the 26th December was.

"Yes!" snarled Scrooge. "You want both days off and that means I'm still having to pay you but get no work in exchange. If I refused to pay you, it would be all, "That's not fair Mr Scrooge," and, "It's Christmas Mr Scrooge," wouldn't it, hum hum?" demanded Scrooge in his best nine-teenth-century manner.

"Well, it's only once a year," replied Bob, "and they are Public Holidays."

"That's irrelevant. Public Holidays, too many Public Holidays. What do the public need holidays for anyway? Just to get up to no good Sir, that's what! And I still pay a full day's wage for no work. So called labour market, where is my compensation? Do I get an extra day's work for free? No, Sir, I don't, Sir! It's disgraceful," snarled Scrooge, channelling Mr Bumble again while conveniently forgetting the regular, unpaid, overtime Bob did during the summer when Scrooge didn't shut the business until 6 or 6.15 pm. "So, just make sure you're here early the follow day to make up for it or you could be starting your new year by searching for a new job!"

Bob promised he would and, overflowing with the joys of the season, he threw caution to the wind, grabbed, and shook his employers' hand and wished him a Happy Christmas!

Scrooge snatched his hand away as if he'd been bitten. Looking at Bob Cratchit in total stupefaction he said quietly, "Happy Christmas? In this day and age? And you, with a wife and how many kids to support and you still cling to this foolish notion of a *Happy Christmas*. Either you're blind or a fool Bob Cratchit. I suppose you'll be saying there's still a Santa Claus too with your next breath. No!" Scrooge held up his hand as Bob opened his mouth to speak, "I prefer you to keep whatever you're going to say to yourself and preserve my sanity. Goodbye Mr Cratchit! And remember, early as I said, **early**!" And with that, he strode through the door, slammed and locked it behind him, and was off down the street muttering, swearing, and barking at any Christmas shoppers who got in his way.

Bob stood watching him for a moment, then, humming his favourite carols as he went, he set off for the tube in the other direction. An underground ride in a crowded train full of happy Christmas goers and he would soon be home to have a wonderful evening because he had promised to sing Christmas carols and play games with his children.

Chapter 4 Marley's ghost

Scrooge, being both a man of habit and extreme miserliness, headed to his usual restaurant for his usual dinner. I say "restaurant" but perhaps the words "Hamburger Takeaway" would be more exact. Scrooge didn't really like hamburgers, but, for less than eight quid he could get a burger, chips, and a large coffee and that was enough to fill his stomach without emptying his pocket, so he considered it an acceptable deal. Pleasurable and more fulsome eating was saved for business dinners when someone else paid the bill.

Having eaten his dinner while reading the free copies of the daily newspapers, all stamped DO NOT REMOVE FROM RESTAURANT, he tucked them under his arm and filled his pockets with sachets of sugar, salt, pepper, sugar substitutes and paper napkins. He also filched any unopened sauce sachets, dipping sauces, or sachets of syrup that had been left by other diners, popped them into one of his other pockets then proceeded to walk the one and a quarter miles to his apartment.

How can I describe Scrooge's house to you? Ok, I've got it. Imagine a delightful Victorian style, Howards End type, London residence. The trees, the bay windows, the roses, the intricate fretwork...Got it? Lovely. Now imagine it subdivided, gutted, remodelled, added to, repurposed, and turned into 4 "luxury" apartments that have totally missed the mark of style and elegance, but cracked it as a discombobulated disaster. The mix of old and new trying to exist alongside each other and failing abysmally. A place where the architect could have chosen several themes to work from: Victorian, Edwardian, Early Modern. Art Deco, Modern, Post Modern, but instead he skipped all these, and just went straight for profit.

Adjacent to this building there used to be a vacant lot, where kids and teens could hang out, smoke cigarettes stolen from their parents, score soft drugs, hard alcohol, and light a bonfire every Guy Fawkes. Now it had been reclaimed and turned into yet another high-end outdoor "Metro Market" where everything from 50-kinds-of-imported-cheeses to dozens of varieties of homemade bread, game meats, craftwork, expensive blend (grind your own) coffee beans, spices, organic veggies, leatherwork, candles etc were sold to those who wandered around sipping upmarket £8 a cup takeaway coffees and who could still afford to indulge in overpriced Knick knacks and exotic foodstuffs. Opposite, in an old Victorian park, where nannies and ladies used to push upper class babies in fashionable perambulators, customers now double parked throughout the day into early twilight. Dawn gave rise to food vans, that parked up from 4 am, luring delivery drivers with the scent of bacon-butties and strong espresso coffee.

The entrance to the apartments was a small flight of pebble dash steps leading to a heavy, one-hundred-year-old, copper banded solid oak door, put in place to help give the building an appearance of taste and quality.

It didn't.

This was the building where Scrooge lived. Actually, it was Marley's old place, but Scrooge had received it along with all of Marley's otherworldly goods, and, once moved in, he'd sold his own house for an excellent profit, banked the lot, and not once muttered a word of thanks for his good fortune.

This place was closer to Scrooge's office, and he could walk to work. From his old house, he used to take the tube, the small daily savings on fares was a constant source of satisfaction to Scrooge.

In the last seven years he'd lived as solitary as a snail, never responding to friendly overtures from neighbours, never pausing in the foyer while collecting his mail to pass a word or two about the weather , never stopping to inquire of anyone's day. That his neighbours talked about this unfriendly behaviour behind his back had no effect on Scrooge. Friendship had no cash value.

The interesting thing about this place, apart from being insignificant and dull, was no one outside realised it housed four apartments. From the exterior, it blended into the skyline and faded away, with people walking past it for years, never realising what it was. Even those who worked next door and stood outside it several times a day having a coffee or a quick cigarette would have argued the fact that the building contained living quarters, thinking instead it was the home of bland and unnamed offices for similarly bland and unknown businesses.

This is where Scrooge arrived home every evening. He walked down the road, past the large outdoor Metro Markets, past several retail shops, including *Olives Objects of Virtu*, which sold antiques, *Gregory's Informational Superhighway*, which sold newspapers, magazines, cards and cigarettes, and past the curiously named *Hermie's 7 Day Emergency Gift Boutique*, which, as the name suggested, opened 7 days a week, 365 days of the year and sold a variety of gifts and foodstuffs from handmade chocolates and champagne to bath salts and lavender bears.

Paying scant attention to all these neighbours, Scrooge, chin against his chest to keep out the cold, would walk up the steps, through the old oak door and up several flights of stairs to his apartment. He never varied his pace and arrived home at exactly seven o'clock each night, in time for the news.

Ebenezer Scrooge was unique in that he had extraordinarily little in the way of imagination or creative eccentricity about him. Nothing enchanted him, captured or enraptured him. No film or play moved him. No music stirred his soul, no painting captivated his attention. Nothing frightened him, nothing disturbed him. Nothing at all. He didn't jump at sudden bangs and clanks. If anyone was brave enough to sneak up behind him and shout in his ear, "GOOD MORNING MISTER SCROOGE!" He would not start in surprise. He was numb to all-natural human reactions.

So, it must be said that when what was about to happen, happened, Scrooge's reaction was unusual, very unusual. You see the old oak door had been dragged into our modern times by being fitted with a keyless entry lock, which meant each tenant gained entry by punching in a unique six-digit code. But this night, just as Scrooge entered his code into the lock, the silver keypad transformed, morphing into the face of his dead partner Jacob Marley.

Honestly, Jacob Marley!

Scrooge was so startled he stumbled back at the sight, nearly tripping down the steps, but Marley's face stayed there, staring out at him. It bore the same expression Jacob wore for as long as Scrooge had known him, morose, surly and miserable. That's how Scrooge knew it was definitely Jacob Marley.

Then just as unexpectedly the face faded away and it was the keypad once more. Scrooge looked around. The lighting was fine, murky, and dim, but the same as usual. He tapped the keypad, but it seemed ok. He looked at it from both sides but saw no evidence of tampering. Shrugging at this mystery, he looked over his shoulder again, then hauled on the heavy door and stepped inside.

Scrooge climbed up several flights of stairs to his flat faster than usual and arrived outside his door, breathing heavily. With his fingers trembling, he fumbled his key into the lock and rushed inside. Slamming the door behind him, he slipped the deadlock and, just in case, shot home the two bolts and safety chain which had been fitted courtesy of the metropolitan police. They'd offered upgraded home security for everyone in the borough over sixty, free of charge (of course). If it hadn't been free Scrooge would have refused and continued to use his own security device of pushing a large, solid mahogany bookcase in front of the door each night. But it was, so he gladly accepted the offer, and saved himself the ongoing difficulties of shoving the bookcase and, of course, the backache.

Scrooge thought it best to have a look around the place just to check things were ok. Not that he was scared! No way. For security reasons you know, check the windows and things. Just make sure it's locked up. However, this did involve a bit of a kerfuffle as Scrooge didn't have any bulbs in his ceiling lights. Remember my friend with the grapefruit? His idea of thrift was to have light globes only in the rooms he used. Scrooge's idea of economy was to have two light bulbs in the whole flat. One to use, and a backup, in case the first one blew, or he dropped it, which happened occasionally.

In each room he had a standard lamp and it was his habit to take the globe he was using from room to room, screwing it into each lamp as needed. The fact that he walked in darkness until he screwed in the bulb didn't bother him. Darkness was cheap, and bulbs, expensive.

Once again, when modern technology had revolutionised lighting, Scrooge had a terrible time replacing one of his blown bulbs, discovering the cost had gone up by some two thousand per cent. No amount of explaining that these new globes were better, lasted longer and helped the environment shifted Scrooge's apoplexy at the cost. Having been told the globe would last thousands of hours he set to with pencil and paper recording every time he used it and was delighted when it didn't go the distance. A scathing letter produced a free replacement, so Scrooge recorded that too.

When that also fell short, he wrote again and was ecstatic to get another free bulb. However, the third, fourth and fifth letters following another failure got him nothing more than a polite reply and an invitation to try a different company's product.

A light bulb in hand, Scrooge now went room to room, screwing and unscrewing, and checking each one by the dim 40-watt glow. This didn't take long because the whole apartment was sparsely furnished so his investigations were fast and easy requiring little effort.

No one in the bedroom-check.
Nothing under the bed-check
Nothing in the closets-check
No one in the bathroom-check
Ditto kitchen-check
Dining room-empty-check
Upstairs study and spare room-check
Sitting room clear, everywhere normal. Jolly good.

All the windows were tightly shut in every room. Nothing to worry about there. Each window in the apartment was so gummed up with layer upon layer of thick gloss paint, opening them would have needed a crowbar and the assistance of a large muscled man called Dave, who could bench press twice his own weight.

Once Scrooge had checked everywhere to his satisfaction, he changed into his pyjamas (bought for three pounds from a discount store, a "bargain" he was very proud of if you like dressing in emergency room scrubs that is) an old but warm jumper went over them and an equally old, long , grubby dressing gown was tied down over the lot. He also kept his socks on and finished with a pair of ancient wool fleece boots. Combined, this incredible ensemble meant he didn't have to turn his fire on for warmth.

He dropped his ill-gotten gains of sugar, salt, pepper, and other pieces of stuff from the restaurant into several containers on his kitchen bench, then prepared to relax for the evening.

Scrooge sat himself down in his semi-comfortable chair by his television set. Semi-comfortable because this also used to belonged to Marley, and because of his shape, he had strained the arms of the chair into a wide "V" and his large bottom had pushed the seat of the chair into such a deep depression that when Scrooge sat on it, his knees were almost level with his chest.

Settling himself, he flipped on the news and tried to relax. The television was another legacy from Marley. For himself Scrooge had previously thought a TV to be an outrageous indulgence and regarded a radio sufficient enough to keep informed with the world. However, when the TV came with the flat, Scrooge wasn't going to turn it down.

Paying the license...Well...That was a different story.

Tonight though, he was distracted. Usually he had heated conversations with his television set, especially during news and current affairs programs. He would shout his objections, bang his foot, and thump his hands on the arms of his chair. It was a nightly routine that satisfied him immensely. But tonight, he was distracted. He kept going over and over the sudden materialisation of Marley's face, and consequently the juicy news stories glided past him with no comments or outbursts. Politicians and pundits got away without a word. Even the final wishing to our viewers of, 'a Happy Christmas', received not a murmur from Scrooge. All he could think about was Marley's face.

Finally realising he had been sitting for ages just thinking, he decided he'd better try to forget it and picked up one of his stolen newspapers. He was scrabbling about for his reading glasses when he heard a very strange noise. The downstairs buzzer rang. This was the door buzzer at street level that anyone could use to be let into the foyer of the building. Not strictly weird on its own except for two reasons:

1. It was 11.30 at night and who would be calling then?
   and
2. His buzzer had been broken since July and as he never had visitors, he'd never got it fixed.

But there it was, buzzing away. On and on and on, for at least a full minute! Louder and louder until, when it was so loud it was deafening, it stopped! Like a snap of the fingers!

Scrooge looked around him trying to figure out what was happening.

The face, the buzzer. Was this some kind of trick? This had to be a practical joke, right?

"Rubbish and nonsense" he muttered to himself.

Then, to add to his annoyance, a new and equally strange noise echoed throughout the building. It sounded for all the world like someone was hauling some sort of heavy, clunky equipment up the fire stairs, step by step, using a chain or a cable. Slowly, step by step by step.

Heave... clunk! Heave... clunk!

Again the sound grew louder and louder. Scrooge wondered where were all his neighbours? They must be hearing this, why was no one opening their doors and yelling, "What's all that racket!" Were they all deaf, or had they all got their televisions up so loud they couldn't hear it? Oh for goodness sake, he thought, throwing his newspaper moodily to one side, did he have to do everything!

The noise finally reached a crescendo right outside his apartment. Scrooge was on his feet, headed for his front door, ready to throw it open and give the noisemaker a piece of his mind...

But before he touched the handle, and without him undoing any of the locks, through the door stepped Jacob Marley.

Honestly, Jacob Marley!

Well, I say Jacob Marley. Not actually him. Not his body, for after all, he was dead. We established that when we started. No this was Jacob's ghost or apparition. A phantasm of what Jacob once was, looking precisely as he did the last time Scrooge had seen him, which wasn't exactly flattering as the last time Scrooge laid eyes on him, he was dead, flat on his back, stuffed into his coffin. It wasn't like he was just back from a fortnight sunning himself on the beaches of Ibiza. No, this figure was ghastly, pale, with dull black eyes, his hair falling limp and lifeless. His fat body was transparent, his hands were painfully twisted, and he gave off a smell of mouldy old blankets and those horrible cigarillos he used to smoke. He was altogether a very unpleasant manifestation of the former, equally unpleasant Marley. Moreover, the ghost was also attached to the most astonishing sight Scrooge had ever seen. It was burdened down with a monstrous spectral chain, with heavy links, like an anchor chain, clamped to his wrists, wrapped around his waist, and falling to his feet.

Fastened to the other end was a ghostly iron chest, like a pirate's chest, with a central combination lock. The chest was huge, half as tall as Marley himself, and half again as wide. Banded with spectral iron straps and bolts it dragged on the chains around Marley's waist, obstructing his efforts to stand upright. The chain itself was such a heavy burden, but the chest doubled the tremendous load, making it almost impossible for the ghost to move.

He stood before Scrooge, making no other movement, but simply lingered, silently waiting. He didn't try to enter further into the residence, nor did he say anything. He merely stared at Scrooge, biding his time.

Scrooge was undeniably shocked at the state of his old business partner but having a guy seven years dead walk through his front door in the middle of the night didn't seem to shock him as much as you would expect it should.

Once again, I pause and refer to Shakespeare and this time to his "Scottish" play, to question how someone reacts to a ghost. While we all know *Macbeth* is just a play, it's interesting how Shakespeare's eponymous character reacts to the appearance of Banquo's ghost. Unlike Scrooge, when Macbeth gets the shock of his life on seeing the ghost of Banquo calmly joining the guests for dinner, he turns a perfectly nice evening with friends into a chaotic event. This could, of course, be explained by the stress he was under, the fact that he had ordered Banquo's murder, the ear bashing he was getting from the wife or the Scottish weather. As lovely as Scotland's rugged beauty is, I suggest it's the latter as the unpredictability of the Scottish climate is enough to drive anyone to the edge of reality. Just trying to decide what undies to wear would have been difficult enough, given the weather's changeability.

Scrooge kept his wits about him and stepped backwards into the room whilst challenging Marley's ghost. "So, what do you want at this time of night?"

"Everything," answered the ghost simply, his voice echoing as he spoke.

"And just exactly what are you...? I mean... Who are you?" Scrooge questioned aggressively.

"You know who I am. I am your business partner Jacob Marley. This is my flat and that," he pointed to the armchair, "Was...is...was my chair."

Scrooge looked at the chair then back to the ghost. "I see. Well, why don't you sit down?" Then thinking about this he asked, "Can you still sit down?"

"Yes, I can," said the ghost.

"Well, sit then," snapped Scrooge, as if he were talking to a dog.

Marley's ghost obliged and although it appeared to sit upon his chair, in fact it floated just an inch or so above it. Looking directly at Scrooge the ghost said, "You don't think I'm, real do you?"

"No, I don't. I do not!"

"Why is that?" asked Marley. "Your senses can see me, hear me. You can even smell me. Why not believe what they're telling you is true?"

"Because," Scrooge answered sarcastically, they are too easily tricked into imagining things that are not real. They can be easily influenced by anything. The heat, for instance, or a migraine can affect them, Or...Or.... Too much wine! You could be an illusion because I'm so tired, or the result of some underdone chips or meat I ate tonight or any amount of different things." Here Scrooge forced a laugh "You're probably the result of some poorly cooked gravy, rather than an actual ghost come back from the grave!" he said wittily.

In truth, Marley's spectre was upsetting him more each minute. The sitting figure was completely still, there was not a single movement from it. The black, dead eyes didn't move around in his face but stared straight ahead. With the chain bunched around his feet, the ghost looked at Scrooge, but never blinked and showed no emotion on its face.

"Look here," Scrooge said, picking up a safety pin that he used occasionally to pin his shirt. "Do you see this pin?"

Marley nodded affirmative.

"How can you? Look at it...," commanded Scrooge waving it back and forth in an annoying fashion in front of the phantoms face, trying to move those dead, black eyes. "You're not looking at it!"

"I can still see it though," answered Marley.

Scrooge gulped a lump of fear and replied, "Well If I swallowed this pin, my mind could convince me I was being eaten alive by devilish pixies all the rest of my life! So, no! I don't believe it. None of it. It's all rubbish and nonsense! Rubbish and nonsense!" rejected Scrooge loudly.

At this dismissal, Marley's ghost jumped to his feet and, raising his manacled arms, hands tightly closed, he crossed them before his breast. As Scrooge watched in bewilderment the spectre threw back its head, and without warning, let out a horrendous sound that flew around the room, hitting Scrooge like a fist and bringing him to his knees. Every window in his apartment slammed open with a loud bang, thundering in rapid succession like a fusillade of gunfire, letting the night's mist sweep in and the cold wind's howl mix with this terrible cry.

It was the sound of terrible suffering, and a despair so deep, Scrooge was horrified. Intense remorse at chances ignored and lost; sorrow that was so palpable he could feel it go right through him, and suddenly he was horrified at the intensity of Marley's feelings of desolation, despondency, and misery.

Tethered together, wrapped in and around each other, was a scream, bound to a cry, pinned to a wail. Grief, pain, and hopelessness were all born from the sound Marley made, and it washed over and through Scrooge as he cowered petrified on the floor.

Yet terrified as he was, Scrooge had to steal a glance at the ghost and was sickened to see that, by opening his mouth to scream, Jacobs jaw had detached from his skull and dropped down onto his chest in a stomach-churning sight. His face was now a cavernous oversized horror that made Scrooge feel dizzy and nauseous. The freezing air and fog whirling in from outside was making him shiver with cold as well as fear. He begged, gibbering for mercy from the apparition that stood over him.

Marley looked down at his old partner, his voice echoing as he said, "Ebenezer, it was always the same with you. You never let yourself believe anything unless you could touch it or feel it. But here I am, in front of your eyes and you must decide, right now, do you believe I am real or not?"

"Yes, alright, alright, I do, I believe you are real," Scrooge replied, "but why, why are you here Jacob? What on earth has brought you here to visit me in this way?"

Marley began to speak, quieter now, but still with great passion and intensity. "Nothing on *earth* has brought me here. My message comes from a different place and you need to listen closely old friend if you are to learn the reason for my visit...

"We are all born innocent into the world, and as we grow, we learn we're bound by our humanity to help our neighbours, our community and those who need us. To give of ourselves freely, honestly, expecting nothing in return.

"It is our destiny to seek and find love. To marry and have children and be part of the greater good. To care for those who need care. To share our good fortune without restriction of colour or creed. To learn patience, kindness, and acceptance of our fellow man with no prejudice in our hearts. This

50

is why we're created, so we can be a part of something, and to give back. That is the purpose of our existence...

"Those of us who refuse and deliberately turn our backs when we're living are bound to wander the earth after death, unhappy and alone, compelled to see what a life filled with such joy we could have had if we'd not closed our hearts, shut ourselves away, turned our back on others, and thought only of ourselves. Now we are left in bitterness and all alone, hoping for forgiveness, praying for release"

Here Marley again cried his terrible cry and shook the chains that bound him.

"All around there are ghosts, suffering the same as me, twice cursed, twice punished. Not only did we turn our backs on love and family, but we used our money, our power, our position to injure the innocent, and fill our pockets. It was never enough, we always wanted more, and in chasing more we injured so many, and gave not one a single thought."

Scrooge's voice trembled as he asked, "But why are you shackled like that? I don't understand."

Marley looked at his chains and pulled them to hold some links in his hands as he said, "These are the chains I made for myself. Every day I was alive I made this link by link and yard by yard." He pointed to the huge box he dragged behind him. "This chest is my burden, my penance. It too is of my making. It holds every offence and injury I ever committed. Every wrongdoing, every wickedness, every misdeed and every sin. It holds the debt I owe in everything I said and did, every possession I seized in lieu of payment, every penny I took against all decency. All the interest I charged that was usurious and wrong. Every scheme, every plot, every twist and turn I used to make more and more money, with no thought of anyone else or of the unhappiness I left behind me"

Scrooge risked a glance at Marley as he spoke, "But the chest is closed Jacob, how do you know what it contains? It could be empty!"

Marley shook his head, "The chest is full. The misery I caused, the sins I carry, are so heavy on my soul, I feel their weight. They pull me down as I move and whisper to me if I am still. I will never be rid of their presence, not until I have repented for every single one."

Marley looked again at Scrooge, "Even this chain, I forged it with every extravagant meal I stuffed in my mouth, every bottle of wine I drank, and with each costly cigar I smoked," here the phantom laughed bitterly, "that

51

is the supreme justice, for with my greed, my indulgence, my gluttony, and all those cigars, I killed myself.

"I did this with the money I should have given to those who needed it. Money I left to you old friend, and what have you done since then? Where is that huge amount of money I gave you seven years ago? Squirrelled away so you can worship it as your personal golden calf, while those in need still pass around you, just as they passed around me, invisible in your eyes, or at best, ignored." he alleged.

Then shaking his head, he continued, "I made this chain, just as surely as an ironmonger forges his wares, and every day I added to it. Tell me, old friend, does it look familiar to you?"

Scrooge shook his head; he couldn't understand the question.

"No, I thought not. Seven years ago, when I died, your chain looked exactly like this does now. And for seven years, you've added more links, more misery, more sorrow, until your chain, Ebenezer, is now so long and so heavy it is a terrible and frightening weight, a heavy penance, waiting for you to die."

Scrooge's blood ran cold, and he looked around him, expecting to see the chain appear at his feet and grab onto his arms; but nothing happened. He risked another quick glance at Marley and cried, "Jacob, why did you come here then? Is there nothing hopeful you can tell me about your situation?"

"No," replied Marley, "I can't. Hope comes from others, from better men than I ever was, and it's offered to those who want it and will benefit from it. I never would've. I never looked outside our office doors to see the world and the light. I never looked for someone who could have been my helpmeet, changed my purpose. I might have even had a family that I loved and cherished. But no, I never wanted to share what was mine with anybody else."

Marley closed his eyes for a moment, as if composing himself, then went on with a regretful voice, "I chose to stay within our office walls and serve the god of mammon, and now my punishment is to walk the earth alone. I can't stop, I can't rest. I can't even tell you much more about why I'm here. I'm not allowed to. My journey is never-ending, I am tired, very tired, but I must keep going."

Scrooge didn't move. He stayed on his knees, his eyes on the floor, but in a manner curiously professional he said, "You're obviously taking a long time about it Jacob, do you ever stop?"

"I have a never-ending journey, full of pain and remorse."

"Surely, I mean if it was me, I would have gone a little further. Could you have gone any further?" hinted Scrooge. "And lost a little weight if, if you can that is, I mean, if you're travelling, continually, all this time....?"

Marley screamed that dreadful scream again and shook his chains, loud and harsh, echoing like thunder around the room, deafening Scrooge.

"Here I am, bound with the burden of my making! Wretched, and regretful, and you make jokes!" He shook his head, sorrow in his eyes, "I never thought of love or charity. Or that I had an obligation to help others in the world. I didn't care when I was living, squandering every chance I had to change and be someone better. If I'd only stopped being selfish, owned my sins, admitted my wrongdoings, and started to make amends......But I didn't, I wasn't that man." He lifted his chains again, "I am forever this man...," He looked sadly at the huge burden of his chains, piled around his feet, "and now that I'm dead, no amount of remorse will alter my punishment."

Marley continued to stare at the chains by his feet and said, softly now, so Scrooge had to strain to hear him, "I have often thought, in my arrogance, of all the money I had when I died, that I would give every penny just to have one link in this chain removed. But now I know that every penny of every fortune in the world couldn't buy my soul free. When I've finished my penance, then, only then will I..."

"But Jacob," interrupted Scrooge, "what does that matter? You were always the best businessman! I never saw a better man at business than you."

"You think that makes me feel better?" Marley shouted incredulously. "Business be damned! Out there...," he said, pointing to the windows with his manacled hands, "those people should've been my business! I should've been occupied with their lives. Their hopes and dreams. Their needs, their wants. I should've been kind, tolerant and understanding! Instead, what! I thought just about money and profit. What's that, against someone's needs?"

He held up his chains again and then sobbing, threw them with a great clunk to his feet. Choking back more emotions he said, "This time of year is the worst for me. I see so many people, families and friends, making plans, even strangers who greet each other warmly, all living the true spirit of Christmas. I suffer to know I could've had such times myself.

"All Christmas Ever meant to me was uninterrupted days when I could eat more fine food and drink more champagne. It meant nothing more than that.

"Oh! Why did I never think about the heavenly message which brought the shepherds to the stable that Christmas night? Why did I never look up to see the star that guided the three wise men to the manger! But no, instead what did I think? That it was beneath **me**, that **I** was too clever for it, too sophisticated to be trapped by it, and only **fools** believe in Christmas.

"And now, I'm ashamed when I see total strangers helping those not as fortunate have a better Christmas, with gifts of food, presents and money. People like the two men who came to see you today, Ebenezer Scrooge, who you threw out of your office," Marley paused then said, "Our office."

"Jacob, no! Why are you thinking like that! You were an entrepreneur! One of the best I've ever seen. You made important deals and lots of money. Not since your death has there been a better negotiator, with more cash value than Jacob Marley!" cried Scrooge passionately.

Jacob stared at Scrooge with pity, "So you still measure everything by its cash value. All the time we worked together, you only talked about the cash value. Shall I tell you what value cash has in the life beyond? Nothing! Nothing, and less than nothing! You can die with a fortune in the bank and be buried in a solid gold coffin. None of it has any meaning after death. Money becomes exactly what it is. Pieces of paper with pictures on."

Scrooge made no answer. Marley too was silent for a time. The only sound in the room was the whistle of the freezing wind blowing through the windows.

"I have to go soon," said Marley, "but you need to listen to me. How you can see me now is a secret I can't explain. In fact, I have been here many times before, standing over there, just staring at you."

Marley, an invisible presence, watching him, over and over, frightened Scrooge even more and a cold sweat broke out all over his body.

"Watching you each night has been a painful part of my penance because it was like looking in a mirror. I remember being just like you, thinking like you. Then I drew my last breath and it was too late to make amends," said Marley mournfully, "But tonight I'm finally visible, to tell you there is a chance, a hope for you to escape this penance and punishment. I have secured this chance for you, a chance to make amends, now, before you die, and escape my eternal suffering."

Scrooge reached up a hand to try and touch Marley, his voice abject, even humble. "You and I were always good friends Jacob, working together, do you remember?" He said as Marley stepped beyond his reach "I...I... Thank you for your help, Jacob."

"So, you're going to have ghostly encounters with three different Spirits.," Said Marley flatly.

Scrooge's jaw dropped, his voice changed abruptly, "Say that again? Is that your idea of a chance to make amends?"

"Your only chance.," replied Marley succinctly.

"Ok, well, no, not for me Jacob," said Scrooge getting creakily to his feet. "Thanks very much for thinking about me though. Was there anything else before you leave?"

"WITHOUT THEM YOU CAN'T POSSIBLY CHANGE AND AVOID ENDING UP LIKE ME!" stormed Marley, his deafening voice reverberating around the room, making the windows rattle and glass shake. Scrooge retreated to his knees, ducking his head down and cowering with his arms defensively.

"They will appear here for the next three nights. Look for them and go with them when they arrive. Do not turn away from them, take this chance that's being given."

"Appear, where, what, make sense Marley!"

"The first Spirit will materialise here, tonight as the church bell tolls one. The second will appear tomorrow night at the same time. The last ghost will rise up just as the old church clock strikes midnight on the third night." instructed Marley.

"They keep rather late hours do they, Jacob? No thought for those of us having to go to work in the morning then?" muttered Scrooge.

"THIS IS NOT A JOKE EBENEZER," roared Marley, "you must see all three Spirits, or you will still suffer my fate!"

"But why one by one Jacob?" whined Scrooge. "Can't they come all at once so I can get it over with? You know, get everyone together, so we can brainstorm this thing, get around the table and really talk it through, save a bit of time."

"No," snapped Marley. "One at a time, as I say, is your only hope. Don't look for me again. I can't ever return to you after this visit."

"Look, Jacob…Aren't you exaggerating your situation just a bit?" cajoled Scrooge. "Can it really be that bad, you know, being a ghost? Flying here and there. I think I could do that if I had to," Scrooge said, flapping his arms like a chicken and looking hopeful.

Marley was quiet for a few moments after this foolish remark, then ordered in a voice that brooked no-nonsense, "Get up Ebenezer, and follow me."

Scrooge scrambled to his feet and saw Marley too was standing again, his chains back around his waist and thankfully, his jaw back into its proper place, the yawning maw no longer on view. He began to back away from Scrooge, towards one of the large open windows, and with each step, Scrooge could hear, louder and louder, strange moaning and wailings coming from outside. The sound was filled with sadness and an overwhelming, deeply painful sorrow.

Scrooge ran to look out, and was shocked to see hundreds of spectres, phantoms, and ghosts; Men, and women, all chained as Marley was, moving slowly here and there, going nowhere, but pacing, floating, and drifting in an endless rhythm of desolation.

Stretching back over hundreds of years, each ghost was dressed as they had been in life. Medieval knights wearing chainmail mingled with sixteenth-century puritans dressed in black, while Tudor men and their tightly laced womenfolk passed Wall Street warriors wearing two thousand-dollar suits, each faltering under their own burden.

Twenty-first-century women dressed in figure-hugging jeans and high heel shoes walked with black frocked matrons hiding their hair in simple white caps. Nineteen twenties flappers in knee-length frocks and pageboy haircuts joined in penance for their earthly sins.

Eighteenth-century vagabonds clothed in greatcoats and tricorn hats grouped with highwaymen, pickpockets, and footpads, dragging their penitential loads. And yet more souls, clothed from history, also burdened, travelled as they could in their ghostly states, each regarding the others, all labouring under the same sentence.

Scrooge was spellbound by the phantoms, so many in the night sky he lost count. None were free of a burden, toiling under the weight of their mortal sins. They could not speak to each other, not to offer any words of kindness or compassion. They couldn't touch each other either, not in a gesture of love or support. But they could see one another, labouring under their terrible burdens, and hear the lamenting of each other's souls, the howling of their hearts, their sorrows, and regrets.

"You see," said Marley, "This is not *the easy way out* Ebenezer. I'm not alone in my punishment.

There are so many of us, unlamented, unloved.

No one cried at our passing.

No one mourned at our grave.

Now we see one another for eternity.

Hear one another for eternity.

We can never be alone.

We can never be silent.

We can never be still.

We cannot put down our burden.

We cannot "Rest in peace."

We do not sleep… It never stops.

Listen to them Ebenezer, crying in desolate misery,

"Do you honestly think you could endure it better than anyone here?" Marley said, sweeping his hand to indicate the other ghosts.

As Scrooge's eyes adjusted to the darkness he could see more of them. Like a busy London street, they struggled past each other, never touching.

"There's no exaggeration in this," said Marley. "There's only intense sorrow and regret. We would give anything to change our lot but have nothing, nothing to give. Our earthly power is meaningless in the life after death. Only love, compassion and humanity follow beyond the grave, so we suffer a just and perpetual punishment."

"How…How long does it last?" asked Scrooge.

"Do you know the story of the sparrow?" Marley said, answering with his own question. Scrooge shook his head, he didn't know.

"Once every thousand years, it brushes its wing against an iron ball the size of the earth, and it is only when the iron ball has been completely worn away by the sparrow's wing, that eternity will have begun." Marley looked at Scrooge, "Each of us here still has the chance to make amends for our wrongdoings. Our burden becomes lighter as we serve our penance, atone for our wrongdoings, and finally come to terms and admit what we did was wrong. When our penance is done, and no one knows how long that will take, we are released and can go on, as others do, towards the light," Marley looked again at his chains and burdens, "But for many of us, eternity must pass first, so we wait, we atone for our sins, and… we hope," he said.

As he watched the different ghosts, Scrooge saw some of them stayed together, huddled with their like, drawn in by their sins, shuffling along in their common misery. One group caught his eye because they were each carefully following in the steps of the other, as they bore the weight of their penance. All had committed the same kinds of sin against innocents. The liars, the cheats, the con-men, the dodgy dealers, the get rich quick merchants, each one who took innocent people's money, broke their dreams and left them holding nothing. There was no leader of the group, they walked a never-ending circle, around and around, one following the other.

An old ghost, who stood out from the others in his eighteenth-century clothes, was burdened with his sins of double dealing, fraud, and manslaughter. A liar and a cheat, at the start of 1820 he'd beguiled the dreamers and the hopeful, who imagined owning their own land in the Americas, invented a utopia and enticed hundreds to this new paradise, where, he promised, the land could be bought for just two shillings an acre. All lost their money, scores lost their lives, and with no earthly justice holding him accountable, his ghost had been locked into a pillory and had walked the circle for over a hundred and seventy-five years, his burden so severe, he could still barely take a single step.

Some who walked the circle with him were the romance scammers, who down through the ages had cheated the lonely out of considerable amounts of money. Now it was done by computer, convincing the vulnerable to send cash to silver-tongued lovers who never existed. Leading them on with lies and stories. Playing on their solitude, breaking their hearts, pushing them into deep despair. Their penance? Shackles. Heavy manacles twisted from the broken hearts they'd left behind them. Stuck, fused by their heartlessness, these broken hearts bound them to their penance because a broken heart takes longer to heal than an empty pocket, and cries with a lingering pain that needs more than time to recover.

Scrooge looked upon the myriad of ghosts, from modern computer scammers to fake mediums, spurious fortune tellers, and false prophets. Each imprisoned by the tears of those they'd wronged, tears that were bound to their chains, like dewdrops, glistening in the dawn light; but their weight was onerous, for each little drop carried the torment of broken hearts, of wounded souls, and of sadness, unable to be dispelled

"There are no children bound here?" Said Scrooge.

"No," answered Marley. "You won't see any children here, or teenagers, and few young adults. Everyone is held blameless until they mature enough to fully understand their actions. They have time to learn and mend their ways.

"If they don't change, their sins will burden them eventually, and with no repentance, they will become like everyone here, with a penance to serve."

Scrooges fascination in the ghosts had, up to now, been uninvolved, dispassionate, as everyone other than Marley was either from the distant past or unknown to him. Now his composure was shaken as several of the ghosts coming into view were people he'd known when they were alive! Suddenly the consequences beyond the grave meant more to him than Marley's testimony.

He could see with his own eyes people he'd had business dealings with and remembered well. What's more, he would never have thought anything they did when they were alive deserved such penance after their deaths. Sure, they were tough businessmen, they played the game to win, as he did. They weren't murderers or robbers, these associates of his, so why did they merit such dreadful punishments? They weren't like the swindlers and miscreants they walked with. They were men of business, professionals, used to dealing with substantial amounts of money, making important decisions. What? Because they didn't buy the right flag or push a coin into the right tin they were condemned to this purgatory?

If they were so severely punished, thought Scrooge, what about him?

Among them, Scrooge recognised a mortgage manager, a man he knew who'd foreclosed on so many houses he'd boasted he'd lost count. He spent his days putting people out of their homes without a second thought, selling houses out from under them to pay overdue mortgages, sending in the bailiffs to force the families onto the street. He'd been deaf to any appeal, once claiming the only sound he could hear was money talking. When he passed his burial was conducted with pre-arranged efficiency, according to his own instructions. It was quick, with no mourners, only his employers sending a corporate wreath.

Within the week his position was filled by a younger clone, programmed with the same ideals, destined to grow old walking the same narrow minded career path to the same deplorable end.

This ghost was grieving terribly, drifting along, trying to see a woman and her child, huddled together for warmth in their car, the woman softly singing carols to her sleepy child, a little Christmas tree standing on the dashboard at the front. The car was parked on a quiet side street, and the ghost was reaching, struggling to get to them, wanting desperately to help, but now he'd no power. The influence, the control that he'd wielded on earth, which had made him feel he was in command, was meaningless after death, and now he, like so many others, finally understood if he had helped one person, just one, rather than turning everyone away, there would have been someone in the world who would have felt sorrow for his death, and their mourning would have saved him from his fate.

Then came another disturbing sight. Scrooge recognised an old curmudgeon he had known well in life and had admired for his hard-line approach to business. This man, he remembered, had died a week or so ago, and Scrooge had thought in passing to attend his funeral, though inevitably, he'd found a convenient excuse not to go. Now, with Marley by his side, he watched this ghost as it appeared amongst the others, not yet burdened, but confused, not understanding where he was or what was happening.

Marley said softly to Scrooge, "I was like this man once, pre-penitent, heedless of my sins, oblivious to my price. His judgement will be swift, and his punishment fair."

"Why is he here?" asked Scrooge quietly, a little fearfully.

"He's here because he passed with no recognition. No one grieved for his loss, no one felt sorrow for his death, no one sobbed by his grave. So there was no one to vouchsafe his journey into the light. Now his life must be weighed and balanced, to see if he can continue, or if he has a penance to serve." explained Marley.

"I knew him," said Scrooge, "before he died. I dined with him and spoke to him many times."

"Then watch what happens and learn from him old friend," said Marley, "while you have the chance."

Slowly the other ghosts began to swish and swirl past the man, whispering of all the deeds in his life as they went. Closer and closer they passed, quietly, gently, for it wasn't their task to terrify him but to evaluate his life and forge his spectral chain. With each grievous deed, a link was added, with each righteous deed, a link was removed, and for this man, the chains grew quickly at his feet.

For each unmourned soul, their life was weighed in such a manner. And while some were judged to have a penance to serve, many were not, and they passed through the place of wandering ghosts on towards the light.

And when each of the ghosts' penance was done, they too would go on, into the light, sins forgiven, soul renewed. For no penance, however long, was unending, and no soul, however much burdened, was forever condemned.

Over and over, the soft, gentle swishing of ghost after ghost, passing and passing again, and a heavy chain was forged. Finally, they all whirled around him together, as a gentle dancing wind, and as they whirled the chains they had fashioned clamped to his wrists and locked, only to be removed when his penance was done.

While he looked at the chains, confused at their meaning, his judgement was determined, and his burden appeared. Fastened to the other end of each chain was a name plaque, triangular metal, an everyday item found on an office desk. Scores were joined, one for every offence, emblazoned with his name, though small, the weight was onerous and severe. For the weight was made of the high opinion he'd always had of himself when alive, the piece of metal he'd polished each day, his symbol of self-importance, which had closed his eyes and ears to everything around him. Those who needed his help, kindness, understanding and compassion, who he so easily dismissed. Now his burden was proclaimed, and his penance had begun.

"So was my life examined. Weighed and balanced, my chain was forged, and my life was judged. Locked inside that chest are all my earthly sins, and for each one I must serve penance, as I will do, for the chance to make amends. Though we cry out in lamentation for the opportunities we have lost, we atone, for however long it takes, and pray we will be forgiven," Marley said.

Scrooge was trembling with shock at what he'd just seen. "Is there no hope, no chance to prevent this?" He asked fearfully.

"Everyone has chances Ebenezer, but mostly they are ignored. Tonight, you have your chance. The question is, are you going to take it?" Marley asked as he looked at Scrooge, who was still watching the ghosts.

Now Marley's voice changed as he spoke urgently, his voice forceful and loud to be sure Scrooge was listening, "Remember this Ebenezer Scrooge, you can see these apparitions because you needed to see them, to help you understand my message, but soon they will disappear. Don't be fooled. That doesn't mean they're gone. They'll still be there, atoning for their sins, but invisible from the mortal world. Keep them in your memory, never forget them, don't let their torment be in vain," he warned.

Neither said another word for a long time as they stood watching the phantoms in the cold misty night. At last Marley's ghost whispered softly, "My time here is ended. You must look for the three Spirits old friend if you want to avoid this fate. Don't waste this chance because there will not be another."

And then, before Scrooge could ask a question or say another word, Marley stepped up onto the windowsill and looked out at the night sky. He turned back to Scrooge one final time and said, "Goodbye old friend." Then he simply stepped out into the night, into the company of all the other ghosts, the heavy chest following behind him. He soon disappeared amongst them, his covenant now complete, to continue his relentless purgatory.

Scrooge stood looking out of the window for some time as the ghosts slowly faded into the London mist, and the sounds grew softer until they stopped. The night was clear now of shadows. No noise could be heard, the streets were so quiet it was eerie. Scrooge went to check on the door Marley's ghost came through. But it was still locked tight. No sign of tampering. He mumbled to himself that he was very tired. The day had been a long one, but now he found himself facing a dilemma and one he must reason through if he were ever to sleep tonight.

Scrooge was a pragmatist. What he'd seen and heard rocked his little world and he was muddled as to how to react. Was it real, or not? If he decided, it was real, it meant he had to change. But he didn't want to. If it wasn't real, it meant no changes and he could go on as normal. But why the ghostly appearance if it wasn't real? There had to be a reason to explain it away. As he'd told the ghost himself, his senses probably caused the hallucination, and after much pacing, he hit upon the perfect rationalisation that would explain away the evenings mysterious phantasmagoria and allow him to continue as normal. His dinner that evening, of course! He'd ordered something new, different to his usual meal. It had included a burger with the extra hot jalapeño chillies and a side salad of cucumber, onions, chillies, and mayonnaise. He'd bought and eaten these not because he liked chillies or any spicy food, but because he saved more than a pound on his order.

The explanation was staring him in the face! Of course, it was the chillies, had to be! Ah, now he felt much better. His digestion, coping with the foreign and too spicy food had caused a bilious attack. That, in turn, had disturbed his senses!

But wait, what about the windows? The windows were all still open, letting in the freezing air of the London night. He'd never been able to open them before, no matter how much he'd pulled or banged on the wooden surrounds. Now they were all wide open. Pushing at one, he found he couldn't now force it closed either. He tried another, then another, then one more. All were stuck open when before they had been jammed shut.

What had been the cause of this?

"Wind and rain!" he dismissed. "Wind and rain shook them loose. Shook them loose and made them fly open. It was lucky I wasn't hurt. I could still catch my death of cold, yes I could!" he thought, "if I can't get the damn things closed again." It wasn't good enough. He'd see to it in the morning, oh yes, he would, drag the building manager out of bed to fix it and damn Christmas Day! Lucky for the man he didn't do it right now! And he would, were he not so tired. "Rubbish and nonsense, all of it," he grumbled, "rubbish and nonsense. None of it has any C..C... cash..." he stuttered, pausing awkwardly over his usual dismissal. Correcting himself, he shouted helplessly, "None of this makes any sense!"

By this time, he was feeling dreadfully exhausted and, let's face it, real or not, Jacobs ghost had been difficult to deal with. So had the phantoms outside his window, stirring up too many foreign emotions, and the whole evening had gone on so long it had wearied him. He wasn't sure he could rest with all these imaginary happenings buzzing in his head, but he walked along the short hallway to his bedroom and lay down on his mattress. Before he could even pull his blankets up around him, he fell into a deep sleep.

If he had looked up, just for a moment, he would have seen that every one of those windows that had inexplicably flown open, had once again, silently, and mysteriously, closed.

Chapter 5: The First Spirit

Scrooge woke suddenly in a room so dark he couldn't distinguish anything inside it, or make out the windows beyond, which were usually visible thanks to the streetlights outside filtering through the heavy curtains. He didn't know the time but could hear the familiar and comforting sound of the church clock begin to chime. He was surprised when it chimed its way through one, right the way up to ten, then eleven, then twelve. Twelve! Hang on. It had been past twelve when he'd fallen asleep.

"I can't have slept through the whole morning, can I?" Scrooge thought to himself, pulling himself up and moving to look outside. He was so preoccupied that he could have slept so long, he didn't pause as he drew back the heavy curtains and peered out through the windows, expecting to see midday. The fact that the windows, which had been gummed shut for decades then suddenly thrown open so dramatically last night, were now once again tightly closed, simply didn't register in his brain. Instead, much to his relief, he saw that the streets were still quiet and dark.

Returning to bed, Scrooge felt a little better knowing it was still night. He made up his mind to settle back to sleep and wake up tomorrow with all these strange goings on behind him.

No sooner had he closed his eyes when another thought crowded into his consciousness.

If the church clock chimed twelve, and it was still dark, it had to mean he'd slept away a full twenty-four hours! How was that possible? He'd never slept that long in his life!

And now the visit from Marley's ghost was tumbling through his thoughts again, further waking his sleepy mind, forcing him to remember.

He asked himself repeatedly, did it happen, or was it just a dream? Scrambling to his feet again, he began to pace the room thinking it through. Whenever he convinced himself it WAS a dream, the certainty of Marley's ghost and its prophecy set him worrying all over again.

Jacob had predicted the first Spirit would arrive at 1 am and now that Scrooge could no more go back to sleep than he could fly, he decided to wait up and see what, if anything, happened.

Slowly the nearby church clock ticked its way through the quarter hours as Scrooge counted down to 1 am.

Ding dong ding dong-A quarter past, nothing.

Ding dong ding dong-Half past, nothing.

Ding dong ding dong-A quarter to, still nothing.

Ding dong ding dong-1 am,

"It's one in the morning, and nothing has happened," Said Scrooge gleefully to himself, "I knew it, rubbish and nonsense!"

Unfortunately for Scrooge, however, he'd said this just as the church had finished chiming the Westminster Quarters but not yet tolled the hour. Now its mighty, brass-cast, one-hundred-year-old bell pulled the hammer back and sounded out a loud, resonant, *ONE...!*

A huge burst of light, like a bolt of lightning came flashing through his window, its intensity hurling him backwards on the bed. It lit up the room like thousands of LED lights, too strong for his eyes to focus. He threw his hands up to shield his face, trying to see what was glowing in the intense light. As the brightness slowly dimmed, he gradually saw, standing in front of him, a figure unlike anything he'd ever seen, or imagined, before.

It could have been a juvenile , but it clearly wasn't because it had a shock of long white hair, like an old man, spilling down over its shoulders. Though its face was that of an older person, it had no wrinkles or signs of ageing. In fact, it looked very healthy, youthful, almost ethereal with piercing eyes above a gentle smile. Botox perhaps? Scrooge thought. It was small, like a child on the edge of puberty, but it had muscular arms and hands, like an adult who was used to hard labour. A little person maybe? Its feet were petite, sweet, and dainty, and it wore no shoes or footwear of any kind. It was dressed in a long, hooded tunic, like a monk's robe, but without sleeves. The tunic was a soft white, a belt around the middle, and spring flowers floating in a garland around its hem. Scrooge looked at the Spirit in amazement. Fancy dress party perhaps? Whatever the reason it was going to freeze in that getup, Scrooge thought.

Scrooge could see this because the Spirit wore a band on its head, like headlamps cave explorers wear, a bright blaze of light streaming from it, dazzling his eyes.

Perhaps to see the way, Scrooge wondered. Okay, he summarised to himself, was he looking at a little person, probably a manual labourer, possibly in his 60s, who'd recently had Botox and was now on his way to a fancy-dress party wearing a torch on his head so he could see the way?

Sounds perfectly reasonable thought Scrooge. Mind you, after his night of ghostly encounters, a purple dotted elephant with two tails, wearing ballet slippers and a pink tutu, standing on his doorstep singing Christmas carols would've sounded perfectly reasonable at this point.

He stared at the apparition. It seemed to come in and out of focus, Scrooge knew it WAS there, he COULD see it. But the light ebbed and flowed onto different parts of the Spirit, now he could see more of the robe, now more or the face. Then he could see the limbs and the light made it look like the Spirit had more than two arms and legs! Then just the head would be visible, no body! Finally, the whole Spirit stood in his bedroom looking at him.....

What Scrooge had just seen was the phenomenon known to us as "Beaming" or I should say that's the closest description and easiest way to understand what had just occurred. Unfortunately, it must be reported that Scrooge was one of those sad, few, strange, weird individuals who clung to the very edges of our society, uneducated and uninformed because sadly he'd never, ever seen an episode of Star Trek in his life. If he had, he would have instantly recognised that the Spirit was beaming in from another dimension and therefore not been quite so stunned at the phenomenon he'd just witnessed. But he hadn't. He also didn't know what a Tribble was, nor had he ever heard the magic words, "Beam me up, Scotty" which is a great pity in my view.

"Are you the first ghostly visitor Jacob Marley told me about?" Scrooge asked grudgingly.

"Yes, I am," replied the Spirit. Its voice surprisingly sweet and gentle.

Scrooge, determined to gain the upper hand in this new relationship, growled, "So who are you then, what's your name?"

The Spirit smiled and said, "I don't have an earthly name; I am the ghost of Christmas Past."

"Christmas Past, eh?" replied Scrooge. "How far back in the past? 200 years ago, 300, 500? How far back do you go?"

"No," answered the Spirit, "you misunderstand. I'm from the Christmas's of your past."

Scrooge grunted his dismissal of this statement, but still striving for dominance he stared rudely at the Spirit and said, "Why is that light you have so bright? It's very uncomfortable to the eyes you know and not necessary. We have electric light in the modern world," he said sarcastically. "Turn it off, you're giving me a headache!"

"Pardon me?" answered the Spirit gently. "Did you hear nothing of Jacob Marley's warnings? Didn't you listen to anything he had to say? If you did, you would remember his advice. Do you really want me to turn out the only light that can lead you to understanding and change, right now, before we've even started?"

Scrooge angrily replied he'd meant no such thing, and anyway, what exactly was the Spirit doing there at that hour of the morning?

"I am here for your benefit," replied the Spirit.

"My benefit!" Scrooge muttered. "Some such thing! The only thing that would benefit me right now would be a night of unbroken sleep!"

"Call it your re-education then," said the Spirit. "Get up Ebenezer Scrooge, you must come with me." And taking hold of Scrooge's arm the Spirit pulled him to his feet.

Scrooge grumbled at the Spirit as he grudgingly stood up. "Why all this bother?" he said. "Why all this airy-fairy nonsense with Jacob and you? If you want me to change, can't you just wave your magic wand or do some jiggery-pokery and be done with it? Then I might be able to get some rest!"

The Spirit looked at Ebenezer with a mixture of irritation and sorrow. Looking him squarely in the eye the Spirit said firmly, "I'm not your fairy godmother Ebenezer Scrooge, nor am I a Genie from the lamp, here to grant you three wishes. To use your earth terminology, this is an intervention. You and you alone are the one to decide about your future. My task is only to chaperone you through your past."

Scrooge was going to plead that it was late, that he was cold and tired, he was still in his pyjamas and didn't know where his proper shoes were, plus a dozen other reasons not to go, but he found his aggressive bluster was useless in the presence of the gentle Spirit, and he could not resist the pull on his hands as it steered him towards the windows.

As he drew near, he finally realised that the windows, blown open so dramatically during his visit with Jacob Marley, had, of their own accord, closed just as tightly as if they'd never opened. Now, as he and the Spirit stood before them, he exclaimed, pointing, "The...The...windows! Look...they're...closed again!"

As the Spirit slowly walked backwards, pulling Scrooge along with him, he suddenly understood that not only did it intend to step through the glass, but it was determined to pull him through it too! Scrooge jerked backwards and cried, "No wait...Stop! I'm not a Spirit like you, I'm a human, a person, I'll be cut, I'll fall!"

The kindly Spirit, placing his hand on Scrooge's chest, smiled reassuringly saying, "You won't fall. All I have to do is touch you here, and you'll be able to follow me to more places than this." And holding tightly onto Scrooge's hand, it pulled him closer and closer towards the window. Ebenezer shut his eyes as the two of them passed through, and like *Alice Through The Looking Glass,* everything familiar in the world disappeared.

The flats, the markets, the road, the car park and the city all evaporated around them as he and the Spirit beamed into the distant memories of his past.

Chapter 6: Memories Of Yesterday

Scrooge and the Spirit appeared on a country road where fallow fields were bordered with hedgerows, all under a heavy burden of snow. Silent, cold, and crisp, the day had dawned with a soft, misty light and before them, in the far distance stood a grand old building. This then was the countryside of the 1960s, when everyone could still make a living off the land before visitors from the big smoke turned the farms and villages into theme parks of English Country Life. To be precise it was December 1968, and celebration was in the air.

"Bloody hell!" enthused Scrooge unconsciously slipping into his schoolboy vernacular and earning a disapproving look from the Spirit. "I... I know this! This is where I went to boarding school! I practically grew up around here!" he said, remembering his many years in this place. He breathed in the crisp country air, heavily scented with smoke from cottage fires, and punctuated with the sweet smell of cow dung. He could clearly hear the sounds around him, how easily his ears were tuned to the countryside and not the loud, brash noises of busy London. Here, the calling of the birds, there, distant farms with a morning cacophony of animals; sheep, chickens, horses and the steady rhythm of chop and clatter as someone close by cut wood for their fire. The local junior school, the children and their noise and the faint tolling of the old church, all blended into a symphony of the countryside and reminded him of lost joys and sorrows he had known when he was there. Wiping his eyes that had somehow watered (perhaps it was the cold air?) Scrooge looked at the Spirit as it asked him, "Can you remember the way then?"

Remember it! He could walk it blindfolded and in the dark. Confidently Scrooge set off towards the memories of his bygone days.

As they walked and the day unfolded, Scrooge's memories seemed to take over and overwhelm his natural disagreeable, rude state of mind. He became carefree, relaxed, and full of remembrances. Tapping each post and tree with his hand, he talked unconsciously about his past until in the distance a little market town came into view. Scrooge pointed out the old church that had stood for several hundred years near the town and had, in 1535, become one of the first new Churches of England under Henry VIII. There, of course, the ubiquitous gentle river that wound its way through the town, like many rivers in small towns and hamlets throughout England did then, before modernisation and subdivision ruined it all. He talked about the small footbridges that stretched over them, making great places where schoolboys raced leaf boats to see whose came through to the other side first and where he and a friend had stood to drop rocks into deeper water, just as springtime couples canoodling in boats came out from under the bridges, soaking them in river water. How occasionally, when some of the boys came back early from the long break, they would sneak extra food from breakfast, or pester the kitchen staff for a few sandwiches, and all set off for the day, to picnic on the riverbank where the water was deepest, swimming in the brackish pool during those last weeks of summer before the days grew short and the weather chilly.

All the boys knew the village shop where you could buy the best sweets ever, a quarter of a pound for thruppence or half a pound plus a sherbet lollipop for a sixpence (this was before decimalisation of course) and where they could get the new Boys Adventure Magazine every month. He told the Spirit how he and his best friend would collect all the empty beer and lemonade bottles from the neighbourhood and take them back to the Rose and Dragon Pub for the deposits so they could buy comics and ice creams. Weekends they would sometimes go scrumping, not just for apples, but pears, cherries, even damsons if they could get away with them, then sell them, three for sixpence in their dorm.

Look, there was the town hall where the scouts met weekly. Scrooge had five badges on his uniform, but some of the boys had lots more. Old Ernie Pinkle had 22 badges! But then his Uncle was Akela of the troop, Scrooge said with a little smile. Over there he said, pointing to a hidden area behind the clubhouse, was where he used to watch the public-school lads play conkers and marbles against the town boys and farmers kids.

And there!! His only triumph! He stopped at the village green, with its tea house, benches, scoreboard, and markings on the grass for every sport from football to lacrosse. This was where, he told the Spirit, he had opened the batting for the first XI of his school every year since he was twelve years old. Cricket season was the only time anyone knew his name, he said with a sardonic smile. Once it was over, everyone forgot about him again...

He talked about it all to the Spirit who said, "It's so strange Ebenezer, up until now you'd forgotten all of this hadn't you?" Scrooge, realising this was too true, nodded as the Spirit smiled and said, "come on, let's go, we've still got a lot to see."

Then over the hills and down those narrow country lanes where you could stretch your arms wide and feel the hedges on both sides, a group of young lads on their bikes, including Scrooge's younger self on an old Raleigh he'd found in the gardener's shed, all raced into view, yelling out to each other, sprinting then stopping, cold, breathing frosty breath and having a marvellous time. Not so for drivers in cars trying to squeeze past on those tiny country roads, with the boys making it difficult by deliberately cycling in a slow, leisurely zig zagging way. When several of the boys were admonished by one frustrated driver and told to get out of his way, a young lad answered succinctly, "It's everyone's bloody road mate, not just yours!"

This language sent the driver into a fury and he loudly declared that if the lad was his child, he would receive a jolly good hiding for swearing! Scrooge smiled, then laughed aloud. He knew what would happen now because he remembered it from his childhood. The best answer to any adult who ticked you off about using the "B" word. All the boys stopped their bikes in a row across the road. As the man fulminated against them, standing by his driver's side door, one of the lads waved his fingers like a conductor and said, "One, two, three..." And altogether they chanted,

"Bloodies in the Bible, bloodies in the book.
If you don't bloody believe me, have a bloody look!"

And, finishing with a group raspberry and a couple of double-digit gestures, they turned tail on their bikes and headed for the hills, laughing all the way. Scrooge laughed along with them and was still chuckling to himself when the Spirit touched his arm and said quietly, "Ebenezer you need to understand everything here is from your memories. They can't see us, and we can't touch or interfere with anything we'll see or hear."

Scrooge nodded, but kept watching the boys, remembering their names as they raced away from him and the Spirit. He began to feel differently. His cold heart was warmed by their shouting back and forth and he felt emotions he hadn't experienced for as long as he could recall.

They turned off the small country lane into a magnificent sweeping driveway which lead up to Shirringdon Hall, a beautiful country house built in 1525 by one Edward Shirringdon. It was an exceptionally large two-storey house where Shirringdon, it was whispered, had lived like a king. Inevitably the hall was seized by the actual King over 'questionable allegiance to the crown' but Edward Shirringdon eventually resolved the problem to everyone's satisfaction. He'd persuaded the crown of his loyalty by gifting to His Majesty the hall, the 50 acres of farming land, the 200 hundred acres of forest and its access to the river. In return the King allowed Edward Shirringdon to keep his head.

The hall passed through many hands through the years. From 1815 it billeted French officers captured during the Napoleonic war. They were given conditional parole and a regular stipend allowing them to come and go, mix with polite society, use the local libraries to perfect their English, occasionally even staging wonderful concerts for their new friends to enjoy. All terribly civilised.

It fell empty until it was commissioned again during the late 1800s, this time as a hospital for TB patients. Though many patients passed through its doors on two legs, a number left carried shoulder high, to the grief and sorrow of their loved ones.

The house saw service one last time during the Great War, as a hospital for wounded soldiers sent home with every injury imaginable. Returned home with burns, lost limbs, lungs that were dissolved thanks to mustard gas, battle fatigue and blindness, hundreds of men came home, broken, but not defeated.

Finally, it was bought nearly four hundred years after it was built, by an unnamed philanthropist brimming with good intentions. Renamed *Shirringdon Hall House* its doors were opened in the early-20th century as a boarding school for young gentlemen between the ages of 8 and 18. When Scrooge attended its lofty halls it was the perfect preparation for gaining entry to the universities of Oxford or Cambridge.

As Scrooge and the Spirit reached the front of the school they saw teachers and house masters draped in impressive robes, and students bursting to pack up and leave for the holidays, all milling around talking to nattily dressed parents. Chauffeurs, porters and helpers made sure everything was packed safely into car boots and onto roof racks for the journey home. Scrooge named all his friends, bright young lads, running in and out of the main entrance, yelling to each other, getting into their cars as one by one they took their leave. Scrooge waved at each one, even though he knew they couldn't see him, listening to the shouted calls of "Happy Christmas!" As they drove away to their homes, his smile faded. A Happy Christmas? What was that? When had HE ever had a Happy Christmas? What good was it really, to him, to anyone!

Soon, almost all the cars had gone, and the school was quiet. The day was becoming overcast and cold. Scrooge wasn't as cheerful as before; he sat on the steps watching the last car drive away and now waited to see what the Spirit wanted next.

"They went home for Christmas?" The Spirit said, looking down at him, "Did all your friends go too?"

"I only had a few friends, four or five. I was a bit of an outsider here, but I had some friends and yes, they went home for Christmas," said Scrooge.

"You know, the school isn't empty of all students...Someone is left behind," the Spirit said.

"No... Really? You do surprise me," sneered Scrooge.

"Perhaps you know who's still here?"

Scrooge, brimming with rude sarcasm replied, "Yes... Of course, I do." He pulled himself up and turned to the entrance, leading the way.

They went through the main doors into the foyer which was as cheerless as the outside. It was cold and empty except for a few old paintings of hunting scenes, several imposing portraits of forgotten benefactors and one picture of an unnamed woman in riding dress. It was rumoured to be painted by Gainsborough in the mid-1760s, however, it was too high up on the wall for anyone to bother to check, especially if it turned out not to be true. It was more pragmatic to reflect in its anticipated glory than finding out for sure.

Fixed to the wall, barely visible in the dingy light was a leader board for sports glory, one for school captains, one for scholarships, and finally several severe photographs of deceased headmasters. The windows were too small to allow any real warmth or light in, so it was echoey, dark and dismal. They walked past offices, reception rooms, matron's room, the bursar's office, and the downstairs cloakroom, all shut for the season. Each was cold and dreary. Finally through a back corridor of the building, they entered a quiet, dark common room for the boys aged between 8-13 years old. Here there were a few old sofas and easy chairs, some bookshelves stuffed with well-used tuition books. A snooker table, chess sets, table football with several "players" minus heads, all at the ready. There was an old Zenith stereo record console and some records, plus a black and white TV, ancient by today's standards, all of which supplied to help the students relax in the few free hours between after school activities, homework, supper, evening prayers and bedtime.

However, in the entire room, there were no signs of Christmas. No paper chains, no tree hung with handmade decorations, no bells, no bunting. No 'Merry Christmas' signs or cards. Nothing to tell a stranger that at Shirringdon it was time to celebrate Christmas.

There was one lonely occupant in the room. Sitting in an easy chair under a dim lamp, was an eight-year-old child. A couple of small wrapped parcels from his friends were on a table in front of him. Scrooge's younger self was reading. His eyes, fixed determinedly on the book, were glowing with tears.

"I remember reading that book!" said Scrooge looking sideways to read the title. Again, his memories overwhelming his natural dismal attitude. "Robinson Crusoe was one of my favourites. I loved all the classics. I could read properly by the time I was five and read every book in the library, imagining the characters coming to life right here in front of me, just for me!" he said.

"All these books were such wonderful friends, they helped fill in many lonely hours. Ali Baba and the 40 Thieves. Kidnapped, Treasure Island, of course, H.G. Wells, Shakespeare, George Orwell. Great Authors. Sooo many books...all...to myself." Scrooge looked at the boy intently and pulled up another chair. He felt his own eyes moisten as he watched his younger self struggle to focus through his tears

"...But then," Scrooge continued, "I was alone many times. I learned... to...see the books...Like plays...in my mind. I had this room all to myself. I

74

had no one to share with, I could read any book I liked. And I could watch anything on the television I wanted to. No arguing with the older boys. I watched what I wanted to for two whole weeks. It was...good...you know...the telly and the books all to myself, in the quiet here...like a little holiday."

The young boy turned a page and used the back of his hand to wipe his eyes and nose, drying it on his trousers. He was breathing heavily, trying to stop crying and focus hard on the page in front of him, he couldn't stop the tears oozing from his eyes.

With nothing to distract him from what he was feeling, nothing to gruff or grumble about, Scrooge, watching his younger self struggle with his tears, finally let all his heartache go and began to weep. Putting his hand into his pocket, he searched for his handkerchief. Not finding it, he too wiped his eyes using the back of his hand saying, "I'd like to...If I could...Perhaps...well, it's too late. I suppose..."

"Problem?" asked the Spirit.

"Nothing really," said Scrooge. "Some children were singing at my door last night, I wish I'd given them some money, some encouragement, that's all."

The Spirit made no reply to this, but simply said, "We need to move forward to another Christmas time."

Giddiness overcame Scrooge as the images blended and he saw his former self grow a little older. Maybe now he was nine or ten, not much more, and again, alone in the room, sitting under the same light, reading. Through the door, one of the schoolmasters bustled in asking, "Are you ready then my boy, all set for Christmas Dinner?"

His younger self put down the book and got respectfully to his feet answering, "Yes Sir, thank you, I'm ready." The man, who was in truth the Bursar of the school and a very kind man, laughed and threw an arm around his shoulder saying, "Into the car then lad, my family are waiting to meet you and lunch smells magnificent. Also, I've just picked up a parcel from the Head for you. So, when you come back this afternoon you can open it. Something to look forward to, eh?"

"A parcel, from whom?" young Scrooge asked as he wrapped up tight against the cold.

"I don't know my boy," said the bursar, "but the postmark's from Scotland if that helps."

Scotland? Fan! Fan was in Scotland or was the last time he spoke to her. It had to be Fan!

"It's probably from my sister Sir," Scrooge replied, from deep inside his "big" coat.

"Well, that's nice. You can see what she sent you later. Come on, old fellow," called the bursar from the doorway. "Sprouts wait for no man you know!"

"Your sister sent you a gift?" asked the Spirit interrupting Scrooge's reverie.

"Yes, that was the first time. She came for Boxing Day every year after that, but this year, she sent a gift."

"What was it, do you remember?"

"Yes, I do. It was a jar of Scottish marmalade, shortbread in a tin and a photo of her at Stirling Castle. I made the shortbread last until April," Scrooge remembered smiling.

"Let's look once more at another important Christmas here," said the Spirit.

The room whirled and swirled around him again, faded in and out of focus and became older and shabbier as Scrooge's former self grew up, four or five years this time. The windows became grubby and some were cracked and patched. Parts of the ceiling had fallen in, revealing the beams above, and the floor was worn down and scuffed. The room smelled musty and damp with the unmistakable scent of mice mixing with the odour of dust and decay.

Scrooge watched his other self now grown into a teenager, pacing up and down, occasionally stopping and looking past them to the door, as if he were waiting for something. He was still pacing when a young woman came in almost dancing with delight.

Scrooge's older self stood stock still as he watched her enter the room. "Fan," he whispered, "Oh Fan, you're here. How can you be here again?" And he stared at her, overwhelmed, his shrivelled heart filling with love, his mind, remembering that love, edged with sadness.

"Spirit," he called his attention, "Its Fan, Spirit! I never thought I'd ever see her again."

A little older than the teenage Scrooge, she was smaller than him and stood on tippy-toes as she hugged and kissed him, identifying him as, "My wonderful baby brother." Slightly built and very pretty, she laughed and hugged Scrooge over and over, then twirled about the dusty room like a wood sprite saying joyfully, "Guess what Buzz, pack everything! I've come to take you home with me!"

Scrooge's former self though happy to see her and beguiled by her joy and enthusiasm, couldn't help but look nervous as he replied, "Home Fan, are you serious? Home?"

"Yes!" she laughed. "Home, and to stay! You're not coming to this dusty old place ever again that's for certain." She took both of his hands in hers and looked up into his eyes. Pure green looked into deep blue as she said, "Everything at home is so different now. It's all okay. When I was saying goodnight to Daddy on Sunday he looked at me so differently and spoke so softly and gently that I said to myself, just ask him one more time about Buzz, so I crossed my fingers and toes and said, Daddy, I really think it's time Ebenezer finally came home to stay don't you? The past is the past now and can't be changed, how about he comes home for Christmas and stays, never goes back. Hasn't he been there long enough? And he said YES! It was about time you came home to stay and then he said, Frannie, I'll get a car to take you. You can be the one to bring him home before the end of the week if you like. And I kept reminding him and reminding him and ta-da! Here I am!" Kissing the palms of both his hands, she laughed and said, "We're going to have such a wonderful Christmas, all of us together! I've made great plans; it's going to be fantastic." She whirled him around and around, laughing with so much joy Scrooge finally relaxed and laughed with her.

Scrooge's younger self said in a kind admiring voice, "You're so grown up Fan, look at you. You're not just my big sister, you're so beautiful now."

Fan laughed, hugged, and kissed him again. She pulled him into her arms and humming a tune they waltzed around the dusty, gloomy room together. The more they laughed, the more they tripped and laughed some more, so much so they couldn't dance any longer and just held each other, hugging, their eyes sparkling.

A cockney voice yelled loudly, "Can we 'ave Mr Scrooge's luggage h'if you please?" And holding hands, they both rushed upstairs to hurriedly pack up the few of his things not already kept in the trunk at the foot of his bed. A final look round and the porter was called to take his luggage out to the car.

Hand in hand, Fan and Scrooge flew downstairs again towards the main entrance and the car that would finally take him away from this place forever.

The Spirit was looking at Scrooge intently. "You were here for many years?" he questioned.

"Yes," answered Scrooge, his voice distant as he looked after his younger self and his sister. "My father brought me. He...He didn't care for my company. I never knew why. My mother died, and then he brought me here when I was quite young. Fan, she was like a mother to me. She always visited me when she could, not just at Christmas, although that was the best. She wrote to me often with all her news, called me on the phone at least once a week, and always told me she loved me."

"Did you ever go home for Christmas?" asked the Spirit.

"Once. In the first year I was here," replied Scrooge. "As I got older Fan would come on Boxing Day like I said, to bring me a gift and spend the entire day. Actual Christmas Day I used to spend here, on my own mostly. One year, another boy from the upper sixth had to stay at the school too. We had an enjoyable time, despite our age difference. He was the one who taught me how to play chess, I remember. When Fan came all three of us had a terrific day.

Another year I had lunch again with the bursar and his family, they were genuinely nice to me, even gave me a gift, a pair of hand knitted gloves his wife made for me. They were all right, but I was the outsider. It was better when my friends came back. I enjoyed it better then, school, but Christmas Day, no, I was usually alone."

"How long were you here, at the school?" asked the Spirit.

"Nine...Nine years," replied Scrooge. "But there were times it felt a lot longer than that."

Meanwhile, as Scrooge's trunk was being finagled into the car, the headmaster had appeared and intercepted Fan and Scrooge, insisting on them drinking a toast and eating some cake. Caught on the hop, neither could think of a reason to refuse so, following him into his study, he served them each a glass of dry sherry, with a slice of equally dry Christmas cake.

Perhaps it was because the room had no comfort. No warm, bright lights, no decorated Christmas tree, no cosy fire, no television tuned to a welcoming show. Perhaps it was because the headmaster had already said everything he could say about Christmas many times before. Or maybe it was just their impatience to get away, but when Scrooge and Fan were told his luggage was finally loaded, they made no effort to stay. Quickly drinking the rest of their sherry they said a hurried goodbye to the headmaster and rushed off, leaving the school forever. As they scrambled into the car Scrooge could hear Fan say, "Come on Buzz, no need to worry. This is the beginning of your whole new life! Start as you mean to go on."

The wheels of the car crunched through the slush and snow. Scrooge and the Spirit could hear Fan laughing and talking a mile a minute as it drove away.

"She was always a very caring person," said the Spirit. "Gentle and loving, she'd an enormous heart, filled with love."

"Yes," said Scrooge. "She was very special. Everyone loved her. I... I loved her very much. She was the only person I could relax and be myself with. With everyone else, my father, at school, sometimes even with my friends, I had to push my feelings down and be someone different, but with Fan, I could just be me. She was always so kind to me. She helped me as I grew older. Everyone loved her. She was one of a kind, and incredibly special."

"Did she ever have children?"

"One," said Scrooge.

"Of course, your nephew Fred," said the Spirit. Scrooge said nothing and looked away.

"You never came back after this day?" the Spirit asked.

"No, never. This was the last time I ever saw it, until now."

"And your friends? Did you ever hear from them at all?"

"No, none of them. No answers to my letters either. I wrote to my friends, but no one wrote back, none, not ever," Scrooge said sounding like a child.

The Spirit looked sympathetic as it replied, "They never answered you because they never received your letters. Your father gave the school orders to destroy any letters you sent and not to pass them on to your friends."

"Oh, I see," said Scrooge shortly, at once hating the Spirit's sympathetic tone.

"Doesn't that upset you?" asked the Spirit.

"There's not much I can do about it now is there!" snarled Scrooge suddenly defensive. "Anyway, we were bound to grow apart. Their parents sent them to university, most became Cambridge men. My father said I should go out into the world as soon as I was old enough and got me a business apprenticeship where I could learn all about finances and commerce. 'Earn your own way boy,' that's what he said, 'Go and be a man, no free rides,' so I was packed off as soon as I was old enough to be out on my own.'"

Scrooge's demeanour had quickly changed from the mellow smiling person who'd been reminiscing with the Spirit, back to the sour and hostile, impatient old man from before. "This is ridiculous!" he growled. "A waste of my time and a waste of yours. Why go on? Why keep going over ancient history. Why are you wasting your time with all this nonsense?" he demanded.

"It's not your place to judge whether my time is wasted or not," replied the Spirit kindly. "Time spent here is especially important for you, only by following your past can we change your future. But now, let's see you as the young man who was sent out into the world at such an early age." And with a flick of his hand, he and Scrooge travelled forward in time, into a different era of his past.

There has been a great deal of mystery concerning Scrooge's sister Fan, and whether she was older or younger than him. Some people, including her father, have said that she was younger. She was short of stature, with a sweet nature and always full of joy; A tiny sweet Christmas doll you could hang on your tree. But my research shows Fan was not a "porcelain doll." Fan was a fighter, determined and resolute...

However, her petite size, and the fact that she and her brother were only separated by 14 months, meant that people made the common mistake that Fan was indeed the youngest, a fiction her father promoted to continually deny his son existence.

Nevertheless, Scrooge always said, quite clearly, that his father dumped him at the school some years after his mother died and we know she died in childbirth with her son, not her daughter. (Associates of Augustus Scrooge confirmed he always blamed the boy for his wife's death and had as little to do with him as possible.)

A search of medical records for Mrs Theresa Scrooge shows that both Mr and Mrs Scrooge were warned after the birth of their first child, a daughter, that a second pregnancy could be extremely dangerous, and it was recommended they take every measure to prevent

it. Whether they tried contraception or not is unknown. According to the same friends of Augustus, once the second pregnancy was confirmed, he was in favour of immediate termination of the child, something his wife flatly refused to even consider, no matter how much he coerced or bullied her. Sadly, in the same medical file is a copy of Theresa's death certificate dated the 18th of September 1959 and giving the cause of death as maternal mortality due to eclampsia. The child, a boy, was born 4 weeks premature by emergency C-section.

The earliest age a child could attend an English boarding school was usually around eight years old, but rules can be relaxed if you have enough cash and are loudly insistent. After Ebenezer's father, who, let's face it, was never going to win "Daddy of the year" sends him away, his sister almost immediately starts a campaign to bring him home again.

Fan was determined not to abandon her brother and continues using all kinds of communication with him including visiting whenever she could. She has a big sister relationship with her brother that Daddy dearest couldn't break, much to his annoyance. She insisted on seeing him in the school holidays and every Boxing Day, which shows her resolve not to cut him out of her life no matter what her father said. A brave act in the face of a man who can only be called a bully.

Obviously she shares that same streak of determination that her mother had, and, even though her campaign was hindered by her father sending her to finishing school at Stanglynton Ladies College in Scotland, she was resolved never to give up and eventually wore her father down, getting the all clear to bring her brother home after nine years of never ending persistence.

After extensive research of all the available facts, census, and parish records, I have concluded Scrooge was younger than his sister Fan by approximately fourteen months. Following his mother's death due to complications in childbirth, Scrooge was looked after by nannies and nursemaids but also had a loving relationship with his sister who, let it be remembered, also lost her mother when she died. Their relationship continued even after his father sent him away to boarding school.

After closing his heart to Ebenezer, Augustus Scrooge could no longer bear to look at him, a living reminder of his own guilt in the death of his wife.

Scrooge and the Spirit arrived in the hustle and bustle of the early nineteen seventies and found themselves in an area of busy shops and warehouses. Cars and trucks, delivery bikes, mopeds and people were everywhere. Bright lights and decorations said it was Christmas here too. The Spirit guided Scrooge to a business complex and a particular warehouse door and asked him if he recognised it.

"Of course, I do!" Scrooge answered. "I had my first job here! This is Fezziwig's warehouse! I worked here for years!"

Scrooge and the Spirit moved through the wall into the high ceiling warehouse where old Fezziwig was seated at a grand desk.

"Holy sh...!" exclaimed Scrooge, quickly slapping his hand over his mouth to cut off the obscenity in the Spirit's presence, who smiled and nodded his approval. "Old Mister Fezziwig, there he is, alive again!"

We need to pause here to set right a long-standing mispronunciation of the Fezziwig name. Generally, it is pronounced FEZZ-EEE-WIG but that is in fact incorrect. The pronunciation should be FET-ZEE-WIG. Just as the double ZZ in PIZZA makes a "T" sound, it does in the Fezziwig name, changing the pronunciation to FETZIWIG. But if indeed you are used to pronouncing it the old way, continue to do so, Mr Fezziwig wouldn't have minded.

Mr Fezziwig was a chubby little man about five feet five who had a perpetual smile, an infectious laugh, and a soft heart. He ran his business honestly and fairly but was known to be a bit too indulgent with credit and as a result was owed a lot of money by his customers. While he would never be very wealthy, he was loved by everyone who worked for him, which included Scrooge's younger self.

Fezziwig looked at his watch, then closed his big accounting book, took the phone off the hook and shouted, "Benny, Dick, come on lads, look lively, let's be having you. Chop chop!"

The Spirit turned towards Scrooge, his eyes twinkling with amusement, one eyebrow lifted questioningly, "Benny?" he said in amusement, but before Scrooge could say anything, his younger self came running into the office along with another young man approximately the same age. Both were wearing the fashion of the 70s: flared blue business trousers with sharp creases down the front, matching waistcoats, crisp white business shirts with oversized collars and ridiculously patterned wide ties. Both sported fashionable sideburns, shoulder length hair and looked...er...Interesting from a modern point of view. Embarrassing is another word that springs to mind.

"Oh, my goodness!" Scrooge said to the Spirit and grabbing his arm in excitement, "Is that Dick? That's Dick! Dick Wilkins! We were inseparable Dick and me when we worked here. We both started at the same time, I never thought I'd see him again!"

"That's it," shouted Fezziwig, "done and dusted for today, time for our Christmas celebrations!" Rubbing his hands together, he said, "Righto you two, let's get cracking! Everything away, locked up and room made. Off you go!" And waving them on Scrooge and Dick took off running, closing windows and doors, moving equipment to the sides of the huge warehouse floor, and bringing out collapsible tables and stackable chairs which, under Mr Fezziwig's direction, they quickly arranged into settings of two, four and six around a central area designated for dancing. An elevated area at one end of the warehouse was arranged as a stage with a curtain of glittering lametta shielding the wires of the microphone and spotlights. Strings of coloured lights, Chinese lanterns and tinsel were hung around, and candles in wine bottles were plonked onto tablecloths and lit.

Through the back dock, the DJ arrived with a van full of equipment. Offering him a helping hand, Dick happily moved, stacked plugged and finally tested all the equipment to make sure it was working, the DJ making good use of him as he did his sound check.

From somewhere a mirror ball made an appearance and was hoisted into place, a flick of a switch and the brace of lights that illuminated the DJ burst into life and suddenly the magical illusion of an exclusive Christmas restaurant was complete.

A tooting horn announced Mrs Fezziwig arrival; her Mini Clubman Estate stuffed with large containers of wonderful smelling food. As happy and pleasant as her husband, Mrs Fezziwig was everywhere, directing Ebenezer and Dick as they opened each container and arranged the placement of the food and drink.

Her three daughters, Petunia, Maria, and Scarlet arrived one at a time, Maria with her fiancée and Petunia and Scarlet with boyfriends in tow. While the guys tried to look cool and relaxed, everyone there knew they were hopelessly enchanted by each girl; these three young women, who'd inherited all that was good from both parents.

Mrs Fezziwig immediately put these star struck lovers to use, helping Ebenezer and Dick unload the car and set everything out on buffet tables for their guests to enjoy.

From 7.30 pm people began to arrive. Employees who had popped home to drop the little ones off at the babysitter's place, now returned to the warehouse with their significant others, dressed in their glad rags and ready to party.

Forty-something men wore flared trousers and flower power patterned, large collared shirts, while high waisted dress pants, silk shirts and leather jackets were favoured by the younger generation. It was not yet the era to wear jeans to a formal "do," not to the office Christmas party anyway. Older gentlemen who'd been with the company for years wore their Sunday suits and crisp white shirts.

Women wore long sleeve frilled blouses, psychedelically patterned slacks, maxi length peasant skirts and suede fringed jackets, while others were drenched in a variety of kaftans. Big blue eye makeup abounded. Hairstyles that screamed, "Welcome to the Country and Western Music Awards," competed with huge curls and backcombed bouffants that were lacquered into place long before anyone had heard of split ends and breakage.

Drinks in hand, work colleagues would, for some reason, stand and talk to people they'd known for years as if they were strangers. 'He' would complain about how long it took 'her' to get ready and 'she' could say, 'oh this old thing', when complimented on her dress.

More and more people arrived as the party warmed up.

The Fezziwig's neighbours came.

Old Mrs Patel from number 27 came, on the arm of her son Isaac. Mrs Patel used to babysit the Fezziwig girls when they were younger, and they'd all had a crush on Isaac at one time or another.

Mrs Fezziwig had invited all the girls from tennis, and Mr Fezziwig all the lads from football.

Maria, Petunia and Scarlet had invited their friends, who all turned up well buffed and starving, after being in the pub for an hour.

Charlie, the night watchman, arrived with his significant other, Barry.

The local Bell Ringers Society, where Mr Fezziwig went every Tuesday evening, all arrived, packed into three cars, joyfully tooting their horn, and wishing the Fezziwig's a Merry Christmas.

Everyone came, Families, couples, groups, friends, and singletons. Off they all went, talking, laughing, mixing, chatting, drinking and enjoying themselves immensely.

Guests could choose from Red or White wines. Classics like Blue Nun, Mateus Rosé, Black Tower, Rioja, or Chianti, all provided by the Fezziwig's. Guinness and Cider were laid on. A keg of beer was flowing nicely. Port and the best Amontillado Spanish sherry were available as a pre-dinner aperitif.

Sweet chilled Lambrusco or glasses of champagne were served for the more sophisticated. Add fresh orange juice for a ritzy Bucks Fizz cocktail. Young ladies drank Baby Cham, while the kids enjoyed Tizer, Pepsi, Lemonade, and Dandelion n' Burdock as they eyed the crisps, cakes and jellies on the big banquet table.

Ebenezer and Dick were everywhere, introducing everyone, making sure their glasses were full, and they knew where they were sitting. Ebenezer was pouring another order of drinks when two dainty hands covered his eyes from behind. He quickly turned around and shouted, "Fan, you're here!" And whirled her off her feet, around and around. Fan was the embodiment of a 1970s fashion magazine. She wore a long sleeved multi coloured mini dress, a thick belt and white knee-high boots. Her pin straight hair was held back in a matching headband and blue/purple eyeshadow with dramatic eyelashes and "nude" frosted lipstick framed her pretty face. He immediately took her to meet the boss, who kissed her hand and loudly asked how on earth did 'Benny' have such a beautiful sister. Fan giggled while Scrooge agreed, grinning. He'd never felt so happy in his life.

Mrs Fezziwig bumbled over like a mother hen and took command of Fan, telling the "boys" to leave Fan with her, she would take care of her tonight. She took Fan's arm and steered her away, introducing her to her daughters and their boyfriends. While they were chatting Mrs Fezziwig grilled Fan in that kind, motherly way that caring people do, and eventually discovered Fan was still single. Tutting several times, she announced that would not do and, taking Fan's hand, declared they were both on a quest to find her a nice young man. Fan, who'd never ever met anyone as kind and loving as Mrs Fezziwig, was a little alarmed at this wave of maternal attentiveness and looked to her daughters for help. However, all three just laughed, saying Fan may as well give in to the inevitable. Raising her glass in a salute, Scarlet said, "Go on, off you go. Have fun," and giggled into her drink as her mother tucked her arm around Fan's waist and bore her away in search of an eligible bachelor.

The buffet table staggered under its burden of roasted chicken pieces, curried chicken wings, shish kabob's made with chicken, lamb, and beef. Three big bowls held potato salads, garden salads, egg salads. Silver covered serving dishes revealed freshly roasted pork with delicious crackling, beef with juicy gravy and ham on the bone. Mister Fezziwig served whatever anyone wanted, and jugs of gravy could be poured all over the delicious meat. Mashed potatoes, mixed vegetables and roast potatoes were under another covered dish. There were platters of pate with crackers next to a dish of cocktail prawns swimming in thousand island dressing. Sausage rolls made to Mrs Fezziwig's special recipe sat next to bowls of potato crisps and nuts. Cheese and pineapple porcupines stood invitingly near cocktail sausages on sticks. Mini quiches nestled next to compartmentalised plates of pickles, gherkins, beetroot and pickled onions, salad cream and mayonnaise. Crispy bread, garlic bread and herb bread was there for everyone to enjoy. Fresh fruit on cocktail sticks lay near a huge wobbling trifle that took centre stage. Cakes and pies were pushed in wherever there was space and a big Pavlova balanced on one end of the table while at the other end a tower of homemade mince pies was going fast.

Mrs Fezziwig had been always a woman after my own heart. In my opinion, she'd brought the most important ingredient to any social occasion, large or small. From her little car, she produced a great stack of paper plates and bowls, plastic cups, wine glasses, knives, forks, spoons, and paper napkins. Honestly, who wants to get stuck with the washing up after a big party.

Then when everyone finally had enough to eat, the DJ changed the soft background music to something livelier, and the evening's entertainment began.

The Fezziwig's opened the night with a dramatic tango, gliding across the floor to whistles and applause. Once the ice was broken, couples followed the siren call to Waltz, Mambo, Twist or even try their hand at the Funky Chicken. The DJ, acting as emcee, mixed his discs, encouraging everyone to dance and have fun. He'd chosen his music well, with tunes for

everyone. Even the Charleston and The Stomp had a few willing partici-
pants, some having learned it from their parents many years ago. Polkas
followed disco dances like the Hustle and the Jive, then a foxtrot or two.
Rock and roll had ladies of a certain age kicking off their shoes and dazzling
the room with moves they didn't know they still had. When everyone got
their second wind, the big band sound of the 1940s boomed out for swing
dances, the Lindy Hop and the Jitterbug.

Meanwhile Scrooge, clearing away paper plates and cups, was looking
around for Fan and noticed a tall, good-looking bloke trying to tempt her
to her feet with promises of teaching her some simple disco steps. Not to
be swayed though, she stayed sitting at their table until it was ordered everyone up on the dance floor for the Wigan Slosh. (She could do easily as she
and Buzz learned it together when they went on holidays at Butlins the previous July.)

The Wigan slosh is one of the dances unique in the annals of history. Its
esoteric popularity is matchless and the simplicity of its steps, along with
your level of enjoyment, is directly related to how much alcohol you've con-
sumed first.

But that wasn't the end of the group dancing. While they were all still on
their feet, puffing and blowing, happy and laughing, the DJ split them up
and everyone fanned out into circles on the large warehouse floor for a loud
and energetic round of the Hokey Cokey.

Or Hokey Pokey depending on where you come from.

**There are differences, not just in the name, but in the lyrics and ac-
tions which can vary widely and, I've discovered, cause fervent
debates on which version is correct. Having made the mistake of doing the incorrect Hokey in conjunction with the incorrect Cokey, or
Pokey, in the wrong hemisphere, you can take my word for it, never
mind debating the complexities of politics or religion, get tangled up
in that disagreement and its teeth and hair all over the place.**

Finally, a Conga Line peeled away and set off around the warehouse, out
the front door, round the business complex and in through the receiving
dock, bringing everyone back to their seats in exhaustion, just in time for
the main event.

Mrs Fezziwig had stayed behind and, together with her daughters, she'd plated and poured brandy over a huge twenty-pound Christmas pudding. The lights were dimmed, and Mr Fezziwig dramatically set the pudding alight, flaming the brandy as it sat in the centre of the large table, to the cheers and applause of the guests. While Mr Fezziwig disappeared, generous portions were served with cream or custard to the waiting crowd, coffee and brandy quickly followed, and everyone agreed they'd all had an exceptional dinner.

From behind the glittering curtain of lametta, a jolly "HO-HO-HO" was booming over the speakers. Mr Fezziwig, now dressed as Father Christmas, a vision of red trimmed with white, appeared from behind the lametta carrying a large sack. Ringing a bell and shouting, "Merry Christmas," old Mister Fezziwig, with Dick as his helper, went around all the tables, sharing Christmas greetings, while Dick handed out the Christmas crackers that were specially made for tonight. The ladies had pink, the men, blue, and all the children received a yellow cracker. Hot as he was in the stifling red suit, Mr Fezziwig made sure no one was missed as he toured every table on the large warehouse floor. With a final, "Merry Christmas" he bid everyone farewell and disappeared back behind the shimmering curtain.

The large Christmas crackers were an enormous success. In each there was a special gift. Ladies received a silver charm in a velvet pouch. The men, a silver tie clip. Kids got sweets and a lollipop. Well, it was Christmas after all, and if the sweets caused cavities and wobbly teeth, at least the Tooth Fairy would still have a job for another year.

Before the DJ closed the evening's dancing, Mister Fezziwig, now stripped of his Father Christmas persona, made a quick speech to all his staff and friends thanking them for coming, and to everyone who worked for him for another fabulous year in business. So pleased, he said, that Mrs Fezziwig was giving every member of staff a small envelope containing a Christmas bonus, with much appreciation from them both.

Dick jumped onto the stage and grabbed the microphone, calling for three cheers for Mr and Mrs Fezziwig. An impromptu chorus of, "For he's a jolly good fellow" followed, as Scrooge presented Mrs Fezziwig with a huge bunch of flowers Fan had sneaked in earlier, and Dick gave Mr Fezziwig a bottle of black label scotch whisky.

The DJ closed the evening by playing a few waltzes and slow dances. Young and old danced; Shuffled steps or canoodled to the softer music. Fan danced with her handsome stranger under Scrooge's watchful eye. Sleepy children snoozed against mum or dad, while older kids found a place out of the way and skated on the cement floor in their socks, played at twizzies or did handstands against the wall, all in between sucking on lollipops or sherbet lemons.

Encouraged by the Fezziwig's to take home doggie bags of leftovers, people began to leave, saying goodnight, all wishing 'Happy Christmas' to the Fezziwig's with thanks for the party as they left.

At last, it was just Scrooge and Dick remaining to clear away, re-stack chairs, fold tables and bin rubbish, while Fan sat and watched, nursing a cup of coffee, and telling her brother about the bloke she danced with. The Fezziwig's had gone home, but not before they had wished both men a 'Happy Christmas', slipping a bonus into each one's pocket.

Standing with the Spirit, Scrooge had again kept up a running monologue of remembrances while he was watching. He'd been in the moment all through the night, reliving everything and had enjoyed it all once more, especially when he'd again seen his beloved Fan. He'd chatted and talked to the Spirit about this person and that, not even realising he was feeling so much happier than he'd been for years. Listening now to Dick and his younger self talk about the evening as they cleared the rest away the Spirit said, "An awful lot of brouhaha for such a small thing, don't you agree?"

Scrooge turned to look at him, frowning his disapproval. "Small, what do you mean small?"

"Well, let's face it," said the Spirit, "what would this have cost him at the time? A handful of your earthly money? No more than ninety or a hundred pounds surely. Hardly worth all this praise," he said, gesturing to Scrooge's younger self still talking about Mr Fezziwig.

"No Spirit you're wrong!" Scrooge shouted in his passionate answer. "A hundred pounds in the seventies was worth a lot more than it is now, but the money is nothing to what's really important. Mr Fezziwig could've made our working life happy, cheerful and interesting, or damned miserable. Every day with what he did or said, our day could be good or such a horrible time we dreaded going to work! He could've paid us thousands each week, but if he made it difficult and uncomfortable, the money would...Be no...Compensation for...The stress we...And the misery we...Lived...Under..." Scrooge dried up as he finished his sentence and became quiet.

"What's up?" asked the Spirit.

"Nothing, nothing's up," said Scrooge. "I just thought of something I'd like to say to my clerk, Bob Cratchit, you know him. Well, I just thought I might...Well anyway, I can't so..."

The Spirit looked up at the sky and said, "My time is running out. I must leave you soon. Quickly, look at yourself as a grown man..."

Scrooge and the Spirit materialised at the back of a school assembly hall. It was dark outside, obviously late evening and raining heavily. Several rows of chairs were filled with eager looking people listening to the lecture being given by a middle-aged man holding a microphone. Behind him were posters and diagrams of pie charts, free-standing blackboards with baffling figures written on them and overhead projections of colourful graphs, each showing increasing money investments of tantalising amounts. Scrooge looked at the Spirit and was about to say something, but the Spirit put a finger to his own lips to silence him and said, "You remember what happened here? Something of great significance in your life Ebenezer."

The speaker was reaching an enthusiastic crescendo, talking earnestly about stocks and shares: the money market: investments and loans, when, at the back of the room, near to where the Spirit and Scrooge were standing, the rear door to the hall slid open with a squeal, and a young woman entered soaking wet, looking like a drowned rat. She tiptoed to the nearest chair, waving to a friend who had, along with everyone else, looked back to see who'd just come in. Finding a tissue she blotted some of the rain off her face, but unfortunately, most of her long red hair had escaped from her ponytail, and dripped bedraggled curls around her eyes and cheeks, while pools of water trickled from her raincoat and gathered at her feet.

Microphone man was at the end of his lecture and summarised the points for his audience. As a final flourish he strongly admonished his students to, "Remember, to get on in business, everything needs to be measured by its cash value. If something within your business structure can generate a cash payment, keep it in your business. For instance, say you have this pen, it has value, because you can sell it and receive payment for it. Therefore, it has cash value. But what about something doesn't have cash value? Let's say a few flowers from someone's garden that they've brought in to brighten up the office. They may look delightful, but they can't be sold so they have no cash value. Cut them loose, waste no more time on them. Don't let sentimentally or persuasion cause you to keep anything that can't generate its own value in cold hard cash. No cash value, no place in your business. Thank you."

His talk was finished at last, and he received a polite round of applause from the audience. More than half of those present had shrugged the evening off as a total waste of time, nevertheless, there were a few budding business moguls in the group, a glint of fanaticism in their eye, who'd been trapped in his tempting pecuniary web.

Mumbling conversation broke out as each person stood up ready to leave. Chairs screeched as they were shoved backwards, picked up and clunked together, as several helpful people began stacking them. Meanwhile, others were checking their watches, wondering when the next bus was due, or where the nearest pub was.

At the same time, the friend went over to the dripping young woman exclaiming, "What the hell happened to you? You look like you've been through the rinse cycle of a washing machine."

The woman laughed. "It's bucketing down out there! If I'd have known I'd never have asked for a lift after night school, I'd have taken the bus. Just five minutes walking here, and I'm drenched," she said, still trying to dry herself off. "And this thing is no good." She held up the now soggy tissue as they both laughed.

"Allow me," said a deep, warm voice as a hand offered a dry handkerchief. "You may have more success with this."

Standing beside both women, holding a snowy white handkerchief, was a tall, dark-haired man with deep blue eyes.

"But I have one condition," he said smiling. "I'll give you my handkerchief if you tell me your name."

"Err...Bella," replied the redhead. Captivated by his charming smile, she took the handkerchief, her ice-blue eyes shining under the lights. "Well, it's Annabelle really," she rushed to explain. "But everyone calls me Bella." She giggled. Bella never giggled.

Bella's friend looked from one to another, then snapped her fingers in front of her friend's eyes. "Hello, excuse me, introductions?? I am still here you know!" As Bella turned to look at her, an absurdly silly smile on her face, she muttered, "Oh great, wonderful! Rhett bloody Butler has rendered her speechless..."

The kindly stranger smiled at Bella and replied, "Glad to meet you, Bella. My name is Ebenezer. My sister calls me Buzz and my friends call me Benny.

91

We're all going to the pub, would you and your friend…?" he looked questioningly at the woman by her side being shoved and knocked as everyone jostled past her through the door.

"Oh, I am here, I was wondering. Trish is my name, thanks for noticing me, I feel my existence is validated…"

Ebenezer smiled again "…You and Trish like to come?"

Still with the silly smile, Bella nodded while Trish rolled her eyes and thumped her friend in the arm to break her trance. "If we're going to the pub you're going to have to change or you'll catch your death. Lucky you, it's Wednesday, I've been to the laundrette and got dry stuff in the car. Do you think you can tear yourself away from Cap'n Butler long enough to get changed?" Grabbing Bella's wrist, she steered her towards the main doors yelling, "We'll meet you at the pub," while Bella looked backwards over her shoulder at Scrooge, the daft smile still on her face.

The image swirled and blurred as the Spirit moved them forwards in time, and as he watched, Scrooge saw a movie roll of pictures and snapshots, memories, and moments, all showing himself and Bella as their relationship developed. Bella and Benny, love's young dream Trish called them. Beginning with the laughter and fun, the dinners and dancing, romantic moonlight walks, going to the movies and plays together.

When he introduced Bella to Fan and how well the two girls got on, declaring themselves sisters from a different mister and lifelong friends.

When they all went out together, Trish and her fiancée, Fan and her boyfriend, Bella, and Benny, loves young dream…

That time he and Bella's went on that last-minute mini break to France and forgot the bag with their underwear, saying they invented "going commando."

The day Bella made him eat winkles on holiday in Padstow and laughed at his face when he tasted them.

A long weekend in Scotland, where they'd bought a lobster at the dock and were told to drown it in freshwater, but it came to life again, scuttling around the floor of their caravan, so they released it back into the sea and ate cheese sandwiches instead.

… And in all this time they fell in love…

Finally, that wonderful day when it was pouring down again. She'd been mildly grumpy because he was dragging her to Wales for a day trip, *Wales for goodness sake*!

And she really didn't want to go!

And he was supposed to check the weather before they left, but said he forgot!

And it had been periodically pissing down all the way, but he flatly refused to return home! Walking around Barry Island, the heavens opened again, soaking them both, which did nothing to improve her mood. They bolted for a little café to get out of the rain and, probably sensing her mood, he jumped up to order coffee rather than hanging on for the waitress. Still grumpy and uncomfortable, she sat looking out on a turbulent Whitmore Bay and tried to dry herself with several serviettes. Having no luck, especially with her hair, Benny offered her his handkerchief like before, but this time when she unfolded it, there was a beautiful engagement ring inside.

Dropping to one knee in front of the whole place he proposed to her and when she said yes, everyone whistled and applauded. Benny was so happy, he swept her off her feet, full of excitement and told her Wales was the only part of the British Isles that had rain that weekend, that's why they drove all that way, to re-enact their first meeting!...And she kissed him and said he was an adorable idiot, and he had never felt so wonderful in all his life...

But then...

Then came the slow but definite changes.

It started the day he resigned from his job, Mister Fezziwig clapped him on the back and wished him the best of luck with his new business venture.

Then there were no more walks by the sea. He told Bella it was too cold.

No more romantic dinners. He told Bella he was too busy.

No more mini breaks. He told Bella they cost too much.

She couldn't remember how long it was since they went to the movies together, he said renting a video was cheaper.

The last time he'd asked her if she fancied a romantic evening of dinner and a movie, she'd opened her front door, dressed up in a soft pink sweater, jeans, jacket, and boots, all ready to go out. However, he'd arrived carrying an Indian takeaway, a VHS copy of "King Kong" bootlegged from somewhere, a box of microwaveable popcorn, and two cans of lager. Not even a bottle of wine! He brought lager, like she was one of the boys!

Arguments kept coming, he was always late, and she felt like she was always competing with the business, and Jacob Marley, for Benny's attention.

Benny knew she didn't like his business partner. They'd met once over dinner, and that had been enough for Bella to announce any future entertaining involving Jacob Marley, meant she stayed home. As far as she was concerned, he was loud, fat, greedy and rude. He didn't seem to know what a knife and fork were for, licked his fingers suggestively as he ate, and belched loudly without covering his mouth, in between gulping great mouthfuls of wine.

When she'd rebuked him for burping impolitely *for the third time*, he'd declared superciliously, "My dear girl, belching after a meal is the ultimate compliment to the chef. It indicates one's extreme pleasure in the meal!" And belched again.

On the way home, she told Benny to count her out of any future meetings with Jacob Marley.

The time between them was still short. Then Benny had the idea if they lived together, he would have more time to see her. It was true his driving from his place, to hers and to the office did cut down on the time they spent together. If she lived at his place, when he got home, he was all hers he said. So, she crossed her fingers, gave up her flat, and moved her life into Benny's three bedroomed villa. It was nice to be together all the time, and they did have more time with each other that was true. But still rushed, snatched moments between phone calls, or in the car as he drove her to work, or at night before they fell asleep. But full days, the weekend? Very, very rarely.

Their life became one long discussion about money. Saving money, making money, investing money. The money market, the stock market, and the value of the pound against the US dollar. It was monotonous. If they weren't talking about money, they seldom talked at all.

Spending money, buying anything, was a no-no, but as Trish said, it was her money, she could spend it on what she wanted, couldn't she? She paid her fair share of the bills, she'd insisted on that, but she still felt guilty and got used to hiding her shopping away from Benny, just so he wouldn't start an argument about her making "frivolous purchases." That pressure she didn't need.

All the joy had gone. They saw each other less and less. The new business meant he had to work long hours she told Trish. Even weekends and Bank Holidays. No time off to be together, not even one evening when she could cook a meal, and they could watch a movie together. Every time she tried, it was ruined by him either being late, or he spent most of the time looking

94

at figures or contracts, while she watched the film on her own. Whatever she suggested they do together, he usually had a ready and plausible excuse not to go, and she was made to feel childish and greedy by just asking.

She'd spent the millennium watching coverage on TV rather than being out there, celebrating with her friends, letting in the new century. Then they'd had a row.

He missed her birthday, protesting his innocence that he just forgot, then he missed his, not turning up at home on time and ruining the surprise party. By the time he walked through the door at 1.30 am, everyone had gone home.

She stopped trying to get him to come out with her and began to spend more time with Trish and her old friends, just like before she'd ever met him.

Then came the final limit. Trish's wedding. Bella was her maid of honour and had stayed overnight with everyone at the hotel where the reception was held. Benny was supposed to be best man, and due to meet Ross at another hotel, but when the day dawned, no one could find him, he didn't answer the phone at home, and he wasn't at work or at his house when someone went looking for him, no one knew where he was.

It was only because Ross had made contingency plans, with a reserve best man that the ceremony had been saved. But that didn't stop Bella from burning fury all through the reception.

When Benny finally turned up, three hours after the bride and groom left, detailing a cock and bull story about a new client in Manchester, not being able to find a phone and missing his train, she was furious. But it was after a blazing argument, when she'd finally cooled down and they'd kissed and made up, when she'd said light-heartedly, "I hope you won't do that at our wedding," that he had shattered her completely with his reply. As he made a cup of coffee he'd simply said, "Oh you and I won't be getting married for years yet…"

The image rolled over just once more. It stopped with them both sitting in a small, quiet pub, Bella was looking terribly upset. It was only a few months since the incident at Trish's wedding.

Scrooge was still pleasant looking, his eyes still twinkly and blue. He was a man at his best, but here and there the symptoms of avarice and greed had become more visible. He was impatient and kept looking at his watch. His back was a little bent from leaning over his accounting books all day and his right leg jiggled when he sat still, like he was aggravated by something. His glasses perched on his face like a pince-nez and made his nose seem sharp and beak like. Right now, he was tapping his fingers rudely on the table all the time and looking at his watch again, begrudging how long he was sitting here and not working. His eyes scraped around the pub with a glare so sharp you could almost hear it making a sound like nails on a chalkboard. As he glared, he shot angry looks at all the prices. He'd snarled at the cost of Bella's orange juice, ordered only water for himself to save money, took both to the table and waited for Bella to tell him what was so important he had to leave the office in the middle of a working day.

Finally, after sitting for over half an hour while she quietly explained herself, sipped her drink and oozed tears, he said impatiently, "Bella you're making no sense, it's all just emotional and not logical. I can't understand you. Your argument has no cash value."

Bella was twisting her hanky as tears welled up and ran down her face. Hiccupping and hiccoughing, sipping at her juice as she tried to compose herself, she replied, "It doesn't really matter. Something stronger than me has taken over. Now you're only occupied with that one thing. All other matters, all decent things, all joy, all living, have been crowded out, and I along with them," she smiled wanly.

"And that is?" asked Scrooge sarcastically.

"Money," she replied. "Money is now your main objective, and everything else, including our engagement and marriage, comes after that now."

"Totally ridiculous," Scrooge snapped. "What would you have me do? Go back to Fezziwig's so you can have more of my time?"

"No one's saying you shouldn't concentrate on business, but your obsession with money is verging on the unnatural."

"This is Trish talking isn't it?" asked Scrooge. "You spend too much time listening to her."

"Believe it or not Benny, I do have a brain in my head and..."

"Well use it then!" Scrooge cut across her angrily. "I'm trying to build a business here Bella, a future for us, for you and me. That takes time. It's not like the days when I was working as a wage slave." He banged his fist on the small table, upsetting the glasses, spilling half which he hastily had to blot with napkins.

She put her hand on his arm saying, "At least then we were happy, but now you're so scared of the future and what may happen, you don't see what IS happening in the present. You used to have moral values and ideals, but, one by one, you've dropped them to chase the almighty dollar." She paused to wipe her eyes. "Benny, I fell in love with you the moment I laid eyes on you, but now, it's like you're a different man. You're not the same man I fell in love with."

Scrooge retorted, "I haven't changed. I'm still the same, especially in how I feel about you. That's never altered, no matter what *other* people may say."

"Was working for Mr Fezziwig that bad?" asked Bella. "Back then we had time, we had friends, we had savings..."

"Not enough," interrupted Scrooge.

"We had seven thousand pounds!"

"That's not enough to do anything..."

"It was enough for a deposit on a house somewhere..."

"Nowhere ideal, not anywhere I would want to live, it wasn't enough Bella."

"It was enough for you to withdraw the lot from our account without asking me and use it to set up your business!" she flared, getting cross and upset.

Scrooge ignored her and drank some of his water.

She shook her head and answered softly, "Look, we got engaged years ago when we were both earning very little and were happy sharing the same dream of working and saving, so we could marry, buy a home, and start a family. But now, you've changed too much, and it's just about money, money, money." She ticked off on her fingers. "You don't want to go any-where because it costs money.

"You don't want to do anything to save money. You don't want to visit friends because we may have to spend money. If I buy anything you tell me I've wasted money.

"You don't even want cod and chips by the seaside as a treat, because its 'spending money' for heaven's sake.

"What did you say the other day when I said about getting a puppy? You said, 'pets have no cash value'. I mean, really? And now you don't want an engagement party because it will cost too much. Another thing we can't do in order to save money. I think the best thing is to call it off. We can stay friends, but we really need to call it off."

Scrooge replied, "Bella have I ever said I didn't love you?"

"You've never said it no, but how do you think all this makes me feel? It's like you look at me but think I'm not worthy enough. Tell me, honestly, really, the truth now, if we met today, as I am, would you think I was good enough to marry you?"

Scrooge was silent.

"I thought so. No, you need a wife of value. 'Cash value' preferably with her own fortune who can bring money and prestige to your business so you can show off as rich and bask in her reflected glory. I'm not beautiful or rich. If we married based on our longstanding commitment, we would be miserable within three months. So," she said, removing her engagement ring, "I'm calling off our engagement. We'll put it on hold for a while. I still love the man you used to be and hope someday to see him again." She turned slightly away from him, "I'd like to think this would be a difficult break for you, but I suspect it will only come as a relief. The part of me that still loves you wants to wish you a happy life." With that, she dropped her ring on the table, stood up and clumsily pushed her way past him.

Scrooge grabbed her hand, stopping her leaving and saying, "Look, we're both upset, how about I come home early, and we sit and really talk about this tonight. I'll bring some takeaway and wine. We can have a nice dinner, and really talk things through, find out where we want to go, make proper plans. I can be home by seven. What do you think Bella, will you wait, and talk to me tonight? Don't do anything before we talk ok. Please Bella, okay, okay?"

Bella looked at him with tears in her eyes. "Okay Benny," she sighed, "One last chance. Seven o'clock tonight. But I'm holding you to that. After that, no more chances. Tonight then, we'll talk." She turned and left, dabbing at the tears in her eyes.

Scrooge's younger self also stood, watching her go. He looked at the ring she'd dropped on the small table. She hadn't picked it back up to put back on her finger, so he slipped it into his pocket, hoping after tonight she would wear it again. He looked up once more in the direction Bella had gone and remembered he had an appointment with a new client. If he was to make it home by seven, he had to get a move on. He drank the last of the juice and water rather than leave them to waste and left the pub in a hurry.

At 1 am Trish was woken up by Bella knocking on her front door.

When Benny arrived home an hour and a half later carrying a bottle of warm champagne, a stone cold Chinese take-away and a bouquet of her favourite white roses, withering on their stalks, he saw Bella had packed up all her belongings, left her keys on the kitchen table, and was gone.

"Spirit!" said Scrooge impatient and rude, "can we leave this place now? My breakup with Bella was years ago. I don't see the relevance."

The Spirit held up a hand and replied, "It's relevant because there was never another woman like Bella. The money took over just as she predicted it would. It became your golden calf. Look now and see, there is another place you must visit, and see what might have been." And with a touch, he and Scrooge moved in time again, forward many years and materialised into a new room. It wasn't grand, but it wasn't a shabby room either. It was a simple everyday room of an everyday house, and it was dressed for Christmas. A tree in the corner shone with lights, ornaments, and homemade decorations. Christmas cards were pinned in a star shape above the fireplace. Tinsel was looped around the walls. Children's homemade Santa's and reindeers flooded the mantelpiece, with stockings hanging over the fireplace and snow scenes and figurines dotted here and there to complete a Christmassy room. It was warm, welcoming, bright, and festive.

Sitting on the floor by the fire, was a girl who looked so like the one he'd just left that, for an instant, Scrooge thought it was her. Then he saw Bella. Sitting in a rocking chair, older, but timeless and lovely. She carried her age well, she'd been younger than Scrooge after all, and now all these years later her face showed very few lines, her hair still glowing that wonderful shade of red. He remembered seeing her hair the first time, wet, bedraggled, framing her face. She was sitting talking to her daughter. He couldn't believe what he was looking at, the two so alike they could be sisters, one with that rich red hair, one with soft blonde, and he smiled at them sitting in comfort, mother and daughter in a room full of love and warmth.

Scrooges reverie was interrupted as he realised there were several more children in the room, all waiting, it seemed, for their father to arrive home. For whatever reason, it appeared that this year, Father Christmas would arrive through the front door and not down the chimney, so every child was listening for the tell-tale sounds of their father's car turning off the road onto the gravel drive to their house, and for the sound of his boots crunching on the newly fallen snow.

After what to them seemed like aeons, the sound of tyres pulling into the drive was heard and the kids exploded in a mayhem of excitement and delight. Rushing to the door in their enthusiasm, Bella had to fight her way to the front. After a lot of shushing she finally managed to get the door open and let in her cold but parcel laden husband.

He was accompanied by a friend from work who was also carrying lots of gaily wrapped presents. Her husband cheerfully informed Bella that his colleague was going to be all alone on Christmas, so he'd persuaded him to come and spend the day with their family instead.

The kids quickly relieved both men of their burdens, happily taking them into the sitting room and piling them up by the tree. A quick cup of coffee was made to warm the two men, then the presents were given out.

Like all children they tore at the coloured wrappings, ripping them to get to the booty inside, piling the paper behind them or rolling it into balls for the cat to play with. The toys inside were the prize. Each child yelled their appreciation and thanks, calling to their mother to see what they'd received.

Then father gave his special gift to Bella. An antique sapphire and topaz bracelet to 'match those ice blue eyes' her husband said. She instantly loved it but protested it was too expensive for her.

"Too expensive for you my darling?" her husband shouted, "nonsense! What do we think kids, is this bracelet too expensive for Mum?"

Shouts came from the children as they all insisted Bella was worth the bracelet and even more. "There you are you see!" her husband exclaimed. "You're out voted, come on, hold out your wrist, it looks better when you put it on." Leaning over he kissed his wife as he fastened the clasp, while the kids marvelled at the bracelet and said again how much their mum deserved it.

Now it was Bella's turn and she coyly handed her husband his gift. Her husband travelled so much you see, she presented him with a bespoke, handmade, book style, leather travelling wallet, with 'pages' for passports, papers, credit cards and, "A special section where you can carry my picture, so everyone knows you're married," joked Bella. He roared a huge belly laugh, especially because, instead of having his name 'Harry Davenport' stamped on the leather, what was embossed on the wallet, in clear gold lettering were the words,

Property of BELLA DAVENPORT'S HUSBAND.

Next, the children had a serious inspection of everyone's toys. Batteries were inserted, parts were assembled, dolls were pried loose from twisted wire packaging that kept them firmly imprisoned in their cardboard king-doms. Adults had coffee and mince pies while the kids played with their toys with one eye watching Christmas cartoons.

At 1 pm came Christmas dinner, the Queen's speech followed at 3 pm, then several Christmas comedy TV shows, a movie and finally the kids were off to bed, toys, and all, to fall into an exhausted but happy sleep ready to do it all again tomorrow. Father's guest left soon after, off to his rented apartment, thankful for the company and conversation rather than a day alone. The only ones left awake now were the master of the house, our tired but happy Father Christmas, his wife Bella, who was sipping some sherry and stroking a cantankerous old cat sitting on her lap, and their daughter, so like her mother, sitting on the floor beside her, like peas in a pod. The girl was looking at the 24-Carat gold locket she'd received this Christmas Day.

"Bella," said her husband, quite suddenly, breaking the gentle quiet. "You will never believe it, but I saw an old friend of yours today."

"Oh?" she answered.

"Yes, do you want to have a guess who?"

"Go on Mum, have a guess," challenged her daughter.

"Oh no, Rose," she said to her daughter, "you know I don't like guessing games, just tell me," she said turning to her husband.

"Well, it was Scrooge! I couldn't believe it. He was sitting all alone in that office of his. It was dark as pitch because he only had one light on and he was working on his books! His books! Everyone knows his partner died last night and old Scrooge was working on his books!" He shook his head, "I did feel so sorry for him."

"Spirit," Scrooge whined, "I can't see any more, I refuse. Let me go home."

"Remember what I said at the start," said the Spirit, "everything you see comes from your past. What you see here is directly related to you and can't be changed, if you don't like what you see, blame yourself, don't have a go at me!"

Scrooge watched the scene a few moments longer. The little family talked together in a pitying manner about Scrooge on Christmas Day, and then moved on to happier subjects.

"This lovely family could have been yours Scrooge. Bella, children, a home and hearth. But perhaps a family had no cash value eh?"

Scrooge turned to the Spirit and said, "I can't see anymore. I don't know what you want me to do. I can't change any of this, none of this can be altered so why bother seeing it now?"

"You sold a life of happiness and love for money and power and paid for it with this," the Spirit nodded to Bella. "Family is the currency you used, Ebenezer Scrooge. You need to remember the choices you made were made voluntary and could have been changed if you wanted it." He turned Scrooge around, "Now we will go backwards, a few years before this Christmas to another day in your life…"

Scrooge had been reading the newspaper when Fan arrived, breathlessly at his front door, that wonderful Sunday morning when the church bells rang, and a warm sun still shone. On page five of the Sunday supplement was an article which bore the headline, 'Environmental Entrepreneur Celebrates Wedding Anniversary at Zoo'. A large photograph showed a tall, attractive man looking with a happy expression at the beautiful woman by his side. She was wearing an autumn dress, cardigan thrown over her shoulders. Her face was radiant, and she was smiling that wonderful smile he knew so well. Relaxed, Belle looked so happy and carefree it brought a lump to his throat.

He'd been engrossed in reading the full details when Fan arrived, and he was grateful for her visit to stop him wallowing in self-pity.

Fan was beautiful that morning. She always came around on a Sunday because, as she said, "Everyone has to have some time off and you'd be in that office seven days a week if I let you!" Sunday was her day she declared. The day they spent together, no business, no talking about money, stocks, shares anything. A day to relax, go to the movies or have lunch or even take a long walk by the sea and catch up.

Today she was all happiness. Giggly and fun, full of laughter and smiles, hugging him over and over. He made some coffee, loving her excitement and joy, and then she dropped her bombshell, hugging him repeatedly she said, 'Buzz, I'm going to have a baby!"

Her flirtation with the handsome stranger at the Fezziwig Christmas party years ago had blossomed into a serious relationship and Ebenezer approved of her choice, inasmuch as he thought no one would ever be good enough for his sister, but Samuel Brown had earned his vote of approval with his attentiveness and care of Fan and willingness to do anything for her. Now she glowed with her news and then flashed a beautiful emerald engagement ring Sam had given her to 'match her beautiful eyes,' he'd said.

Ebenezer was stunned, excited, and overjoyed at the idea of being an Uncle with another little Fan running around.

"Just think Buzz, a little boy you can play cricket with," she giggled, showing her preference.

"What if it's a little girl, a tiny little girl just like her mother? I could put her in my pocket and carry her around all day," he teased.

"Watch it with the short jokes junior, or you won't be Godfather," she said, "and no jokes about making me an offer I can't refuse either!" They hugged and laughed and made plans. It was only with his sister that Ebenezer totally felt himself. Calm and relaxed, everything was good around her. She always gave him complete happiness and love.

As for Fan, she'd seen the negative changes in her brother since getting bogged down in business and splitting up with Bella. The two women still talked occasionally, and Bella always asked how her brother was, even though she'd been happily married for a while now, she still thought about him and agreed with Fan that the business may not be the best for Ebenezer's future. Fan hoped that the new baby would help bring the old Buzz back to her.

She enjoyed being pregnant, although neither of them could remember their mother, she was determined to be the best mum she could, reading every book she could find, from natural motherhood to Dr Spock. "Start as you mean to go on!" she told her brother, as he stared at this bewildering array of maternal literature that had taken over her house. However, as she ticked off the weeks she was mostly alone while Sam flew all around the world for his company. Meanwhile, the morning sickness seemed to never end, and she was always tired.

"Nothing to worry about," said her doctor cheerfully, "often happens with first babies. Try to get more rest and keep taking your vitamins. See me again in a month."

But a month later she was still feeling unwell and the headaches had started. She tried to make light of it at home, "I swear my boobs have dropped to my knees," she would laugh, but that was a brave front everyone saw through.

"I can hardly drag myself up to do anything doctor," she said on her next visit. "My boyfriend is away, and my brother helps, but I'm just so tired."

"Don't worry so much, I've never lost a patient yet," joked the doctor, but Fan felt a chill go down her spine at his words. By the next visit, she was feeling worse and Ebenezer insisted on coming with her to see the doctor.

"Look here," he said, not mincing his words, "she's vomiting, has pain in her back, she's uncomfortable all the time. I mean is that normal for a woman six months pregnant? Wasn't that supposed to be over by now?"

The doctor seemed more concerned but reassured them that some women did have a tougher time than others during pregnancy. He said her small frame may have something to do with it, for she'd always been a petite person, however, in response to Ebenezer's questioning, he drew some blood to send off for testing and again told Fan to rest.

Then came the Sunday Ebenezer was at Fan's house helping paint the nursery while Sam was away, yet again. She'd stopped with the brush in her hand and said she had to sit down. She'd been feeling a little better the last few weeks, and now she'd passed the seven months mark could see the end in sight. She'd put on more weight lately and, as her brother put it, 'was looking a bit chipmunk cheeked, like Henry VIII,' but feeling okay if not glowingly wonderful. She could eat soups, eggs, and toast. Tea and salads were ok too, so she was having them until her 'grand opening" as she put it. This made her feel better because she'd thought she she'd been too thin throughout the pregnancy. The doctor seemed pleased, noting she still had headaches and swollen ankles. Once again, he said to rest with her feet up. She had weekly urine tests, but just couldn't wait for it to be over.

She'd invited Buzz over to help with the nursery and to chat as she knew he was still 'a bit off' since Bella and Fan wanted to talk it out with him. But just then she'd felt woozy and dizzy.

"Buzz, I have to sit on the couch for a few minutes, okay?"

"Yup, fine," he answered, "you waddle in there and I'll bring you some tea."

"HA -HA!" she answered with heavy sarcasm.

Fan got herself comfortable as Ebenezer brought in a cup of tea and chocolate bickie.

"You do look a bit peaky," he said. "You should rest. Close your eyes for a while."

"And let you ruin my nursery with your radical ideas, no way, I'll be back in a minute."

Ebenezer put up his palms in a surrender sign and went back to decorating.

"Mind you," he called to her, "I still say we should do one half for a boy and one half for a girl, with a line down the middle. What do you think? Batman motif on one of the walls and Barbie on the other side... Clever idea, eh, Fan... Fan? A clever idea? ... Fan... are you asleep already... Fan...?"

Ebenezer hurried back into the sitting room to find Fan had slumped to the floor. She was unconscious.

***

Scrooge rubbed his eyes trying to stay awake. He was trying to concentrate on what the doctor was telling him, but mostly the words were just bouncing off his brain he was so tired. He had called an ambulance and got Fan straight to hospital where they'd done tests that revealed she had Eclampsia and had gone into a coma. Scrooge didn't know what Eclampsia was, but as next of kin he'd given permission for them to do an emergency caesarean. Fans baby boy had been born at 7 and ½ months. Small, but healthy, they said. He hadn't gone to see the child. They'd asked did he know what she wanted to call her baby? Crossly, he said he didn't, couldn't they wait until its father got here? Scrooge had been here 30 hours, waiting for Sam to return from Australia, where he had been on a three-week business trip. Anyway, Scrooge was just concerned with Fan. Concentrating on Fan, willing her back to consciousness. The baby...If it wasn't for that baby, she...He'd see the baby later, when she was awake, when she was better.

"What's the point of this?" snarled Scrooge to the Spirit. "So my sister died, so what? I'm not the first and I won't be the last who's had a sister die. It's over, done. I won't see any more!"

"You will see a little more Scrooge," said the Spirit and before Scrooge could object again, a new image was before him, a place he hadn't remembered for many years. The Spirit had brought him to an office. The first office he shared with Marley when they were both young and just starting out. He remembered moving in, Fan and her boyfriend helping over the weekend, the hustle and bustle of getting the second-hand furniture in and arranging it, hanging the sign, installing the phones. It had been a success from the start. Fan had been their receptionist for a few weeks while things were being sorted out. Doing what she could to encourage her brothers'

105

new venture, every morning she'd reminded him and Marley, "Start each day as you mean to go on," and with her positive attitude, and captivating nature, she helped to woo some important investors and the business went from strength to strength.

He recalled one evening, a few days before they opened, all four of them sitting on the floor eating fish and chips. None of the chairs had fitted in Marley's little car so everything was being done standing up or sitting on the floor. He remembered them all giggling at the ridiculousness of it. "Certainly, Mr Morgan, your contract is ready, if you'd just like to squat on the floor and sign here!" They'd all laughed so much.

For a moment Scrooge could attach no recall to this new memory the Spirit had brought them to. He was at his desk, staring blankly out at nothing. There was no movement around him. The place was dark, closed, the office seemed empty. There was no work spread before him on his desk, no accounting books, no contracts, no letters, or papers of any kind. Yet here he was, obviously late in the evening, sitting at his desk. Staring into nothingness.

Then the connecting door between his and Marley's office was abruptly thrown open and in stepped his business partner. Short, fat, brusque, business-like, and smelling of the disgusting cigarillos he constantly smoked. "I've finished the contracts for Robertson," he said, "all ready for them to sign tomorrow." He looked at Scrooge's desk.

"Come on now old son, work still has to be done, contracts have to be drawn up and signed, money still needs to be made. You can't keep sitting like a stone you know; you've got to snap out of it and continue with life."

Scrooge's former self looked at Marley. "Why?" he said. "What's my life now? She was the one good thing in it, now she's gone. What can I do now?"

"Business old son," boomed Marley. "There's always business. Money to be made. Bring the pennies in," he said, rubbing his thumb and forefinger together. "Anyway, why the sad face? She's left a child, hasn't she? You're still 'Uncle Ebenezer!' You have some family! Be satisfied with that. I have no one, and does it bother me? No! Business, that's the way, that will keep you so busy. You won't miss her. Business, making money, doing deals, that's my advice. Concentrate on business!" exclaimed Marley, slamming the door as he left and leaving the stink of his cigarillo in the air.

Business thought Scrooge. Business and a nephew. A nephew, Frederick. She'd wanted the boy named after him, her boyfriend said, so the baby would be christened Frederick. That was Scrooge's middle name, Ebenezer Frederick. Little baby Fred, a new life, new family joy and happiness, but not for Scrooge, not without his beloved Fan. He drew a deep breath and made his decision.

Not anymore. No, No more.

Too many times he had been affected, (he'd never admitted he'd been hurt) no *affected* by the actions of others. It wasn't going to happen again.

Fan, the only person who genuinely loved him and today...Today he had gone to her funeral. He had buried the only person in the entire world who'd ever really shown him any love, or affection, warmth, or interest.

He'd stood by her grave in the pouring rain, among all her friends, Samuel, even Bella was there, heavily pregnant herself, watching as Fan's coffin was lowered into the ground, and his heart had broken. He had felt real pain as it had broken and emptied of all the love and emotions he had left.

After the service, Sam shook his hand, tears in his eyes as he reminded Scrooge of the christening taking place in ten days' time. Dry eyed and stoic, Scrooge replied that he wouldn't be attending and walked away, refusing to listen to anything Sam tried to say to him. He didn't answer any calls or return any messages. His decision was made. Nothing else would get close enough to hurt him again, no, not *even the new baby*.

In the darkness of the quiet office, Scrooge's former self put his head on his folded arms and mourned all his losses, for the very last time.

"**This** is where you started to harden your heart and close it to all feeling in the world," said the Spirit. "You choose to walk the path that led you here Scrooge. As you said, others have lost family, lost a fiancée, and had cold and distant parents, but you'd still known love in your life and could have carried that love forward, as Fan would have wanted you to, with her son. A life with love in it, with family, was still possible, but you turned it down. You chose another way and travelled a bitter road alone."

And as the Spirit spoke, it showed Scrooge a tableau of his nephews' early life. The baptism he chose not to attend. Fans little baby boy, swaddled in white, nestled in his father's arms.

His first birthday, toddling around holding Sam's fingers, giggling, with cake all over his hands and face, his bright green eyes dancing with joy. He looked so much like his mother, Scrooge thought.

Laying sleepily in his Grandma Nanni's arms while she read him a story, Scrooge could almost reach out and touch him...

Then moving ahead a few years to his first day of school, Fred grinning with excitement as he entered the school gates and turned back to wave to...

The Spirit whirled the images away with his hand. "You refused to attend the christening of your nephew, even though you knew your sister wanted you to be his Godfather. You broke your promise to her that day to love and protect her son. You had little to do with the child as he grew up, and less to do with him as a man. You chose to repeat the sin of your father and burdened your nephew with your sorrow when you know he is no more responsible for Fan's death than you were for your mothers...Look at that road, Scrooge, not just selected memories, but the whole truth of your life," said the Spirit.

And finally, as he faced his past, Scrooge knew that it was he and he alone who had hardened his heart and shut down his emotions. In his business with Marley, the more the money came in, the more his morals, his humanity and his character dwindled, leaving only the Scrooge of today where that younger man used to be. Now he was old, heartless, greedy, sinful, and filled with anger and bitterness. It hovered around him like a dark hulking shadow, and now he could see clearly that he was, and always would be, completely alone.

Scrooge had watched and couldn't take any more. "Let me leave here damn it! How dare you judge me! Why shouldn't I stay as I am? Yes, I chose to empty my heart of all the love that was left there. I chose to let it all run out and do you know why? Because that way no one could come along and rip pieces out and cause it to bleed in pain anymore. An empty heart is better than a bleeding one and mine had bled enough. Whenever I've had happiness or the chance of happiness, something has always come to take it away from me. Nothing comes to take away misery or sorrow. Nothing ever snatches your resentment away from you like it does your joy. So yes, I kept my anger and my sorrow because that won't be taken from me like love, friendship and happiness were every time I had them. Every time!" Scrooge clenched his fists and pressing them into his head he screamed, *"Don't show me these things anymore, what's the use, the past can't be changed as you said yourself. I can't get that chance back. I can't go back in time. I can't undo what I've done!"* He shouted, **"Don't you think if I could change it, I would?"** As his misery overwhelmed him, he pushed at the ghostly apparition, begging for it to take him home.

He struggled with the Spirit, but it offered no resistance and he found himself pushing and pulling a defenceless figure. As he did, the beam of light coming from the Spirit's headband seemed to get brighter and more dazzling, hurting his eyes. In desperation, Scrooge grabbed for the light to yank it away or turn it off. When he couldn't remove it, he pushed his two hands over the headband, flat together, pressing down to try to cover and extinguish the light. But the dazzling beam would not go out. It spilled over the Spirit, shone down, bathing it in a cone of light, and hitting the floor in a great flood of illumination. Scrooge kept his weight against its head, and as he did the Spirit collapsed under him, and the light finally gutted out like a candle flame, leaving only a soft glowing circle spilling onto the floor like a puddle of water. Scrooge pushed again for good measure and finally when the room was in total darkness, he felt a huge wave of weariness and nausea. He was in his bedroom. How or when he and the spirit had returned he didn't know, and right now, he didn't care. The nausea was so bad he had to lie down. Groping his way to the bed he managed to collapse on top before he fell into a deep and fitful sleep.

And for the first time in countless years, Scrooge had the dream about his childhood that he'd only ever had before when he was terribly upset, before he'd taken such iron control of his life. The last time was the night Fan was buried, when he swore he would never again let anyone touch his heart. Now he tossed and turned as it threaded its way through his mind once more, silenced all this time, but not exorcised, and tormenting him as it had before. And now, as then, he couldn't wake until he'd seen it to the end.

Scrooge's Dream

Scrooge knew his dream was real because he remembered bits from his childhood, but what played out was not fragmented traces of memory, but a full Act, as if he was watching a play or movie. It was no less disturbing, however, than if he was reliving his ordeal every time he dreamed it.

A 1960s opulent Volvo Station Wagon Deluxe, complete with uniformed chauffeur, motored up to the front of the school he'd spent so many years at. As it drew to a stop, the impressively gowned headmaster appeared at the top of the cement steps, accompanied by a motherly, tweedy matron in her forties and a sporty, friendly looking chap in cricket flannels. The chauffeur opened the rear door for the occupants then went to the boot. The chap in cricket flannels ran down the steps and helped the chauffeur remove an exceptionally large, exceptionally heavy, travelling trunk from the back, and unload it on to the gravel drive, where it made a distressingly permanent sounding "thump" as it landed. The two occupants, father, and son walked independently up the steps to shake the hands of the welcoming committee and were shown inside for tea.

Invited into the master's study, father and son sat separately, the boy saying nothing while his father, Augustus Scrooge, rolled off a list of instructions regarding his expectations and requirements for his child's education. Tea and conversation lasted about forty-five minutes and the man in white flannels, who was introduced as the boy's new Housemaster, noticed the young lad made no move towards the tray of tempting cakes and treats served with tea. Neither did he ask his father, or anyone else for permission to take one.

Augustus Scrooge, however, without invitation, ate several and didn't stop until he said he must be heading back to town. He quickly donned his overcoat and scarf, picked up his expensive leather gloves and strode back outside with everyone following in his wake. The child came last and saw the trunk had disappeared from the gravel drive, and the chauffeur was already by the car's back door, waiting for his employer.

Standing close by, pausing to light a cigarette, his Housemaster overheard Augustus' parting words to his son. With no fatherly encouragement, kind words, or comfort in his voice, he said to the young boy, "I expect you to do well while you are here."

That was it. During the entire time of their visit, since their arrival, meeting, and his departure, these were the only words the father spoke directly to his child. Ten words in one hour; that was all.

Shaking hands with the headmaster and matron, Augustus Scrooge proceeded to pull on each glove before reaching out to shake his sons' hand, almost as if he didn't like to touch the boy with his own flesh.

This didn't go unnoticed by his housemaster, who walked over to stand by the boy on the steps. He was still smoking his cigarette as Augustus Scrooge offered him his hand to shake. However, the Housemaster had already decided he didn't like this odious, bombastic, greedy little man, so, rather than returning the pleasantry, he flicked his cigarette away with thumb and forefinger, and instead, placed his hand on the boy's shoulder. Unperturbed Augustus Scrooge turned on his heel and walked down the steps, without so much as a backward glance.

Getting into the car he neither looked at his son nor waved goodbye. The chauffeur dropped into the driver's seat and the Volvo drew away, leaving the boy looking after them.

The other adults returned inside while the Housemaster squatted down beside him. "Your trunk is in your room old chap," he said kindly. "Come with me, I'll show you where that is." The boy, still looking after the car, nodded. "I'm your Housemaster my name is Mister Beare, but the other boys call me Teddy. What's your name?"

The boy was confused and brimming with tears, "I'm Ebenezer Scrooge," he replied, watching the car as it finally disappeared.

"That's a long name to remember," said the man. "How about I call you Ben instead?"

The little lad nodded as he looked up at the man, his eyes still full of tears.

"And how old are you, Ben?" asked Teddy, taking his hand as they walked inside.

"Six," said Ben, looking warily at the stranger. "I'm six."

111

Intermission

Give me the boy until the age of seven and I will give you the man.

Ebenezer's father had control over him until he was six.

Six years of fearing his father, of subliminal negative programming, of always wondering why.

And then, nine years of Ebenezer's schooling began.

Nine long years of being shut away from the only source of love he knew.

Nine years of occasional visits, letters, and phone calls to connect him with a source of love and kindness he could hang onto and trust.

Nine years in which he learned more about becoming his father's son than he would have realised.

Nine years to mould a boy into a perfect clone of the typical English drone.

Such were the indoctrinations at English public schools, their mission wasn't to turn out a sensitive new age guy. SNAGs were decades away and no one was interested in namby-pamby Californian ideas of talking out their feelings. Of course, one never said anything to their wives or family if one was feeling stressed; One may occasionally mention it to the chaps at the club or during a round of golf that one was feeling a bit snowed under, but that was as far as sharing your problems and 'talking things over' went in those days.

Give me the boy until the age of seven...

Finish him off over the next nine years.

....And now, behold the man.

Part Two

We left Ebenezer sleeping in turmoil, dreaming a childhood dream that he'd only had before when he was terribly upset. During his travels with the ghost of Christmas Past, he'd journeyed back into his youth and saw many things he'd blocked from his memory. Now we will see what happens when he meets the next two ghosts soon to arrive and guide him on his way.

Chapter 7: The Second Spirit

Scrooge woke himself up with a loud and ungentlemanly snore. For a few moments he wondered where he was and what had happened to have him asleep, on top of his bed, rather than in it. Then the memories of the first ghost returned, then his childhood dream, and lastly, the words ran through his head, "Family is the currency you used to pay for wealth and power, you made that choice willingly."

Still, though his stubbornness hung on. He knew, without understanding how, that it was the now second night, when Jacob had promised another phantom would arrive, and this second ghostly visitor was now imminent.

He decided this Spirit was not going to startle him like the last one, so to prepare himself for another dazzling arrival, he sat up and plumped his pillows, enabling him to see both the sides and the foot of his bed clearly. Scrooge waited, eyes peering into the darkness, filled with suspense, wondering if the second Spirit really would appear and prove this wasn't all just an elaborate dream.

As we've discussed, Scrooge was not a guy who was so full of experiences or imagination that he could envision strange things in daily life and absorb them with a certain level of equanimity. If it didn't revolve around money, he seldom bothered with it and certainly never tried to understand it. That's why now, Scrooge, who had decided he was not going to be surprised by the second ghost as he was by the first, ended up being just that, surprised.

If you think about it, if you suspect you're going to have a surprise birthday party, and you arrive and no one is there, you don't really know what to do next do you? Are you early? In the wrong place? Were you not getting a party after all? And you naturally wouldn't sit like an idiot, but get up and look around to see what's going on, right?

Scrooge had prepared for something to happen, so he wasn't ready for nothing to happen, and when nothing did, he sat in his bed, his whole body shaking with apprehension, as the hour went from one am to a quarter past one with no result.

Having no ability to think why nothing had happened when he'd been promised a visitation from a ghost, Scrooge stayed sat on the bed for a further fifteen full minutes watching the clock. Finally, as it was approaching the half-hour, it occurred to Scrooge that the clock was illuminated very brightly, more so than usual, and looking towards its source he saw a light shining from under his bedroom door that was so brilliant, it couldn't possibly be caused by any natural phenomenon. Scrooge decided to explore this mystery and shoving his feet into his boots he padded across to the door and down the hallway to the sitting room. The second he touched the door handle, a voice with a warm Yorkshire accent called, "Come in, that's right, come in and say hello, let's get to know each other better."

Turning the handle and opening the door, he stepped into his own sitting room, that was true, but one that had undergone a remarkable makeover. Gone was the plain and boring furniture, gone were the cheap and nasty bookcases. Gone was the chipped paint and old wallpaper. In its place was a room so welcoming that Scrooge felt himself instantly relax. Filled with everlasting greenery, holly and ivy, mistletoe and berries, a roaring fire in a room with no fireplace made the whole feel welcoming and safe. Chestnuts roasted near the fire, crackling, and smelling delicious, while dates scented the room with their rich toffee smell. Tangerines, sugar mice, walnuts and brazils were in huge bowls. And chocolates... Boxes and boxes of chocolates. Some open and half eaten, some on trays, some ready to open and enjoy, all richly enticing.

On a separate table, a tower of glasses filled with pink champagne that bubbled and popped, next to huge trays of sandwiches, sliced meats, cheeses, pickles, and fresh bread rolls. Game pies, sausage rolls and a huge sliced turkey that added to the room's delicious, mouth-watering aromas.

In the corner was a large ornate chair, almost a throne, and seated on this was a huge but gentle looking giant, dressed in wintergreen, with a white beard, twinkling eyes, and a warm, welcoming smile. The very image of an eco-friendly Father Christmas. In one hand he held a turkey leg that he took great bites from, in the other, a massive tankard of ale that left a moustache

116

of foam around his already bearded face. At his feet were cream cakes and petit fours, tea cakes, and Christmas puddings. On the tables were bowls of pink punch and piles of crystallised fruit, more boxes of chocolates, mince pies, Christmas cake, gingerbread cookies, spearmint sticks and lollipops as big as saucers. Fruit from the four corners of the earth lay temptingly on trays alongside chocolate Santa's in gaily wrapped foil. Endless food and fortune were in this one room.

"Come on, young man, that's the way. In you come so we can get to know each other," said the Spirit again.

Scrooge took a better look at this incredible figure who, unlike the last Spirit, at least looked more like a normal man. The green garment was like a dressing gown or robe, trimmed with white, it was much too big for the Spirit, but he didn't seem to mind. It opened at his chest, so it couldn't be very warm, but that didn't seem to matter either. This Spirit, like the last one, also had bare feet and Scrooge wondered if they were to go travelling as he'd done with the last visitor, how this one would fare with the cold ground and freezing temperatures. This Spirit too wore something on his head. It was a crown, made with holly and berries, icicles and water crystals that glittered in the light. The Spirit had shoulder length curly hair and had beside him a torch that looked uncannily like a cornucopia, or horn of plenty, in which light beams crackled and spilled out from brightly, like a thousand sparklers all fizzling and glowing at once.

The Spirit was spectacular. Like a giant character from a storybook, he bedazzled Scrooge not with intense light as the first Spirit had done, but with his sheer size and fascination. Scrooge stood before him, tongue-tied and feeling insignificant as he said timidly, "You're very...You're large...You're very big, aren't you Spirit?"

"Aye," he replied in that warm northern accent. "It's true, I'm a bonny lad for my mother. Why so tongue-tied young man, I'm can't be the first visitor you've welcomed to your house. Surely you must have met some of my family already?" Asked the Spirit kindly.

"Your...Family? Now, what...? Who are they?" Scrooge replied questioningly.

"Who are...? Ebenezer, there have been more than two thousand of my brothers that have come here before me, more than sixty since you were born, do you mean to tell me you haven't met any of us before?"

"No, I don't think so. I'm not sure. No, thinking about it, I don't know if I've met any of them before," he answered. "But two thousand brothers, it's a marvellous family to belong to. So many of you to be cared for. It must be difficult in this modern age, prices being what they are," Scrooge said.

The Spirit looked at him, as if calculating his rudeness as one would a child's. Irritated by no answer, Scrooge grew bolder. "You're not much like the first Spirit. Who are you? And what's *your* purpose here? Tell me, how can a Spirit understand enough about human beings, or the modern world, to tell me how I should live in it?"

The immense Spirit rose to his full imposing height, towering over Scrooge. Looking down on him the Spirit intoned, "Man of the mortal world, I am the ghost of Christmas Present. While it's true I am from the here and now, understand this; members of my family don't just appear for a few hours on Christmas Day but live among you for an entire year before returning home. I was born out of Christmas a full year ago today, in full belief of its meaning, sustaining the messages and morals of Christmas throughout the year, just as the child who was born today carries His message into the hearts and souls of everyone who follows Him. I am not here to tell you how to live, nor am I here to force you to make changes in your life. I am here only to guide you: To show you the world you are blind to. To answer any questions. Tell me now, man of the modern world, are you ready to discover the true meaning of Christmas?"

Scrooge took several steps backwards at the size of his guest and hastily put his hands together saying, "Spirit, I... I didn't mean to be rude. Please, take me where I'm going. I went last time because I was forced to, but I saw some things I had forgotten and, well, now I want to go, wherever you need to take me."

"There's still a lot for you to learn. Last time you discovered how you closed your heart to a future of love and family. Now you need to understand the real meaning of Christmas. If you're ready, hold onto my coat and see what you can learn from the present."

Directed by the Spirit, Scrooge reached out and touched the fabric. Instantly everything in the room, the holly and ivy, mistletoe and berries, the bags of chestnuts and dates, the wine, the sandwiches, turkey, and Christmas crackers, everything around them, even the room, disappeared, as Scrooge and the Spirit beamed out of his apartment, and materialised on a suburban street, early on Christmas morning.

It was bitterly cold, and everywhere there was snow, the old kind of intensely white, almost blue, deep snow, piled up around doors and windows. Men with shovels were digging paths to their houses so guests could get to the door, while their kids slowly got wet through, dodging snowballs, pretending to be snow angels, building snowmen and ice castles, while waiting for their relatives to arrive, or for the call from mum that hot chocolate and mince pies were on the table.

The Spirit, who had materialised at Scrooge's side, was reduced to the size as a normal man, no longer towering over him like a colossus. Scrooge noticed he didn't seem to suffer at all from the cold, even though his ill-fitting garment offered no warmth or protection against the chilly wind that blew or the snow that was still falling gently around them. It hung open to the chest, and he strode around with great affability and enthusiasm as if it were a bright, sunny August day. Neither did his bare feet trouble him as he walked along the freezing ground. Making his way through snow and slush, through puddles and on ice, with no apparent ill effects, while Scrooge dodged around, avoiding the soggy ground as much as he could, trying to keep his dried boots from getting sodden, and his feet from numbing completely.

Scrooge looked around him and said to no one in particular, "It's always snowing," and it was. Sleet and slush were everywhere as cars and a few busses passed up and down, making road maps of once brilliant white into muddy direction lines crossing and crisscrossing the roads. More loud and happy kids skidded in their knock off Nikes as they surfed the sleeted streets in front of their houses or tower blocks. Those who'd already opened their presents tried new bikes or skateboards, wobbling dangerously on icy footpaths, and bouncing into the soft snow when they inevitably fell off. That was the way to learn to ride. Landing on soft snow was much better than splatting into a hard pavement or scuffling headfirst off your skateboard into the pebble dash footpath near your house.

The weather itself was a bit too cold and the sky gloomy. Low sunlight, fog and more snow threatened, but this was Christmas Day, and there was no chance of anything stopping anyone's fun.

Shops were open here and there. Deregulated trading hours and multiculturalism meant small independent shops, pubs, petrol stations, newsagents and others could stay open when once they had been forced to close for days.

Takeaways opened later in the day so if worse came to worst anyone could celebrate and welcome the baby Jesus with hamburgers and fries, cod, chips, and mushy peas, a roast chicken dinner or a tandoori with rice and poppadoms.

Twenty-four-hour family-run mini marts were trading and still selling Christmas foods; oranges, lemons, peaches, and plums, all brought from warmer countries for Christmas. Fancy stuff like prawns, smoked salmon and champagne nestled seductively next to jars of caviar, pate, and soft Brie all there to be enjoyed. Traditional plum puddings (add your own 50p pieces), and that fruit cake that no one ever ate on Christmas Day, but everyone bought in case unexpected guests arrived, could still be had, and anyway, even if it wasn't eaten over Christmas it was lovely fried in butter on New Year's Eve and served hot with cream or custard.

Pubs being open meant you could pop to your local before your Christmas dinner for a pint or mixer to sharpen the appetite, sing a Christmas pop song and get a bit merry while mum or dad struggled with the turkey and the kids played with their presents and watched TV.

But before all of this, at eight am the bells of London's churches began to ring. Even in these days of instant music downloads and twenty-four-hour pop, the bells that rang out across the capital did so with a great sound of celebration and joy that was unchanged for over three hundred years. They set the heart pumping and the spirits soaring, crashing, and clanging, ringing, and singing as they announced to one and all that today was Christmas Day, the birthday of the King of Kings, and they called the faithful to celebrate the birth of Christ.

Scrooge and the Spirit watched and listened to all of this, and Scrooge noticed that the Spirit had brought his torch with him, its crackling light now a soft glow.

"Why did you bring that?" questioned Scrooge, "what's it for?"

The Spirit of Christmas Present smiled and said, "It contains blessings from my family. I'll give them to everyone we meet on this special day, but to those who are poor or underprivileged I'll give more."

"And why do they get more?" Scrooge asked.

"Because they need it more," answered the Spirit as if it was obvious and strode off, leading the way forward.

Their walkabout quickly brought Scrooge and the Spirit to a picturesque terraced house at the end of a line of similar houses. With the large front bay and second floor gabled windows, heavy with snow, it looked like a Victorian picture postcard. In the small front garden, encircled by a black iron picket fence with gate, stood a slightly wonky, but proud snowman sporting an old bobble hat and matching woollen scarf. Scrooge was at once reminded of the snowmen he'd made with Fan when she'd visited him at school. Unaware he was smiling, he patted the snowman, looking at his unusual features...

The annual migration of snow persons to Camden had gone off without a hitch this year. Each front yard played host to a migratory visitor built with love and fun, created using snow, old clothes, and, this year, a twist in their facial features. This snowman, and the ones in the other nine gardens down this side of the street, plus the eight on the other side, had all been made using pebbles for eyes, fat round snowball noses and twigs for mouths, rather than the traditional coal and veggie components.

That was mainly because in the last three years, every snowman in this road and all the surrounding ones, who'd had coal eyes, carrot noses and coal buttons had mysteriously been ravaged prior to Christmas and lost both their means of vision and their ability to smell, along with their very buttons on their bellies, sometimes more than once.

Though foxes had been the prime suspects, the culprits were finally tracked and discovered to be the residents from number 327 Albany Court, who lived two streets over.

The biggest clue was their roaring outdoor fire pits, together with plenty of pit roasted veggies, especially the honey soy carrots on a stick, at their annual outdoor Whisky and Haggis Hogmanay, held successfully for the last three years.

Unfortunately, nothing could be proved, and anyway, who was going to call the cops over several pounds of coal and carrots? Therefore, this year all snow personnel within a ten-street radius had new facial features, and all had, thus far, been left mostly untouched, although several snowmen were sadly decapitated early in December.

The ghost of Christmas Present stopped at a certain door and blessed it with great handfuls from his torch. A Christmas tree twinkled its lights through the frosty bay window, from where a small boy looked out intently. Ebenezer could just see through the window that the whole room was decorated for Christmas, with tinsel hanging from the ceiling, balloons in each corner, dozens of cards above the mantle where he figured they would constantly fall off, and a wonderful tree standing pride of place in the window, glowing under the weight of lights, ornaments, balls, crackers and tinsel. Underneath peaked wonderful things, waiting to be unwrapped.

As Scrooge and the Spirit entered the warm kitchen, filled with the sounds of happy children and the smell of delicious cooking, Mrs Cratchit appeared. Amy Cratchit was dressed in seasonal, though second-hand, clothes from the last church jumble. Wearing a pair of red poly fleece track-suit bottoms that fitted nicely and helped smooth her Mummy bubble*, together with a sweater featuring a snowman embroidered motif, she also sported a skew-whiff Santa hat, from which her long plaited hair lay over her shoulder and soft wisps escaped around her face. A winter pattern apron completed the ensemble and looked rightfully festive. She'd laid the table and was cooking dinner with the "help" of her children. Belinda, her second eldest daughter, also dressed in preloved Christmas finery, was working diligently on a pan of applesauce. Her son Peter had taken charge of peeling and boiling the potatoes and steaming the sprouts, which he was testing now and then by surreptitiously eating one to see if they were done, a ploy that caused hot water to dribble onto the cuffs of his shirt and give away his guilty secret.

The smashed mashed would be for the kids, while the roasted spuds for the adults were already in the oven, sizzling alongside the cooking bird, wallowing in delicious goose fat.

Two of the smaller Cratchit children came running into the kitchen, singing the praises of the cooking goose and the glories of sage and onion stuffing with thick juicy gravy, both of which smelled so yummy they could taste them already. The excitement in the house was building, and Mrs Cratchit had to shoo the children from the kitchen several times as they coaxed, cajoled, and begged to know when dinner would be ready.

---

* It's particularly important not to confuse a Mummy bubble with a muffin top. Both are separate figure conditions that may look similar but are quite different. When one has a muffin top, one's chubby tummy hangs over the top of jeans, pants, shorts, or skirts in every direction of the body circumference, rather like a muffin baked out of its paper shell. Hence the name. With a Mummy bubble, one only pops over at the front. No love handles, no back fat. Viewed from the back, one has a beautiful figure. Only at the front does one have a popped belly, which makes buying jeans, trousers, skirts, and dresses exceedingly and irritatingly difficult. Also, take it from someone who struggles with a Mummy bubble, asking, "When's the baby due?" is not funny, especially when fifty million smart arses have already asked you that before.

Chapter 8: Meet The Cratchit Family

The Cratchits were a large, noisy, exuberant, passionately loyal family. There's Bob Cratchit whom we've met already. Bob is forty-four years old and exactly six feet tall. He'd left school after the prerequisite education required by the state and continued his tuition through the night school system that's been popular in Britain since the 1940s. These classes taught interested and forward-thinking students "computer science" as it was then called. The forerunner of all the skills needed to be able to understand and use the home and office computers that would eventually revolutionise the world and increase workplace efficiency. Four years of night school and Bob also emerged with diplomas in accountancy, finance, and contract law.

Bob was a plain man. That's not to say he was unattractive, actually, he was quite a dish. No by plain I mean he was not a man who needed "things" to make him happy. He didn't need the latest car, the expensive suit, the best address. He preferred to live simply, minding his own business and expected the world to return the favour. He was a trifle shy with the girls, but it wasn't a problem because he'd met Amy Loveridge, a girl with waist-length mahogany curls and captivating violet eyes, married her and fathered his first child all before he was twenty-one.

Amy, short for Amalia, was very much an earth-mother type, an extremely resourceful woman who was also a whizz at money management, natural remedies, home cooking and make do and mend, all of which she learned as part of the gypsy upbringing and heritage that she was extremely proud of. To emphasise this, she'd a gypsy flag tattooed on her upper left arm. She'd also planned to get her children's date of birth tattooed under the flag, but it turned out that even though she could manage labour pains, after all, she'd had eight kids, the agony of someone scraping around and injecting ink into her raw skin proved to be a bit more than she could tolerate, so she'd stopped at the flag.

Amy stood 5 feet 5 inches in her stocking feet and had an excellent command of the Queen's English, despite leaving formal education at the age of fourteen. She was known at her children's school not as the earth-mother but as a tiger-mother and anyone doing anything to upset her offspring had better have a damn good reason. That said, her children knew they were at school to learn and not there to be rude, difficult or a smart arse.

She'd a unique way of managing her children when they inevitably began using the thrilling profanities their friends did. Rather than get annoyed, they were handed the dictionary and told to write down five alternative words, and their meaning, that they could have used instead. Interestingly, when her two eldest children recently went out into the big wide world with the rest of humanity, its rudeness and demands, they finally benefited from Amy's annoying five words deterrent, as they could now swear at anyone in an argument without that person realising it.

After they married, Amy and Bob had been unanimous in wanting children and Bob had said he wanted more than one as he'd been an only child when growing up and was consequently very lonely. Amy of course, grew up in a large family community of extended Gypsy relatives so, "definitely more than one" to her meant anywhere between two and fifteen. They had stopped at seven after Tim had been born, but little Abigail had popped up a few years later to even out the number to eight. This made their house full to the brim with Martha, oldest at eighteen, Peter, seventeen, Belinda fourteen, the twins, Mathew and Eliza were ten, Simon eight, Tim seven, and the eight month old baby, Abigail, who Mrs Cratchit affectionately called her 'never say never again baby'. That was the human contingent of the family.

They also had a scruffy white Australian Terrier called Digger. Not for obvious reasons, but because of his breed and because he was a real old soldier when he got hurt. Digger's main pastime, which he took very seriously, was popping bubble wrap, bubble by bubble. He had several half-popped sheets in his collection and any attempt to remove them was met with great resistance. Still, everyone knew where to look if they needed a bit of bubble wrap for something. Groomed, he was a handsome chap, but it was unnatural for him to be all primped and powdered, the rough and ready look suited him better; and, while he tolerated a warm bath, he disapproved

124

of being dried, brushed, combed or clipped and would grumble ominously, wiggling in protest, until you gave up and left him to his own devices. Thereafter he would dry himself by rubbing up and down on the carpet in the hallway, and spend the following two hours sucking his feet, biting his toenails, and spitting them out. He was currently sitting under the table where Amy Cratchit was working, hoping for titbits, and waiting for her to drop something tasty.

They also had two dwarf lop rabbits named Stew and Casserole, who lived entirely by munching the back lawn and eating kitchen scraps. Everyone had their job to do in the Cratchit household, and it was the rabbit's job to keep the lawn trim so Bob or Peter didn't have to mow it. Bob would facetiously chuckle that their names served as a warning if the job wasn't done properly. The rabbits lived a serene existence, sunning themselves on pleasant days, sleeping on wet days and mooching around the garden the rest of the time. They were often mistaken for garden ornaments rather than live bunnies because they moved around at speeds somewhere between dead slow and stop. The only time they ever moved any faster was when their hopping and nose twitching so irritated the dog, he would lie in wait behind the shrubbery then jump out, barking loudly. On those occasions, they could move amazingly fast and would shoot across the lawn and into their cage faster than the *Energizer Bunny* on steroids.

Added to the rabbits was a mixed breed, short-legged, fat-bodied, long furred emotional support cat called Crisis. This cat earned her name within the first three days in her new home by causing chaos, mostly due to her short legs and ambitious ideas. The results were upset glasses, cups, and plates, with food spilled everywhere as she tried, several times, to jump onto the dining room table or kitchen bench. When she inevitably missed, she would break her fall by grabbing onto anything within reach, such as tablecloths or tea towels, and pulled the whole lot of food, drinks, dishes, and cutlery with her, landing in a messy *plop!* on the floor. She'd then spend the rest of the evening sitting with a wounded air, licking food out of her fur, and glaring dangerously at anyone who dared laugh at her. She also left claw holes in the curtains due to her stubbornness of wanting to sit on the pelmet and admire the view. When Amy declared, "This cat is causing one crisis after another," her unique name was born. Now older and wiser, she'd learned how to manipulate her family so jumping, climbing, and clawing was no longer necessary. Crisis was black except for four white paws, a white tip on her tail, white ears, and a tiny splash of white on her nose which annoyed her and caused her to go cross-eyed until someone coloured it in black with a permanent marker, a job that had to be repeated every time she washed her face. She was Tim's emotional support animal and she'd a permanent chip on her shoulder because, whenever she meowed, she didn't make a sound, other than a strangulated "Glek" noise as if she were about to vomit. Nevertheless, she slept on Tim's bed, ate his scrambled eggs when Amy wasn't looking and chased the rabbits when bored or feeling the need for exercise.

To round out this menagerie was an inseparable duo known as Titch and Quackers, who the Cratchits had been asked to look after for a couple of weeks while the owners went on holidays. When the two weeks were up and they tried to return the pair, they discovered the owners had in fact moved to a new house, left no forwarding address, and changed their mobile number.

Quackers was a three-year-old white Pekin duck who couldn't fly.

Whether this was due to a feeling of inadequacy or because he didn't need to as everything was provided for him on land wasn't exactly known, but it was probably due to the latter rather than the former because ducks aren't idiots and don't tend to wander away from a good thing.

Titch was a three-year-old blonde ferret. She never tried to escape either, possibly because she also thought she was a duck, plus her life was far too entertaining where she was. She'd a large group of furies to tantalise and fight with, a garden full of places to hide, a big brother to call on in a scrap, and lots of humans who thought she was cute.

She and the duck had it made. Ducks are sociable animals needing lots of attention, and Quackers was known to waddle into the kitchen and throughout the house looking for company and interesting conversation. The ferret would tag along, searching for the open pantry door and direct access to chocolate biscuits. Both were known for playing right under Amy's feet, usually when she'd something hot in her hands, and the cry of, *"Will someone get this bloody animal out of here!"* was constantly heard. At night they could be found cuddled up asleep, with Titch wrapped in one of Quackers' wings. Their days were spent either swimming or paddling together in the pool Peter made for them or strolling around the garden like a couple of old Etonians discussing the weather, nosing into everyone's business. During these walks they mostly ignored the rabbits, evidently considering both well below their status, and avoided the cat whom they viewed as a troublemaker and rabble-rouser after watching her chase the bunnies into their hutch.

Quackers was a very emotional duck who was dedicated to his whole family and enjoyed nothing better than watching TV cuddled up with the kids until Amy shooed it out of the house. He would also sneak surreptitiously up the stairs at the sound of running water, and join the younger children when they had their bath, while the ferret, never far behind, nosed around the bathroom floor exploring the cabinets, the laundry hamper, the base around the loo and canoodled with the doll who had the spare toilet roll shoved up her dress, an idiosyncrasy typical to British households and one that makes absolutely no sense at all. Once the bath was over the duck would waddle out again, leaving webbed footprints in a watery trail out of the bathroom, across the landing, down the stairs and across the kitchen floor as a clue to its escapade.

Bob had made the decision not to try to rehome these two, as the twins had fallen in love with them, the ferret was hysterical to watch and, as he said with a teasing smile, if worse comes to worst they already had Sunday lunch walking around the back garden.

Neither of these animals had names when they came to live with the Cratchits and had only ever been referred to as the duck and the ferret. Finding ones to suit had been a challenging task. I mean, naming a duck is not as easy as naming a dog and naming a ferret not as simple as naming a cat. Several names were put forward, and suggestions included such names as Charles and Camilla, Taylor and Swift (*Martha's suggestion. She was a devoted fan.*) Coke and Pepsi or Little and Large. When none of these seemed to fit the duo, Peter had the novel idea of swapping over the first letter of each animal's name to the other, which could have succeeded, but for one unfortunate spelling problem.

Although it would have been fine with those living near to the Cratchits to hear anyone in their back garden calling for a "Derret," yelling for a re-christened duck, whose name now began with an "F," would have definitely caused an upset with the neighbours.

The Cratchit house and gardens were spotlessly clean and tidy, warm, and comfortable, friendly, and safe. While furniture may be on the older side or second hand, it was a wonderful place to cuddle up under a soft duvet and a hot water bottle if you were ill. Herbs abounded in the front garden, with Azaleas in pots by the front doors. Flowers, veggies, and roses abounded in the back. Birds were fed, squirrels had nuts, foxes were chased away. It was all very Beatrix Potter.

Mrs Cratchit checked her watch and said with exasperation, "Where are your father and Tim? And what time did Martha get here last year?" It wasn't this late was it?"

Martha had a wonderful job in Shepherd Bush, where she also lived in a tiny shoebox flatlet with three friends who shared the rent and other costs. This enabled her to give some money to her parents each week to help with their household and other more important expenses, which will be explained shortly.

"Look! Here's Martha mum," cried Simon, who had been looking out of the window for her. "Here she is," he said again and waved frantically. Martha, who'd struggled, burdened, out of a friend's car, was walking down the footpath, smiling and waving back with arms full of bags and gifts. The twins, Mathew, and Eliza, who was still dancing around underfoot took up the cry, yelling, "Here's Martha, she's here Mumma, here's Martha," and as she came through the front door, "Hurry up Martha, come and see the goose, you must come and see the goose."

Barely giving her time to put down her bags, which held some excitingly wrapped parcels, they dragged her into the kitchen and Mathew opened the door of the Aga so she could fully appreciate the smell of the cooking bird. Immediately his mother shut it again, fluffing her tea towel at him saying, "It won't cook with the door open. I keep telling you, go on the both of you," chasing the twins from the kitchen.

Giving Martha a big hug she said, "Happy Christmas sweetheart. You're late you know. What on earth kept you so late? I was beginning to worry." She hugged and kissed her daughter again, hustling her on to a chair at the kitchen table and filling the kettle for a cup of tea in one fluid motion.

"We had tons to finish after closing, it took us half the night mum," Martha answered. "Then we got there early this morning and finished the rest, so we don't have to go back until the 3rd of January. Oi! Out you two!" She called to the twins who had spied the parcels in her bag and were gingerly feeling through the wrapping paper to guess the contents.

Mrs Cratchit smiled at her daughter. "Well, at least you're here now," she said. "You stay by the oven, drink your tea and warm up... Ooh, I have missed you," she said as Martha wrapped her cold hands around the steaming mug.

But before she could answer her mother or even take a sip of the tea, she was seized again by the twins who'd abandoned the bag saying, "Wait! That's dad back. Go on Martha, hide somewhere. We'll say you couldn't come, then you can jump out at him in surprise. Go on, hide Martha, hide!"

Martha left her tea and squeezed herself into the broom cupboard to wait for her father. In came Bob, his old scarf wrapped twice around him, his Macintosh barely keeping off the snow and rain, pushing Tim, in his wheelchair decorated with tinsel and covered with thick plastic to keep him dry. Bob gently helped Tim up and the boy ran to his mother to receive a hug and kiss. Tim then plonked down on the seat nearest the Aga (just vacated by Martha) where it was warm.

Bob clapped his hands and rubbed them together as he looked around the room asking, "Is Martha here yet?"

Amy Cratchit, who hadn't spent three seasons at the East Camden Amateur Dramatic Society for nothing, winked at Tim, put one hand on her hip, and with the other gestured to the wall phone saying, "Oh, yes, I was going to tell you, she's not coming today."

"Not... Coming... Today," repeated Bob. "Did she say why?" Poor Bob. He had been looking forward to seeing his eldest daughter on this special day, indeed on having all his children once more under his roof to celebrate Christmas. After pretending to be Tim's racing car all the way home he'd been full of frosty joy and glowing with Christmas merriment. Now his balloon had burst, and he looked blankly at his wife.

"Nope, there was just a message on the machine about having to finish up from last night and that she *may* get here later. I tell you, Bob, I'm furious about it!" Amy replied, wiping her hands on a tea towel and throwing it dramatically on the table, she glared angrily at Bob with this terrible news. Bob however, knew that Amy had never been furious about anything in her life, and even getting her cross took some doing. Then, seeing the second mug of tea on the table, he smiled saying, "Wait a minute...!" At the exact moment Amy's bravura performance crumbled and she burst out laughing. Martha crashed from the cupboard amongst brooms, mops, and the cordless vacuum, dropping them all behind her and ran into her father's arms wishing him a Happy Christmas. Bob laughed and hugged her back as Amy said that's exactly why she didn't do four seasons at the East Camden Am-dram.

Meanwhile, Scrooge had been puzzled by the appearance of Tim in comparison to his lusty and vigorous brothers and sisters. The boy stood out so obviously from the crowd, Scrooge's eyes kept flicking back to him as he watched the entire Cratchit family.

What is it that makes Tim stand out among so many Cratchit children? Well, sadly, Tim was not the best. Although he was seven and a half years old, one could be forgiven for thinking he was as young as five or six. Physically he was a pale, thin child who was easily tired. Not usual in a child his age and certainly not in a family whose kids bounced off the walls with good health and vitality. But you see Tim was fighting leukaemia and had been for a long time. The treatment was difficult, made him sick and, this is the bit he really hated, affected his growth, which was why he looked so small for his age. But he was an affectionate, intelligent, and observant child who was well loved by all his family. He also had a strong determination and was blessed with a deep faith which he needed at times. All those who treated him, from his doctors and oncologists to the nurses, even the ancillary staff who brought his meals when he was in the hospital, had a soft spot for Tim. He didn't exactly suffer in silence, he wasn't a martyr, but he was brave, and always had a smile for everyone he met.

Oh, and as mentioned earlier, it was for him that Martha got a job after leaving school, rather than going onto further education, which she could have easily done, winning a full scholarship to university. But by moving out and finding employment, it gave her family one less mouth to feed, and she could contribute some money to help Bob and Amy with those costs of Tim's treatment not covered by the NHS. Hidden costs, like travelling back and forward to specialists and the extras that were important to ensure the rest of the kids didn't feel abandoned.

Whatever she could do, she had said to her parents, at the family meeting to discuss her future prior to leaving school, she was more than happy to do. Tim was everyone's priority; the scholarship would wait a few years. Seriously, she told Bob and Amy, she wanted to help.

Her dedication to her family and her little brother was no surprise to her parents. They were extremely proud of their beautiful eldest daughter. She had stood in the sitting room, passionately voicing her intentions and commitments to them, while simultaneously flipping Tim upside down and hanging him by his ankles until he called feignights.

Finally, it was just Amy, Martha, and Bob alone in the kitchen as the children played cards and games in the living room in front of a noisy TV. They'd been banished there by Mrs Cratchit so she could finish her cooking in some semblance of peace and quiet. Martha was a spare pair of hands, helping her mother and catching up on all the gossip at the same time.

I must pause here for a few moments, to pay tribute to Mrs Cratchit and her skills regarding the Cratchit Christmas dinner.

Firstly, unlike most families, the Cratchits traditionally ate goose, not turkey, and secondly, as we all know, turkeys, ducks and geese are outrageously expensive just before Christmas, when supermarkets take full advantage of this culinary tradition. A tradition founded, as indeed many other British institutions were, by Henry the Eighth. However I'm sure Henry didn't envisage quite how costly the humble Christmas gobbler would become some four hundred and ninety odd years later. Particularly one big enough to feed such a large family.

I must admit, on occasions, when I was unable to afford one of these Yuletide delights myself, I wrestled with the idea of wandering down to my local duck pond at the crack of dawn, a stocking full of rocks in my pocket, to wait for an unsuspecting candidate to waddle by, so I could thump it on the head and smuggle it home stuffed inside my puffer jacket.

The only time I ever got close to trying it, I moseyed down there with as much subtlety as a pantomime villain, to discover there were only swans swimming on the pond and nary a duck in sight. They say all the swans in London belong to the Queen. I'm not certain if that's true, but if it is, one would expect them to behave with a certain amount of regally appointed dignity. However, as I discovered to my cost, while searching amongst the reeds for my Christmas lunch, a graceful swan gliding serenely by can turn into a pissed off pterodactyl in less time than it takes you to shriek, "Oh shit," and run for your life!

Amy however, got their goose through her family network, via her great grandfather Bartley, who kept a van parked near Camden Markets from late Spring right through to December 12th, where he sold trinkets, observed divination, and forecast lottery numbers for enthusiastic punters.

131

You may have seen him if you shop there. His large painted gypsy caravan appeals to the public, and every other weekend in Summer, he brings along a huge Clydesdale horse named Leander. A gentle giant, he doesn't mind being in a selfie or two as long as you bring him an apple. The horse that is, not Bartley.

I've known their family for years, ever since Bartley read my palm when I was six years old and predicted I would be a famous opera star. Between you and me, I couldn't carry a tune in a bucket, but then again, he's the first to admit he doesn't have the gifts Gaia bestowed on others in his family.

Getting back to Amy and her goose; every Sunday Bartley barks up business for his daughter, Amy's Grandma, Masilda, who uses a handmade silver bowl, river pebbles and water to divine someone's outlook for the next few months. She has a large clientele because she is extremely accurate, and because she only charges a tenner an hour.

Amy comes into the picture by lending a hand every Sunday, noon to four pm, from Spring, right through to the end of Autumn, using her Dowsing Pendulum to help pick out lottery numbers for enthusiastic punters.

Since she was 5 years old, Amy had lessons in using the pendulum and now in front of everyone, and with no movement of her hand, it would move left to right, backwards and forwards or round and round. Her Dowsing Pendulum would dance, and the customers loved it.

The upshot of this tale is her Great Grandpa knew a bloke, who knew a bloke, who knew a farmer who farmed free-range geese and goose eggs. He also liked a flutter on the lottery and would come regularly to see Amy, swearing she always picked his winners.

The farmer *was* a regular winner, the jammy bastard, so not only did he gift her the odd half dozen goose eggs every now and then, but he also presented her with a free-range goose each Christmas. Refusing any offers of payment, he insisted it was a thank you for all his lotto luck throughout the year. Amy initially refused his offer, but when he pointed out he'd won over eight thousand quid in one year, she decided it was fair do's, and picked out a fat, juicy goose for Christmas dinner.

It wasn't just who you knew, it was sometimes what you knew and how to turn it to your benefit, she told her children.

Bob was sipping a cup of coffee when his wife asked, "How was Tim at Mass? Was it ok?"

Bob smiled a smile of deep love for a child so, so precious... "Better, much better today my love than he's been in a while. He asked to sit in the middle rows of the church with his chair on the end of the aisle where everyone could see him. When I asked him why, he said he wanted everyone who came to church to notice him so they could remember that the child born today became the man who made the sick better, the blind see and the lame walk. I was so proud of him Amy. Everyone walking past said, Happy Christmas, and smiled at us, even the vicar. I think he's feeling stronger today darling, a little stronger, perhaps it's his Christmas Spirit." Bob smiled at his wife and drank a little more of his coffee before adding quietly, "Then he said the strangest thing, he asked me, did I think it would be okay if he said a prayer for Mr Scrooge."

There was a loud and sudden clanging in the kitchen as Amy dropped the ladle she'd been using to baste the goose and looked up at her husband in astonishment. "He didn't!" she exclaimed totally surprised.

Martha, equally startled, her eggbeater frozen in mid-air over a bowl of custard, blurted out, "Prayers! For old sourpuss!" Then, looking at her parents' faces she said more quietly, "I wonder why?"

"Well, I asked him just that, why? And he said he wanted to pray for Mr Scrooge because he hoped he could change and be happy."

"Happy?" said Martha scornfully. "Ebenezer Scrooge! That'll be the day. I reckon he spent all last night heating up pennies for carol singers!"

Amy gave her daughter a playful poke. "Shush you," she said with a laugh, "back to your lumpy custard." Martha giggled as Amy turned to Bob, "God love him, but Tim won't ever understand there are people like Scrooge, who just can't ever be happy because they prefer being miserable," she said.

"Tim always thinks the best of everyone," interrupted Martha again. "It's one of his most endearing faults."

"Virtues," corrected her father. "You mean virtues."

"I know what I mean," said Martha, licking the custard off the eggbeater.

"What did you say anyway?" Amy asked as she drained the juices off the goose and wrestled it onto a serving plate.

"Well, I just said I was sure Mr Scrooge wouldn't mind a prayer or two," said Bob. "So he closed his eyes for a while, said some prayers and then told me he was sure Mr Scrooge would be okay."

Martha rolled her eyes, muttering something about flying pigs while her mother, making gravy, added the goose juices to a pan.

"Well," Amy said from underneath a cloud of steam, "I'm sure they're the only prayers he'll get unless he undergoes some radical change of personality. But it's nice Tim saying some for him anyway..." She paused, tuning into the noise the rest of the kids were making in the other room and asked loudly, "What ARE they all doing in there?" She set off to see for herself, leaving Bob and Martha to ponder on Tim's motivation a little longer.

Scrooge was confused. "Why would the boy say prayers for me Spirit? I don't know him, I've never even seen him until now. He's sick. He should pray for himself if he wants to pray. I'm not interested in his salvation!" he said scathingly.

The Spirit answered softly, "Whether you're interested or not, the boy feels you need help. He doesn't need to meet you. His intentions are honest, and his prayers are offered with a pure heart. It's a wonderful gift inspired by Christmas, Ebenezer. His faith is so strong, he's relying on it to help you. Never turn your back on a gift of hope and faith, even if you don't believe, it's still given from a place of true love and is well meant."

The children came racing back into the kitchen, the games obviously no match for the delicious smell of Christmas fare, and now Bob, Tim and Martha were here, they would not be put off any longer from their dinner. Peter had Tim in a piggyback while Belinda struggled with the smaller children, trying to keep them away from the hot stove. After finishing making the custard, Martha had left the kitchen, returning with her baby sister who'd just woken from a nap. Tim sat again by the oven while his brothers and sisters busied themselves with last minute jobs handed out by Mrs Cratchit, while Bob set about making his famous Magic Christmas mulled wine.

I say famous. Bob's Magic Christmas mulled wine was only famous within his family, but they all enjoyed the drink and the magic part, so he was careful with both. Bob's Magic Christmas mulled wine is a homemade recipe he dreamed up himself. The basic mulled part of the recipe is like any you can find on the internet. For those interested though, here's Bob version.

Three days before Christmas, Bob added sherry, cinnamon quills, nutmeg, golden syrup, and raspberry jam into a pan on a low heat.

Then he needed the skin of one apple. Tradition (Bob's own tradition) holds this must be peeled by one of his (unmarried) daughters over the age of thirteen and peeled in one long piece to infuse the "magic."

Strict adherence to the apple skin folklore also says the daughter's hair must be left untied and flowing over her shoulders during peeling. Like all women of gypsy descent, the Cratchit girls have long hair as it's rarely, if ever, cut. Once peeled, she throws the skin over her left shoulder and looks to see which letter of the alphabet the skin resembles, giving her the first initial of her future husband's name...

So far Martha's husband would have a first name beginning with a C, J, L, O, R, P or V and Belinda's future husband would have a first name starting with an A, O, Y, V, L, S or N. So theoretically, as a predictive system, it's not very dependable.

The peel is cut, added to the pan together with cloves and diced apple flesh and simmered very gently for one hour.

Bob then removes it from the heat and once cool pops it into the fridge.

Come to Christmas Day when the goose and veggies are being cooked and Bob undertakes the second stage.

Into a pan goes two bottles of red wine.

In a mortar and pestle, or in his case a coffee cup and the end of the rolling pin, he grinds the zest of an orange, cardamom pods, vanilla extract, ginger powder, and a white peppercorn or two. Once mixed, he adds it to the pot with the juice of the orange, light flower honey, soft brown sugar, blackberry jam and blackcurrant squash and the previously infused mixture from the fridge. Warmed on a low simmer for forty minutes to dissolve the sugar, jam, and honey then strained through muslin or a fine sieve to remove the bits, he would pour it into a ceramic/heatproof jug and place it into the oven at a very low temperature until served. Just before serving, he adds two cups of sweet sherry if you fancy a little more alcohol in your mulled wine. This is totally optional.

Bob **NEVER** adds chilli flakes to his mulled wine.

Several things were strictly forbidden from entering the Cratchit house. These included such things as opals, umbrellas, frogs, dream catchers, double-sided mirrors, scented candles, ouija boards, politicians, wind chimes, feng shui nonsense, pay-tv, smokers, rocking chairs, garden gnomes, God botherers, white cats, hermit crabs, pet

rats, guinea pigs, dirty feet, estate agents offering to value their home, or anyone who could spend hours talking about golf.

As well, certain foods don't make it across the front steps either. Foods such as chilli, sushi, octopus, garlic, fresh ginger, kale, coriander, faggots, broccoli, desiccated coconut, silverbeet, bay leaves, tripe in any disguise-including that made into any form of "seafood," flat leaf parsley, or fennel.

Each of these discriminations, and many others, were backed up by cogent family superstitions or practical reasons.

For example, any blond-haired young boy dressed in white who stopped to sing a few Christmas carols at the Cratchit residence, would immediately be greeted by a horrified scream, and have the door slammed in his face. All the curtains would be drawn, and Amy would then go from room to room, burning white sage to purify and bless the house. She wouldn't open the curtains or answer the door again until it was done, sometimes leaving Bob or any of the kids freezing on the doorstep, pounding feet, and blowing on their hands, until she declared it clear. The boy, having no idea he had just been responsible for absolute panic by awakening an old family legend about death, would probably skip onto the house next door, where hopefully he'd get a more friendly welcome.

The embargo on guinea pigs came from Amy's childhood when a relative told her if you hold a guinea pig upside down, its eyes will pop out.

As for the chilli, ginger, coriander, bay leaves and fennel, etc. their prohibition was more compelling. Both Bob and Amy were united in their dislike of them and claimed that they ruined the taste of everything else on the plate.

Never get into a discussion about chilli with Bob because his loathing of it was so vehement, he'd written hundreds of letters to cooking shows and famous TV chefs bemoaning their addition of chilli to a recipe and why, in his opinion, it ruined the dish. He was once offered chilli crab while out to dinner and his reaction was apoplectic.

As for the reasons why the others weren't allowed, that's a story for another day.

Finally, the Cratchit family could sit down to eat. Bob and his family said grace before meals so held hands and bowed their heads in prayer. Bob said a simple thank you for the fine food and the family all replied, "Amen." Each still remembering last year when Peter had been called upon to say grace and had dashed off irreverently, *"Thank you, Father, Son and Holy Spirit, to eat the most you've got to be in it to win it!"* Which drew a giggle from his sisters, a laugh from his father and a playful cuff around the ear from his mother.

While everyone pulled their crackers and donned their silly hats, told their terrible jokes, and looked at their tiny toys, Bob set to, carved, and served the goose with some stuffing on everyone's plate. They passed around the potatoes, excellently mashed by Peter to a delicious creamy mush, the sprouts, expertly strained by Martha and therefore not squidgy, and the apple sauce cooked to perfection by Belinda. The adults added roast spuds to their plates and lashings of gravy rounded it all off; from then not a sound was heard until Eliza declared it simply too yummy for words and was there any more gravy left? Everyone said what a great meal it was, and everyone had seconds. Even the baby had cheerfully finished a plate of mashed potatoes and sprouts mixed with gravy, although Bob said they were sure to regret it later when Abigail, a particularly windy baby, farted.

Scrooge had been watching in silence and now muttered, "Not exactly a big meal, for such a large family."

"Aye, but one gratefully received by everyone here," the Spirit replied. "In fact, the Cratchits would tell you they were much blessed in what they've just had, much better than many others in this world."

But now, the air was charged with tension as this was the serious part of the meal. Yes, the goose was delicious and important, but it was for naught if what followed now was a disaster. The dirty plates were removed, clean bowls placed at Mrs Cratchit's elbow, next to the huge jug of custard. Silence and anticipation sat all around the table. She looked gravely at her family, then quietly left the room. They could hear her moving about the kitchen, but no one would dare ask if she needed any help. Time passed. Three minutes, five, seven. Clanking and all sorts of noises came from the other room but still they held to their seats in desperate anticipation. Finally, she called out loudly, "Ooooooookaay!"

Simon jumped to his feet and, as was his special duty, raced to turn off the main light, while Mrs Cratchit entered the room, carrying before her a plate bearing a huge, flaming, deliciously smelling, Christmas pudding. Everyone clapped this glorious vision as Amy put it on the table. Simon flipped the light back on and took his seat again.

Now came the test as Mrs Cratchit cut a piece with her spoon for Bob, then, adding custard, passed it to her husband.

What if it was underdone, or too much flour! Not enough fruit, or too much so it fell apart!! A bundle of nerves, she couldn't relax until Bob had tasted the pudding she'd made and laid by last *Stir up Sunday* when she'd banished everyone from the house for the day. That way she'd had complete peace and quiet to perfect her own recipe and concentrate on her pudding. With the help of several cookbooks and one or two glasses of red, she'd produced her pudding dancing around the kitchen to Queens' greatest hits. Finally, it was ready, to wait silently until Christmas, so it could mature and deepen in flavour, and come to the table today, ready for Bob to give his verdict.

The children passed the pudding down, each sniffing in anticipation on the way until it got to Bob, who also sniffed the bowl. He lifted it in his hand and felt the weight, then pulled some custard off to see the fruit inside. At last, he portioned a piece of pudding and custard onto his spoon and popped it into his mouth. All waited, watching him chew slowly, his eyes closed until he finally opened them and smiled broadly at Mrs Cratchit saying, "Amy, the pudding of ninety-eight was good, the one of two thousand and one was remarkable, in two thousand and twelve what can I say, it brought tears to my eyes, but this, this? I can safely say that is the best, sweetest, and most flavourful Christmas pudding you have EVER made during the entire time we've been married!" And he took another huge spoonful to emphasise his delight.

The children cheered as Mrs Cratchit blew out a sigh of relief, confessing her worries about fruit and flour while she dolloped out portions to her waiting family.

Before they could dig in and eat, it was Tim's turn to follow another Cratchit family tradition. Standing up, holding a creased piece of paper, he coughed nervously and said the little rhyme he'd composed in honour of the pudding.

Christmas pudding round and bright,
Grace our Christmas table tonight.

Full of fruit and spices too,
Boiled then cooked for me and you.
Bless our family upon this day,
With thankful hearts, we stop and say,
Christmas blessings and all that's good,
We wish to everyone as we eat our pud.

The whole family clapped and cheered Tim, who looked pleased as punch and sat down beaming. Now they could dig into their bowls, the children, who ate it with extra custard, yelling gleefully as they found the pound coins Mrs Cratchit had slyly pushed in as she served each bowlful.

Abigail enjoyed a bowlful of custard.

And so, the afternoon passed. The mountain of dishes were washed, dried, and put away amongst wistful talk of one day owning a dishwasher, and the gas fire was lit in the sitting room. It was a small fire, but if the doors were kept closed it could warm that room well and it was here the family had gathered, sprawling on an assortment of easy chairs and on the carpet as they peeled and ate the chestnuts cooked while the dishes were done. The whole family now sat in a semi-circle around the fire, as Bob served his famous mulled wine to everyone, mixed with varying quantities of lemonade depending on their age, and when they all had a filled glass he called, "A Merry Christmas to us all, God bless us." Everyone raised their cups and glasses in a toast and cried, "Merry Christmas" while Tim shouted, "God Bless us all, everyone one of us!"

The room was warm and comfortable, and Scrooge noticed that Tim sat very close to his Dad and that Bob, for his turn, was always in physical contact with his son. Either by holding his hand, or an arm around his shoulder or Tim just leaning against his father. It was as if Bob knew that Tim's time was short and so dreaded the idea of losing him that he needed to continually make sure his son was still by his side.

Scrooge turned to the Spirit and asked, "What's wrong with the boy? Is Tim going to be okay?"

The Spirit closed his eyes briefly, then shaking his head no, he said, "I'm not able to see far into the future. That's not within my province. Nevertheless, I can see the family in dreadful sadness and tears, mourning his loss, with visitors dressed in black, his photograph carefully preserved on the mantle for everyone to see. He's going to die if there are no changes in the future."

Scrooge was jolted, feeling an emotion almost foreign to him, and urged, "Spirit can't YOU just change the future?"

"No Ebenezer," it replied. "Neither I nor my family have any power over the future. My time is here and now. We are not magicians. We cannot say a few words of incantation and set the world to rights. Only people can change human destiny. The future can only be altered by what's done in the present. If the present isn't changed, he will die. If Bob can't make any changes, neither I nor my family can help Tim. All we can do is make a place for him in our house and give comfort to his family."

The Spirit looked directly at Scrooge, his Yorkshire accent now hard and disapproving. "But then if he is going to die, perhaps he should just get on with it eh? Do away with himself, quit this world, cut short his life, stop cluttering up the streets, sucking up your taxes and decrease the surplus population?"

Scrooge was ashamed to hear his callous, thoughtless words quoted back to him by the Spirit, and was unable to look him in the eye.

The Spirit though was still talking. "Look at you," he said gently now, "so positive who is surplus according to YOUR values. What makes you so important that you decide who lives and who dies? Why do you weigh one life as more important than another?

"Why do you believe, because someone lives a life on the street, or is sick or poor that their life is not important? Why do you presume they have lost the right to their own humanity?

"Do you believe the gates of heaven will open for you, just because you have money or earthly prestige when you constantly ignore the teachings of my family?

"I tell you truly Ebenezer, those who spend an hour each week down on their knees, repeating sacred words they don't even follow, can't secure their place in heaven, not while they turn their backs on the suffering and distress of their fellow man.

"Sundays spent holding a hand up to God, glorifying our teacher's name is not enough. Praising the glory of his sacrifice, and the words of his scripture mean nothing if you don't try to live his teachings each day. Teachings of love, acceptance, and, kindness. Of forgiveness, respect…and most of all a belief in each other. Then and only then will a place in heaven be secured.

"Heaven's gates will open a million times over for Tim, Bob, and his family and all those who try and live these teachings throughout their lives. But for those who rely on their money and power, believing that will secure them their place in heaven, those same gates will shut in their faces unless they change. Those earthly powers they hold so much reliance on, mean nothing. Money, power and earthly prestige will never buy them entry."

Scrooge was still looking at the floor as Peter shouted, "Toasting everyone, lets toast like we always do. Toast and make our magic wish with Dad's Magic Christmas mulled wine. Go on Martha, start us off, you go first, give us a chance to think of something," he said grinning.

After a few seconds, Martha began their traditional round where everyone made a Christmas toast and then made their magic wish.

Martha toasted Mrs Cratchit for the fine meal and closed her eyes to wish...
Peter toasted Mr Cratchit for the delicious punch, and he wished that...
Belinda toasted Christmas and wished she would get a...
Eliza toasted Martha for coming home, wishing they could both...
Mathew toasted Peter for leaving school and he hoped, well it was really a wish for...
Simon toasted Tim on looking so well and he desperately wished that...
Tim toasted the Queen and wished she would always...
Mrs Cratchit toasted all her family and her wish was that they could always...
The baby burped and giggled...

At last, it was Bob's turn and Scrooge heard Bob Cratchit call his name. "Mr Scrooge!" he shouted lifting his glass, "How about a toast to Mr Scrooge everyone?"

A stunned silence descended with a thump on the frivolity as they all looked first at Bob, then cut their eyes to Mrs Cratchit, who put her glass down with studied gentility saying, "A toast to that miserable old... I don't think so, Robert. Not that he'd ever be allowed across my front steps, but do you know what I'd do if I had him here?"

All the children shook their heads no, waiting curiously to see what their mother would say.

"I would sit him down to lunch and as soon as he'd that sour mouth of his full, I'd give him such a piece of my mind he wouldn't know what hit him. Look here Ebenezer Scrooge, I would say, here's a lesson in the real world and what it's like to live in it... And no Bob, before you say it, it's not the wine talking. I wouldn't allow him to move until he understood what it's like trying to manage every single day with a boss like him. You know how he is Bob; no one knows better than you."

"Darling," said Bob, "please... We should set a good example to our children on Christmas Day."

"Oh, sweetheart," said Mrs Cratchit sighing, "It's only due to Christmas that I'd ever contemplate drinking a toast to the likes of Ebenezer Scrooge. I've never met anyone as objectionable as him, so impolite, money-grubbing, miserable, mean..." Bob started to say something, however she lifted her hand to stop him interrupting, "BUT...," she went on, "I'll drink his health just because you want to Robert," and she raised her glass, took a deep breath, saying tonelessly, "Long life to the wretched old bugger...er. Ahem," Amy stopped, catching Bob's eye, "I mean, *children*... To Mr Scrooge, I hope he has a joyful day and is very Merry. And a Happy New year. Cheers!" and she jerked her glass in an "up yours" motion reminiscent of Bette Davis and her celery stick.

Everyone raised their glasses and repeated, "Mr Scrooge" but it was mechanical, monotonous, and dreary. No enthusiasm, no joy. Scrooge could not help but see how the toast to him was so different from those that had gone before. No laughter, no fun. Just... Nothing.

"Mumma," came a little voice, "have you ever met Mr Scrooge?"

Amy looked at Simon who had asked the question. Such a quiet, delicate child, he wanted so much to find the good in everyone. "Yes, I met him once, when I had to take some papers into the office your father had accidentally left at home."

"What was he like?" Breathed Mathew, full of excited curiosity, as if they were talking about some wild exotic animal.

"Rude," said Amy, "very rude" and she refused to say anymore because it was Christmas Day and, said Amy, they weren't ruining it talking about Ebenezer Scrooge.

What had been a happy family atmosphere had changed at just the mention of his name. Scrooge was the ogre of their family and his name could still even the busy Cratchit twins and cast a temporary gloom over them.

"Do you remember that meeting with Mrs Cratchit?" the Spirit asked Ebenezer.

"I remember her bringing in the papers, yes."

"And..."

"And I may have been a little brusque with her."

"No Ebenezer, you were bad-mannered and disrespectful. You snatched them off her, said she'd taken so long to get there it was too late, and called her useless!"

"I, well...Perhaps I was..."

"She dropped everything to bring those pages in, asked a friend to collect her children from school and took two busses to get to your office, yet not once did you say thank you. You pushed her out of your building to wait for over an hour until Bob came back to take her home!" Reminded the Spirit.

Unexpected Martha piped up, "Mumma, whenever we mention Mr Scrooge you say it isn't the time to talk about him. Any time of the year, not just Christmas. On an average day, you say it's not the time to talk about Mr Scrooge. When is the time to talk about him! Seriously, Mum, I want to know, out of the whole three hundred and sixty-five days of the year when can we talk about Old Scrooge!" she grinned cheekily at her mother.

Amy took a sip of her drink and cocked her head to one side, thinking. Then she also grinned and answered, "Hallowe'en. That's the day we can talk about him. It's full of scary monsters, so he'll fit right in," she said, tipping her glass again in a mock toast. Martha and the others laughed and with that, Scrooge was forgotten, unable to ruin Christmas.

Scrooge had listened to this exchange of words and felt himself flush with embarrassment and anger, not only at the way Amy talked about him in front of her children but at the way all the family had laughed. Not looking at the Spirit, he muttered angrily about setting a good example and not talking impolitely about someone behind their back. The Spirit didn't look at him, but agreeing said softly, "Aye, talking about people in a disrespectful way is something no one should do, no matter what their age." He left Scrooge to realise the irony of his complaint in his own time.

The merriment continued as the Cratchits all swapped news.

Martha, who was an apprentice to a very exclusive and expensive couturier, told how much she was enjoying her job and that she'd even served a famous TV star who'd arrived in a big white convertible! The television star had been extremely impressed with Martha and said she was a helpful young lady, telling the *vendeuse* she was pleased with the service! The owner was teaching her dress design and Martha passed around some of her drawings to show her parents.

Meanwhile, the younger Cratchit's were talking and shouting over each other in a cheerful din. Eventually, Bob called for silence and announced that, as Peter had finished school that summer and was now old enough for full-time employment, it was time for him to move on from his part-time work collecting shopping trolleys and start a proper career. What's more, Bob knew of a place that would suit him AND would pay a very generous salary for a youth his age, and he had even gone so far as to arrange an interview for Peter on the 28th December at 2 pm. This caused a great flutter and Mathew, Eliza and Simon proceeded to shout "ruff-ruff-ruff. Pet-er, Pet-er, Pet-er" over and over football fashion while his sisters hugged him saying he would soon be a pukka businessman with his own bowler, brolly and briefcase and could then buy his own shirts and ties, instead of wearing Bobs which were always too large.

Let's just screech to a stop for a moment, and take a good, long look at the Cratchit family.

So far, who thinks this family are too nice for words? Come on, hands up, you can be honest. Surely all that sweetness, kindness and family togetherness can't be real!

Have we all been transported back in time to an American sitcom circa nineteen ninety-five? Full of family values and important life lessons we've all got to learn within twenty-eight minutes of commercialised amusement.

Morality with humour.

IT'S NOTHING LIKE REAL LIFE!

Where's the fighting, the yelling, the sibling rivalry? What's happened to the sniping, effing and blinding, storming out in a mood, slamming doors? I don't know about you, but growing up, my family only ever communicated through heavy sarcasm, so they would be totally baffled by the Cratchits.

Are they real, one asks oneself? It's true, they sound so incredibly sweet anyone reading this could be in danger of contracting diabetes, but to be honest, their reality is more understandable.

Like any family in similar circumstances, the Cratchits were devastated by Tim's illness and had been fighting it on and off for years.

Periods of remission were followed by setbacks, hospitalisation, intensive treatment and for such a long time they had lived with no certainty or ability to plan too far into the future.

It was around Tim and whatever his life was going to be next, that his family organised their lives. That was why they wasted no time, they didn't argue overmuch, and Bob stuck like glue to his job, working day in and day out for the delightful Ebenezer Scrooge. He needed a secure, regular wage to support his wife and family, and pay for anything Tim needed either for medical, or palliative care and nothing anyone would do or say, not even Ebenezer Scrooge, would get in his way.

Tim was the reason Martha left school at seventeen to find employment and why Peter had a part-time job even while he finished high school.

The Cratchit's managed everything in the simplest and clearest way. They knew life was too fragile to waste and were determined to shower Tim with love.

Oh yes, the kids squabbled, and yes, they exchanged hot words, no one is saying they didn't.

And no one said Amy didn't cry into her pillow at night, because she did, quite often.

Nor did anyone say Bob didn't lash out in frustration either. In fact, he still bore the scars from when he thumped the wall outside the oncologist's office and broke two bones in his left hand. An understandable, but bloody stupid thing to do, as Amy never ceased to remind him.

Everyone coped as best they could.

Amy, being the one Tim turned to the most, grabbed a full day of me-time when she sometimes sent everyone out to the countryside for a day, to visit her family and "blow the cobwebs out". Then she'd treat herself to a full day of R&R, beginning with a massage that did wonders for built up tension, followed by waxing, threading, face pack, manicure and a hair colour, all thanks to her best friend and beautician, Li. Half an hour of meditation, a long hot bath, and by the time Bob and the kids got home, she was relaxed, radiant and ready to face the world again. Pizza in the oven, a glass of wine in her hand, she'd be dancing around the kitchen to Queen's greatest hits.

Bob liked to garden. He burned up his stress and anxiety moving soil from one side of the yard to the other, building and pulling down pergolas, Balinese courtyards, cottage gardens, vegetable runs, and an ultra-modern low maintenance backyard Amy described as "bland." Now it was a higgledy-piggledy combination of everything which was a colourful, relaxing space. Alas, his constant activity disturbed several moles which had taken up residence under the lawn. They were cute and adorable, but as far as Bob was concerned, they were vermin and caused a lot of damage. There're several ways to deal with a mole problem and Bob's preferred method of eradication involved the flat side of the garden shovel and a good aim. However, he was outvoted by his horrified family, so if he caught one of the little buggers, he dropped it into a sack, and resisting the temptation to let it go in Regents Park, drove via the A40 to Harmondsworth Moor where he could safely dump its furry little ass.

Back in his garden, he planted daffodils and marigolds to discourage new residents, and pinwheels that added colour and gaiety, making the backyard look like the Cratchits lived "Sur la Mer" rather than in deep suburbia. For Bob, his garden was a place to turn frustration, anger, and despair into something positive and beautiful. Just don't mention moles.

Martha had been known, on occasion, to go on a girl's night out, get tiddly and dance like a madwoman until the sun came up, just to have a few hours stress relief. A kebab on the way home, followed by a hot bath, and she tumbled into bed at 7 am feeling no pain. Both her struggling finances and the banging headache she woke up with, made her swear she'd never go out again.....

Peter punched the bag and lifted weights at his local sports centre a few times a week. The punching disciplined his mind and relieved his stress, and the weights helped build his strength and concentrated his thoughts. He burned up his frustration at the world, and emerged calm, tolerant and in control. Plus, the redhead on the refreshment kiosk gave him free smoothies.

Belinda baked. Cakes, cookies, slices, muffins, meringues, macaroons, you name it. She was a born baker, exceptionally good at it and hoped for a place at one of the top cooking schools in the country.

The local community centre benefited from these stress-related culinary outbursts, all of which sold well for morning teas and bake sales. So much so, on special occasions, such as the day the Mayor came to open the new wing, the entertainment committee wrestled with the ethics of deliberately increasing her stress levels, just so she would respond with more deliciously baked goods and relieve them of the difficulties of arranging the catering.

The twins swam laps, had diving matches, and underwater contests at the same sports centre Peter went to and would race each other all day if they could. They would emerge, wrinkled, eyes stinging from the chlorine, worn out, and sleep like babies. Tomorrow they would wake up fully recharged, and ready to help their mother with anything.

Simon, studious and shy, retreated into his books. Ask him about Tutankhamun or the Titanic however, and he would come to life and talk for hours.

Abigail sat on her blanket with her soft toys and Digger for company, watching the Little Mermaid on a loop and gnawing on her rusks. Digger sat looking at her until she toppled over asleep, then gently removed the remaining rusk from her hand. After alerting Amy, who put the baby down for a nap, Digger would settle on the blanket and finish the rusk in comfort, also watching the Little Mermaid. Then he fell asleep too.

And how did Tim cope with the inevitable frustration of his condition? Believe it or not, he played the electric guitar. Very well for a child his age. He had been given a second hand one by a charity a year ago and slowly taught himself to read music. It was hard, time-consuming and just what he needed to keep his mind busy. He composed songs for his mum, songs for his sisters, and songs for the nurses who took care of him in hospital. When he was better, he said shyly, he'd give a concert for everyone. Tickets fifty pence each, all proceeds to cancer research.

All the family members still got depressed, worried, anxious, frazzled, and snappy, but soldiered on. Fishing trips to the seaside, picnics in the countryside to visit the moles, fairs when they came around, afternoons at the park feeding the ducks with Quackers on a lead, all if Tim was well enough and the weather was warm, and of course they went to the movies and the British Museum; anything that helped keep the tension and worry to a minimum.

No false sweetness. No unreal "Hollywood script" of family life.

Just keeping it together, doing their best and making happy memories with Tim every chance they had...

Makes them human really, doesn't it?

As the afternoon wore on the chestnuts went down with the punch and the twins reeled about, pretending to be drunk, singing Christmas carols loudly. Eventually, Mrs Cratchit clapped her hands for order and declared it was time for presents. Everyone was immediately still. Tim had the honour of handing out the parcels and settled himself by the tree so he could reach everything. Not having a lot of spare cash, most of the gifts, like most of their clothes, had come from charity shops such as Oxfam and the Salvation Army, but careful shopping and a keen eye for a bargain could snap something that was virtually new, and any gift was still exciting. As each child tore off the wrappings from their little pile of presents, lots of hugs and kisses were exchanged.

Martha's gifts were unwrapped and while the children received toys, she'd been hard at work on her lunch breaks making separate gifts for her parents, Peter, and Belinda. Her mother received a multi-pocketed apron, handmade from linen in a beautiful cornflower blue. Amy laughed as she remembered talking to her daughter saying the best gift for a busy mother was an apron with lots of pockets. One for keys, one for the phone, one for a pen, one for reading glasses... And Martha had remembered and made the apron for her. Made it and hand painted the bib with a Clydesdale Horse.

Her father received a hand stitched, fine cotton business shirt, as did Peter. Made to measure they were beautiful, soft, both a perfect fit. Belinda, much to her delight, opened a sweet summer dress and though it was December, she went upstairs at once to put it on and wore it for the rest of the day.

The younger children settled down to play with their new toys, leaving a mountain of wrapping paper and bubble wrap for the cat and dog to explore while Amy, Martha and Belinda went to make coffee, change the baby, and talk girls talk. Peter was dragooned into assembly duty, putting together the twin's toys that came boxed in pieces. Simon took the pillows off the other sofa to make a cubby house and disappeared inside with his new Harry Potter, not to be seen again until teatime, and Bob settled comfortably on the sofa to snooze his way through the Christmas afternoon movie and kids' cartoons.

By the way, don't think the Cratchits had made the children wait all this time with no gifts. Father Christmas had visited everyone overnight and left a pillowcase full of goodies at the end of their bed. The "big presents" though, were always opened after Christmas dinner. That's also, coincidentally, how we did it in my house when I was a child and how I do it now I'm an adult with my children. The pillowcase was just to keep them busy for a few hours, while Amy and Bob finally got some sleep after their last-minute orgy of gift wrapping, and Christmas Eve preparations. Drinking the milk left out for Santa, or if he was lucky, a nice espresso coffee, (never Port or Brandy, thanks to the "don't drink and drive" campaign. Apparently it applies to Santa being drunk in charge of flying reindeer!) eating the homemade, slightly crumbly mince pies the kids had baked, and, of course, showing where Rudolph had got in via the chimney, by stamping reindeer hoof prints on the lino with white poster paint and a hoof stencil carved from a large potato.

Oh, general tip. If you are going to do the hoof thing in future. You MUST destroy the potato shape completely when finished. Don't be an idiot and just toss it in the kitchen bin as I did one year. I was ruthlessly cross examined and made to explain what Rudolph's shoe was doing in our bin. Eventually, after what felt like hours, I finally managed to convince my daughter that Rudolph must have broken his shoe when landing on our roof and needed to put a new one on before he could go any further. So, he must have changed it while Father Christmas was busy putting the presents under the tree, and that's why he'd left the old one in our bin. Yes, of course, all reindeer shoes are made from potatoes! It's a well-known fact. No, I know it's not mentioned in any books or movies about Rudolph's hoofs, but it's one of the things they tell mummies about just in case they wonder where one of their potatoes have gone on Christmas Day.

She grilled me unmercifully for half an hour about that.

She was four years old at the time.

Scrooge was still watching the family. Bob had managed to fall asleep amidst the group of yelling kids, a baby crying in the kitchen, plus a dog that seemed to be popping bubble wrap blister bubbles one by one, then barking at them. A cat was sitting amongst the used wrapping paper having a bath and the TV was loud with Christmas cartoons, but there was Bob, chin on his chest, glasses on the end of his nose, snoozing contently on the sofa oblivious to all that was going on around him. How could Bob sleep among all this chaos, noise and mess? How could he be so relaxed? Surely, he should insist the children tidy up and put things away, turn the TV down, and put that noisy dog out? How could he sleep with all this turmoil around him?

The fact that this turmoil, this chaos, was at the heart of Bob's contentment was something Scrooge couldn't understand, no more than he could understand a conversation in Gaelic.

Suddenly the Spirit turned to Scrooge and said, "We need to leave here very soon, and continue our journey into Christmas, take your leave of them all Ebenezer, we must move on."

Scrooge found leaving the Cratchits difficult, even though they couldn't see or hear him. Their warmth, humour and family atmosphere was so comfortable, he'd slipped right in and felt at ease in their company. Now he knew he had to leave but he didn't want to go. Mostly he didn't want to leave Tim. The knowledge that a small boy, very sick himself, would feel a need to pray for him, had taken hold of his sad and empty heart and shocked it, like a defibrillator, but instead of bringing back life, it had brought back the seed of human feelings. Hope and joy.

No, he didn't want to leave, so when the Spirit finally said there was no more time, he looked at Bob's family and felt a loss in his heart. But it was different this time. When he felt his heartbreak, it didn't empty of all emotions, it flickered back into life, a small spark lighting his way.

Chapter 9: The Meaning Of Christmas

Outside it was snowing again. The weather was cold and sharp, a strong lazy wind was blowing. The snow came down heavier and the wind cut like a knife. As Scrooge and the Spirit walked past the houses, Ebenezer pulled his robe close around him trying to keep warm. The Spirit, however, still strode around in his ill-fitting gown and bare feet as if it were a sunny afternoon.

Scrooge found he could see, (though he wasn't sure how), the warm fires in cosy houses as they passed. He could look into all sorts of rooms in all sorts of houses. Here a room with a table set, ready for Christmas dinner, warm and full of love and laughter. In a house across the street, the door blew open and family spilled out, shouting 'welcomes' to a married brother and his wife. On the other side, married sisters, aunts, and uncles were pulled inside from the cold, disappearing inside houses filled with a similar warmth, light, and love. Boots full of snow were banged out on the doorstep before they went inside. Further down another door opened, this time to let out several young women, all dressed up snug in coats and hats, on their way to a nearby party, where inevitably, when the coats came off, they would sparkle like winter fairies and hopefully capture more than a few of the boys' attention. To each the ghost passed blessings triumphantly from his generous hand, all touched by it were bright and cheery with the Spirit of Christmas.

But then, with no warning, the Spirit and Scrooge beamed away from the intense cold and snow, over an exceedingly long distance, where it was a warm still night, with no wind, and where millions of bright stars could be seen in a cloudless sky. They were standing on a viewing platform, above a huge alien landscape that was made from the red earth below them, like the unearthed city of a lost civilisation. Cut deep in the earth, the sides glowing from intense lights at the bottom, was a shape, a scar, like an inverted pyramid. The lights shining on its step-cut sides made beautiful colours and illuminated a wavy track coiling its way from the bottom, several hundred metres below, round, and around, to the top, close to where they were standing. Below, small dump trucks, like toys, crawled up from the 600-metres depth, lumbering along the track on their long journey to the surface.

"What's going on here?" Scrooge demanded, puzzled and alarmed. "Where are we? This isn't home."

"This," said the Spirit as he opened his arms expansively, "is one of the largest open-cut mines in the world. It's called a Super Pit and is far from where you live. They mine for gold here, scraping back the sand and rock for that metal you humans desire so much. It's three kilometres long, one kilometre wide and six hundred meters deep. Sixty million ounces of gold have been mined out of here. It's so big it can be seen from space," the Spirit said, as he leaned on the fence rail and looked down into the mine.

Scrooge followed suit, slowly and gingerly, as if the platform might give way and they both fall into the deep hole. Like the Spirit, he grabbed the safety rail and leaned over to take a better look. The lights shining on the sides emphasised their beautiful colours, glowing in the dark like an ancient pharaoh's burial tomb.

"Mining can still be dangerous though, even today," said the Spirit, "there are many brave men who are remembered more for the circumstances of their death, rather than the accomplishments of their life."

A loud rumbling, the powerful smell of diesel, and one of the trucks that had seemed so small crawling its way up the track, finished its journey to the surface. The giant behemoth, its powerful high beam lights flooding the way, carrying two hundred and forty tons of rock to be processed, lumbered into view.

The driver's seat was empty and the huge truck so intimidating, Scrooge was struck dumb. He looked at the Spirit who chuckled at his confusion "Satellite, Ebenezer. Satellites and remote control. These huge trucks are driven from over three hundred miles away. Modern technology keeps these trucks working day and night in a never ending cycle. One operator can drive four trucks at a time you know. This whole place is a constant hive of activity and has been for over a hundred years." Then he laughed again at

Scrooge's bewildered expression saying, "Don't be too impressed, I got most of that from Wikipedia."

Near a small office, a good distance away from the pit, a cheerful group of people were sitting in outdoor chairs at picnic tables. Mosquito coils burned to keep the bugs away, and leftover food on the tables was covered to keep off night-time crawlers and flying bugs.

A few of the people were dressed in Hivis shirts, hard hats at their feet, others wore jeans and tee shirts, all were holding beer cans or coffee mugs, except one, who played the guitar whilst others softly sang a Christmas tune. One or two were tapping away on phones or computer tablets, while several were standing slightly away from the rest, talking on their mobile phones. The Spirit inclined his head towards them and said, "Calls home to kids, wives, husbands, parents.

"These are some of the miners. They labour over a kilometre deep inside the mine, but they all know me.

"They haven't seen their families for many weeks. They're called FIFO workers, fly-in, fly-out. Both they and their families have difficult lives, separated for long weeks by huge distances. The separation is exceedingly difficult for everyone. Nevertheless, at Christmas, wherever they are, here or home, they still stop and remember my family. They celebrate and rejoice, however they can. And even though are so far away, they still remember to send each other Christmas greetings, joy and above all…love."

As the night wore on, the huge trucks, now relieved of their loads, rattled and rocked down the track once more, shrinking again to a child's toy, until reloaded, they began their return journey and their metamorphosis back into the giant workhorses of the mine.

Meanwhile, Scrooge and the Spirit watched the little group of people relaxing and talking, swatting bugs, and mosquitoes, sitting under the dark sky, enjoying the soft breeze, out in the middle of nowhere.

***

Pulled through time and space, with a flurry and a twist Scrooge and the Spirit had moved again. Ebenezer Scrooge slowly looked around. He could see that they were at a military base, the unmistakable union flag flying proudly as it whipped back and forth in a strong, cold wind. There were several assorted vehicles dressed in camouflage, parked up neatly outside the cookhouse, and several personnel entering and leaving. It was daylight again, a bright sun shone down, warming the chilly air, and in the far distance, snow could be seen on the mountains.

A VIP was visiting the forward base, and making sure everyone knew about it, even though the visit was supposed to be "Top Secret." This political dignitary from home, a target dressed in black amongst a sea of desert camouflage, had flown in aboard a Chinook MK6 helicopter, the bigger the 'bird' the better as befitted his status. It had been loaded with resupply cargo for the personnel on the ground. The press agent was hard at work, giving introductions and directing the photographer and cameraman to take pictures which would made his boss look professional, down to earth, humble, responsible, and trustworthy. He'd already got the sweet shot of him leaving the heli, striding down the back ramp, bulletproof vest on, an impressive photo for the political website.

The soldiers, support staff, ancillary personnel, in fact, everyone there, were a cynical bunch. They didn't get butterflies when informed of the impending arrival of the VIP, rather they viewed it as an intrusion into their too few leisure hours and a total waste of their time. Soldiers of both sexes, dressed in beige camouflage uniforms, were busy queuing for their Christmas dinner. They weren't interested in the VIP trying to get political mileage out of their situation and, more to the point, once you had been shot at by a fundamental idealist with an AK47, a bloke from Whitehall wasn't so important that you'd happily interrupt your dinner or smile for photographers while your scran was getting cold.

Then again, the VIP and his team had a mission too. To get as much political kudos as they could while simultaneously making the VIP look proud and concerned about the sons and daughters of the voting public back home. Therefore, they'd carefully decided on the photographs and video footage they wanted, which included the prerequisites of him:

Touring the barracks, CHECK!

Standing in a watchtower, looking into the distance, while someone holds a map, CHECK!

And not forgetting:

Talking to a group of young soldiers in a concerned, Churchillian manner. CHECK!

After these were taken, the official photographers relaxed and snapped off a few more pictures showing the human side of the political visitor. A

154

photograph of him serving meals to the soldiers was thought a ~~vote winner~~...er, a good, heart-warming picture. Eating with the ranks, not with the officers, there was time for some informal chit chat and a few selfies. The press agent directed the photographer to take more "natural" happy snaps, all of which were useless because, as a military base, this was a strategically sensitive area, and no photographs would be published, not even by the right honourable VIP, without the expressed consent of the M.O.D

An interview followed, during which he was asked carefully crafted questions by his own press agent, and gave carefully crafted answers such as how, "wonderful and privileged" he felt visiting the men (and indeed women...) at Christmas. What an excellent job they were doing, it made everyone at home immensely proud; proud of their soldiers, proud to be British!

One last photo of him exchanging a firm, resolute handshake with the base commander, and he hightailed it back to the Helipad where this time an impressive Puma HC2 was sitting ready to go, blades whomping as they lazily turned, the pilot calmly waiting. This heli had side doors, so to embark the VIP could, if he wished, bend and run under the rotor blades to make a great last photo for his press agent. Resisting the temptation to throw a final Yankee-style "commander in chief" salute, our VIP hopped aboard, the rotor blades increased speed, kicked up dust and the Puma lifted off, nose down for a tactical, combat exit from the base and, even better, an impressive final shot for the cameras.

After being on the ground for a total of five and a quarter hours, the helicopter returned the VIP to the secure billet of his five-star hotel, while the security detail at the base breathed a huge sigh of relief now that nonsense was finally over.

Meanwhile, amongst the soldiers, the atmosphere was more relaxed than usual with some leeway given because it was Christmas. Paper hats from Christmas crackers were worn while off duty, festive Christmas karaoke with alternate lyrics was sung in time to a music CD. Square stockings were passed around together with mail from home, and Jesus's birthday was toasted by soldiers drinking non-alcoholic beer. A little dancing took place, and there were a few speeches to get through. While some were serious, humbling, memorable and unifying, most took the piss out of senior officers. This was followed by a strange looking Father Christmas dressed in Red Camo, carrying a bulky black kit bag. The F.C. went ahead to give out yearly "awards" to several personnel, ranks and officers alike, for questionable habits or status achieved during the year that are too gross to mention here. However, it induced a great deal of raucous laughter and the recipients seemed incredibly pleased, so I suppose that shows you what being far away from home, living under constant threat of attack, in a ridiculously hot climate does to people.

"Come here, Ebenezer," said the ghost of Christmas Present. "Look at all of these people. They come together to celebrate but still miss the Christmases at home surrounded by family or friends. Some miss the shopping, the carol singing, the festivities, the family parties. Some just miss the weather.

"Their only contact with home is by phone or email and loneliness can be tough. But even now, they still know me, and let the joy and love of Christmas touch their hearts."

As he'd been speaking the Spirit blessed the rowdy group with large handfuls from his torch, while the soldiers loudly whistled, and shouted over the emcee, as he awarded another ambiguous honour. Every now and then they broke into a Christmas carol, sung with lyrics unique to their particular regiment, the soldiers punching the air with hand gestures at the more descriptive parts of each distinctive ditty; if one listened carefully, one could say that culture was alive and well in the British Army!

"Know you?" Said Scrooge as he watched the presentation of another dubious award to a fluky winner. "They may know you Spirit, but they're not exactly decent with their celebrations, are they? Hardly 'glad tidings of comfort and joy,'" he quoted.

"So, they celebrate with rough words and questionable traditions," answered the Spirit. "They are soldiers. They can't do here what's done at home. It wouldn't fit. They might behave like this now, but sometime in the next twenty-four hours each will stop, think of their loved ones and smile; and I will have done my job."

As they listened, the Spirit went to the window and looked at the sky. Then, calling to Scrooge, it hurried him along saying, "We must continue our travels Ebenezer, there are still many places where you can learn about Christmas, and why it's not just a word…"

***

Scrooge felt the pull again, and they were travelling another long distance. Heavy rain clouds hung in a grey stormy sky. He could hear the crashing waves filling his ears, rolling from the depths of the sea and bursting to the surface. Now they were standing on a huge floating rig, its footing deep into the water. Cranes swung out and over the boiling sea. Lights and ladders leading to the drilling module and its support module stood out, the whole rig glowing in the overcast sky. Gantries led off into a maze of walkways, leading to storage units, power units and production modules. Then there were the accommodation modules, offices and sleeping quarters. The Heli-deck stood empty in the darkness. A gas flare burned bright like a lighthouse at sea. The Spirit shouted above the noise of waves and wind, crashing into the platform, and whistling through the machinery. "This place is where I'm also welcome. We're in the North Sea, high off the coast of Scotland," he bellowed, "they're drilling here for oil and gas."

Scrooge followed the Spirit and pulled himself along the outside walk-ways until they, at last, came to a door that brought them inside and away from the noise, cold and wind of the tempest blowing around them. A quick walk down a short corridor and they entered a large café type dining area, furnished with tables and chairs, comfortable sofas, armchairs and coffee tables, giving the room an uncanny resemblance to an airport departure lounge. Aligned against one side wall were the ubiquitous machines for fizzy drinks, coffee, tea, chocolate bars, and crisps for anyone who needed a snack between meals, while the whole other side adjoined the kitchen and meals serving area.

A pool table, video screens, X Boxes, and even a foosball game like the one that was in Scrooge's common room at his school, were all laid on for relaxation and a large TV screen, fastened up high to give a clear view, brought news from a satellite digital TV station.

The rig ran twenty-four hours a day, seven days a week, but getting most of the big maintenance jobs done before today meant everyone could have a couple more hours to relax. Once a shift was over, workers would shower, change, and go in search of the amazing Christmas dinner prepared for them, before they had some downtime to call home, see a movie, watch some TV, and get some sleep, though not necessarily in that order.

This year the servery held a fabulous Yuletide feast, offering choices from turkey, goose, or ham with all the trimmings, to a seafood spread fit for the best restaurants in London. Even this far out in the North Sea,

157

Christmas dinner was enjoyed by the more than two hundred personnel that kept the rig operating.

After this wonderful feast, several groups congregated on the deliciously comfortable sofas, coffees in hand, watching the furious waves spray water against the windows as it grew darker outside.

The Spirit joyfully passed amongst them as they swapped 'Secret Santa' gifts while a cheerful Father Christmas distributed parcels sent from home.

Fair-isle jumpers, comical onesies and sheepskin boots seemed to be a recurring theme, with beer can hats, socks with 'DO NOT DISTURB, THE FOOTBALL IS ON', embroidered on the feet, coffee mugs sporting messages from, 'World's Best Dad' to 'Miners Have a Big Drill' and karaoke CDs of songs to sing in the shower were amongst the favourites this year.

A tough as nails shift captain, who was known lovingly to his men as Barry the Bastard, was moved almost to tears when he opened a card from his five-year-old daughter. Inside was a drawing of himself in work clothes and a hard hat which had the words, 'I love my Daddy' written in her wobbly crayoned hand.

Others were making full use of modern technology, face-timing family, and friends, loved ones and children directly on computer screens, tablets or mobiles. Some checked on Facebook or logged onto Instagram to see a stream of photos of Christmas Day at home. Parents with little kids Skyped with their children, where they could have long conversations about important things. Santa, Rudolph, presents and chocolate.

"You see," said the Spirit as Scrooge was watching the joy on their faces, "like those people we've already visited, everyone working here does it to provide a better life for those they love. Your world needs fossil fuel to survive and people like these keep the exploration going. Working on a rig like this is hard and it stops for nothing. At any time of the day or night, when other people on the mainland are sleeping or celebrating, it's still working and so are the people who run it. It costs millions of pounds to keep the exploration going," said the Spirit, " but without it, your world would soon run dry of the oil and gas it desperately needs."

Scrooge had only been half listening to the Spirit, but at the mention of money his ears pricked up as the Spirit finished speaking,

'Yet everyone here remembers my family and rejoices. They still take the time to stop and celebrate even if it's only for a few hours."

As the day wore on, everybody got to talking about Christmases at home. Well, it's what you do isn't it, share tales and stories, chat about families and friends at home, past celebrations with partners and kids, everyone has a tale about Christmas...

The letters that were written to Santa Claus and sent up the chimney in November, so he had plenty of time to get everything on the list. Some so long they read like a toy catalogue while others were weighted down with technology requests for phones, iPads, drones, computer games or laptops.

One woman told how her son, fed up that Santa didn't get it right last year, wrote his list in such detail there couldn't possibly be any mistakes this time. Not only did he list his toys, she said, but he even went to the trouble of listing the store, and the aisle they were in at that store! Short of drawing a map, Santa had no excuse this year for not getting precisely what her son asked for!

Remember trying to get some sleep on Christmas Eve? Almost impossible with the kids waking up at midnight, two, four and six am, desperately waiting for the goodies to arrive.

Or difficulties of trying to sneak past their bedrooms, not making a sound, suppressing your giggles as one of you tiptoe down the stairs with armloads of gifts while the other one keeps watch.

Sharing a laugh about wrapping footballs, scooters, or bicycles.

And why did the kids suddenly need something particularly important from the attic, just when they knew you were keeping presents up there?

Ebenezer was listening to their conversations. He had never imagined that the bothersome habits of children could bring delight and laughter! He was listening to their parents talk about their naughty behaviour, yet they didn't seem angry about it. They told the stories with love and affection. He thought the children were very disobedient and he would have smacked their bottoms, he would! But their parents just laughed with love and didn't get upset.

Once again, *he couldn't understand.*

Then... at the end of Christmas Eve, when the kids were finally sleeping and all the presents were piled under the tree, the wrapping paper was cleared away and a stocking full of treats was at the bottom of each child's bed for the morning, Mum and Dad could finally settle down for a few hours of well-deserved rest.

All their stories were similar... The Spirit called Scrooge over to listen as Jack told his...

Last year, he and his wife could finally, contentedly go to bed and sleep. It was two o'clock in the morning, everything was prepared, and they tumbled into bed, happy but exhausted. Comfortable bed, warm duvet, soft pillow. Morpheus come, thought Jack as he burrowed down. Take me to the clouds of Olympus so I may rest.....

Snuggled eyes closed, at the edge of slumber... When suddenly!

Oh **f*#*k!.** Santa didn't eat the cookies or drink the milk that was left out for him in the kitchen! Rudolph hasn't left his footprints by the fireplace! Damn it, I just got comfortable!

No... Wait, it's okay... I'll keep my eyes tight shut. Perhaps the wife is already asleep.

"Darling...."

Oh Great! She's awake!

"Darling...?"

Keep my eyes tight shut like I'm sleeping.

"Darling, are you sleeping?"

Tightly closed... Can't feel her fingers softly stroking my leg.

"I said are you asleep...?"

Fast asleep. Ignore the fingers... Ooh, she smells good...

"Hmmm...? Darling... are you awake...?"

Ignore the hand... ignore the stroking up and down my thigh, I'm asleep... deeply asleep. Don't want to go downstairs in the cold.

"Is my huggy lover bear fast asleep?"

Nope, not going to answer. I'm not falling for that one. I'll snore a little to put her off...

"Darling...?"

Not feeling anything... Especially not feeling her soft, warm body pushing into my back and her hand stroking up my thigh, getting closer and closer to my...

"Sugarplum, are you really sleeping?......"

No..Can't...Stop...Myself...Must...React...To...Hand...To...Fingers...

"Ooh, Ahhggg..."

"Oh, sweetie did I wake you?"

"Yes!"

"Sorry Darling, it's just that...are you listening?"

160

"Uh-huh."

"Oh good, well it just that we forgot to…"

"Drink the milk and eat the mince pie I know!"

"And stamp Rudolph's hoof prints around the fireplace."

"It's too cold."

"But the kids will be so disappointed."

'It's still too cold."

"We don't want them upset on Christmas Day."

"I'll get upset if I get cold."

"Darling…for me?"

"Why can you go?"

"I just got comfy."

"I'm bloody comfy!"

"It won't take you long."

"I'll play you for it."

"What?"

"Paper scissors rock, best out of three, the loser goes."

"Is that really necessary at this hour?"

"Play or you go, that's fair."

"Okay, if you insist."

"PAPER, SCISSORS, ROCK"

"Hah! You lose!"

"PAPER, SCISSORS, ROCK"

"One all darling."

"PAPER, SCISSORS, ROCK"

"Shit!"

"Remember to drink the milk darling, the kids will know if you've just poured it back it the carton and I'll know if you've poured it down the sink. Don't turn the light on when you come back in. Love you, Mmwwah!"

Revenge was had though, he laughed when he, the unwilling messenger, returned to bed with cold feet and wicked thoughts of retribution.

The Spirit laughed at this story along with everyone else. Scrooge didn't get it, not at all.

The Rig crews' discussion changed to buying gifts and presents, and the old hands who'd been married for years were explaining the 'rules' to the young blokes who were recently wed.

"Never buy her clothes or makeup, she'll take it as a criticism; perfume is okay, but it has to be expensive. You can't go wrong with jewellery but make sure it is elegant and classic, nothing cheap and nasty," said Jack, grinning.

"Cuddly toys are ok, but don't overdo it, she'll say you're pushing her into having a baby," advised Bryn.

"Don't ever buy her a kitten because cats' crap everywhere, and the little bugger will leave its fur all over the bed," added Andy.

"And never, ever, under any circumstances, buy her a vacuum cleaner..."

"Or an iron..."

"Or a washing machine!" advised several other voices of experience, who went on to explain the dire punishments they had suffered for similar transgressions.

Graham, who was newlywed last year, told the group he thought he would buy his wife Dianne something intimate and stimulating for their first Christmas together. That is, intimate for her and stimulating for him. However, as he was offshore and couldn't get to the shops, he ordered some sexy lingerie for her over the internet. A day later he ordered a nightdress and robe for his mum, Deborah, also from the same store. Both were gift wrapped and sent directly to their homes. "Unfortunately, you guessed it," he said in his strong welsh accent, "they sent the parcels to the wrong addresses. Both were addressed to Mrs D Williams, but Dianne got Mums and Mum got Dianne's. I got in late Christmas Eve and didn't think to check, I just said put it under the tree for tomorrow."

Of course, come Christmas Day, his wife opened a nightdress and dressing gown designed for a woman over fifty, embroidered with the words 'Not fat, Just cuddly,' while his mum opened a lacy push-up bra and matching panties with a note that read, "Doctor's prescription. Fill immediately and return to bed for three days."

The company dissolved into howling laughter and spluttering coffee, as he went on to explain, "Mum was okay with the present. Dad thought it was brilliant. It was just my wife that was really pissed off!" he said. "I spent the whole Christmas Day in the doghouse because Diane said she was so embarrassed. She said she could never look my parents in the eye again, now they knew what I'd originally bought her for Christmas. She didn't forgive me until I went out and spent three hundred and fifty quid on an eternity ring!" he finished, leaving the group laughing even more.

And that's how their day passed…

Occasionally someone would wish they could be at home, and the others would remind them of the delights of a family Christmas…

Uncle Brian who invariably gets drunk and spends the day snoring in an armchair..

Aunt Sylvia, who constantly buys your wife a gift from Ann Summers and makes sure everyone knows it.

The kids who fight and argue, and the diplomatic skills needed to resolve the issue, so no adults throw a shit fit defending their offspring.

Your best mate, who loved the York ham so much last year, that you went to considerable expense buying one again this year, suddenly announces to everyone that he's gone vegetarian.

Cousins Angie and Marie, who nearly come to blows over the annual, "My child is more gifted than yours" discussion.

Brother John's rude and churlish demands asking, "How much did this lot cost you then?" as he walks around the house, filled with jealousy.

And remember last year, for three days afterwards no one could find the television remote? It was finally discovered at the bottom of the fish tank. Thirty-five quid it cost to replace his last year, said Hari.

Not to mention all that washing up, which no one ever helped with. I mean, you say, "No, it's fine, don't worry, I can manage," but it never means "I can manage…" It means, "Yes, help would be very nice actually. After all, I've fed you, the least you can do is help with this mountain of dishes!

And to cap off the day, there's your wife's best friend, who asks smugly,

"Don't you have a dishwasher? Oh, we'd be lost without ours wouldn't we darling, we do so much entertaining. In fact, we had to cancel an important engagement today but I said, No! Nothing was stopping me from sharing Christmas Day with my best friend."

"Tupperware Christmas party?"

"Certainly not! Oh, ha ha ha, no it's just we're in so much demand socially, aren't we darling? Darling? I'm saying we're always going out. Busy, busy, busy! And at home, so many dinner parties, Sainsburys can hardly keep up with our orders! Thank goodness we have the dishwasher. It's such a Godsend. Such a useful thing to have don't you think? It's a shame you can't afford one, but I suppose you're being more environmentally friendly than us, ha ha ha!"

Last year Peter couldn't stop himself in time. Too much booze and bull-shit and he blurted out, "Hey, Luce, was that you I saw at Tesco last week, buying all those microwave dinners for one?"

...And the melancholy mood would pass. The TV filled the air with noises of worn out sitcoms and variety programs bursting with humour, seasonal songs, and chronicles from around the world.

Outside, nature unfurled her Christmas lights as far as the eye could see. The Aurora Borealis flashed colours across the sky, while in the water, bio-luminescent algae sparkled like blue diamonds, glittering in the ocean. It was as if heaven itself had turned on its lights, which glowed across the world in celebration.

Chapter 10: Fred's Christmas Day

Then, from nowhere, Scrooge heard a merry, deep-throated laugh, which he recognised as coming from his nephew, Fred. They were in London again, and the Spirit had brought Scrooge to Fred's house where it was warm, bright, and decorated for the season. Both he and the Spirit stood watching as Fred talked to all his friends, breaking into fits of laughter as he held forth about his recent visit to his Uncle, Ebenezer Scrooge.

Truthfully, there is nothing more beneficial to your body than a good laugh. There's no denying laughter lowers stress, strengthens your immune system, diminishes pain, keeps you focused and fires off brain connectivity. Everyone one loves a good laugh, right? And who amongst us hasn't had a fit of the giggles just when we need to be serious. Take me for example, I once had a shocking fit of the giggles thanks to some wag honking their Colonel Bogey horn right outside the cathedral, in the middle of midnight mass at the moment the congregation has two minutes of silent reflection. It was awful, Tears were streaming down my face, I nearly choked stuffing my hanky in my mouth trying not to laugh. I even tried covering my face with the hymn sheet but that looked even worse! I would have gone outside to calm down, but I was in the front row of the choir at the time....

Why was it so funny? Well, where I'm from we have slightly different lyrics to Colonel Bogey, and not the ones you're thinking of. All I could hear as the horn blew was "Bollocks, they make the best meat pies..." And that was me, totally destroyed!...

Anyway, we know that a good laugh is so beneficial it's even used as a form of therapy in Laughter classes and therapy groups. Ever seen those bumper stickers saying laughter uses up as many calories as walking and is a terrific way to lose weight? Or is that sex? I suppose either one will do.

Well, whatever it is, a Fred was now wiping his eyes and catching his breath as laughed his way through recounting his last conversation with Scrooge.

"What he actually said was, 'Christmas is crap,' right to my face, I couldn't believe it!" He laughed again. "But, Scrooge will be Scrooge and of course, he was deadly serious!"

"Well," said Kate, Fred's wife, and Scrooge's niece by marriage, "I'm sorry, but that's a bloody horrible thing for anyone to say. It's very rude, especially about Christmas of all days! Even if he doesn't believe in it, it's still very rude, I don't care who he is, manners don't cost anything, and he should learn to use some!"

Fred smiled at his wife, so angry at this figure of disrespect she'd never met. He wondered why he never felt anger at anything his Uncle had ever done and for a moment, he let his mind drift back over the last 30 years of his life, and the part his Uncle played in it

Since he was a child, Fred had heard all about his Uncle, Ebenezer Scrooge. His father, Samuel, had talked about him often as he was growing up, telling Fred that Uncle Buzz was Mummy's brother, whom she loved very much. But he explained to the little boy, Uncle Buzz was terribly upset when Mummy died, and so he didn't want to come around to see them just now. He would come very soon, Daddy said, but for now, wasn't it wonderful they had all these lovely pictures of Mummy and her brother to look at? And Uncle Buzz always sent presents for Freddie's birthday and Christmas, never missing once, that's how much he loved Freddie, loved him very much.

As he got older Fred began to hear that Mummy's wonderful brother was not as wonderful as Daddy said he was. Oh, his father would never hear a word against him, that was true, but according to his grandparents, Ebenezer Scrooge was a hard-hearted miser, who'd walked away within a week of Francesca's death, and never bothered to find out how Freddie was in all the years that followed. On top of that, they said, all the gifts supposedly sent by his Uncle were bought by his own father!

Samuel though, would take his son to one side and tell him that his grandparents were angry with his Uncle, but they didn't know the full story. Ebenezer had a difficult upbringing his father said, and it was still tough for him to come to terms with Fan's death. Freddie shouldn't judge his Uncle until he knew the full story.

Growing older still, Fred decided to take the bull by the horns and after a bit of detective work, he found his Uncle's office and simply walked in after school one day and introduced himself. To say his Uncle was surprised was an understatement, but he had grudgingly offered his nephew a seat and spent fifteen torturous minutes asking him about himself, before telling the boy that he had to go so he could get back to work. As his Uncle hadn't thrown him bodily out of the office, Fred considered this first visit a complete success.

He subsequently conveyed the news of his adventure to his astonished father and soon formed the habit of dropping in on his Uncle at least once a month. While his grandparents couldn't fathom why Freddie would bother with a man who never bothered with him, Samuel encouraged his son's efforts to break down barriers and continued to do so until his death.

"One thing you have in common with your mother, Freddie," his father always said, "is her determination to hang on to family ties, especially when it comes to your Uncle Ebenezer."

And so, month after month, year after year, Fred continued his habit of visiting his Uncle unexpectedly. He invited him to his wedding, Scrooge never came, and to his father's funeral, Scrooge never came, but he did send a sympathy card that Fred suspected came from Bob on his behalf. On Scrooges birthday Fred brought him a cake and a candle and wouldn't leave until he had blown it out, and every 24th of December,Scrooge was invited have Christmas dinner with all the trimmings. Nothing had happened so far, but Fred had another thing in common with his mother. He was a cockeyed optimist, and never gave up hope...

Now he looked at his wife and said, "Oh, don't worry yourself darling, don't get upset, he's a sad, grumpy old man who cuts off his nose to spite his face, that's all. I can see in his eyes, he's interested sometimes, but then he retreats into his nineteenth century 'Bah Humbug' persona and that's it, you can't shift him. No," he said, "I still won't hear a thing against him, I still reckon he's worth the effort," and he clinked his glass with his wife's in a mock toast to his Uncle Scrooge.

Kate shook her head in exasperation. It wasn't worth her saying anything. Fred's mind was made up. He may have visited Scrooge 156 times to no avail, but as far as her husband was concerned, 157 could be the charm.

His cockeyed optimism was one of the reasons she loved him...but it still drove her mad.

Freddie's wife Kate was a talented, creative, left wing, socially conscious bohemian who managed to live outside the 9-5 rat race. She did so by selling her paintings and sculptures and by selling the carefully restored vintage jewellery she collected from charity shops and jumble sales. She enjoyed dumpster diving for old furniture, which she cleaned, repolished or repurposed, and sold for an excellent profit.

In the evenings she sewed intricate quilts from vintage fabrics and her greatest passion was restoring antique wedding gowns.

Kate was very successful, her work sold everywhere from Chelsea antique stores to the best bridal shops in London.

She had a mild form of Tourette's, but managed her tics and clicks with music, pharmacotherapy, colourful language, and meditation. Kate was a born-again Wiccan with Catholic predispositions and had adopted 4 stray cats she named Eanie, Meanie, Miney and Mo.

Kate was an artist. If she was stuck for ideas, her way to unblock the artistic flow was to move the furniture around. There were times when Freddie came home in the evening, wanting to drop exhausted into his favourite chair in front of the TV, only to find she'd shifted it to another room.

Since marrying, she'd moved her workroom to the back of the house, which was light, sunny and warm. Many evenings, when she was absorbed in her work, Fred would be greeted by the dog, the cats, no wife, and no dinner in the oven. Just a note in the kitchen which read, "I fancy an Indian, the washing needs to go in the dryer, and none of the animals have been fed. Kiss Kiss."

All this in one 5 foot 8 inch package was why he loved her.

"Well, you're the one who keeps saying how rich he is," said Kate. "I suppose that has importance."

"Not as much as he thinks my love. Like most rich people he thinks his money excuses his manners. But so what if he is loaded," replied Fred. "His money is of absolutely no use to him at all. It's like he doesn't have any."

Ticking off on his fingers so his gathered friends could see, he continued, "He doesn't use it to make himself comfortable. His house is always freezing cold because he won't use his fire so as to save on the gas bill. He washes in cold water to save on his heating bill. He doesn't help anyone else with the money, he certainly never donates to charity. He walks to work through freezing ice or blazing sun to save on a ten-pound cab fare. And he plods along in those same awful clothes and shoes just to save a few pounds!

"In the winter, rather than heating that cold office, he prefers to layer two or three sweaters over his shirt, then his suit jacket. Under his trousers he wears long johns. He does. I've seen the bottoms of them sticking out above his shoes. He ties that awful old mackintosh down over the lot, so he ends up waddling around like a duck, looking like the Michelin Man!"

To his immediate left came a coughing, choking sound, followed by a spray of liquid from one of Kate's friends, who'd spat out her wine in strangulated laughter at the image of Scrooge waddling around like a duck.

"You okay there?" Fred asked, jumping to his feet, fetching a tea towel and tissues to help her dry off and drifting into a separate conversation with her in the process.

Kate sighed and said to the rest of group, "He always does this, gets off track from what he was talking about...Honestly, it's so annoying! FREDDIE!" she called, tapping the table, "About Uncle Ebenezer...?"

Fred looked back at her. "Oh yes, sorry, well, I was just saying that his money is no use to him. He keeps it in the bank and worships it like a golden calf while living like a pauper, hoarding all sorts here and there. Do you know," he said, wine glass tipping dangerously threatening to spill, "the last time I was at his place he had at least five hundred packets of take away sugar in a bowl on the counter? Why? It makes no sense to me. He won't put his hand in his pocket to make even his life easier. He scrimps and saves and counts his pennies and for what? I could understand if he did something beneficial with his money, but he doesn't. Certainly, the thought of helping us has never crossed his mind," said Fred sipping more of his wine, then with a great laugh he yelped, "He'd probably say we had no cash value!"

"Oh his kind of people make my teeth itch," declared Kate. "I've never met him, but I just know I wouldn't like him," she said as her friends nodded their agreement. "I've got no time for him."

"Oh, I have," said Fred. "He's a study of human nature and a work in progress for me and honestly I just feel sorry for him. Really, he doesn't make me angry, couldn't if he tried. I mean, who really suffers for his silly moods and snubs like today? He does! So, he said no to coming to lunch, what happened? All he's done is deprive himself of a..." Fred tapped his fist on his chest as if to burp, "...rather indigestible dinner."

"Hey!" Kate said, hurling a chair cushion at him. "That was a good dinner!" Turning to the others, she said, "Wasn't it?"

Everyone agreed the dinner was a masterpiece.

"Well, I'm glad you all think so," said Fred, mock burping again, "because I don't have much faith in these newfangled cooks." He grinned cheekily.

Kate poked out her tongue at him.

Fred laughed and said to a man standing near the window, "What's your opinion of the meal then Topper?"

Tom Topper, who was always called, Topper, or TT for short, was determined to remain neutral and raised his hands in mock surrender.

Fred pressed on, "A masterpiece in cooking or a young wife's best effort?"

Topper was six feet four, drop dead gorgeous and knew it. Unfortunately, he was also quite bashful, which, despite his looks, made dating exceedingly difficult. The problem was, no matter how much he tried not to, he always ended up saying the wrong thing when making conversation. Right now he fancied one of the women in the group, so, in an attempt to make a good impression, he proved his unerring ability to put his foot in his mouth by saying he was a just a friend, and couldn't possibly pass judgement, as he was not overly familiar with Kates cooking, but suspected she'd done the best she could.

Fred, roared with laughter at this response, embarrassing poor Topper, who chugged the rest of his wine and prayed for the floor to open up and swallow him.

Kate, who'd had enough of this disparagement on her Christmas luncheon said sweetly to her husband, "It's okay darling, you'll have enough time to judge for yourself, because you're doing the dishes," before poking her tongue out again and making Fred laugh even more.

"But what's the use of inviting him every year if he just keeps saying no?" Asked Dee, another of their guests, returning to the enthralling subject of Ebenezer Scrooge. "Why even bother making the effort?"

"Because one day I hope he's going to realise the only result of not coming to dinner, is he's lost an afternoon of happy memories, among pleasant company. If you think about it, he can't have that many to begin with and he certainly won't find any in those stacks of files or the mountain of papers in his dreary old office. I feel sorry for him. I really do. For how he is and how he lives. But he's the brother my mother adored and, because of her, I'm going to keep going in every year until he cracks, or croaks," explained Fred.

There was a momentary pause, then Kate reached forward and took her husband's hand. "And you would like to know more about your mum, wouldn't you?" She turned to their guests. "Uncle Ebenezer can tell Fred all about Fran when she was younger. What she was like, what she did, how she was. Fred needs to know all that, and only Uncle Ebenezer can tell him those things."

Fred smiled at his wife, "That's true my love." He coughed a little and rubbed his nose with his hand, then said briskly, "I just think one day, one year he will be in a better temper and something will come of it. Even if he just gives poor old Bobby Cratchit a Christmas bonus. Bob's worked for my Uncle for over twenty years and he's very loyal to him, even though he's had several offers from other companies. God knows he's certainly earned a bonus. No, I'll make my annual pilgrimage, if only for Bob's sake. Therefore, I still say the toast is, Uncle Ebenezer!"

Everyone lifted their glasses and obediently toasted Scrooge. Fred and Kate encouraged them to relax and be happy, and his friends being easy going and good natured, all promised to be nice to Scrooge should they ever meet him.

Scrooge turned to the Spirit and whispered, "I never knew he wanted to hear about his mother when she was young," he said. "Why didn't he talk to me?"

"Would you have listened?" replied the Spirit. "You fail to realise Ebenezer that you are the custodian of some very precious memories, and only you can pass them on to the next generation. Our family memories tell us who we are, and if there is a gap in those memories, it can leave a big hole in a person's heart."

"Okay," said Topper, putting his glass down and looking directly at Fred. "Here's my question Freddie. What would you say to old Scrooge if he walked through that door now?"

"No thank you, not today," guessed Anton, interrupting.

"Sorry old chap, the fancy-dress party was last week!" Added Dex with a smile.

"If you're the stripper the hen party's three doors down," said Kate's sister humorously.

"I know that face, give me a minute, I'll get it...It's...Tuesday night bingo, right?" Said Jamil.

"Mum! There's a strange man looking like a dead clown at the door. Mum, MUM!" Paul yelled as everyone laughed at all the suggestions.

Topper held up a hand, saying, "No, I'm serious everyone. Come on Freddie, he's just walked in, you must have thought a thousand times what you'd do, what is it?"

Fred slapped his knees as he stood up, "Easy, I'd shake his hand and welcome him in."

TT was stumped. "That's all? No 'what's your game, why's it taken you so long, why are you always so miserable' none of that?"

"No, of course not," replied Fred, shaking his head. "If Uncle Ebenezer did come for lunch it would mean he'd had a tremendous change of heart. If I started turning on him like that, he would be out the door in a flash and I'd never get him back!" he said, and draining his glass of wine, went to the kitchen to brew some coffee.

"Would he really do that?" Scrooge wondered aloud.

"Why would you think otherwise?" asked the Spirit.

"I don't know. I haven't been very approachable in the past; I wouldn't blame him if he turned me away. I would, after all this time."

"Don't judge everyone by your standards, Ebenezer. Your nephew is cut from a different cloth. He follows his mothers' path, not yours. If you knew him better, you'd see how much like his mother he is."

After coffee, Fred brought up the subject of the afternoon's entertainment.

That meant one thing: Games. Christmas is the one day of the year when adults can be kids and abandon themselves to silliness and fun, and any invited guests soon realised that a Christmas dinner at Fred's place always came with a side order of parlour games.

Freddie's games catalogue always started with an ice breaker; Pin the balloon on the donkey... A modern variation of the classic sure to break down any barriers of shyness.

Is it just me or have balloons got more impossible to inflate? I can't count how many times I've ended up pop-eared, cross eyed and rubber cheeked just trying to get one going. Even those manual pump things are difficult to use. Am I the only one to get scores of balloons just within tying range, only to have the rubbery wretch shoot off the pump, fart around the room and die at my feet like a flightless, featherless bird?

When they'd run out of balloons and all their cheeks were rubbery and popped from blowing, they moved on to Blind Man's Bluff. Everything that could be, was pushed, bumped, knocked, and shoved throughout the whole game. Working in teams, the men tried to catch the ladies who hid behind the curtains, dodged behind the sofa, squeezed in the corner, and sat on the bookcase, but were always found. As each woman was caught, they had to pay a forfeit.

These included ten star jumps in high heels or singing "Silent Night" in French. To paint their fingernails with the brush in their teeth or to juggle three tins of coconut milk (in lieu of real coconuts.) As each were caught and paid their forfeit they were out of the game until the only one left was the girl who Topper had taken a fancy to. At last, she was cornered, and Topper, bolstered with that extra glass of wine for liquid courage, removed his blindfold to claim his prize of a chaste kiss on the cheek.

Then it was the girls turn to catch the guys and plunging right in they soon had them doing one arm press ups, sit ups, reciting Hamlet's 'To Be' soliloquy on one leg, spelling the word Supercalifragilisticexpialidocious backwards or shaving their legs as their forfeits. Topper was the last one left and in a shared attraction, was caught by the woman he'd taken a fancy to. To convey her mutual interest, she took her forfeit in the form of a deeply passionate kiss.

Scrooge had been watching the whole interaction quietly, the games and music drifting through his mind, and he had to admit to himself he was finally regretful of all those years of happiness he'd voluntarily turned his back on. If only he could have softened and cultivated some kindness and care in his life years ago, he could be part of this wonderful circle of friends and family. Instead, what "Christmas memories" could he boast of? The year he buried Jacob Marley. And even then, he hadn't attended the funeral.

Kate didn't take part in blind man's bluff, thanks to a bizarre and unforeseen bout of seasonal claustrophobia, she sat cuddled in an easy chair by the fire, her feet curled under her, a pure Chaeneice* blanket draped over her legs, writing up stickers for the next game.

Who Am I, is that typically middle class, dreadfully conservative game whereby the name of an obscure but famous person is written on a sticker, which is then stuck to someone's forehead. They then must guess who they're supposed to be from questions asked of the other players.

Several rounds smoothly segued into the Christmas favourite of charades. It's true some play charades more seriously than others. Especially if you split into teams, then it can become a serious business. At Fred's house however, as with all games, it was played for fun, and anyone getting too serious was immediately disqualified.

Scrooge and the Spirit were standing behind Kate's chair so they could see and hear everything. Soon Scrooge was so caught up in the excitement of trying to guess the answers he was shouting out, forgetting that no one could hear him. The Spirit watched him closely and was happy to see the change in him; how he'd relaxed and joined in so easily. When Ebenezer asked if they could stay until the last guests had left, the Spirit shook his head, saying there wasn't enough time. Scrooge became quiet, dejected, even sulky at the refusal.

"But we can watch this last game before we go," the Spirit promised as if speaking to a crestfallen child.

This last game was one many of us will have played, in cars, on long journeys or in the lounge during power cuts. Simply put, the company had to find out who Fred was thinking about and he could only answer YES or NO and BLACK or WHITE to guide their thinking.

During the quick-fire questions, Fred said he was thinking of an animal, it lived in London, was white, very disagreeable, moody, growled when spoken to, lived alone, had no mate, wasn't a pig, cow, horse, dog, or cat. With every answer, Fred burst into fresh bouts of laughter and had great pauses while he recovered enough to splutter yes or no to the questions. The whole group was laughing at this unfortunate creature without knowing what it

---

* Chaeneice is an exceptionally soft, warm fabric made by weaving camel down, taken from the wild camels found in the Australian outback, with the wool of merino sheep. The camels return to the desert once the down is collected and the sheep are farmed for their wool and not for slaughter.

was until Fred's wife exclaimed, "I know who it is, it's Uncle Ebenezer isn't it!?" Fred confirmed it was and once again they all laughed in merriment at the joke.

"Well," said Fred once again, "he's given us a great deal of fun this afternoon and we would be mean not to drink the old man's health." Picking up his glass, he encouraged everyone else to do the same, "he wouldn't let me say it to his face, but I wish him a Merry Christmas, Uncle Ebenezer."

"Uncle Ebenezer!" chorused the group who raised their glasses and drank the toast.

Scrooge had, up to this point, been very enthusiastic about the game. He'd been thinking hard about the clues to guess the animal and was enjoying the conundrum, but when Kate guessed the answer, and everyone had laughed, he felt empty. The laughter overcame his excitement and left him dismayed. The toast Fred had made to him had been appreciated, so much that he wished he could have returned the gesture and thanked Fred for his kind words and merry afternoon's entertainment…but…still, to be the object of such amusement? Was this how he was viewed by everyone?

Their time at his nephews' house was done said the Spirit, and they couldn't stay any longer. The two left the warmth and comfort of that happy home, Scrooge with some regret, for he'd seen more of his nephew in that small time than he had for years, and he admitted, if only to himself, how much he missed his sister's son.

***

Journeying again, he and the Spirit, sometimes in silent company with each other, travelled backwards and forwards in time on this Christmas Day, they went so far and saw so many things Scrooge had never considered before.

From Fred's house, they first visit was to The Salvation Army.

Now it was early morning, so early it was still dark, the sun's rays not so much as a grey glimmer in the cold winters dawn. Dozens of volunteers were hurrying around like worker bees, putting the final Christmas Boxes into delivery vans, and, with a thump on the rear doors, sending them off to deliver the last of the hundreds of hampers to those in need this Christmas. Mountains of donated goods had been painstakingly split into boxes with food, drinks, sweets, pudding, gifts, and party favours for each family. A huge whiteboard with lists of suburbs ticked off, showing deliveries made, while pages and pages of forms filled out by those asking for help were hanging on clipboards and stamped as completed. On one side of the white-board, a merry little elf was running a baked bean and beetroot tally. Of all the things gratefully received by the 'Sally Army', they got more tins of baked beans and beetroot than anything else.

The volunteers were exhausted but feeling happy. Many would go home now and have Christmas with their families knowing a monumental task had been achieved. They'd helped as many as they could, yet even now, those who were staying behind to volunteer again were busy with the Christmas dinner that was being cooked at every Salvation Army hall over the country; The same too at drop-in-centres, Church charity halls, street outreach organisations and city missions, every one of them cooking and serving Christmas dinners to street dwellers, the homeless, addicts and those on the edge of society.

All the charities were busier this year. But that wasn't unusual. Every year increasing numbers turn up. Not just those who were homeless, those who lived along the borders of society, being ignored by everyone else, but also the new "working" poor. Parents who worked hard every day but received such low wages they could barely manage and couldn't provide a Christmas for their families or gifts for their children. At the Reach Out, Family Assistance Trust, ROFAT as it was known to everyone, no matter who they were, everyone was served a full Christmas dinner, with pudding and custard, in a festive atmosphere while a band jollied the place up and sang Christmas songs.

Toddlers and small kids, unaware of things like finances, payday loans or bills, danced and jumped about, joining in the actions to songs about Santa and reindeer, while their parents, just hanging on financially, were happy and relieved when the kids received a present or two from Father Christmas, and, despite their age, they could still believe in him, because here he was, giving gifts to their children and sharing the Christmas celebrations they couldn't afford to provide.

These mums and dads, for one happy day, didn't have to worry about money and bills and juggling finances, but could enjoy the meal, hug a volunteer, kiss the man in the red suit, wipe away their tears and thank them all for still being there, and know that sometimes, the world was still a good place.

Scrooge looked on, trying to understand why anyone should deliberately involve themselves in trying to help a total stranger feel better. Why bother?

It wasn't your fault, you didn't even know them. Why concern yourself with their problems? Everyone had difficulties one way or another, didn't they? People should learn how to manage their own affairs. Make them stand on their own two feet and don't waste your time, he thought, otherwise they'd just keep coming back again and again.

As if the Spirit were reading his mind, he turned to Scrooge and said, "Ebenezer, you don't need to know a person to show compassion and offer a helping hand. People give up their time, not just because they want to ease the burdens of those less fortunate and needing support, but because the idea of walking away and leaving them to struggle is as foreign to them as the idea of helping is to you. Whether it's their nature or they have learned by example, they know that if they can help, they should at least try. Can't you remember any time in your past when you helped someone just because they needed it and not because it benefited you?"

Scrooge looked at the Spirit and almost growled his reply, "No, I don't remember. Maybe when I was younger, when my sister was alive, but since then, no, there's nothing."

The Spirit shook his head sadly. "Understand, if you are going to make changes in your life, the difficult part will be changing your thinking. Once you achieve that, you can be of real help to those who need it, but until then, you can't empathise, and without empathy comes judgement and no one who asks for help likes to feel they're being judged."

But empathy is not easy to learn, the Spirit knew, and judgement sits more comfortably in a person's mind. "Think like this Ebenezer, if you are walking in the wind and the rain, and someone slips and falls beside you, would you stop and help them up? Or would you keep walking, leaving them on the footpath all alone?

"Then ask yourself, what if it was you who stumbled and fell? And everyone hurried by, leaving you to struggle, offering no help. How would you feel watching everyone go past? To get help, you must give help, willingly, with no conditions, expecting no reward. Only then will you finally understand it's not the getting that brings the rewards, it is, and has always been, the act of giving that brings fulfilment."

Now, the Spirit hoped to change Scrooges judgment on some of places he usually avoided. "Common" places, full of the "great unwashed" as he liked to call them. This was where low-income families or those on the dole lived; in council flats and tenements, surviving day to day on a pittance, most below the poverty line.

Here, the residents were criticised, denied their humanity, judged, and repudiated in a single glance. Scrooge never went near them because he wasn't interested in how those neighbourhoods survived. Their misfortunes, their "whining" irritated him and frankly he just didn't give a damn.

They had a roof over their head, provided at a cheap rent didn't they? They should be grateful for that, but no! They lived worse than animals, he said, graffitied the building, the stairs, the balconies, and left rubbish around everywhere. Children roamed the streets like savages, causing trouble, stealing, taking drugs, and the parents were no better. They smashed and trashed every council flat they lived in, drank their dole money, peed in the streets, and threw used syringes everywhere. No, he wasn't interested at all.

And so, the Spirit took him to a housing estate. Here it chose a huge tower block from a group of three and motioned Scrooge over. Together they walked around it, past the frozen grassed surrounds where children were playing, past the few cars that were parked up near the garages and around the back, where dumpsters overflowed with rubbish, and garbage bags were heaped around in piles because there were too many tenants and not enough bins.

Then together, they climbed several flights of stairs, and with every wheezing step, the Spirit listened to Ebenezer mutter and complain. They climbed for ages, it seemed to Scrooge, but finally the Spirit walked along a balcony, stopping in front of a glossy red front door bearing a handmade holly and tinsel Christmas wreath.

Scrooge trailed behind, coughing and panting, trying to catch his breath. Leaning heavily against the door he asked, "Why…did…we have to…struggle up all of those bloody stairs…when…You...can…move us…around…like…" he whirled his hand in explanation, "why did we need…to walk...all...the…way up?" he said, putting his hands on his knees and bending over trying to draw breath. "Oh God, I'm going to have a heart attack!" he finished dramatically.

"No you're not," replied the Spirit who wasn't at all winded. "That's exercise, you're unfamiliar with it I know; stand up Ebenezer, take particular notice of how you're feeling. Part of your education is not only to see how people live, but to experience it. Now you know how it feels to struggle up all those stairs. Imagine doing it four times a day, even more, while carrying heavy bags of shopping, being old, or in pain, pregnant or with small children, struggling up and down daily because the lift is always broken," said the Spirit. "And think about having no one who listens to you when you complain, because they consider you're not important enough."

Scrooge continued this coughing and spluttering while the Spirit looked serenely out over the balcony, watching the kids playing below, running in and out of flats on different levels, screaming their excitement because of the day.

At last Ebenezer drew a calmer, albeit raggedy breath and stood next to the Spirit, gazing out from the tower, a lighthouse in an urban storm.

"Where are we?" he asked, listening to the children's voices echoing all around, "that's not a London accent, where is this place?"

The Spirit smiled, "It may sound incredible to you Ebenezer, but there's more to the British Isles than just London. There's a whole wide country way beyond the banks of the Thames you know.

As for where we are, welcome to Manchester. One hundred and sixty miles northwest of London, it was first established by the Romans. Its Britain's second-oldest city with a current population of over two million, seven hundred thousand.

By 1835, it was the greatest industrial city in the world, and it was an important area for the establishment of the Labor Party and the beginnings of the Suffragette Movement. It's called the birthplace of modern football and is sometimes referred to as, *the rainy city*, although," the Spirit said looking wryly at the overcast, thunderous sky, "I can't understand why."

Scrooge looked at him sceptically, "Wikipedia again?"

Laughing the Spirit answered, "Of course Ebenezer, of course!"

Two loud and happy children, rugged up warm, noses and ears pink from where the cold had nipped their faces, ran past and opened the red door behind them.

"Ah, here we go," said the Spirit and gestured for Scrooge to enter the flat behind the two excited kids.

This flat was home for a family of three. A mother in her mid-thirties, her son about ten, and daughter aged six. The family obviously had very few belongings but the flat was festive with homemade decorations and a small Christmas tree that stood on a table by the window.

The Spirit blessed them all, as the children dived under a blanket on the sofa to watch cartoons and eat dinner off plates on their knees. Does the indoor picnic in front of the TV ever cease to thrill!

Scrooge looked around him. The room was clean and tidy. Everything had a place, toys in the toy box, books on the shelves, rubbish in the waste-paper baskets, no dust or dirt. It was not at all what he'd expected.

"Remember Ebenezer," the Spirit said, "It's bad enough being labelled as ignorant, lazy, a dole bludger or slovenly just because you live here, have limited income, if you are a sole parent, or aren't white. Take the time to get to know people because everyone is not the same. Yes there are those who live in some of these flats that are no better than feral cats, but there are over fifty families in this tower alone, and most try very hard with the little they have. They deserve recognition for their efforts, not just contempt because of their address."

Descending the stairs again the Spirit turned to Scrooge and asked, "Tell me Ebenezer, what's the one difference between these people and those who live in places like Chelsea, Kensington or Hampstead?"

Scrooge shook his head, he didn't know.

"Matter" answered the Spirit "that's the difference, *"matter."* Quite simply it's the belief that those who live in Kensington, Chelsea, and all those suburbs, *"matter,"* while these people and those like them, don't. If every person mattered equally, if those who live in messy homes, who wear unwashed clothes, surrounded by unemptied garbage bins, unwashed dishes and filthy floors, mattered as much as people from the affluent suburbs of London, there would be more amenities for them, more rubbish collection, more street cleaning, more community care, more family support, more of everything.

But instead, there is this ignorant assumption that these people don't matter as much. That it's not worth struggling to improve their attitude or expectations.

Not until everyone matters equally, will enough progress be made to stop the kind of poverty and ignorance that causes people to live in squalor."

"But," Scrooge interjected, "wait a moment, the people in those places in London and the like, they pay more taxes than those who live here. Why shouldn't they get better service if they pay more? Surely that's fair, I mean, people like this, they pay less, so…"

"…So because they can't afford as much they don't get as much, that's your reasoning. Yes, yes, Ebenezer I see what you're saying…" interrupted the Spirit, stroking his beard as if he was seriously considering Scrooge's objection. "I see your argument, but answer me this, does the fact that they pay less, automatically mean their humanity is diminished as well? Are you honestly suggesting the further a person lives away from the centre of affluence, and the less they have, that it automatically follows the less they need? Only those who are prosperous need a green, leafy park with safe, clean equipment for their children to play on. Only the successful should have access to a public library with the proper number of research tools, computers, and books? And only the wealthy need a strong social safety net to protect their children from danger and crime?

"Is this the only way your civilised society can order itself, the haves and the have nots. Them and us?"

"But can it be done, what you say? Changing people, attitudes, turning things around for these communities. Could it really be done?" asked Scrooge.

The Spirit smiled, "It could certainly be tried," he said, clapping him on the shoulder.

***

A different place, where cars were few, busses were less, not as many people walked back and forth.

And as they both walked along, they watched people setting up tents and tarpaulins, with bags and backpacks holding all their possessions. Some had better tents than others, bought from Azda or Aldi, or occasionally provided by well-meaning peoples who may not be able to find them a bed, but did at least help with a dry place to sleep.

Everyone was in the same boat. Without homes, forced to live on the streets. There was safety in numbers protection from the yobs and troublemakers, so they reunited as the day wound down, a transient neighbourhood, pulled back together, like moths to a flame.

Nowhere to go, nothing to buy, no money to pay for it anyway. Just this ever-moving tide of makeshift dwellings and people settling in shop doorways, car parks or pieces of wasteland that hadn't been gated off, with the hope of a few hours of unmolested sleep.

Those who'd missed the free Christmas dinner celebrated the coming of the King of Kings with a burger and fries and wondered when his teachings would come true.

The mortal and the Spirit walked past. Scrooge saw how diverse these homeless were. No drunks and druggies, not in this group, just sad, exhausted people who had nothing left to give and nothing left to sell to rent a place and make a home.

There were adults of all ages, singles, couples, parents, friends. Some who'd lost their homes, maybe they'd never had one, some who couldn't afford one. The longer they stayed on the streets, the rougher, the dirtier they looked, the more they smelled, of body odour, of desperation, and of fear, the less likely that anyone would rent them a place.

Mums who'd taken their children, toddlers and babies alike, had grabbed a few belongings and run, looking for safety. Anywhere was better than living in terror at home. They couldn't get into a shelter because they were over stretched and wouldn't ask social services for help and risk losing their kids. Couldn't get into a safe rental, not yet. Couch surfing when they could, staying one step ahead, struggling to keep their kids with them, always trying to prevent them from being taken away. A few nights of accommodation here, a couple of nights there, and now they were huddled together to keep warm, the kids hoping Father Christmas would still be able to find them, even on the streets.

Teens who'd fled their homes for awful reasons, searching an indifferent world, looking out from fractured eyes. They silently waited for the days when things would get better and be like the shows they had seen on TV. When could they start the lives they desperately wanted to live?

Single men who tried, but couldn't live inside society's rules, so chose to exist outside, living their version of freedom, and paying the heavy price of social isolation, rejection and the loss of their humanity.

Some people were lucky, they could sleep in their cars and didn't have to worry about the police or welfare agencies coming along to push them out or take their kids, they parked in different places each night, keeping one step ahead of family services.

Everyone was struggling to keep their families together, themselves together, not fall into risky traps, but when you have no money and your choices are limited, you do what you can, cross your fingers and hope.

182

The final nail in the coffin, once listed, for whatever reason, on the Bad Tenants Database, it made getting a place even harder. Yes, it's true, there were trashers and smashers amongst them, but most had done the right thing and still couldn't get into a basic, clean, safe, one-bedroom flat. And if you had children, who wanted to shift to Brighton and try to keep them secure in one room of a clapped out hotel that also lodged drunks and druggies?

"How many of them are there?" asked Scrooge.

"Thousands of people live on the streets, Ebenezer," said the Spirit. "Even the richest countries in the world won't invest in homes for its citizens. It happens here and in every wealthy country all over the world. And every day people walk past them, not even seeing them, at best ignoring them. You have no cognisance of these people, yet you've walked past them twice a day, every day, for the last two years."

"Is there nowhere for them to go?" asked Scrooge.

"Such as those places for the homeless?" the Spirit said sarcastically, referring again to Scrooge's own words. "No. People need help with their own place to live, not just a bed among strangers. But the homes are not built, because society automatically thinks homeless people are offenders and law-breakers, so why waste money on helping them? That attitude needs to change before people can get the help they really need..."

"But these types of people, they clutter up the pavement so you can't get past and they're always asking for money," whined Scrooge.

"Then give them some," answered the Spirit, "then they won't steal just so they can eat. Ebenezer, no one knows why someone ends up on the streets, it's not written on their forehead. Each story is different. Just as it is for these people. Remember, they're not statistics, but individuals who've washed up here through a series of unknown events. Show them kindness and compassion. Listen to them and help if you can..."

The Spirit put his hand on Scrooges shoulder and turned Scrooge to look into his eyes. "But now you need to follow me and see for yourself what happens behind these places."

Scrooge and the Spirit walked quietly behind a supermarket where several large skips could be found. To Scrooge's astonishment, a group of people were standing on boxes and crates rummaging through the bins. So far, their foraging had produced several loaves of bread, miscellaneous fruit and vegetables, eggs, meat, pizzas, and butter, all of which had been simply thrown away.

The people worked together quickly, quietly, with great efficiency, but suddenly, when a torchlight was spotted, a lookout called, "Heads up, security!" and the group gathered what they'd collected and rapidly dispersed, disappearing into the night, off to rendezvous somewhere and share out the evenings' catch.

Scrooge stood in open mouthed amazement as the Spirit said, "It's called dumpster diving. Day after day, good food, which should be given to hungry people, is just discarded as waste. Some shops even lock their bins because they want people to come in and buy food rather than take it from the rubbish. It's of no use to them, but they deny it to the poor and hungry because it's supposed to be damaged, unsaleable, or because of insurance liabilities. A few stores have security guards or call the police to arrest anyone trying to go through the bins, and so food constantly goes to waste, left to be eaten by rats or seagulls at the rubbish dump, instead of being given to needy people.

This can happen anywhere that sells or serves food; supermarkets, restaurants, Farmers Markets, you name it. Yes, there are a few places that will donate this food to charities, but not enough. Still too much is wasted.

"I ask you Ebenezer, is this reasonable? Wasting food while people go hungry? Is it right arresting someone for just trying to eat?

Is it fair that the burden of feeding so many people falls to overworked charities, rather than governments who are accountable, and politicians, who each day devour fine meals at public expense?"

"But I don't know these people," grumbled Scrooge. "It's not my business."

"It's everybody's business," said the ghost abruptly and walked away.

***

Continuing their journey, Scrooge became outraged at the next place they visited, because this time they went, not to another hostel or some place of sanctuary, but to a men's prison.

Here, as the jolly Spirit passed among the inmates dispensing his blessings, Scrooge squeaked resentfully, "Why did you bring us here. To a prison? You're giving blessings to the guilty, to those who have broken the law?"

"Yes, I am," replied the Spirit.

"Why?" asked Scrooge. "Surely, by their crimes, they have forfeited any rights to your comfort?"

The Spirit smiled, "Ebenezer, it's always easier to believe only the good should receive blessings from above. But remember, even a common thief was promised paradise at the crucifixion.

"I am not insisting on mortal forgiveness of their crimes. Nor am I here to say they should be given chance after chance to change. Each of these men has committed crimes and must serve earthly punishment for them. I am here to reclaim the soul. To stop it falling into further sin. By bringing the guilty to the brink of repentance, they can choose a new path. Because without repentance there is no forgiveness. But, if they take the step to true repentance, they can be absolved, and their soul redeemed. That is why I visit here, and that is why they are blessed," said the Spirit.

"But Spirit, what about the innocent people these criminals have harmed? The people they've robbed or injured," cried Scrooge. "What happens to them?"

The Spirit turned to look fully at Scrooge and sighed, "Do you honestly think I, or any of my family, would ever abandon them, now or at any other time in their life? We care for everyone who needs our help. We know the road they've been forced to walk is not of their choosing and is arduous and full of sorrow, so we never let them walk that road alone. We will walk with them, by their side, holding their hand, bearing the weight of their pain as they need us to.

"Throughout their lives, we give comfort and peace to the bereaved. Courage and resolve to those who are hurt. We give comfort and strength to those who are frightened and give reassurance and hope to those who are despondent. We keep them all within our sanctuary where they can find rest. Just as I am here with you, I am also there, with them today. No one is ever forgotten, no one is ever abandoned. No one is ever left to struggle alone."

Scrooge thought about what the Spirit said then asked, "What about people who do all that stuff in your name. Robbers and murderers. Those kinds of people who say they do it all for you. What about them?"

"In my name?" asked the Spirit.

"Well, in the name of your family certainly," said Scrooge.

"There are lots of people who claim to know my family," said the Spirit "and commit many criminal deeds in our name. Deeds of murder and of lies. Of jealousy, prejudice, hatred, and robbery. Of wounding, or fraud, of terror and of violence, all in our name. But I guarantee, they're unknown to us, to all my family. I do not know them, and no one in my family knows them. They use our name because they think it frees them of their responsibility in the eyes of man and God. But the decision to commit these acts was theirs and theirs alone. Blame them for what they do, not us."

"Can't they just be stopped before they commit these crimes?" asked Scrooge.

Here the Spirit paused thoughtfully before answering, "There are those who ask how a merciful God could let terrible things happen? I have heard this said in my time on earth. The answer is as deep and complex as the ocean and as light and simple as a feather.

"Ebenezer, humanity is comprised of individuals. Individual people to whom He gives an important gift," said the Spirit. "You each have your own free will. It is second only to the gift of love.

"But free will is a double-edged sword.

"On one side it will lead you to compassion, empathy, understanding and faithfulness. It will lead you to happiness and joy. With it, you can study the very origins of the universe, unlock its mysteries, and see into the stars. Doctors can explore the human body, save lives and cure people of diseases that used to be fatal. They can even assist in the creation of new life.

"With free will, you can experience pure and profound love. Love of each other. Love of a mother for her child, so unconditional that she willingly bears the pain of its birth. Love of a friend, so strong, that one will lay down their life the other.

"Yet there are those who use the other edge and turn their free will to something wicked and sinful. But to deny their free will, to stop them before they commit their sins, would mean denying free will for the whole of humanity, and God will not take back from the many because of the few.

"Free will is your gift, so you can choose your own destiny. Guard it well Ebenezer, never surrender it to anyone, because once you do, you no longer live your life by your choices, but by someone else's fears."

…And even further they travelled into Christmas Day, stopping at many churches and places of worship, where people gathered to pray and welcome the Christ child. And at these places, Scrooge noticed that the Spirit was noticeably quiet and respectful.

Dropping his naturally strident voice to a whisper, Scrooge asked softly, "Being in a church makes you more reverent Spirit, it is the church then, that's so important?"

The Spirit shook his head, "It's not the building that makes a church Ebenezer. What is a church? The bricks and mortar? The statues, the pictures, and carvings? A gathering under the open sky is still a church but has none of these. No, It's the love that brings these people together in peace and harmony, that's what makes a church and that is what I honour. At this time of the year the love of the people is so strong it's miraculous. I venerate the love that brought all these people together because there is no other force like it in the world."

Scrooge was thoughtful for a long time after this, as he and the Spirit travelled through many places of worship, he watched as everyone smiled and prayed and wished each other a Happy Christmas. He saw how strangers clasped the hands of those near them and wished each other Peace. How various places celebrated this holy day, with children dressed as angels and shepherds, choirs singing about the birth of the King, candles and communion, services, and traditions and how they varied in the form but not in the message of Christmas.

Scrooge recalled his religious upbringing at school. How the boys were instilled with the pompous Christianity, which taught that God was white, protestant, and English and how strenuous rounds of cricket, rugger, or polo could cure every sin, problem, or transgression. Any boy, after admitting a misdeed, would be given punishment, never prayers. No, *Our Fathers* or *Hail Mary's*. No lap of the *Rosary* to obviate their sins, for that was Catholic doctrine and not practised in Protestantism. Their punishment was never anything more severe than showing busloads of weekend tourists around the historic school, and at least you could vent your frustrations by being superior to groups of day trippers paying five pounds sixty each to tour the magnificent four-hundred-year-old building. Play your cards right and you could even earn a few pounds in tips...

Finally, after he'd been turning something over and over in his mind for a while, Scrooge couldn't contain himself any longer and blurted, "Spirit, I need to know the answer to a question. There is so much unrest and fear now. There is hatred and retribution that's built up between religions, theologies and ways of worship," he said.

"You must know. Tell me, what does God want?

What religion should we believe?

Which way is the right way?"

The Spirit shook his head, smiled at Scrooge again, and spoke once more in that soft, but persuasive tone, "There is no 'right way', Ebenezer. God has never commanded everyone worship in the same way. In fact, He doesn't command you worship Him at all. He leaves that choice to your own free will.

"But what He does want, is for every living soul to commit to the morals and decency fundamental to all humankind.

"That you treat each other with kindness, dignity, and respect.

"That you care for one another as if everyone were a member of your own family.

"That you believe everyone else's welfare is as important as your own.

"And that you welcome each other with an open heart, with love, and compassion, not with prejudice or judgement.

"If you follow this path, you will have the belief you're looking for. Belief in each other, in humanity, in your brother and sister, no matter who they are, where they are from, or whatever their colour.

"You will accept anyone who wants peace, goodwill, solidarity, acceptance and equality for all people, no matter if they believe in Him or not.

"Think of it Ebenezer, a world run in such a way would have no wars, no hunger, no poverty, no pain.

"This is the belief God wants you all to have in your hearts.

"As for religion, does He favour one form of worship over another? Of course not.

"No one religion has a monopoly on Him, nor can it profess to speak for Him in everything. Many religions argue theirs is the one, true faith, but that's not so. God listens to all those who have a kind heart, compassion for others, love, and acceptance for everyone.

"As for how and when God speaks to a person, that is something only they will know, and everyone must accept that, and be at peace."

***

All through that day they visited scores of places and the Spirit blessed everyone he met. As the time passed Scrooge thought they couldn't possibly be seeing just one Christmas Day, but many days, for he saw so much, and they went so far, as they travelled all over the world. Yet it was just that one

Christmas day, as the Spirit guided him and they chased the sun back and forth, as it moved around the earth.

Something strange was happening to Scrooge...

His barriers were starting to crumble, the barriers he'd spent a long-time building, which kept an unapproachable distance between him and the outside world.

And his iron beliefs were starting to melt. Beliefs that kept troubles of others out of his mind. He was beginning to think about these people, people he'd never seen before, even when he'd walked right past them in the street, he'd never seen them. Now he couldn't get them out of his mind.

And why wasn't he feeling that "quick to temper" feeling that sat in his chest, waiting to fire at the slightest provocation? Waiting to snap and snarl at anyone who even slightly inconvenienced him. Where had it gone?

Something was happeningand he couldn't understand...

They didn't just visit places of Charity or redemption, our two travellers in time and space. Scrooge and the Spirit paused at many places made of joy and laughter, of giving back and sharing, not for charity, simply for love.

Such as groups of giggling children, visiting retirement homes. Nanas and grandpas too old to live alone, all together on Christmas day, loving the entertainment especially arranged while they waited for their family to visit.

These children were giving concerts and singing Carols for no other reason than it was a nice thing to do. Giggly scalawags in handmade costumes dazzling in glitter and bedecked with tinsel. Feathered wings, aluminium foil halos and pipe cleaner antlers, everyone now assembled, holding large cards with letters on, ready to turn over, one by one, as they all sang in unison...

C is for the candy trimmed around the Christmas tree,
H is for happiness with all the family,
R is for the reindeer prancing by the windowpane,
I is for the icing on the cake as sweet as sugar cane,
S is for the stocking hanging on the chimney wall,
T is for the toys beneath the tree so tall,
M is for the mistletoe where everyone is kissed,
A is for the angels who make up the Christmas list,
S is for the Santa who makes every kid his pet,
Be good and he'll bring you everything in your Christmas alphabet!

And when they were finished and the residents applauded, they mingled shyly with the nanas and grand pops, youth among age, finally finding common ground as shyness gave way to curiosity, until it was time to go home, leaving more than traces of glitter behind them...

Scrooge noticed that the Spirit beside him was beginning to grow older. As they continued the Spirit was slowing down. His back had become stooped and his hair and beard were streaked with grey, but he still laughed and spread his blessings to everyone they met, as the sky grew darker and the day turned to night.

"You're old," said Scrooge at last. "You have grown older, so fast, are Spirit's lives usually that short?"

"My life on earth is indeed short," answered the Spirit. "The year of my life will end at midnight tonight, and I will return home to my family."

"Midnight!" shouted Scrooge.

"Yes, my times nearly done," said the Spirit. "Soon, I'll leave this earth forever. I must admit, I will miss it."

Scrooge was suddenly feeling quite melancholy at the idea of losing this kind companion and stared at him to fix his face in his memory. He was looking intently at the Spirit when he saw something odd about his clothes that puzzled him, so he asked, "I'm sorry Spirit, but......, you've got something strange poking out of your jacket. It doesn't look like it's part of you, but it looks like it could be a foot perhaps, or a claw..."

"Yes," answered the Spirit softly, "it could easily be mistaken for a claw, for its nobut a little hand with no flesh on it, it's wasted and shrivelled. Do you want to see Ebenezer Scrooge...?"

But quickly, before Scrooge could answer, the Spirit dragged into view, two unfortunate, diminutive children, who crouched at his feet and clung desperately to the outside of the robe with skeleton-like fingers.

Scrooge jerked away at the sight of them, his stomach lurching in horror. Not normal children as we know them, these were thin, cadaverous, wretched, and desperately heart sickening to see.

"Look!" Commanded the Spirit "You are a man, you wanted to know about them, look, look at the offspring of all mankind!" He ordered as Scrooge tried to turn from the confronting sight.

The children were a boy and a girl, aged somewhere between six and twelve years old, he presumed, their age too difficult to guess more accurately because of their condition. They were small, with paper thin skin stretched over their faces, translucent, their faces not coloured by the sun of healthy play. Their eyes were large, round, and hollowed into their skulls, each heavily drawn with the dark circles of malnutrition and poverty. Where soft and shining locks should have fallen from their heads, matted unwashed hair hung around their faces. Those faces that should have been childlike, were simian, pinched and menacing. Where happy, playful features should have been, now only bitterness and resentment were visible, for truly they were children without hope. No movie director, no special effects technician, no horror writer ever dredged up such a sight from his imagination.

When they looked at Scrooge, their expressions were full of hostility, anger, loathing, and rage, but to the ghost, they were humble and submissive. With thin hands and arms, bones visible like dry twisted wood, they held fast, as they looked, desperately pleading, at his face.

Scrooge thought he should say they were nice looking kids, but his mouth went dry and his tongue stuck to his palate rather than take part in such a lie.

"Spirit are these children yours," asked Scrooge softly, still looking at them.

"No," replied the ghost, "they belong to you. To all of you. To humankind. They hang on tightly to me, begging for help from my family, as their forefathers did with my brothers, now gone, over hundreds and more years, further back than their great, great grandfathers' generation."

The Spirit tugged the boy forward, "This boy represents all the ignorance in your world,"

And grabbing the girl he said, "This girl, stands in place for all that is all that's envied and desired."

He turned back and put his hand on the boy's shoulder, "you must be careful of both of them, but in particular be particularly careful of the boy because in him I see only doom, destruction and despair for the world unless his future is changed."

The Spirit, still with his hand on the boy pointed towards the city and said, "Deny it, turn away from them, say they don't exist. Let the past repeat itself.

"Look down on them from the windows of your concrete castles and tell me it's not true. Just like all of those who have so much and see so far, and still refuse to acknowledge what's right in front of their faces.

191

"Think Ebenezer, think! It's not an offence to be poor or sick, nor is it against your laws to be unemployed. Yet these people are treated as criminals by the very system that's supposed to help them. Looked upon as pariahs, as unpeople, denied their own humanity, begrudged everything they have, with every asset counted against them. Subjected to humiliating questions about their lives, picked apart, before finally receiving a pittance they can just about starve on. The political autocrats who still disavow social equality and blame the undereducated and unemployed for the failings of their government, while postulating that the poor are only poor because they choose to be.

"Social Reformers who have no clue what it's like to live in in never ending poverty, arguing that if they could control how the poor live, poverty will be eliminated!. And after all their conferences, theories and initiatives, all they produce is the same poverty with more red tape, and less real help for those who need it.

"Real changes for these children? That will never happen. Their ancestors have clung to my family for hundreds of years, and as these children cling to me, so their grandchildren and their great-grandchildren will hold onto others in my family, on and on for generations.

"And even while the poor get poorer, and the rich get richer, the privileged will still look down and pass judgement on the less fortunate without ever taking the time stop and say, *There, but for the grace of God, go I.*

"Yes, Ebenezer go and stand with your people and admit it is only for you that society works, you and those like you. Admit you don't want changes because it might affect your way of life, take a little of your time, cost a little of your money, and then finally decide...

"Am I prepared to live with the inevitable consequences of these decisions?"

"And... The little girl?" Questioned Scrooge uneasily "What of her."

"She is all that's envied and coveted by those who don't have what others have. She symbolises what corruptions the mind and body will go through to get those things, and what follows that corruption.

"For the women, there is the loss of virtue, dignity, and self-respect. For the men, there's emasculation, loss of pride, self-esteem, and hope. And for both, their choices lead to the irreparable breakdown of the family, the inescapable vortex of the system and the inevitable penalty of the law..."

Scrooge looked again at the two wretched children and asked, "Don't they have anywhere to go, no hostel, no place of safety, anywhere...?"

"Are there no orphanages?" said the Spirit. "No correction centres or remand homes? And of course, prisons. Are there no prisons anymore?" He demanded, repeating Scrooges words with disdain. Scrooge, once again hearing his foolish words, looked down, ashamed.

The Spirit put his large hand gently on Scrooge's shoulder, "You must ask yourself Ebenezer" he said softly, "What's the purpose of property and wealth. Is it there to be hoarded and jealously guarded as a squirrel guards its nuts, or is it there to be shared and used to help everyone, not just a select few?

"Those who protest and say they follow the teacher of my family can't possibly be doing so, because He told everyone to share their wealth and good fortune among those who had less. But they'll stand and sing and praise His name and drop a few pounds on the collection plate every Sunday, and think they've done enough, then turn their backs and shut their eyes to desperate people for the rest of the week.

"Understand this, someone who's never belonged to a church, never crossed themselves, never said a prayer, but shares their wealth, opens their home, and cares with a loving heart is more welcome in our house than anyone who spends an hour on their knees once a week, and then turns their back and hardens their heart for the next seven days."

***

At last, their travelling was over as Scrooge and the Spirit stopped at a small, quiet park. Rustling sounds in the trees and hedges meant they were not alone, as small nocturnal animals went foraging for their food. A single owl hooted once, then twice, but other than that it was quiet and peaceful.

By now the Spirit was very weary and sat on a park bench. They could hear, in this quietness, a church bell in the distance, ringing the hour. As it counted towards its midnight tolling, the Spirit spoke, its voice tired and weak,

"We have travelled everywhere together Ebenezer Scrooge. You've been to many places, seen many things, and have been fine company.

"It's not my place to ask what you are thinking. But remember, man of the modern world, remember what you've seen today, and learn from it.

"Now, see what's ahead of you. Look there, at the old clock! The future approaches with the tolling of twelve. See what it holds if nothing changes..."

193

Scrooge turned to look into the distance at the old clock tower as it tolled the last of the midnight bells. As the final chime sounded, he turned back saying, "Spirit I…"

But the Spirit was gone. The fine jolly ghost had gone back to his family at last. Scrooge smiled softly, while he was happy his companion had finally returned home he felt desolate, now he was alone.

The night grew darker, colder. He pulled his dressing gown tight around him as he sat on the bench, watching, and waiting. He hadn't been returned to his bedroom to await the next Spirit, and strained his eyes, peering into the blackness, looking for the last and future ghost. Finally, he saw a movement, dark, and almost formless, drifting towards him in the dead of night.

Part Three

It was cold and dark. The echoes of the church bells faded into the distant night and Scrooge shivered as the future Spirit, floated towards him in the inky blackness, bringing with it visions of what lay ahead...

Chapter 11: The Last Spirit

The shape moved very slowly towards him. It was silent, a void of colour rather than a real shape, light poured into it, tall and more like a ghost than the other Spirits.

In the darkness of the midnight hour, Scrooge could detect its shape only by the emptiness of light within it, and by a gnarly outstretched hand. It seemed to be wearing a long, black shroud of some kind, which covered its head, its body and fell to the ground.

Try as he might Scrooge couldn't make out much more of its form. His eyes couldn't penetrate the blackness. Without the outstretched hand, it was difficult to see the Spirit until it moved, and almost impossible as it stood still.

He fell to his knees before the phantom. The unreality of its appearance terrifying him. He asked quietly, "You're the third ghost I am to expect? You're to show me what's going to happen, in the Christmas of the future?"

The shape did not speak, but it seemed to Scrooge's strained eyes to slightly incline its head.

He was, he thought, used to Spirits, after the time he'd spent with the other two, but with this ghost, he was so unnerved he could hardly breathe in its presence. He fancied he could see cold, dead eyes looking at him intently from under a hostile cowl, but truthfully and more scarifying, he could only see the black shape and an outstretched hand.

"You're completely different from the other two Spirits, what are you? Are you death, come for me? Is that what you are, please, speak to me! You look like death, is that the third ghost sent to me? If somehow, I fail this final test, are you death, here ready to take me?

197

"I don't know if I can move, I've never felt anything like this terror. You terrify me, yet I know we must go together. Won't you show me some pity, and please, please talk to me?"

It didn't answer him, simply pointed its hand forward. Scrooge looked in that direction and took a deep breath saying, "Of course, it's fitting. How many times in the past have I not shown even an ounce of pity to those who asked for it. Okay, let's go. *Tempus est transeat*. Go, go, please go. And I'll follow."

And so, the phantom began to drag along, its hand pointed towards the horizon, its long cloak trailing across the ground, pulling Scrooge in its wake, wrapping him in its darkness, as they beamed together into the future, passing from late night into early morning.

Scrooge and the ghost entered the city business district where bank headquarters in glass towers stood proudly amongst the headquarters of corporations from around the world. It was grey and cold here as a wan sun tried to warm the day. He could see his companion clearly now. It was indeed wearing a long black cloak with a deep hood pulled forward to cover its head. It moved silently, didn't speak, or make a sound, yet Scrooge understood it clearly. Though it was tall and compelling, in the light of day he was not as frightened as he had been.

The ghost joined a clutch of power suited entrepreneurs, all carrying the messenger bags, files, laptops, mobile tablets and general office claptrap that were part of the business uniform.

Some were reading the morning newspapers, while several were lost in a trance, captured by the hypnotic pull of their mobile phones, as a few drank early morning shots of expensive takeaway coffee, chain smoking their way into early hypertension. The date on the newspapers told Scrooge that **two years** had passed in this future world.

The ghost pointed his gnarly finger, where a group of three, two men and a woman, were talking in a loud animated fashion about the same deliciously tantalising subject.

"No, I'm not sure either," said Robert, a tall business type dressed in a typical pinstripe suit who was casually flipping through his mobile phone contacts list, "I haven't heard the full details myself. All I got was a text at 5 am this morning saying he's dead."

"Well, when did he die?" Asked Danielle, slightly shorter, willowy, big green eyes who was sipping at her third double shot espresso this morning.

"Last night about...er...tennish I think." Said her Aussie companion Bluey, a nickname he was given simply because of his red hair. "At least that's what's being said. Housekeeper checked him when she returned home after midnight and there he was, dead. Frightened the life out of her. Probably made her drop her bottle of gin," he said rudely. Pausing for a few minutes he cocked his head to one side then said, "I wonder what he died from? I had no idea he was ill."

"God knows, a combination of habitual misery and open wallet stress?"

Replied Robert trying to be funny, "no, he likely just died in his sleep. I thought he was never going to die. How old was he?"

"Cracking on," answered Danielle, "I don't think anyone knew his actual age. I always thought he was in his late 70s, although he could have been anywhere between 80 and 100 for all I knew." She paused for a few seconds, then said, "What I want to know is, what happens to all his money. He had bucket loads in spite of his impressions to the contrary. So, who's he left it to. Did he have a family?"

"That's an interesting question. I could always say I was his long-lost son from the antipodes. I can be c... c... Cold and miserable too," said Bluey hunching over and gnarling his fingers in a Richard III imitation of the dead man while the others sniggered.

Then he went on, "Seriously, I'm sure there is a huge inheritance there somewhere. If not, what? It goes to the government. And if he knew about that, it would be enough to catapult him back to life instantly!"

The three of them laughed, as did several others around them, eavesdropping on the conversation.

"Still," said Robert as his fingers swiftly moved across his phone keyboard, sending text after text, "I reckon it's going to be a cheap funeral. Cardboard box job. And quick. I can't think of anyone wanting to go, can you?"

The other two murmured the negative.

"I suppose we could always draw straws and send a few people there." Finished Robert, finally slipping the phone into his pocket.

"I don't mind going myself," said Danielle tapping her foot restlessly as the caffeine kicked in, "but only if they put on a proper lunch somewhere. The Savoy or Dorchester. Not just a few curly ham sandwiches and a pot of instant coffee. I don't mind if I have a decent lunch. But I'm only going if others go. I'm not turning up there on my own like an idiot. And I refuse to wear black. Hateful colour, it makes me look washed out and attracts fluff like a magnet," she said, fastidiously brushing her jacket sleeves. "Anyway, out of all of us, I'm probably the only one he could call a "friend." We did at least stop and chat occasionally whenever we met."

"That was more his appreciation of your short skirts than your investment know-how," mocked Robert.

Danielle replied with the universal one finger salute.

A small beeping sound came from one of their watches and all three made ready to enter their respective offices. Briefcases were collected, newspapers folded and tucked under arms and the coffee cup was pitched perfectly into an outdoor bin.

Dispersing into their offices, Scrooge could faintly hear Bluey say to Robert conversationally "Do you really bury them in cardboard boxes over here....?" As the automatic doors closed behind them.

Nothing more about the identity of the man they had been discussing was said. He looked questioningly at the ghost as he couldn't understand why he had been made to listen to the conversation, but it gave no hint or explanation.

They moved on. People mixed with each other, men and women, business associates, some Scrooge knew and some he didn't. He again looked at the ghost but still had no idea what was intended for him to understand.

His companion floated towards the main street, now busier with traffic sounds and people hurrying about, and the ghost pointed to two men who had just met each other on the pavement. Scrooge knew them both, having done business with them on a few occasions, and held them both in high esteem. They had made him a great deal of money. So, he stepped closer to hear some sort of explanation of why he was there.

"Morning, how are you?" said the first.

"Oh, getting there, you know," answered the second.

"Well!" said the first. "Old misery popped his clogs then?"

"Yes, I got a text about that," replied the second. "Geez, it's freezing isn't it?"

"Always is at Christmas. You could always warm up by jogging to work if you fancy?"

"No, no thank you. A bit too old for that. I'd probably slip and break a leg or something! I'll have to think of something else." Both men laughed, shook hands, and went on their way. Not another word was spoken. That was their meeting, their whole conversation, and their parting. Scrooge followed this conversation and couldn't see how the ghost could connect anything that ambiguous to what he should be learning. But he understood that there would be a hidden meaning somewhere and tried to work out what it was. It couldn't be referring to Jacob Marley's death because that had happened in the past and this ghost was from Scrooge's future. Neither could he think of any other person of his acquaintance who would fit the bill. Eventually deciding that there was a lesson here, he determined to watch everything that happened very closely from now on and fit it into this puzzle until it was solved.

But… Scrooge began to feel uneasy. A gentle touch of fear. The slight bristle of icy fingers chilling around his neck…

Chapter 12: The Ugly Truth

Scrooge had no more time to dwell on what he had just seen when the ghost moved them to another area, so different that he almost didn't recognise it as part of the same city. He found himself in a lower part of town, where dodgy business was transacted in decrepit lockups under ancient railway arches. Small places where unqualified grease monkeys wound back the miles on car odometers to boost selling prices and sold spare auto parts that could be bought at discount prices for cash with no questions asked.

Scrap metal and timber was heaped up next to recycled plumbing supplies. Cheek by jowl, garment sweatshops churned out knocked off versions of high street fashions. Each establishment was just this side of legal and all were dismal, dripping, and depressing places to work. Fire traps, safety hazards, dangerous conditions that would leave Health and Safety prostrate with indignation were rife in every lockup. Hot and stuffy in summer, with rats and flies for neighbours and freezing in winter. When it rained, the gutters, stuffed with rubbish, overflowed and filthy water ran down the walls. Sweatshop employees were illegal or non-English speaking immigrants, underpaid, cash in hand, no tax, no benefits, exploited with long hours and appalling conditions. Their vulnerability meant they didn't complain.

The whole area was the kind of place you visited only in desperation, looking for knocked off, hooky goods or to fence something fast before the cops caught up with you.

Police knew the area well.

In this group of dubious establishments stood a rundown decrepit old shop. Its faded sign read, "The Cockney Pawn Shop" and below it, suspended out from the wall on a fancy metal grille, were the familiar Myra Balls, named after the patron saint of pawnbrokers, which proclaimed to one and all, that this was a sanctuary of fast cash in a sea of financial hardship.

Curiously, such was the odd positioning of the worded sign and the three golden balls, that the locals referred to the premises as, "The Cock and Balls Pawn Shop" and had done for the last 50 years or so. It was also true that the word of mouth publicity of such a name was so valuable, it couldn't be replicated by any kind of advertising anywhere.

Inside was an Aladdin's cave of trash and treasure, where deals could be made with a nod and a wink. Lawnmowers, garden trimmers, lawn edger's and other garden equipment leaned against second-hand bicycles of various ages, ranging from brand new to antiques from the 1950s. Scooters cuddled up to them with skateboards, rollerblades and ice skates stacked on the shelves overhead. Next to those were a miss mash of musical instruments including guitars, both acoustic and electric, drum kits, scuffed speakers, and several keyboards. Shelves on one side were stacked with incidentals such as Doulton pottery, counterfeit Wedgwood plates that would fool all but the most discerning eye, vases, glass wear, vintage crockery sets for the willing collector and odd and ends for those looking for something unusual. A rusted, reproduction suit of armour stood next to a section dedicated to power tools of various quality. Everything from circular saws to angle grinders and various individual tools by the dozen were on sale, each in differing states of repair. Bread bakers and kitchen mixers, microwaves nestled next to all day cookers and toaster ovens. Cookery books lead to shelf upon shelf of fiction and nonfiction books dating back decades. Many a first edition was found at the cock and ball pawn shop.

In the locked glass cabinets, second-hand mobile phones, SLR cameras and games consoles sat temptingly near Rolex watches, diamond rings, and imitation jewellery that could fool all but an expert eye. Semi-precious stones, amber beads, pearls, garnets, and aurora borealis necklaces were also locked away, temptingly shining in the light, waiting for a buyer.

At the near side of the desk, a locked rail held fur coats, mink, fox, sable and coney plus one or two men's leather jackets in black and brown.

Finally, vacuum cleaners and steam mops leant against the wall near ironing boards and several new indoor/outdoor floor brushes, recently bought for a quid each by the owner, now selling well at five pounds ninety-nine.

The shop sold practically everything, including a various sized false teeth, try them once, no returns. Eyeglasses, crutches, walking sticks, three replacement legs, one foot and yes, even several kitchen sinks, bought cheaply from a local auction when a kitchen outfitter recently went out of business.

In the middle of the shop, stood a large round, doughnut of a desk, an island in the centre of chaos, where an elderly man, approximately seventy-five years old, sat and surveyed his kingdom.

Jehoshaphat Jonnsen was a true cockney. Born within earshot of Bow Bells, this grubby little man beguiled his customers with a blend of Victorian-era flattery, the unique parlance of cockney rhyming slang, and the costermongers' patois from days gone by.

He could slip on this persona at a moment's notice, as easily as stepping into a pair of well-worn shoes, and just as easily shrug it off again, reverting to the canny negotiator many customers had dealt with in the past. Nevertheless, it must be acknowledged that this figure of the loveable old cockney was very advantageous with overseas tourists wanting to see the "real London" or with anyone from the other side of the river who'd ventured out for a day trip to terra incognita.

Joe was "5 foot and a fag paper," tall, plain, calculating, cunning, and all together satisfied with his lot. If ever a person was born to fit contentedly into his predestined future, that man was Joe. Growing up, he'd never been happier than when he was helping his father in the shop, and when it finally passed into his hands at the tender age of 25, he delighted in his good fortune.

Joe eventually married a plain girl from the north of England after they agreed nothing better would come along for either of them and settled into a marriage that, theoretically, lasted seventeen years.

In all that that time Joe proudly boasted that he and the missus never said a cross word. They also never said a pleasant word. In fact, he glossed over the truth that they hardly spoke to each other at all and chose instead to bask in the light of a conventional relationship that only existed in his mind.

They had one child, a honeymoon baby who was fated to have no siblings. Once the honeymoon was over his parents retired to separate bedrooms and from then on preferred to live in sexless serenity.

The child was an intelligent young lad sadly burdened with the name D'artagnan Jonnsen.

Tip for the future, never let the missus watch the shop for a week when you're up before the magistrate on a handling charge. Bored, and with instructions not to do anything but answer the phone and take messages, she'd started reading a ratty old copy of The Three Musketeers. Throw in regretting her loveless marriage, yearning for a handsome lover plus being seven months pregnant, and the poor little bugger's name was a fait accompli.

There was no better pawnbroker in the city than Joe. Taught by the best, who'd learned from the best, he knew the value of almost anything and the resale potential of absolutely everything that crossed his threshold. In fact, so comprehensive was his knowledge of art and antiques that he surprised many pretentious dealers who assumed a pawnbrokers knowledge was limited to the belief that Scrimshaw was a town north of the Pennines.

Joe's father, after owning the shop for several decades, handed it over to him, lock and stock, when he hung up his Myra Balls and retired to Majorca.

Paulie Jonnsen didn't even know where Majorca was, but for some reason, he'd got it into his head that he would retire there, or to Florida. Majorca eventually won out for two cogent reasons.

Firstly he believed he was fluent in Spanish because in 1971 he'd acquired four "Learn Spanish The Easy Way" LPs which he frequently played in the shop, reciting such phrases as, *"I would like a taxi please. (Quisiera un taxi por favor)"* and, *"Do you know the way to the supermarket? (Conoces el camino al supermercado?)"* Once he'd acquired a full catalogue of useful, occasionally asinine, phrases, Paulie was thoroughly confident he could hold a conversation with the King himself.

The second reason was even more tangible. A life-long supporter of the Wanderers Football Club, it was imperative he lived close enough to return to England ASAP, should they finally make it to the FA Cup finals. Weighing all the pro's and cons, Paulie decided that Majorca was the place for him.

So Paulie packed his bags, bought his ticket for a five-day cruise on a small ocean liner and put out to sea. On arrival, he was delighted to find a sunny climate, lots of beaches full of British tourists, pubs that sold English beer, plenty of fish and chip shops and crystal-clear reception of BBC radio. He settled in Spain and, since the Wanderers never made it to the cup final, no one heard from him again.

Before him, the shop had belonged to Joe's grandfather Armand, who, after running it himself for over thirty years, set his sail to retire to the sophistication and grandeur of Brighton, in the company of a twenty-seven-year-old "au pair" named Trudie.

Trudie, five feet two of blonde deliciousness, made a happy man feel incredibly old and spent every penny he had. Still, according to the salacious gossip at his funeral, he left this earth with a large grin on his face and an even larger…well, let's just say rumours at the time suggested it was a couple of days before the undertaker could get the lid down.

Before him, the shop was begrudgingly run by Joe's great grandfather, a dour east end misogynist with the incredible name of Sinbad Jonnsen, who didn't care for Brighton, Spain or anywhere that was full of 'furriners', and who spent his last years shuffling between the Scroungers Tavern, his bookies, the Walthamstow dog track and his front room, where he could listen to the wireless without interruption. He left this world after a sudden heart attack when he realised he'd won a hundred to one chance on a dog with the unlikely name of Shonkies Deal. As his original bet was ten pounds, a huge amount in those days, suddenly finding himself within reach of one thousand pounds was more than his heart could stand and it blew like an over-voltage light bulb.

On the other hand, had he survived, it probably wouldn't have withstood the subsequent shock of finding out the dog running under the name Shonkies Deal was a ringer, and the one-thousand-pound payout had slipped through his fingers.

So the shop had been passed from father to son, as far back as anyone could remember, and scant though it was, Joes family folklore boasted that the establishment went even further back, well over a century into the Victorian era. That had been enough for Joe to use a hammer and chisel on a suitable piece of copper, which he then screwed above the shop door, just beneath the three balls. Slightly lopsided, as such adding to its authenticity, the homemade plaque proclaimed this store was established in eighteen eighty-eight.

While you and I would probably have preferred a year or two prior, or following 1888, to Joe, the significance of that year had no particular meaning, other than that it was a lucrative period in history, with easy money making opportunities driven by spurious tales and rumourology. Most of which he either read in books or made up himself.

Jehoshaphat saw no reason to change a management system that had been successful for more than a century and therefore modern fripperies such as bar codes, computer inventory and scanning systems simply didn't exist within his shop walls. When hopeful representatives would show up, spruiking the latest up to date computer and software packages which would enable him to track his inventory right down to the last teaspoon, he would simply tap his forehead and say, "It's all up here mate, down there for dancin'" and politely suggest they shove off and leave him alone.

It was here then, at this grubby, disreputable establishment, where Scrooge and the phantom appeared, just as three individuals were about to enter the shop.

All three had arrived in separate vehicles. One was a terribly battered, four door, dark blue sedan of an indeterminate make and model, whose age was lost to the aeons. It had just about made it there, grumbling in second gear all the way, belching oily smoke everywhere. The woman driving, one Dolly Butterworth, opened the boot and pulled out a large wrapped bundle of cloth which she'd hastily pushed in not two hours earlier. Once free, she closed the boot by wrapping two bungee cords through the lid and around the tow bar.

Marjory Dilber drove a second car; a white, relatively modern station wagon with the sign, "Domestic Laundry and Cleaning Services" emblazoned on the side next to a colourful graphic illustration of a chubby, friendly looking fairy. The fairy promised, by way of a speech bubble, that she would, *"Give EVERY House a Thorough Going Over"* a message that could be interpreted in several different ways if you had a suspicious mind. Mrs Dilber removed a large, heavy looking bag from the back seat.

The man, who was driving a black, sombre looking private ambulance, complete with tinted windows, was from Truscott Funeral Services. A third generation employee of the business, he was addressed as Truscott, Scott, or Scottie, but *never* by his first name. This was because his mother, who adored the book Wuthering Heights, had named him Heathcliff. As this name was considered unsuitable for one in the funeral business, he used the others instead. In addition to that, "Heathcliff Truscott" sounded more like a stop on the Piccadilly Line than someone's real name.

Like the cleaning services, his car also carried a dedication written on its doors, reassuring customers that, *"With **Us,** Your Loved Ones Will Always **Rest In Peace,"*** thereby suggesting anybody buried by any other funeral service would be eternally dissatisfied and keep popping back through the ether to complain.

Reaching for a small briefcase off the front passenger seat he said to his companion, "Back in a little while, Albert," before he double blipped the vehicle and joined the two women at the entrance of Joe's shop.

These three, realising they were all going to the same shop at the same time, stopped and looked at each other for several seconds then burst into a peal of awkward, embarrassed laughter.

Dolly Butterworth, who never missed an opportunity to state the obvious called out, "Lawd God above, how's yer fancy eh? Look Joe," pointing to herself and the other two people, "All of us got here at the same time! It's gotta be fate, what's brought us all 'ere all at once."

"Well," said Joe from behind his counter, "and why not. What other places would be better for youse all to meet I'd like to know. All got business to transact have you?" Coming out from behind his desk, he hurried them through the door saying, "Best come into the back room then, all of youse. You've been here enough times to make yourself at home Dolly Butterworth, and youse other two ain't just sightseers either."

As soon as everyone was safely inside, Joe cautiously peered up and down the street, slammed the ancient door shut and locked it tightly against any further visitors. Sequestered now from any witnesses to their business, Joe hurried his customers along saying, "Come on, everyone, into the back room with youse and let the dog see the rabbit."

The back room was a small dark space behind one of those coloured plastic strip curtains that are put on doors in the summer to keep flies out of the house while allowing the door to stay open for a cool breeze.

Inside there was a small two bar fire, totally inadequate to heat the room, several knackered old chairs and a kitchen type surface with a small sink and a place to plug in a kettle. One or two wall cupboards held tea bags, mugs and biscuits, and the dim 600-lumen globe shed an inadequate light that cast strange and disturbing shapes on the floor and walls.

Joe bade his customers sit, while he lit the stub of a cigar and blew its foul-smelling smoke around the room. Through canny brown eyes he studied his punters , sizing them up. Truscott, placing his briefcase by his feet, produced a small hip flask, twisted off the lid and took a quick swallow.

Thoughtfully, he offered it to Joe, who waved it away saying, "Naw thank you son, 'ave not 'ad any fancy for the drink. Not since my dear wife departed."

Scott, nodding respectfully at this sad news, took another swig, twisted the flask tightly closed and dropped it back into his pocket.

However mournfully Joe referred to his wife's departure, it's important to know she wasn't actually dead. Aphra Jonnsen had departed, but truthfully she'd packed her bags and quit her marriage fifteen years earlier after she'd had enough of a husband who spent every moment in that grubby little shop, and only came home to change his clothes, criticise her cooking or frighten her son.

Once she'd made her decision to leave, she retrieved from her safety deposit box the many jewels and valuables she'd discreetly acquired whenever she minded the shop and vanished back up north with D'artagnan in tow.

There she invested well and raised her son. It was only when somebody pointed out that her husband could conceivably be entitled to half her money that she finally divorced him and terminated the "seventeen years of happy marriage," that Joe chose to believe in.

As Scott put his flask away, Dolly dumped her bundle on the floor, fumbled in her pockets, and produced a cigarette packet. Tapping one out, she borrowed Joe's lighter, lit up, and breathed the smoke deeply into her lungs.

Dolly Butterworth was the quintessential east end girl. Born in Poplar, she'd lived there all her life, leaving only twice. Once, to honeymoon in the highlands of Scotland and the second time to spend a week enjoying a summer break at Butlins in Yorkshire. She disliked both places, hated the cold weather, couldn't understand a word anyone said and, longing for the familiarity of the place she loved so much, swore never to leave it again. True to her word, she hadn't ventured any further north than Watford since 1976.

Dolly was pukka east end, not always honest, she was nevertheless forthright, and had a personal code of conduct that married a strong set of morals with a flexible set of principles.

Her cigarette lit, she sat back with a contented smile and turning to the other woman she said, "A proper turn up for the books then Mrs Dilber, we couldn't have done this better if we'd tried. Getting here at the same time I mean. But we've all got to take care of our future and pay our bills. S'what he always did, so why shouldn't we eh?"

Marjory Dilber, sitting with studied gentility on the edge of her chair, was one of those women who constantly tried to erase her inconvenient background and convince the world she was born for higher things. In this effort she partially re-educated herself in the "correct" pronunciation of certain words and made a valiant stab at the rest, producing a kind of pidgin English only spoken by those trying to evolve from ITV to BBC1. When she was in the company of her own sort, she could temporarily drop her façade, and act normally.

However, there were occasions when she would find herself involved in a heated conversation and wouldn't be able to resist reverting to her "hoity-toity" voice. Then her pretensions and habit of mumpsimus pronunciations would race to the surface. Her disposition when this occurred was best summed up by friends and neighbours, who described her as "all fur coat and no knickers."

"Yes, that's true," Mrs Dilber answered Dolly's question. "I can't think of any other man who did it more than him!"

"And who's going to know about this, I'd like to know? There's just us four here," said Dolly "We ain't going to grass each other up, are we?"

"No if course not!" exclaimed Mrs Dilber. "Nobody's going to inform on one another. None of us is going to say anything about any of us being 'ere, here," she corrected, the undertaker nodding his agreement.

"Well then," said Dolly. "Everyone's gonna stay schtum right? And no one's going to miss a few trivial things, especially not a dead man, an' not one like him. 'E's got no family to make enquiries about personal items so it's not like anyone's going to cause a fuss is it?"

"No, not very likely, "said Mrs Dilber, with a laugh.

"If he wanted to leave some kind of legacy, he should have been different when he was alive. Am I right? Eighteen months I've worked for 'im and I never met a person like 'im! Such an 'orrible, mean and wicked old man, and so awful to be around he had no one what was willing to nurse him even if 'e paid them. *You know* what he was like Mrs Dilber, seen you 'ave many an angry word with him before now."

"Indeed," answered Mrs Dilber, "always complaining about his laundry or cleaning. Trying to knock something off the bill all the time. Worst customer I had. Fourteen months 'e was on my books, *fourteen bloody long months too!*" She laughed.

"An' now he's gorn. "E went all alone. No one was even willing to hold his 'and when death come for him." Dolly said spookily and shook her head sorrowfully.

"Very true," said Mrs Dilber, her façade slipping, "it's almost like a punishment on 'im as he died. As you sow, so you shall reap," she said piously.

"Yes well, if I can get me 'ands on anything else it will be an 'eaver punishment believe me! Open the bag Jehoshaphat," Dolly said abruptly. "I'll go first. I'm not embarrassed to be first. Give me a price, straight up, I won't be upset at what you say in front of everyone. I think we all guessed when we were there, we were all looking around for what we could have as we done up 'is body for burial. As far as my thinking, it's no sin for me to take some extra compensation for all the hard graft, low pay and sharp words I've 'ad from him. If he'd been a kindly type of person, perhaps I'd be feeling I'd done some wrong, but he wasn't, and I don't. I put up with plenty from 'is mean ways and snappy tongue, so I reckon I deserve all I can get from what's in that bundle there. It's all deserved, I reckon. Go on, open my bag, Joe."

"Hold your horses, " said Joe, "what's in all the bags then? I never knew the old bugger had anything worth selling."

"Oh 'e 'ad it awright," answered Dolly. "send that many people to the wall he could pick what he wanted from their belongings. Kept it in the house, in boxes, in 'is loft, everywhere. It'll take ages to go through it all that's for sure." Winking at Mrs Dilber, Dolly said, "me 'an hers gonna go through it all soon as he's gone. Go on, open my bundle Joe, He's dead, time for the livin' to get their reward."

However, it was decided, after certain amount of animated discussion, that the undertaker would go first, as he'd misappropriated the least. Plus, he was in a hurry, he said. He had just collected another gentleman who'd also passed during the night, leaving instructions with Truscott's for a lavish and expensive internment. This gentleman, advised Scott, the aforementioned Albert, was waiting for him in the car, so to speak, while the undertaker transacted his business with Joe, and both were due back at the funeral home within the hour.

Heathcliff Truscott was not, by nature, a happy person. He was twenty-seven years old, five feet nine inches with nondescript hair and eyes. Pleasant looking, but not so handsome that his looks would overcome his profession enough to make him truly fanciable. Constantly bullied as a child and with very few friends, he grew up an outsider, and even though his father constantly extolled the virtues of his profession, telling the girls at school his old man was an undertaker didn't exactly make him a chick magnet.

Those same squeamish, reluctant women blighted his life even more when he joined the family business, making it almost impossible for him to date at all. There had been a few curious ones who latched onto him for a couple of weeks here and there, but truthfully, once they'd had sex in a coffin, their morbid curiosity was satisfied, and they dumped him soon afterwards.

Nevertheless, he was good at his job. Professional, personal, caring and always helpful to his customers. He was also helpful to himself, usually picking up at least one or two items from his clients which he pawned in one of the many pop shops around London. The proceeds of these "perks" went to support a four-year-old daughter who was the light of his life and a cocaine habit he couldn't kick.

Scottie popped the locks on his briefcase and placed his ill-gotten gains, one by one, on the small table to be appraised. They consisted of one small solid silver bookmark, one engagement ring, one tie clip, a pair of cufflinks, and a twenty-four-carat gold fountain pen and biro writing set. Joe appraised each item and then wrote the price he would give on a slip of paper and handed it to him with the words, "That's my offer. No more. Start haggling with me and I'll reduce the price by a quarter and won't pay a penny more." Truscott looked, read, and was not too happy, but said nothing, knowing Joe was a man of his word.

"Aye," said Joe to the undertaker, "there's not as much left to profit from in death as there was when I was your age. Used to be, the families left it all to the undertaker to take care of, the last few stages before removing the dearly departed that is... Them's was the time you could slip one or two things in your pocket, and by the time the family remembered it was too late. You could say, sorry missus, it was buried with him. Not now, though. Now they want to have laying outs and viewings. Help dress the body and they take everything off and hang on to it. No, it ain't like it used to be," he lamented.

Ebenezer Scrooge, observing this first transaction, felt his stomach turn. Bile filled his mouth as he witnessed this pitiless hawking of the dead man's goods.

Mrs Dilber was next. As the deceased's cleaner, she'd been able to rummage more thoroughly through his belongings without arousing suspicion, and so had been more adventurous and wide ranging with her plunder. Now she produced from her bag, two large solid silver photograph frames, still in their boxes, One rather nice, though small, framed watercolour painting, two pairs of unworn, pure leather golf shoes, gentleman's size nine, two pairs of unworn suede gloves, a hand tooled leather briefcase and a few bits of unworn, quality, gentlemen's apparel. Joe wrote her account in the same way, sucked his breath in over his teeth and handed it to her with the words, "It's a terrible failing I have that I always give too much to my lady customers. It will see me going broke one day, mark my words it will. Mind, you haggle and ask me for anymore and I'll forget being such a gentleman and will relieve you of ten per cent off the price."

Mrs Dilber read her paper and a little more delighted than the undertaker, smiled and nodded to Joe.

Again Ebenezer watched the conspirators in this dreadful deal. This new outrage increased his revulsion. A coldness had spread all over his body, rigors overtook him, his vision blurred, and there was a buzzing in his ears. He was going into shock.

Finally, Dolly could wait no longer. "Open my bundle now Joe," she said, clapping her hands excitedly. Lighting a second cigarette from the butt of the first, she invited the other two, "Youse both must stop and see what I got, I mean, we all knowin' each other so well and you've been so agreeable, lettin' me see what you've brought already," said Dolly, issuing the invitation with a smile. But the smile was brittle, sharp at the edges, her grey eyes glinted like flint, and, although given in a friendly enough way, the invitation was in fact a command for both to remain and be outdone and dazzled by Dolly's cleverness and catch.

Dolly's superior rank within the household was made obvious by her access to the more juicy and matchless loot she'd got her hands on. As housekeeper and permanent resident, she'd not only had the time to peruse the items in the house that were the most valuable but was able to make the first grab for them, once it became apparent her employer was finally wiping his feet on death's doormat.

Joe had to go down on his hands and knees as he undid the ties of the large bundle she'd brought in. Pulling and turning he eventually unearthed a beautifully patterned, handwoven rug.

"What's this, a carpet? A rug?" Joe asked.

213

"Yes!" shouted Dolly in delight. "His bedroom rug. I've had my eye on that for ages. He had no idea what it was worth. But I knew, I knew! It's an 'and woven rug, a Turkish Oushak it is and worth a pretty penny. I was 'avin that and got it 'afore he breathed his last just in case someone else picked it up first." She grinned and clapped her hands with glee.

"You mean you just rolled it up and took it, with him still lying there, dying in the bed?" said Joe, flipping the rug out and laying it on the floor.

"O'course," answered Dolly. "Give it a clean first, with the vacuum like, and then took it. Why should I just stand still when there is something I want within arm's reach? An' it was too late fer him to be putting his feet on by then, 'e was goin' nowhere else that's for sure!" she yelped delightfully, screeching with laughter.

Joe, who knew at one glance the value of the carpet he held in his hands, hid his anticipation, casually rolled up the rug once more and put it to one side, while silently musing on the current market price of such a prize.

Still thinking, he returned to Dolly's bundle and its bulky contents, where he gently pulled free, hastily folded and wrapped in a bedsheet, an exquisite three-piece suit, made from the finest pure wool. Dark grey jacket, waistcoat and trousers, each beautifully tailored, certainly expensive, and top quality. Accompanied by a smart wool, full length black overcoat of equally excellent quality, both made a fine catch. Joe held them up and looked them over carefully in the dim light.

"Now you can look at that suit 'til the cows come 'ome," she said, "but you won't find a 'ole, or stain or a stitch out of place. It was the best he owned. If it wasn't for me, it would have been wasted it would."

Joe looked up at her, "What do you mean by wasted?"

"Well, they were gonna cremate him in it a-course! What was the reason for that? If'n a cheap suit isn't good enough for that I don't know what is," she said, laughing gleefully.

Joe looked at her incredulously and said, "Are you tellin' me you changed his suit as well, right off'n the body? After they'd put 'im in the bag 'n that?"

Dolly smiled and laughed again, "You bet I did."

The undertaker was looking at her intently and broke in, "Ere, I put that suit on him!" he exclaimed.

"And I took it orf of 'im again," she said succinctly. "I'd just of soon wrapped him in a sheet to get that off him if I 'ad to!" she cackled again at her audacity.

214

Joe looked at the undertaker, "Why wasn't he dressed in the funeral home then?" he asked. "Why didn't you take 'im there?"

Truscott shrugged, "He didn't want any service, didn't hold with it, no viewing, nothing like that. Just the bare minimum the state pays he said, and not a penny more."

"'E did, did 'e? Not no service at all?" said Joe ruefully. "No prayers or such like?"

"No," Scottie replied. "Left instructions. Didn't want to pay for it alive or dead. Just cremation and burial of his ashes, he said. The vicar's coming to do a quick 'spectacles, testicles, wallet and watch' but that's it."

Joe nodded to confirm he understood the undertakers' reference, but Mrs Dilber broke in, "Eh? The vicars doing what?"

Truscott smirked, "You know," he said and making the sign of the cross, he touched his forehead saying, "Spectacles"

his waist "testicles"

his left side "wallet"

and his right "and watch."

The cleaning lady pursed her lips and tutted at such disrespectful irreverence towards the church. Removing a few items was one thing, but the mockery of a holy sacrament was another.

"Anyway," he went on, "there was nothing else I could do. Wasn't worth taking him all the way to the funeral home only to bring him all the way back, so I dressed him at his 'ouse and left him there while I get the casket. We're due to pick him up at two o'clock today to take him to the crematorium, then inter his ashes at the Town Cemetery later."

"'An' that's why I got the suit off quick smart, as soon as 'e was gone!" Laughed Dolly, flicking her thumb at the undertaker, "a good suit going to be burnt like that? Tell me!"

"Well," interrupted Mrs Dilber, "at least at the crematorium he'll get a taste of what's to come. Never was a more wicked man in my memory. Destined for the flames of hell that one," she said, her hoity-toity voice rising to the surface.

Dolly covered her mouth as she cackled, "Well, at least 'ell isn't getting 'is best suit!'"

The raucous, unpleasant laughter continued for a few moments until Joe grinned widely at Dolly, puffing his foul cigar saying, "Youse a woman after my own heart you are. Born to make yours fortune."

Dolly demurred coquettishly.

Joe continued an intense inspection of the suit then said, "No doubt, it's definitely a nice whistle, should fit me 'n all." Standing up, he slipped off his old ratty cardigan and began to pull on the jacket of the suit. Suddenly he stopped halfway and looked down at her saying, "Hey 'ang on a minute, he didn't die of anything infectious, did he?"

"Nah, no worries about that." Dolly lifted a hand indicating all was well. "I didn't like being in his company, alive or dead, long enough to get nofink that was catching," she said, the three others laughing together at the joke.

Joe nodded his acceptance of her explanation and pulled on the rest of the jacket. Smoothing it down over his grubby shirt, he modelled it for the others who all agreed the jacket, which was obviously too large, suited him enormously. He sat down and reached again into the large sack, rattled around inside, and produced a gentlemen's 24-carat gold wristwatch. With one cursory glance, he tossed it on the table and grunted, "Paste."

"Paste!" Shouted Dolly, "that's not paste! Don't tell me! That's genuine that is, worth over five thousand sovs!"

Joe paused scrabbling inside the bag and shot a look of irritation at Dolly, offended she would dare question his expertise. "Five thousand sovs? For that? Its paste. It worth no more than fifty sovs and you ain't getting' that much from me! Wait!" He held up a hand to stop her arguing. "You want to take it somewhere else to get five thousand…?" He picked it up and threw it across to her, "Here you go, take it. I never steered you wrong have I. Name once in the past, I done you wrong. Never. You want to take it, find someone else'll give you more'n me? Off you go then, but you take this lot with you as well," and he began to remove the jacket.

"Nah, nah then Joe, don't be gettin' hard, I was only joking at ya." Dolly retreated rapidly. "O'course you neva' done me wrong. You say its paste, then its paste. No worries."

'Awright then," said Joe, waggling his forefinger at Dolly, "no more questioning my professionalism if you please," and kneeling back down, his wounded feelings still on show, he continued to go through the rest of the bundle. Picking out items and placing them one by one on the table in front of him, Scottie and Mrs Dilber watched, while Dolly, not in the least flustered by her argument with Joe, continued her critique.

Scrooge had stood silently beside the ghost and listened to their shameful conversation. The violation of that man's body at his last hour of utter help-lessness still sickened him. That they had picked over his body, through his pockets, his possessions, and had taken his very clothes with no thought for decency, nauseated and appalled him. Watching them gathered in that small room, their stolen goods spread about, with the smell and smoke of Joes disgusting cigar still hanging in the air, Scrooge fought feelings of horror and revulsion that couldn't have been any worse had they brought in the body of the unfortunate man and tried to sell that too.

Furthermore, their humour and merriment at his death baffled him. Try-ing to comprehend all he'd seen Scrooge asked his companion, "Why would they all laugh when they know there was no one with this man when he died. That he was alone, frightened, with no solace when he passed. Why would they be pleased by that?"

A gleeful cackle came from Dolly as Joe produced an old tin box and counted out the money for the rug, suit, overcoat, and other items he'd pulled from her bundle, as well paying Mrs Dilber and the undertaker, who hastily put their money away without counting it. Whatever price he'd of-fered Dolly, she'd been well pleased and pocketed it with glee.

"So, this is how he ends," said Mrs Dilber, slipping back into her middle-class vernacular. "He drove everyone away from him when he was living and now, we make money from him when he's dead!"

"A fitting end for 'im," agreed old Joe, "and you two ladies have landed the job of going through 'is residence, sorting 'is stuff?" He confirmed with Dolly and Mrs Dilber. "You'll be remembering' old Joe won't you, if'n you come 'cross somethin' tasty you'll want to sell?" Though this question too was asked quietly, gently, the threat was crystal clear to the two women. Bring anything of value to me, Joe was saying, or there will be trouble. "You know I likes to see what's goin' first," prompted the formidable old pawn-broker. "I always wants to add to my *special collection.*"

It was rumoured that Joe's "*special collection*" could rival the best jewellery and valuables of minor royals, cash strapped nobility and landed gentry up and down the country. No one had ever seen it in its entirety, but many a person needing money had regretfully been forced to contribute to it, re-ceiving a pittance for long held family heirlooms.

"And what about you Joe?" Dolly was asking, lighting her third cigarette. "Of course, you'll not be 'aving him in competition anymore, will you? I'm sure 'e took many a customer off'n you when they was wantin' to borrow money. You've got a clear field, like to speak, now that 'e's kicked the bucket at last," she laughed.

"Well," replied Joe, "I never take any comfort in anyone's death, you know me, but 'e did steal away plenty of business that for sure. 'Course our lending rates was a bit different and our terms not the same, but business is business and I did suffer from 'im cutting into mine, I won't lie. Still, I won't speak ill of the dead, neither," he finished.

There was a small, quiet pause in the company, then Mrs Dilber let out a tremendous laugh, saying, "Well, you're the only one that won't be!"

Joe put his tin box away and stubbed out his cigar. "Come on, the lot of youse," he said, ushering them out. "I've gotta shop to run and youse all got places to go. I reckon the corpse what's in your van will be wantin' to get a wriggle on Scottie," he said to the undertaker. "And it does nothing for my reputation to have a meat wagon parked outside my doors, so you can shift it if you please."

"Ladies," he turned to the two women and gave an exaggerated eighteenth-century bow. "As always, it's been a delight, but I 'ave to re-open so you can both be on yer way." Unlocking the front door and all but shoving them through, he slammed it shut, leaving the three standing outside, empty bags in their hands, just as it started to rain.

***

Scrooge and the ghost were still watching. "I'm beginning to understand. All this, what we've seen, what you're showing me, you're saying this poor soul could be me? That my life has turned this way already? That I could end up like this man if my life doesn't change. Oh please, where is the man that these three have abused, stolen his possessions, and celebrated his death?" he asked, suppressing a shudder, and even as he drew breath a second later he exclaimed, "Sweet Jesus in heaven, what's this now?"

Scrooge started in fright because suddenly they stood in intense darkness as if all the light had gone from the world with a snap of the fingers. It was too dark for Scrooge to see where it was, he could not even see the ghost he knew was still beside him, all he could make out was the dim impression of the undertaker's trolley and lying on it, the faint outline of a black plastic body bag.

The only light in the room was the glow from a streetlight outside, filtering through the high window, casting a single beam over the image. Though it was silent, the bag screamed its presence by being so shockingly confrontational. Scrooge knew that inside, stripped of every personal possession, unloved, unwept, unmourned, with no one to care about the indignities wrought upon him after death, lay the body of that man. He looked at the vague outline of his body in the bag, he who'd been violated after death, by those who'd picked over his belongings to see what they could take.

Could the lesson now, finally, be learned by Scrooge? He knew he'd committed the same nefarious deeds to the living, plucked their lives apart and taken what he wanted. Then sold the rest, pocketed the money gladly, and never for one moment stopped to think that what he was doing, time and time again, was wrong, immoral, and repulsive to all decency, nor had he even the courtesy to wait until the death of his clients to spare them the humiliation of his actions.

At last, as he stood before this unknown body in the presence of his companion, he finally realised what he'd done to others so many times was iniquitous, and he was at last, ashamed. Scrooge quickly stepped back and looked for the ghost. He could only see the hand, pointing at the bag, to the top where the zip lay. It would have been so easy for Scrooge to pull the zipper down a tiny bit and see the face of this poor man. He knew that would be simple, but he knew he couldn't make his hands do it any more than he could tell the ghost at his side to leave him be.

So, come here dreadful Death, from the shadows where you lurk, with your tools of cold, fear and terror. This is familiar territory for you, this is the place where you dwell. Here you sit, ready to cast dread about you, and upon this ended mortal. But know this before you unpack your tools of terror, that for everyone who has ever felt love upon this earth, this is not the end, and you will have no power to frighten, no power to dread. Come, bring your tools, for it will be for naught. It doesn't matter that the heart that once loved has stopped, and the pulse that flowed is still. What matters is the heart that once beat did with love and kindness. Full of warmth, compassion, and generosity. That the pulse that flowed carried joy and happiness, decency, and humanity along its veins, and with it, all fear was thence defeated. This is what fills the world with immortal love.

Scrooge heard these words, but they were not spoken aloud. Rather, he heard them in his head, as he continued to look at the poor man lying on the trolley. He wondered, would this man, if given a miracle that could restore him back to life, sit up, and think as he used to, of money, business deals, profit, and gain? Or would he grab the chance given to live a different life, a better, more fulfilling one, rather than the one that brought him here, scorned and alone. For now, he lay zipped into a body bag waiting to be transferred into a cardboard coffin for a funeral service that no one would attend. Thereafter would he be condemned to carry his mortal sins in never ending penance, like Marley and the other ghosts he had seen? No one would say to a friend, "I remember when he did this..." And smile at the memory. No one would remember him at all, except to recall his past unprincipled deeds.

How a person's life is measured as one well lived or not, can be judged by those who grieve and mourn their death. For if there are those who weep at the loss of a precious soul, we can stand and say, they, who was loved and will be missed, have lived a life well done. But if they are mourned by no one, what changes should they have made to be more loved, more cherished? For all our lives will surely be measured the same way, and if changes need to be made, make them now, while there is still time, not later when you are all alone, still denying your own faults, and all you have is regret, for your final and only companion.

In the darkness, Scrooge could hear but not see the rats and cockroaches scuffling about, chewing on lino and architraves; but they were there, this man's only company at the end, picking the last detritus from his ignominious life.

Chapter 13: Changing

Ebenezer Scrooge stood beside the ghost, lost in his thoughts. He had asked to see this poor man's body, but now he wanted nothing more than to leave his presence and quell his ominous feelings.

The icy fingers of dread were joined by a rising panic he couldn't control. Sweat formed on his forehead and upper lip, his heart began to race.....

"Ghost of the future, I want to leave here. I understand the lesson in this place, honestly, I do, but I can't stay here any longer. Please can we leave?"

The ghost did not move. Light poured into it and it kept its white, bony hand pointed towards the head of the body bag. Silent but insistent.

"Yes, I understand, and I would if I could," said Scrooge answering the command inside his head, "but I honestly can't. I just can't...I'm too afraid to look, to see what's...In... Please, there must be someone in this city that is feeling something more about this unfortunate man's death. Can't we at least see that first? Please show me that, then perhaps I can look."

In less than an instant, Scrooge and the Spirit were standing outside on the street where the hearse from Truscott's funeral service had arrived. In the darkness of the cold afternoon, here too, it was difficult to see. The street lighting was still bad, a low-lying mist creeping up from the river adding to the strangeness of the moment and although Scrooge looked around to try to get his bearings, he failed to see anything in this future world that told him where he was.

The undertaker had returned to the empty room where the deceased man lay and placed his body into the pine covered, cardboard coffin. In the process of bringing the casket downstairs and putting it into the back of the hearse, a small crowd of nosey parkers and injured parties had gathered. Standing back, Scrooge was able to hear the conversations taking place.

"As soon as I 'eard I came down here," said the woman, "me neighbour says, "did you hear the news, the old skinflint's kicked the bucket at last. The wagon's coming fer 'im soon," and so I dropped everythin' and got down here just to see 'im taken out with me own eyes."

"'E more or less killed my 'usband," said another woman, looking scornfully as the pine box was manoeuvred down the last few stairs, and loaded into the hearse.

"All for five grand it was. He could repay the whole loan, but for the last five grand. All he needed was a month but no, Mr grubby fingers in there, 'e wouldn't wait, and the bailiffs took the lot. Everything my husband worked for, gone for a lousy five grand. Must 'ave been worth five times that and 'e took it all. Had a stroke and died he did, my husband, all because of that man. May God curse him!"

"Mean too," said the first, "wouldn't pay a penny for anything if he could get it for free. Wasn't above pinching a few things rather than buying them either. Seen him take more than one apple from the greengrocer in the past."

"He'll be burning in hell or doing penance for years for the sins on his soul," interrupted a third woman, glaring hatefully at the hearse as if the deceased could see her expression. "Too many people suffered from his wicked ways. Money mad he was, never thought about people at all." And she spat on the road after the hearse as it turned the corner.

'Penance," Scrooge whispered to himself, remembering Jacobs visit and the visions of the hundreds of lamenting ghosts, "What is his penance?" he asked himself uneasily.

And then the dusky street melted away, and out of the cold, up sprung a row of cosy Edwardian houses, each warmly dressed for Christmas.

It was daylight and he and the Spirit entered one of the houses, where he found they were in the company of a woman and her young children.

The woman seemed very anxious, nervous, jumpy to any sound.

She was pacing back and forth, like a lioness, trapped in a cage, waiting for someone. She kept looking at her mobile phone, willing it to ring, and every now and then she stopped and pulled aside the net curtains to peep out of her front windows. When her children called her attention to their drawings and colourings she tried to be interested and encouraging, but her mind was on the front door and her eyes on the mobile phone clock.

At last the front door rattled, and her husband, Leo, came in from the cold. While his children ran to greet him with hugs and kisses, his wife made coffee, and he changed out of his damp clothes into a warm cardigan and slippers. He looked exhausted so his wife settled the kids down quietly in front of the TV while he sat on the sofa with the steaming cup and a few sandwiches she'd kept for him. She sat opposite, watching him eat, and eventually asked, "Is it good news, or bad?"

"It is bad Caroline," he replied, "but..."

"That's it then!" She interrupted, throwing up her hands in a helpless gesture and getting up to stride about the room, while the kids looked up anxiously from the TV.

"We go bankrupt and lose everything then? This house, our cars, everything? All we've worked for. What about the children? How're they going to cope? It's all just going to go to that man isn't it?"

"No, not yet," said Leo trying to catch her hand to settle her. "There's still some hope."

"Oh yes!" Caroline spat. "*If* he relents, and *if* he gives us more time, but that would take a miracle!"

"No miracle needed," answered Leo. "Caroline, he's dead."

Caroline stopped in her tracks and turned to face him looking astonished.

Leo nodded at her incredulous look, confirming his statement. Slowly she broke into a big smile and blew out a sigh of relief.

"I know I should be feeling sadness at the idea that he's died, that anyone's died, but honestly I can't." Then she giggled, "God forgive me for laughing, but it's such a weight off our shoulders."

"Yes, it turns out Ms Dolly Butterworth, that brandy-soaked housekeeper of his, wasn't lying to me when I went to his house last week to ask for an extension. He wasn't just ill, he was dying!"

Caroline looked at her husband and took his hand. Crouching down beside him she asked, "What happens to our loan now. It's unsecured, will we still have to pay it?"

"I don't know," he replied, "I'm not sure what happens when its due, but what I do know is that very soon we will have the money so it's going to be okay. We can sleep soundly tonight darling. We're not going to lose this house or anything else."

And with that good news, as Scrooge and the ghost watched, they celebrated.

The children sensing their parents were relieved, giggled and hugged, jumping about happily, their parents playing with them until bedtime, after which they popped the cork on a bottle of champagne they'd been saving.

As they drank, they toasted each other and laughed, kissed, and talked. Talked of tomorrow, about their children, plans they could now make, dreams they could now fulfil. They were obviously so very relieved that even Scrooge was beginning to feel happy on their behalf.

But then Caroline said something that interrupted his thoughts and reminded him why he was there. Suddenly sitting upright on the sofa, where they'd both been cuddling together in front of the fire, she asked, "Hey, did drunken Dolly Butterworth tell you what he died of?"

"Why would you want to know that?" asked her husband with a smile.

"I was wondering if it was his heart, that's all."

"Why?"

"It's just, well, he ripped the heart out of so many people when he was alive, it would be poetic justice if his ended up killing him, that's all."

Leo laughed, saying, "Trust you to think of that." But then he stared for a few seconds into the fire before adding, "Mind you, you're not wrong. There are so many who've lost so much. So many he's ruined, and he could have ruined us. We won't be the only ones celebrating."

Caroline topped up their glasses and toasted, "To our brighter future then, and to everyone who's celebrating tonight!"

Leo clinked his glass with her saying, "I'll drink to that!"

Finishing their champagne in one joyful swallow, they cast their glasses into the fire, shattering them against the Victorian iron grate, and finally putting an end to the anxiety of the past.

Scrooge was quiet. His gladness for the couple had faded rapidly and now he felt only bewilderment and a heavy sense of regret. All he could see from this man's death so far was profit, revenge, and joy. He looked at the dark shape of the ghost and asked softly, "Spirit, isn't there any kindness or gentleness connected with death in the future? If there is, can we please see it, or I'm never going to be able to forget any of these terrible things"

Whether it was out of pity, or for some other reason he didn't know, but the ghost transported them both to the front door of Bob Cratchit's house. Scrooge had to admit he felt comforted as he and the ghost went inside.

***

The house was mostly as it was before, warm and cosy. There was some new paint on the walls, but it was hung with the same worn Christmas decorations that still shone and glittered, making the house look festive and inviting. Amy Cratchit was sitting with her children around the same small gas fire trying to do a little sewing. School clothes needed different name tags sewn into them for the new year, so she was unpicking old tags and sewing in the name of the next Cratchit to have the hand-me-down garments.

Scrooge became aware it was noticeably quiet. On his last visit, the children had been full of fun and laughter and the twins had been ping-ponging off the walls in their enthusiasm.

But now everyone was still. Studious in fact. Reading or drawing. Eliza was quietly playing with Abigail on the rug, teaching her colours, Belinda was helping her mother by unpicking the old name tags, while Martha was using a handheld sewing gadget to hem pairs of shorts also needed for the new school term. Though the TV was on, purely out of habit, the sound was turned down low.

The front door opened quickly, admitting a cold and red faced Peter who rapidly stepped in front of the fire to warm his hands as he removed his coat and scarf.

"It's getting very cold out there," he said. "I wasn't sure if I would get home before I turned into a block of ice."

His mother gently laughed. "Well you're home now. We're just waiting for Bob, let's hope he gets home soon. There's dinner in the oven love," she said, then added, "How did it go?"

"Depressing," replied Peter, "especially on Christmas Eve. Austerity has really bitten hard this year. So many people with no heat because they can't pay their bills, not enough food and no electricity. They've had no cost of living increase for two years but everything gone up. And many others, who've never been out of work, suddenly don't have a job and have to manage on a lot less. They don't know what to do first. I've spent all day working out household budgets, trying to get appointments with mortgage brokers and advising people where to go for extra help. At Christmas too, it's awful for them."

"God bless them all," she said, "I hope they can get some happiness this Christmas."

The household slipped into a gentle silence as Peter sat and ate his dinner by the fire and Mrs Cratchit continued her sewing. The warm room, and being together reassured them all, each lost in their own thoughts.

Then Amy Cratchit put her sewing into her lap, removed her reading glasses and pinched her nose with her thumb and forefinger. Immediately all the children asked if she was okay.

"It's just trying to focus on this white cotton," she said, unconvincingly. Then she blinked several times, wiped her eyes and said, "all better now. I mustn't look like I've got sore eyes when your dad gets home, you know he'll make such a fuss."

Simon looked up from the book he was reading and said, "If you pricked your finger while you were sewing Mumma, *Odelina The Faerie* would come and grant you a wish, like it says in this folktale." Simon loved books, more so than many boys his age. He'd already read well beyond his age, books were his passion, his addiction. A studious boy, he would rather read than watch TV and called books, "the medium that touches the soul."

"What wish would you make Mumma?" He asked.

"Oh, my darling, there is only one wish I would want, but I don't think even a fairy can make it come true," and she smiled at her son. Glancing at her wristwatch she said, "Bob's a bit late again, should have been home by now," she said. "Shouldn't be too much longer though, or he would have sent a text."

Peter was the one who voiced what they were all thinking. "I think he's walking slower these days mum, remembering different things as he walks, you know."

His mother nodded, but then with a laugh said, "I've known him to gallop home from the station when he's been pushing that heavy chair. Runs like a rabbit with a greyhound after him!"

Peter smiled and said, "Yes, so have I."

"And me," said Matthew from his colouring books.

"But your dad never minds any of that, does he?" said Amy. "Never thinks it's any trouble. Oh look, here he is now."

Amy stood up to greet him as Bob came through the door, wiping his wet feet on the mat before removing his shoes and putting them on the drying rack with everyone's wet trainers and wellies. Amy reached out to give him a hug and remove his coat at the same time. Peter hung it where it could dry while the twin Cratchit's disappeared, returning with his warm woollen jacket and slippers. They then sat on his knee briefly to kiss him as a way of saying, "Don't be upset Pa, we're here, we're here."

Belinda and Martha boiled the kettle and made coffee, bringing in a cup for themselves, Amy, Bob, and Peter, while the smaller kids had hot chocolate, including Abigail who glugged hers happily. Bob was quite pleasant when he spoke to everyone. He looked at the different sewing, the colouring, and the reading, shared a bro hug with Peter asking about his day and tutting in concern at his news, and patted Abigail's head, receiving a grin that revealed new baby teeth in the front. He smiled at his family and said everything would be ready by Sunday.

Sunday....? Scrooge looked at the Spirit. He realised that the whole family was gathered, yet someone was missing. He looked up at his companion and asked, "Where's Tim?"

The ghost didn't move.

Scrooge looked about him again. He checked the children from his memory, but Tim was missing. Turning to the ghost he asked again, "Where is Tim? Is he in hospital? Is he poorly, in hospital?"

Once more the ghost made no movement.

Scrooge looked around and now realised the room was brimming with flowers and cards. Determined to be answered, he left the ghost's side and went over to the mantle to see some of the cards up close. They were all the same nature. 'In Sympathy', 'Thinking of You at This Time', 'In Gods Garden'. Tucked in amongst the cards were hand drawn messages from Tim's brothers and sisters. Rainbows and tears. Love hearts and kisses proclaimed their feelings.

The flowers were all bunches of roses and lilies. Some had dark ribbons, some purple, Tim's favourite colour.

Scrooge picked up a card and read the message. "To Bob and Amy, wishing you our special love at this time." Then another, "To the Cratchit Family, May God's blessings be with you all at this difficult time"

He turned to the ghost.

"Tim? ... Is it Tim? Please, tell me, it's not Tim, it's not Tim!"

The ghost gently inclined its head.

Scrooge dropped the cards and looked around again. This time he realised the family were not in quiet repose but in dreadful mourning. Each one deeply saddened for themselves and for each other at the loss of their little brother, and for their mother at the loss of her youngest son. Each trying to find some cheer in homely tasks or simple entertainment. Even Eliza, playing with Abigail, was struggling to be encouraging as she tried to keep her attention and stop her from getting into mischief.

As the full understanding of what had happened finally dawned on Scrooge, sadness burst from inside him and his eyes spilled over with tears that ran down his cheeks uncontrollably. Wiping them with his fingers, he watched the grieving family and felt compassion for them all. Turning briefly to the ghost, he intended to ask a question, but the ghost shook its head, pointing to the family again.

He turned, obeying the silent command, and stood, a guilty outsider in that small, cosy room, watching Bob's family. Guilty, because Scrooge had never known about Tim's illness before his visits. Never known because he'd hadn't bothered to talk to his clerk about *anything*. Any verbal exchanges between them had only ever been, on his part, a discourteous inquisition about current business matters. Bob, and his day-to-day family misfortunes had no cash value.

Now, in this future world, it was too late.

But even given that, as he watched them all together, and saw how much they drew comfort from each other, as a family and because of their love for Tim, he was granted, by heaven above, a miracle.

While he watched, he could see, standing amongst his family, smiling at them all with a look of pure love, the Spirit of Tiny Tim.

Scrooge brought his right hand up and pressed it against the side of his face, his hand covering it like a mask, his eyes screwed tightly shut, trying to stop fresh tears.

Why was he feeling like this? Had he become so invested in that child, from just one visit with the ghost of Christmas Present that he felt his death so keenly? Could Tim's simple gesture of offering prayers for his happiness have affected him so much, that he was now sorrowful at the thought of his death? *Why couldn't he understand?*

The small flame of humanity that had started to burn within Scrooge, a flame that had been lit by Tim, not only with those few simple prayers he'd said, but with his own compassionate faith, cried out in pain for Tim's loss, and Ebenezer's heart wept for his grieving family...

Tim's Spirit, hearing Scrooge's heartache looked up at him with compassion. Their eyes locked, and with gentle kindness, Tim smiled.

The ghost touched Scrooge with the outstretched hand and pointed to Amy Cratchit. "So," she said, "you did go there today Bob? I thought you might."

"Oh yes, my love," said Bob, "I really wished you could have come with me again today. Maison Valley is such a quiet place isn't it? With all the green grass. Lots of trees, flowers, and birds, it's like his favourite park, you know, where we sometimes take Quackers? I think we did well choosing there. I even thought we would go there often …to visit……"

Bob stopped talking then, trying but failing to stop his tears, he put his head in his hands and softly cried, "Oh God, my child, my little son, please take care of my little son!" And broke down totally. He couldn't stop his tears or the terrible grief he felt at the loss of his child.

Now his family came to him one by one to offer hugs and kisses of love and support. Each one lifted his broken heart and helped put the pieces back together and soon he could smile again. He left them all and went up to Tim's little bedroom where he sat on the bed for a long while, holding a teddy bear, stroking the cat who had not left the bed except for food and the kitty tray for over a week. Bob looked around, drinking in the memories of the son he loved so much and who had fought so hard to live. He thought of the cruel disease that had taken him but remembered too how Tim had fought with all his might, every day, on his terms. And he remembered his commitment to him, "Promise me you won't be sad Dad, promise me you'll still have fun on Christmas Day!" And smiling to himself, he was determined to fulfil that promise. Picking up the cat, he said, "Come on Crisis, you've been moping here too long." Holding her gently he went back downstairs to the rest of his family, putting the cat next to Amy where she snuggled in, watching the fire. As Amy and the girls finished sewing the name tags, Bob mentioned a chance meeting he'd had that afternoon with Fred, Mr Scrooge's nephew. "He saw I wasn't looking too cheerful, you know, and stopped to ask me what was wrong. When I told him about Tim, he was terribly upset for us and insisted on taking me for a cup of coffee. We chatted for a long time. He asked me about the funeral and was there anything he could do to help and said that he was sorry for everything. He wanted me to call him at home or work if there's anything we needed or anything him or his wife, Kate can do for us. When we left he grabbed me in a hug and said, "Bob, please give my love to your whole family, especially to your wonderful wife Amy." Do you know, as I was walking away, I said to myself, how on earth could he know that when he's never met you? But he did."

Amy Cratchit looked up, "Know what my love?"

"That you're a wonderful wife," said Bob.

"Everyone knows that," Peter chimed in, "because she is wonderful. You are mum." The other Cratchit children agreed with their brother. Simon popped up from his book saying, "You're the wonder-fullest mum in the world." Making Amy smile.

"True," said Bob, "absolutely true. He even offered to have the kids for the weekend if we wanted to get away, just the two of us. Oh, and while we were having coffee, he told me that he knew of a place where Peter could be offered a much better training opportunity for his future, and a higher salary. He said he would look into it for us."

"He seems like a very nice person. It appears his apple fell quite far from the tree," said Amy, refusing to explain the allusion to her younger children, while those older nodded in silent agreement.

Bob looked at his whole family, "There is plenty of time to meet him my love," he said to his wife, "but now everyone, we've got to remember Tim as he was. He was kind and patient, but he was a tough little bugger, and determined too! We should talk about him every day. And that will keep him in our hearts. Later when you all grow up, maybe marry and have your own family, you can tell your own children about him. That way, although he's not here, he will always be with us and part of our family forever.

Bob looked around the room at his grieving family. Everyone was nodding and smiling. The girls were oozing tears into tissues silently, while Peter held his mother's hand, a weepy smile on her face.

"We can expect to get a bit teary now and then, that's normal as we adjust, but if we just remember Tim and how he enjoyed Christmas, we will enjoy it too. We should remember what he did over Christmas, things that were fun, include him still in our celebrations. That way, we can honour his wishes and get through this first Christmas without him," Bob said. "It may sound strange, but I'm happy. We need to remember the grief we feel, the sadness, that's the price we must pay for loving someone. Sometimes it seems like it's too high a price to pay as our grief seems endless, and sometimes people say, "Well, I won't love anything so I won't get hurt when they die," but we know our Tim wouldn't want that and we all are better having had his love in our lives. The hurt of losing Tim will go and I know his memory will strengthen us and become something we can enjoy sharing. I'm incredibly grateful for being his father, I will miss him but never forget him."

Amy Cratchit stood up, and, pausing to pick up two sympathy cards that had somehow fallen on the floor, she went over to give Bob another kiss. He smiled at his wife and wiped her tears away with his thumbs. The sweetness of their love for Tim bonding them at this private moment.

Kissing her again, he brushed the hair from her eyes, and she laughed, comforted. Then his daughters kissed him again, each given a few soft words of love, then the twins, who he hugged until they squealed, then Peter and Simon sharing solace with their father.

While Amy made more coffee, Abigail sat on Bobs knee. After seeing everyone else kiss her Dada, she put two sticky hands on his cheeks, looked deep into her father's eyes and gave him a big smacker. Bob laughed, so did Abigail, who then put both arms around his neck and snuggled in for a cuddle.

The Spirit of Tiny Tim, who had been there all this time, smiled contentedly once more, then slowly faded away.

Scrooge too had silently watched, saddened at the loss of Tim as if he was also related to the boy. Drying his eyes, he finally understood the meaning of faith, family, selflessness, the love that Christmas brings and the strength of that love which could even comfort a grieving family. Those two small children, one alive, no more than a toddler, and one a Spirit, still a loving child, had crushed his last boundaries to dust.

For the first time, he knew the message of Christmas.

Here was Bob's family, totally broken by Tim's loss, but lifted, carried, made whole by the teachings, their beliefs, their faith in the saviour who had been born on Christmas Day, and the message he'd brought, *"For God so loved the world that he gave his only begotten Son, that whosoever believeth in him should not perish, but have everlasting life…"* and by living His word each day, the family's comfort was not forced, they didn't struggle to believe it, weren't angry, didn't rail at God for the loss of their son. They knew the same God who gave life didn't take it without a purpose. They simply prayed for Tim's soul and comforted each other.

Scrooge was feeling like an intruder, watching a personal and intimate moment in Bob's family life. He knew he'd been privileged to see the family at this time, but now he had an urgent, pressing matter on his mind. Turning to the ghost, he said softly, "Please, show me the man who lies on that bed."

Instantly Scrooge and the ghost of the future were on a road, walking along the edges of time and space, like they were moving through the sides of a movie, seeing scenes, but not part of them. Through the lives of several businessmen of his acquaintance, stopping for no one but also seeing no sign of himself.

And as they travelled Bob's words resonated deep inside him, "Sometimes it seems like it's too high a price to pay as our grief seems endless, and people say, "Well I won't love anything, then I won't get hurt when they die."

Had he done that? Could he claim his actions, his change in character after Fan's death was that straightforward? Could he...Honestly? Or was it more a convenient excuse so he, like Marley, could stay locked in his office, hoard his money, revel in it, worship it, and never have to live in a world full of comprise and sacrifice.

With every step he took, Scrooge felt the cold grip wrapped around his heart and running through his body, as if ice water ran through his veins. He began to feel sickly and afraid.

Finally, their travels brought them to the street and where Scrooge's office was found, and he looked to the ghost saying, "this is where my business is. It's been here for decades. I can see the sign from here. Let me see what I am like in the future"

The ghost stopped, but the hand didn't point at Scrooge's office, instead it indicated towards the opposite direction.

"No" insisted Scrooge "you're pointing the wrong way, my company is over there," But the ghostly hand didn't move, it kept pointing resolutely away.

Scrooge stubbornly hurried to the window of his business to look inside. It WAS still an office, that much was certain, but it wasn't anything like *his* office. The furniture was new, modern, sophisticated. It had state-of-the-art equipment, pictures on the walls, plants in the corners, and the person behind his desk was someone he had never seen before! But there was Bob, still in his old place, with a second clerk for company. Marley's room had even had the wall removed and easy chairs and a sofa installed for the client's comfort! What was all this change?

Scrooge returned to the ghost, his nausea growing, the Spirit still pointed as before and this time he obediently followed, walking for a long time.

At long last, they reached an incredibly old, very heavy, Victorian iron gate, painted with thick, black enamel paint. Scrooge looked around curiously as the gate slowly skreeked open. Inside was a shadowy old cemetery, the graves dating back to the 1860s. So forbidding, so frightening, so dark and terrifying, any phantom, ghoul or beastie would have felt at home. Walled in, stuffed to capacity, a pauper's burial-ground indeed, but also a necessary place to bury those who had no family, no one to love, no one to care. Simply a last resting place of convenience, not for the dead, but for the living, who saw those unmourned deceased through the final stages of their last journey. Unethical undertakers trying to pack them in here, rather than schlep out of town to one of the bigger cemeteries with more room. After all, the state paid very little to bury these people. Why put themselves out.

Corpses now crowded together. People who would have never mixed in life, now cheek by jowl in death. Buried side by side, top and tail, on top of earlier occupants long since entombed, long forgotten. Stone angels, saints and guardians leering from their pedestals, casting gloom as they watched over it all.

Overgrown with weeds and dying brambles, roots pushed up headstones of ancient tombs. It was eerie, disturbingly quiet, cold with fallen snow and sharp icicles. Sounds of heavy-footed rats and voles mixed with large round-eyed hooting owls that made a spine-chilling atmosphere. It wasn't a pleasant place where people rushed to go, no visitors came to cry and lay flowers. Here a phantom could wander unmolested, with no fear of ghost hunters to disturb their peace. There were only two regular visitors to trouble their slumber; with the dawn came the sun, and with dusk, the moon. Other than that, it was, mostly, left alone..

The ghost moved silently until it found what it was looking for, then it stood, as still as the statues around it, and pointed its gnarly finger directly at a small flat headstone, barely 15 inches square, which marked freshly interred ashes.

Scrooge hung back, a few feet from the spot, terrified.

"Wait!" He shouted, "Wait now! Just a minute, before I look, I need to know, I must know, these things you've shown me today, are they definitely what is going to happen, set in time, or only what could happen if things in the future don't change?"

The ghost still pointed down.

"What we do, every day, has results, if we stick rigidly to our actions, make no changes, yes? But if we decide to change our actions, then surely the future will change too?" said Scrooge.

"If I walk down a road and can turn either right or left, my future will depend on which way I turn. If I have taken a wrong turn, I can alter it by now taking the right turn yes? Please, is that right? I need to know before I look at the name."

The ghost still didn't move.

Scrooge dropped to his knees and inched forward. "If I try to make a change in my life from now on, I could change my destiny yes? And that could change things around me too, right? The future is not decided yet, so it COULD be changed by man's actions...Or what happens to that man. Take floods or things. Lives are changed by what happens to someone yes? So it can be changed again by what someone else does too. That's what the Christmas Present ghost said. I think that's what he said. Am I right, I can change the future if I change, right, yes?"

The ghost made no answer.

"And a positive change in me will surely alter the future of others, like Bob Cratchit's boy, Tim. Won't it, please, tell me, it will, won't it?" He asked desperately, pleading for a response.

Still no answer, so Scrooge, using his fingers brushed the fresh snow off the flat headstone to reveal the name stencilled upon it.

LOT: 682

EBENEZER SCROOGE

"I knew it" Scrooge cried out loud "Before I looked, I knew I was the man lying on that bed!"

The ghost pointed from the grave to him, then back again.

And with his name, he was drowning in the feelings of dread that'd built up within him. Of course, the man was him. Could it have been anyone else with what this Spirit had been showing him? The icy feeling racing in his veins, the dizzy buzzing in his ears, the pounding in his head, and he was retching, retching by the graveside, over and over in fearfulness.

"Oh, Spirits what have you shown me," he thought. "Can this be but the only end for Ebenezer Scrooge?"

He let out a cry of anguish and pain, "No, no, no, oh God, no. Stop it, please stop it now! Ghost of the future, I beg you." Scrooge pulled back from the headstone in horror. "Listen, please, please you must listen to me…" he shouted, as he crabbed backwards away from the grave, frightened the stone would rise, and he would be snatched into a void from which he could never escape.

"I'm not the man who's buried here. That's not me, Not now. Not anymore! I've changed, please you must know I've changed. All the visits from…from you, the different Spirits and Jacob Marley, they've transformed me. I understand now, I've moved on, I believe everything now," he shouted

Sobbing as he spoke, desperately trying to make the ghost believe him, he went on, "Why…Why send Jacob and the other Spirits, why let me see the Spirit of Tiny Tim if I'm still judged to be beyond hope?"

Very slightly, the hand of the ghost began to tremble.

"Please…please let me show you I can CHANGE the future by changing myself. I can do it and I'm resolved to do it by…by…by living a different life! A better life. More fulfilled. More involved. I can do it, I promise."

The hand was shaking even more.

"How can I convince you? I promise I'm not just saying words here, but truly I will keep the Spirit of Christmas all through the year. All the Spirits, you've shown me where I went wrong, when I became corrupted, when my feelings began to die. I must make up for lost time, to everyone I've hurt. Please give me that chance.

"When I saw Fan, I realised how disappointed she would be in how much I'd changed. I must have time to make amends to Fred, for her sake as well as his. But more than that. The future must be changed for others, like Bob Cratchit's boy. I CAN MAKE THAT CHANGE. I want to make the changes to help him, to help Tim. I know I can help that little boy. Please give me that chance. If for no other reason, give me a chance to help that boy.

"I'll never close my mind again to the messages I've seen tonight. I'm going to stop looking to the past, to what has gone and can't be altered. I kept up a barrier of anger and hate and used it to keep my misery going because then I didn't need to adapt. My anger sustained me, and my bitterness carried me, and any thought of change was buried beneath those feelings. You've all opened my heart and emptied it of the anger, and desolation I carried. My heart has transformed and I'm no longer a prisoner of the past!"

The hand shook and trembled so much the ghost couldn't hold it steady.

"And I know I can't shape my future, just by taking care of myself. I must help others, those who need help, are troubled, hungry, needing money, shelter, and care. I'm ashamed I turned my back for too many years on people needing help. How could I do that? I just didn't care, that's how. But now I want to start to try to make amends to all those I walked past and ignored. The ghost of Christmas Present said just praying was not enough. We all had to DO something. I must help and care for others, not walk past them and pretend I don't see anymore. If I can, if you allow me this second chance, I'll repay the whole world for the opportunity I'll be given"

"I've seen love, kindness, and selfless giving. For the first time in many, many years I want to do something, anything, everything to help. Please give me a chance to show you I will share my good fortune, and with your blessings and with the blessings of all the Spirits, I will fulfil all the promises I've made tonight" Scrooge fell back on his knees in the cold thick snow, rubbing at his name on the small concrete tablet he cried, "Help me. Please, help me. Have I still got time to change? Can I yet remove my name from this headstone?"

The ghost, swaying to and fro, it's hand trembling violently, still remained silent to his appeals.

In desperation, Scrooge lunged forward and grabbed the claw that pointed to the stone. He held on fast, but the ghost was stronger and shook him off.

Sobbing, Scrooge held up his hands, pleading for a chance. With tears blurring his vision, he imagined he saw a changeover in the ghost's form. It seemed to shrink, fall away, collapse in upon itself… He stared at the shadow, not understanding the change or its importance.

And then, impossibly, it was gone.

He looked around, searching for the ghost, trying to find it in the darkness. but all he could see was a blur of unfamiliar silhouettes. Then slowly they too transformed and became the hazy outlines of his bedroom furniture in the soft morning light…

Chapter 14: A Second Chance

Ebenezer Scrooge had thrown both hands up in front of his face the moment his bedroom furniture appeared before his eyes. Now cautiously, carefully, he opened them one by one and peeked around .

The room was *his* room.

The bed was *his* bed.

The headboard was his and the coverlet *was his*.

Gingerly he put his hand out to feel them. Yes...yes, they were real!

Solid objects. All the things were real. They felt wonderful, marvellous! Suddenly he felt so relieved he nearly fainted. But he'd no time for that. Oh no! Scrambling to his feet he shouted, "I'm back! I made it. I passed the test. Oh, Spirits, you watch and see, I've got you now! I'll do it, I swear by heaven I'll do it. By all the heavens, by every celestial body in the sky, I swear I'll keep my promises. All of you will live with me. I swear it down on my knees, on my knees!" and falling back down, he put his head in his hands and sobbed, relief and gratitude washing over him.

After a little while, he looked up at the windows and the light that shone through them. For the second time, heaven had granted him his life, the significance of that blessedness crystal clear as he whispered, "Today's the new day. Jacob. A changing day. I've got the time to change now and make amends. I won't let the Spirits down, I won't let any of you down."

He paused for a few minutes as if he was listening for something. His eyes closed, tears still oozing from under his closed lids. "Fan," he whispered, "can you hear me? I promise you too, a new day, a changed day, Fan. From now, I'll start as I mean to go on..."

He scrambled to his feet and started to pace back and forth. "I need to make a plan. Christmas will live in this house and I will give help to others,

237

just as I promised I would. Planning, that the ticket. First things first, best foot forward! That's the way. "Start as I mean to go on," eh Fan? Paper, I need some paper. Make a list, first things first Ebenezer old fool. Write it down, first things first. I don't want to the second thing first or I'll get into a muddle. Then I could do the third thing second and still not do the first thing first and before you know it I'll have done the fourth thing third..."

Scrooge drifted off in this conversation with himself as he busily looked for a sheet of paper.

The rug that lay on his bedroom floor caught his eye and he abruptly stopped pacing to look at it. He'd stepped on it year after year but never really noticed it. Now he dropped to the floor on one knee, almost genuflecting as he smoothed it under his hands, saying, "It's not gone, it's not been taken, it's still here so that means the future I saw, can alter. Everything will be different now, I jolly will make sure of that!"

Pushing himself to his feet again, he told the rug, "and if you're worth as much as she said you are, you're off to auction tomorrow with the proceeds going to charity. I'll get a nice, cheap, poly fibre rug instead," he said, clapping his hands and rubbing them together in anticipation. "In fact, I'll get carpets. Fitted carpets. Damn the expense."

Scrooge whirled about his apartment picking things up and putting them down, knocking things over, looking out of different windows. "I really don't know what I'm doing," he told himself as he staggered about the rooms. "I feel dizzy and lightheaded...I'm not drunk. I know I'm not drunk...I think I'm...I think...I'm happy...that's what it is, I'm happy!" he exclaimed, trying a few ballet steps and a pirouette or two, realising he was experiencing an emotion he'd not felt for many years.

"Hello to the whole world," he bellowed, throwing his arms out dramatically like Jack on the bow of the Titanic. "I wish you a Merry Christmas. I wish ME A MERRY CHRISTMAS!" He sang and two stepped into his sitting room where his adventure had begun only the night before.

"I was sitting here when I heard Marley's ghost," he said, lowering himself into the chair by the TV. He leaned back and briefly closed his eyes, then shot up and pointing he said, "And the door, there, where Jacob came through, wait I must see..." and rushing over to the door, he whipped out his reading glasses, closely inspecting it for any sign of tampering, "No it's definitely still locked." He flipped each lock and saw that indeed they were still in place and shut tight. Turning, he shouted again, saying, "And the ghost of Christmas Present had his chair in that little corner. God knows how it fit. He was a gentle giant, but whoa, so big, huge, big, big guy! Where...where was the fire? Nothing is even charred! All this was filled with cakes, champagne and nuts and berries. Did he leave me any? It looks so tatty and grubby now, I'll have to fix that later. But I remember it all. And the windows look. They all flew open when Marley was here. I couldn't get them open with a sledgehammer before then!" he exclaimed.

Scrooge stopped at the large arch top window and, placing his hand on the glass, he said quietly, "All those poor wandering ghosts, oh if only God could send them some rest. But it's all true. It was all real and it did happen, yes it did, it did."

Walking dreamily back into his bedroom, he stopped short, seeing his reflection in the long wardrobe mirror. His dishevelled appearance, wild and woolly hair that had been blown about when he'd beamed from past to present to future, partially wet dressing gown tied down over damp pyjamas and totally soggy, muddy sheepskin boots was such a ridiculous sight to behold, he felt the corner of his mouth twitching in an involuntary smile. He was the living image of a scruffy, wretched, old Scarecrow! His smile grew larger and was accompanied by a strange churning inside, a feeling so odd that for an instant he thought he was going to be sick.

He felt it in his guts, such an odd bubbling that was so peculiar he didn't recognise it at all. Deciding it was a warning of hiccups to come he self-prescribed a glass of water, but that did not stop the strange, alien, giddy feeling growing inside him. It grew and grew, slowly, like a tickle in his belly, like butterflies, or that feeling you get after being on the waltzer at the fair, and it was making him feel quite weird. Not understanding what was happening and quite unable to stop it, he thought he should try putting his head between his knees, as you do when feeling faint. Quickly sitting in the nearest chair, he dropped his head forwards and sat in that uncomfortable position for a good five minutes, before giving up and realising it was having absolutely no effect, other than giving him a stiff neck.

His next thought was to distract himself from what he was feeling in the hope it would simply go away, so he desperately grabbed a ratty old book from his shabby old bookcase, flipped to a random page, fumbled his reading glasses onto his nose and read an entry on the first line.

Anatidaephobia: *(noun; first use 1988, Larson. G.)* (it read) *is defined as the pervasive, irrational fear that one is being watched by a duck. The anatidaephobic individual fears that no matter where they are or what they are doing, a duck watches.*

Scrooge stopped reading, the corners of his mouth twitching again. Turning the book over he read the title, *Human phobias and cures* then read the sentence again as the curious giddy feeling was now racing up through his body, making his legs and arms, his fingers and toes tingle. Bubbling up, more and more.

Anatidaephobia: *(noun; first use 1988, Larson. G.) is defined as the pervasive, irrational fear that one is being watched by a duck. The anatidaephobic individual fears that no matter where they are or what they are doing, a duck watches.*

This time there was no denying it. What had started as a strange churning down in his belly at the sight of him in the mirror had been hurried along by the entry in the book and finally, it couldn't be prevented. It burst from his windpipe as such a loud and happy belly laugh, you would have considered, if you didn't know him, that it was natural to him and one he enjoyed all the time.

Instantly he slapped his hand over his mouth because, to the contrary, this was not a sound ever heard from Ebenezer Scrooge and he himself was so startled, he tried to silence it. He looked around furtively, feeling almost foolish. He couldn't allow it, not after all these years with no laughter or joy, so he pushed these new feelings back down where they came from, blocking them, shoving them away. But his heart was not in it. In the end, both for his benefit and ours, the effort to contain this new feeling was too hard and finally he gave up, abandoning his struggle. His appearance in the mirror, followed by his imagining of a network of spying ducks had tipped him over the edge and became the catalyst that helped give birth to joyous laughter at last. As much as he tried to silence the sound, it fought to be free of him, because once born, the laughter of so many years would not sit still and demanded to be released.

Eventually he laughed so much he cried, this time, with tears of joy. The teardrops of his new life running down his cheeks.

"I... I wonder what the day is?" he asked himself quietly while wiping his eyes. "I have no idea. I was with the Spirit's for such a long time, it could be any day of the year." Scrooge stood up and, wandering over to the main arched window again, he continued his conversation with himself.

"It could be Spring or Mayday, or August bank holiday," he pondered as he set to and tried to open the window.

"I could have been with them days, (Thump)!

"Month's, (Thump Thump)!

"Even years!

"I'm like a baby," he chuckled, "a newborn baby who knows nothing."

"Grrrrgg…These…windows…are…so…stuck…

"It doesn't matter though, I'd rather be a baby, I'd prefer to be a baby!" And he sang loudly, "Bye baby bunting, Daddy's back from,…flying all over the world learning how not to be a miserable old bugger and how to enjoy Christmas like normal people," he sang in one long breath, laughing at himself.

With one last mighty effort, he managed to wedge his hand under the wooden window frame and push the large window open. "Oh, look at the snow! Everything is new. HELLO EVERYONE!" Scrooge shouted to the world.

Although last night he'd stood and watched the many sad ghosts through this same glass, now he saw only bright sky and fresh clean snow that had fallen all around. Leaning out he breathed in the cold crisp air and felt more alive than he had in years. There was no fog, no low-lying mist. Everything was clear, the sun was shining, on a beautiful, beautiful day!

Seeing a teenage girl walking below, Scrooge bellowed from his window, "What day is it?"

The girl started in absolute fright. She looked around trying to find the owner of the commanding voice but couldn't see anyone.

Scrooge shouted again, "Hey, excuse me, young lady, yes you there, I'm up here! Yes, yes, hello. Good Morning. What day is it?"

The teenager looked up and, seeing Scrooge leaning out of his window yelled, "Geez man!! You scared the hell out of me, nearly give me an 'eart attack yeah?" she shouted angrily, putting her hand on the wall to steady herself after such a fright.

"I'm so sorry my dear," Scrooge shouted back, "I didn't mean to alarm you."

"Alarm me? You scared the frickin' life out of me innit!"

"Please forgive me my love, but I'm quite anxious to know…What day is it?"

"What day is–? That's a joke yeah? Bein' funny yeah? What day is it!"

"No, I'm totally serious," replied Scrooge anxiously. "What day is it?"

"Well 'ave a look around. It's cold, wet and its snowin'. It's obviously 24th of August innit? What bleeding day is it…?" she answered, her voice heavy with sarcasm.

"I'm sorry my dear if I've caused offence, but I'm serious," replied Scrooge anxiously. "I need to know, what day is today?"

"It's…Christmas…Day…innit" replied the girl, very slowly.

"Christmas Day? It is Christmas Day, today? So, everywhere I went and everyone I saw, it all happened in one night?, Ebenezer! You silly fool, of course it did! Didn't I ask if they could all come together, and knock me down with a forklift truck, they did!" And he disappeared inside, laughing in delight and breaking into his happy dance by the windows.

"What?" the girl called from outside.

"What?"

"I said, WHAT?"

"What's what, what?" yelled Scrooge, through the window.

"What. Are. You. Saying?" called the girl. "I can't understand you."

"I was just saying," Scrooge popped his head back out through the window, "that the Spirits have done it all in one night."

"What Spirits?"

"The Christmas Spirits," he explained.

"Uh-huh. Sounds to me like you've already had too much of the old Christmas Spirits already innit," said the girl making a drinking gesture.

Scrooge, however, wasn't listening, as a more sober thought had suddenly occurred to him and he disappeared inside once again. "Oh my Lord. What can I do?" He began to fret, "How can I? Oh no, no, that's not right." And leaning right out of the window a third time he yelled, "It's Christmas Day you say? Young lady, excuse me, excuse me please, don't walk away, I need to talk to you."

The girl looked up again, warily, "Waddya want mister? I'm like, busy, yeah," she replied.

"Er, yes. Could…can you stay there for a moment, I'll come down, just stay there ok, stay there please, yes, stay?" Scrooge pleaded and before she could answer he disappeared from his window, shot out of his apartment and down several flights of stairs to yank open the front door to the bewildered girl in less than a minute.

"Geez man," she said, astonished at his haste. "What's your problem? Chill out yeah....what's your hurry?" Looking him up and down, she took in his dishevelled appearance, unruly hair, muddy boots and with a broad smile exclaimed, "Geeze, what happened to you? Office Christmas party? Or were you attacked by a herd of flyin' reindeer?"

Scrooge, working his way through her accent, grinned in response and answered, "Er, yes. Good Morning, Happy Christmas to you my love. I was wondering, do you know that fancy gift boutique? It's just around the corner. They sell all that expensive food. Chocolates, champagne, perfumes and other things. Do you know it?"

"Er...durr!" replied the girl. "Yeah, of course I do. I like, walk past there every day of my life innit."

"Excellent, so you would know if they have sold that very big Christmas hamper, they had it in the window, the one with all the food and gifts in it, the expensive one," asked Scrooge.

"Nap," she replied, examining her fingernails. "Still there innit, saw it just now. Coupla' people looking through the window, no one buying it though."

"Fantastic!" exclaimed Scrooge, "could you do me a favour? Please? Would you mind? Run there and bring the shop owner here, and please tell him I need to speak to him urgently."

"Err...why should I?" asked the girl. "Wots in it fer me, yeah?"

"Oh. Okay. Bring him back to me and I'll give you five pounds," Scrooge said breathlessly.

"Five quid!" exclaimed the girl, not at all impressed.

"Yes, yes, five pounds if you run and come back with him."

"Why, what you want him for?"

"I want to buy the hamper," said Scrooge simply.

"That thing? It's over four hundred quid innit!"

"It's...a...gift, for a friend"

"Must be a good friend, yeah?" she said suggestively.

Scrooge answered softly, "Yes, a very good friend. Will you run there for me? Please, will you? It's extremely important. I give you my word I'll give you five pounds...I can give it to you now if you like, if you would promise to go, it's so important you see?"

The girl held up a hand, interrupting him hurriedly, "Okay, okay man, stop talking! I'll go for you, but I ain't running. I don't run anywhere; I don't run in the snow and I don't in me good boots, yeah? I could slip and snap off a heel. And I ain't risking them for just five quid, yeah?"

With that, the young woman, walking delicately in her fancy sheepskin footwear, turned around and set off plodding through the snow, back the way she came.

Scrooge clapped his hands in delight and started to retreat inside, but then a thought struck him, and, poking his head around the pillar entrance of the apartment block, he yelled, "If you bring him back in less than ten minutes, I'll give you fifty!!"

That brought her to a sudden stop. She leaned against the wall, pulled off her boots, and wearing only her socks, took off through the snow at top speed.

Scrooge ran back upstairs and began fiddling around looking for paper and pens. "I'll send it to Bob's family," Scrooge giggled. "The basket alone is bigger than Tim!"

His investigation, punctuated by him singing carols, badly and with the wrong words, was interrupted a short time later by the sound of the girl calling up "Oi, mister!" From the street below, and by three heavy thumps in rapid succession on the downstairs door.

Scrooge danced lightly down the steps again. Opening the heavy oak door he observed the woman, boots in hand, standing beside a twenty-something man in a farmer's apron. Both had just exited a black Toyota HiAce, with a white logogram on its side that read, *Hermie's 7 Day Emergency Gift Boutique*.

At her assertion of, "That's him, that's the guy," the man put out his hand for Scrooge to shake and started to say, "The young girl here…"

"I told you, it's Sheila, okay," she interrupted him impatiently.

Curiously, the man was standing with his hand out, staring at Scrooge in astonishment.

"Oh yeah," explained Sheila with a cheeky smile, "I forgot to tell you, He looks like something the cat dragged in."

"Uh-huh. Okay…Shelia says you wanted me urgently. What can I do for you?"

Scrooge invited them out of the cold snow and into the warm foyer and was about to speak when Sheila popped in front of him saying, "Err.... Think it's me first...innit?"

Scrooge thanked her profusely for her help and gave Sheila the promised money, which, despite her alarmingly long fingernails, she managed to take graciously. Then, sitting on a bench by the stairs, she removed her socks, trying in vain to wring out some of the wet slush and snow. Thinking better of putting them on again, she pulled her fur-lined boots over her bare feet, stood up, said to Scrooge, "Thanks mister," and handed him her socks. Stuffing the fifty pounds into the back pocket of her jeans, she gave each man a quick peck on the cheek, bidding them both to "Have a Happy Christmas yeah," and went on her way.

Scrooge and the deli man both waved her goodbye, and Scrooge, having put the socks down, wiped his wet hands on his dressing-gown saying, "I know it's a bit late, as it's already Christmas Day, but could I buy the hamper in your window and have it delivered to a...a...friend of mine in Camden? Could that be done?"

The man smiled and said, "Of course Sir, we can do that. Camden is a bit far from here but..."

"Well of course I must pay for you to deliver it!" cried Scrooge.

"Then I can take it straight away, yes Sir."

Scrooge danced a little two-step, shook the man's hand again and exclaimed, "Excellent, excellent! Tell me, what's your name?"

"Jake, well Jacob really, but I prefer to be called Jake."

Ebenezer paused in his counting of the money. "Jacob?" He said, "Jacob" and with a soft smile at the synchronicity of the moment, he handed Jake Bob Cratchit's address, gave him payment for the hamper, payment for delivery, plus an extra fifty pounds for himself, after all, it was Christmas. However, he said, he insisted on one stipulation when delivering the hamper. Jake wasn't to tell Bob who had sent it no matter how many times he asked. It was to remain a secret, that was especially important.

Jacob left with a wave, promising to take the hamper right away, but as he turned to leave, he called out to Scrooge saying, "Oh, by the way Sir, your buzzer isn't working, perhaps you should get it fixed for the new year?"

Scrooge smiled, nodded, then turned to go back inside. He looked again at the keypad that had become Marley's face and thought of the changes it had heralded for him. He ran his hand gently over the buttons and whispered to himself, "It worked for me. I won't ever forget it."

Back inside Scrooge had a hot bath and could hardly shave, his razor wobbling dangerously as he laughed and splashed about. He finally managed to finish without mishap and began to dress. When he'd been charging around earlier Scrooge had been pulling bits out of his wardrobe and dresser, looking for his best clothes, trying things on and throwing them off in a bid to wear the best outfit he could manage on this new day. Now he had found the wool suit still hanging in his wardrobe, and the woollen overcoat. Putting them on. he smoothed the fabric of the jacket down with tears in his eyes. "They've not been taken," he whispered to himself. "They've not been sold." Blowing out a gulping sigh, he wiped his eyes with thumb and forefinger, then threw a scarf around his neck at a jaunty angle and headed for the door.

Out, out onto the cold streets, he mixed amongst the people he'd seen when he was with the ghost of Christmas Present. Scrooge walked along, wishing everyone a 'Merry Christmas', and collecting Christmas greetings in return as several people stopped and smiled or said, "And you mate, Merry Christmas, yeah." He was to confess many times later, to countless people, that of all the sounds he'd heard that morning, those simple Christmas greetings had been the most joyous to his heart.

Scrooge hadn't gone more than half a mile when he ran slap bang into Mr Huffam and Smyth, the two gentlemen who had come into his office yesterday asking for a donation to charity. Each carried a large box of donated goods and were obviously on their way somewhere, so they made no effort to stop after realising it was Scrooge they had collided with. Neither did either man wish him a Happy Christmas, as they had been doing before, to everyone else they'd met.

Scrooge knew the men were simply reacting to his rudeness of yesterday, and he was determined to right that wrong forthwith. Squaring his shoulders, he whispered to himself Fan's words, "Start as you mean to go on," and blocked the gentlemen's path, holding out his hand.

"Good morning gentlemen," he said. "I am so glad I managed to see you both this early today. I was going to look for you. I imagine you have no desire to stop and talk awhile. I just wanted to wish you both a very Merry Christmas. I hope you had good luck yesterday, really, a very Merry Christmas..."

Both men looked at him, ignoring his hand. They placed their boxes on the ground and regarded him with open hostility until Mr Huffam said quietly, "It's Mister Scrooge, isn't it?" Emphasising the "mister" as Scrooge had done the evening before.

"Yes, and I'm sure after my dreadful behaviour yesterday you have no wish to talk to me. However, I was hoping you'd let bygones be bygones, allow me to apologise for my rudeness and offer a donation of…" and Scrooge took a bulky envelope filled with cash from his pocket and pressed it into Mr Smyth's hand.

Both looked at him in disbelief as Mr Smyth exclaimed, "Wow! That's…goodness me how…geez, how much is that exactly?"

Mr Huffam spoke over him, declaring, "Mr Scrooge, that's quite a large amount, it's very generous of you. You're sure? We couldn't thank you enough for this, it will help so many. You ARE sure? Absolutely sure? Thank you very much."

And as they spoke, Scrooge talked over *them*, his voice an urgent plea, "No no no, no no! Shush…shush…" And flapped his hands, looking about conspiratorially, "You mustn't thank me, please. I don't want thanks for finally doing what everyone else's been doing for years. I'm just sorry I've never contributed before, so that amount includes several years of extremely overdue payments. And you will accept it from me, yes? You will?"

The men were, of course, happy to accept Scrooge's belated but sincere gift and Mr Smyth quickly slipped it into his inside coat pocket for safekeeping.

"Also, well, I was wondering if both of you will come to my office again, as soon as possible?" asked Scrooge. "I want to talk more with you about what you do and how I can help you." Here Scrooge handed the men his business card, "That's got my mobile number on it. You can call me whenever you wish. Anytime, honestly, whenever you want. Will you please come to see me again? Before the new year, perhaps?" He pressed both men urgently.

Both agreed they would indeed come to see Scrooge before the new year, and the offer of a new association was sealed with an eager handshake.

Scrooge continued on his way feeling better than he had in years. He was beginning to understand how giving could make you feel so much happier than taking. Behind him, the two gentlemen called out, "Thank you, Mr

Scrooge, A Merry Christmas, Sir!" And, collecting their boxes they walked away, happily discussing what to do with this new, unexpected endowment.

All at once came the sound of church bells ringing through the city. The unmistakable deep throated "*ding dong*" of larger bells blended with the delicate "*tingle*" of smaller ones so that all around Scrooge was a celebration of sound that danced through the air, singing a wonderful melody on this bright and beautiful day. Scrooge's heart was getting lighter as his walk eventually brought him to the steps of an old Regency church. Tentatively, he followed the people inside. Listening, and I mean *really* listening, for the first time to the words and hymns echoing around him, he bent his head and whispered the ancient prayers he had learned as a child. At the end of the service, he looked at all the people and remembered the ghost of Christmas Present's words, *"At this time of the year the love of the people is so strong it's miraculous in itself. I venerate the love that brought all these people together because there is no other force like it in the world."*

Leaving the church, Scrooge wandered restlessly for the rest of the morning. He didn't want to return to his empty flat alone, so he walked through parks and snow laden streets watching families arriving at houses filled with Christmas joy and children riding new bicycles and skateboards in the streets. Everything he saw filled him with joy and a new-found determination to celebrate Christmas...

Meanwhile, in Camden Town, Jake had found the Cratchit house and was currently trying to deliver the hamper. After ringing the doorbell, he worked his way through several members of the family, telling each one in turn about his delivery.

He started with a lad about ten years old who threw open the door as if expecting someone else and was suitably disappointed at finding Jake standing there instead. After carefully explaining who he was and why he was there, the boy nodded, smiled, and closed the door in his face. When nothing happened for five minutes Jake rang the bell again. This time it was opened by a girl, approximately the same age. Jake smiled, looked at his clipboard asking, "Is this the Cratchit residence?" In the background, he could hear a boy's voice yelling, "I *said* there was someone at the door!"

The girl, smiling at Jake, nodded shyly, and he replied he had a delivery for them. Saying nothing, she smiled again and disappeared, but unlike her brother, she left the door open. A minute later she reappeared, tugging along an older girl, possibly her sister, who wearing a flour stained apron and a pained expression. Jacob repeated the details of his mission and smiled a wide, friendly smile. After all, it was Christmas Day.

The girl looked at the basket on the trolley and suddenly, without forewarning, she threw back her head and shrilled at the top of her lungs, "PEE-TEER!!"

Jake leapt back in fright, the clipboard and pen flipping out of his hands as he was deafened by one of the loudest voices he'd ever heard. Two squirrels eating from a nut feeder shot up a tree, several dogs started barking, and from somewhere or other he thought he heard a duck quacking.

A youth in his late teens, who could only be Peter responding to a command that loud, came running to the door and said to his sister crossly, "Belinda, will you stop yelling my name out like that, I keep telling you. I nearly poured boiling water all over myself!"

The girl looked at her brother sheepishly saying, "Oh...sorry...erm, this guy says that's for us," before she disappeared back into the house.

Peter turned to apologise and shake Jake's hand, but Jake, made witless by the ear-splitting yell couldn't catch his breath. His heart was thumping sixty to the dozen, while his heated, some would say natural, exclamation of "*Geez-us-tonight girl!*" was lost amongst the racket of the neighbours' dogs. As Peter helpfully picked up his clipboard and pen, Jake crashed on to the

Cratchit's azalea pots and was frantically squirting his Ventolin like someone using breath freshener on a first date.

Eventually, when he at last caught his breath, Jake explained again why he was at the Cratchit's front door, with a hamper, on Christmas Day. Peter nodded, then, with the words, "Half a sec, I've got spuds on the stove," he also disappeared, promising to get someone else.

By this time Jake was thinking if he had much more trouble, he was going to give up and drop the bloody hamper off at the Salvation Army.

A young woman carrying a cup of coffee came to the door, followed by a pugnacious scruffy white terrier, who sat at her feet, tail wagging and tongue lolling, hopelessly in love. She listened to Jake's explanation and asked him to step into the kitchen while she went to find her father. Amy offered Jake a seat and told Martha that Bob was still in the garden trying to round up the duck and he better hurry up and catch it if they were ever going to sit down to their Christmas dinner.

Jake blanched, his expression, horrified. Both women laughed, and Martha quickly set his mind at rest telling him the duck was a pet, and not destined to end the day plucked, stuffed, and roasted, then finally served up for dinner alongside sprouts, carrots, and potatoes.

By the time Bob came in, sucking his fingers where he'd been bitten, complaining he should leave the daft duck to fight the foxes off by itself, Jake had accepted coffee and a mince pie from Amy, while she was dealing with her brussels. Jake brought Bob up to date with the whole hamper situation and confirmed while he couldn't tell him who his benefactors were, they seemed like genuinely nice people and wished Bob and his family a Happy Christmas.

A lot of loud discussions later, Bob allowed Jake to bring the hamper in. This wasn't easy as he was now surrounded by the children who were all extremely excited, had to step over the still grumbling dog, who watched his every move, and past the now present duck, who'd apparently wandered in to see what all the kerfuffle was about. Finally, he was about to drop the hamper by the table, when a cry went up and young Mathew disappeared for a second, only to surface holding a ferret, who, it seemed, had followed the duck into the kitchen, and was lying exactly where he was going to dump the large and heavy basket.

Jake finally set the hamper by the kitchen table and asked all the kids who was going to be the one to open it first. By this time, he was thoroughly enchanted with this loud, unconventional, whimsical family and laughed with them all as the youngsters jumped up, hand in the air, shouting "me, me!" in answer to his question. Before he left, they were all on a first name basis, and he'd even promised, although he wasn't sure how, to come to dinner on 31st December and celebrate bringing in the New Year.

After he left, Bob looked at Amy, who shrugged her shoulders and said, "He's right. It says, *To the Cratchit Family*, and the address on the label is ours, Bob, it's got to be for us." No one in the family could think who would have sent it to them, so finally they gave up wondering and Bob gently undid the straps on the big basket, unpacking the contents to the excitement and delight of the rest of the family.

Chapter 15: First Christmas

Scrooge was still enjoying his walk in this new world when, rounding the corner of a particularly busy area, he got caught up in a large group of friends, several sporting Santa hats or reindeer antlers, all rugged up warm against the cold winters weather. Joyfully, they wished him a Merry Christmas, shaking his hand or patting him on the back, so it took him a few seconds to work his way out from the noisy group. Suddenly he found himself facing a young woman. Her beautiful blue eyes shone out from her heart shaped face and her long blonde hair fell in waves past her shoulders. Even though Scrooge had never been introduced to her before, he knew exactly who she was.

She took his breath away, she was the image of Bella as he remembered her. Her long blonde hair the only difference from her mother.

She smiled at him and in a voice just like Bella's offered a laughing apology. Scrooge smiled too, then, before he even knew what he'd done, he'd put out his hand and said, "It's Rose, isn't it?"

Rose stopped and stared at him, looking for a sign of recognition. "I, err, yes, but I'm not sure I know…?"

"No, you won't know me, sweetheart," said Scrooge shaking her hand, "but I used to know your mother when we were both younger."

"Oh!" she smiled. "Oh you did. That's lovely."

"I'm afraid she might not remember me too fondly, but perhaps you would give her a message for me?"

"Yes, ok…yes of course," said Rose.

"Could you tell her that the man she once knew has finally come back and wishes her all the happiness in the world. And say that his biggest regret is that he turned her away. Will you say that?"

"Of course, Mr, err, Mr?"

"Ebenezer. My name is Ebenezer. She, she will know who I am."

"Well, Ebenezer, I'll pass on your message."

"You'll be able to remember my name, my love? Ebenezer, it's quite unusual."

"Oh, no problem," Rose laughed. "We used to have a cat called Ebenezer. It was a fat, bad-tempered old thing. Mum said she called it Ebenezer because it used to eat more than its fair share of food, but she loved it all the same." She smiled again and checked her watch, "I must go. Happy Christmas, Ebenezer."

"And to you Rose, Happy Christmas," said Scrooge.

Rose smiled and walked away. After about twenty yards she turned and waved to Scrooge, who waved back, smiling.

A fat bad-tempered old cat that ate more than its fair share of food, he thought to himself, then laughed aloud as he went on his way.

The opening and closing of doors along his walk allowed the deliciously tempting fragrances of Christmas dinner to waft out into the streets and, unconsciously, his feet guided him towards his nephew Fred's house. As he approached, he could see several people through the big bay windows and Scrooge had to walk up and down the pavement a few times before he'd gathered enough courage to dash up to the front door and ring the bell.

From inside the house, Scrooge heard a dog bark, and several guests all shouted, "Doorbell!" Followed by the unmistakable sound of Fred's voice calling, "Well will somebody answer the door please?"

A woman's voice answered, "I'll get it" then, "Blast it, Lucky would you move..."

The front door was thrown open by an attractive young woman with soft brown, shoulder length, wavy hair and brown eyes who Scrooge recognised from his time with the ghost of Christmas Present as Fred's wife Kate. She was holding a glass of wine in one hand, a tortilla chip in the other and had a large, fat, shaggy dog sitting by her side.

Kate saw tall, thin man in a black overcoat that was smart and classic, and who looked nervous, yet was plainly ordinary.

"Oh, err, hello," she said. "Sorry, the dog keeps sitting in front of the door so we can't open it."

"Well, he keeps the draft out I suppose," replied Scrooge.

She smiled, "Good point, actually he's a she and expecting puppies any day, that's why she's so heavy to move," she said, scratching the dog's ears affectionately. Lucky looked back at her mistress fondly, licking the chip she was holding, then taking it from her hand altogether.

"Anyway, can I help you?" Kate asked.

"Yes," replied Scrooge suddenly nervous. "I...err, yes. I wonder, is Fred here? He...err...he invited me for lunch."

Kate, who knew her husband had asked a couple of people from work over for Christmas dinner, smiled, saying, "Oh yes, of course, he's in the kitchen, come in, come in out of the cold. I'm Kate by the way, go through."

"Thank you my dear, he does know me," said Scrooge with a nervous laugh, as he stepped into the house.

Closing the front door, Kate told the dog off for sitting in the way again, and for being naughty stealing the tortilla chip, both admonitions Lucky promptly ignored. She flopped down on the doormat again and loudly chomped through what was left of the tortilla.

Leading Scrooge into the sitting room, Kate looked about saying, "Everyone, everyone this a friend from Freddie's work. This is the whole gang, gang, this is...oh...sorry, I didn't even ask your name?"

Scrooge didn't answer her. Still nervous he called, "Fred?" very softly, then cleared his throat and called much louder, "Fred?"

A sudden clatter issued from the kitchen and Fred appeared in the doorway with an unopened bottle of red in his hand. Looking completely surprised he shouted, "Uncle Ebenezer!" and rushed forward to grab his hand, shaking it in genuine surprise. Everyone was on their feet in astonishment as Fred hugged him with real happiness.

Scrooge returned the hug awkwardly as he spoke softly saying, "Fred, I've...erm...well, I've come to dinner Fred, if...well, if I'm still welcome."

"Still welcome, of course, you are. Darling, darling, this is my Uncle, Ebenezer Scrooge," Fred said to his wife. "Uncle this is my wife, Kate."

Kate, still playing catch-up about who was who here, was momentarily struck dumb. She'd expected a colleague from her husband's work for dinner, but instead the mild-mannered gentleman in front of her was, according to Fred, his Uncle Ebenezer. Never expecting him to accept Fred's repeated invitation to Christmas dinner, she had no time to adjust to the reality of him standing in her sitting room, with her husband enthusiastically introducing him to all their friends. As a woman who liked to prepare for things, she'd never thought to check with Fred what she should ever do if she ever *met* his uncle. Was there anything she shouldn't mention for instance, any family skeletons in the closet, or subjects she should avoid? But even as all this was racing through her mind, she looked at her husband and said incredulously, *"THIS is Uncle Ebenezer?"* Her voice expressing disbelief as she was unable to marry up the image she had of him as a wicked, shrivelled up, Richard III humped-back old miser, with the mild, slightly humorous man who'd knocked on her door.

Scrooge turned to his niece by marriage and said, "Yes. I'm afraid I'm your grumpy, silly, stubborn, bad tempered, old Uncle Ebenezer. May I stay for dinner?"

She looked at him for a few seconds, then to Fred, then back again. Breaking into a smile, she threw her arms around him and said, "Of course you can, you silly, old, stubborn, bad tempered...what was the other one?"

"Grumpy," everyone answered and then laughed.

"Yes, grumpy Uncle Ebenezer, let's get you a drink!"

Scrooge relaxed with help from the large drink Kate made for him, and Fred introduced him to everyone in the room, all of whom were delighted and very curious to meet him and said they hoped he had a Merry Christmas. And he did. A wonderful meal with champagne and good company helped Scrooge unwind further. He found himself talking quite easily to many of the other guests, including several of the ladies, all of whom were being very polite but were itching to know more about him and why he came to dinner. English manners however, precluded them asking him outright, so although they dropped many light hints, they got no real explanation other than he'd decided he wanted to spend Christmas with his nephew. Unable to break centuries of polite programming, and no one knowing an American they could invite round for afternoon drinks, who they were certain could be relied upon to sidestep decades of hereditary gentility to uncover the truth, everyone had to content themselves with their lot. Even an Australian could probably get the gossip they wanted, but the only Aussie anyone knew was Briana, and she'd flown back to Queensland for a Christmas of sun, surf and seafood and wouldn't be back until after 12th night...

After lunch, Scrooge was feeling very relaxed and happily joined in the games of *Charades*, *Yes and No* and *Who Am I?*, all of which he thoroughly enjoyed.

Later he had a lengthy conversation with Kate in the kitchen, while the two made coffee. Mostly Kate talked about how she and Fred had met, and she told him all about their wedding. Her engagement ring was, as he thought, the emerald ring Samuel had given Fan all those years ago, and by giving it to Kate, it made the whole wedding proposal so much more special and romantic. She said she knew it meant a lot to Fred for her to be wearing his mother's ring.

Scrooge helped make the coffee using their fancy barista express, a completely new experience for him as he'd always had instant at home, and he enjoyed it so much, it took all Kate's persuasion to get him away from the machine when they'd finished. He helped fill the dishwasher, beguiled by its style and function, and gobsmacked his niece by confirming that while he did have a dishwasher in his apartment, he'd never, in seven years, used it. And he was so impressed by the iRobot Roomba when it slid out to vacuum around, that he followed it everywhere it went for a full five minutes, chuckling all the way. To Scrooge all this was new. He'd not only isolated himself from the world but from what was in it and had missed too much.

***

"Tall, over six feet anyway, with blue eyes, sort of skinny, about sixty-ish," said Rose, who was describing to her mother the encounter she'd had with the stranger on her way over. "I can't remember his exact words, but it was sort of, tell your mother that the man she used to know has come back and he hopes she's happy and wishes her a Happy Christmas and the worst thing he ever did was let her go. Something like that anyway. I was too startled to remember it all."

"And that's all he said?" asked Bella. "Nothing else?"

"Only his name. I can remember that because of the cat. He said his name was, Ebenezer."

Bella looked up in astonishment. "Ebenezer, are you sure?"

"Yup, because I said we had a cat with the same name, a fat cat that ate too much, which he seemed to find very funny."

"Ebenezer," said Bella softly. "Well, well, well. So money-mad Scrooge is dead and Benny's finally come back...interesting," she whispered and smiled to herself.

"So, who is he mum?"

"Who is who?" asked a woman entering the kitchen, carrying two empty wine glasses. "These are dead. Wine doesn't last as long as it used to when we were younger." She turned to Bella, "Okay if these go in the dishwasher?"

"Yes, thanks, Trish" answered Bella. Trish disposed of the dirty glasses, then looked at Bella and Rose. "Well then, don't keep me in suspense, who is who?"

Bella nodded to Rose, who said, "I met a man today who said he used to be a friend of mums and told me to give her a message. He said I was to tell her the man she used to know has come back, and he hopes she's happy and wishes her a Happy Christmas, and the worst thing he ever did was let her go."

"Sounds creepy," said Trish. "Who was it?"

"Said his name was Ebenezer," said Rose, "and I'm trying to get mum to tell me all about him."

Trish breathed in sharply, "You're kidding? Ebenezer, you mean Ebenezer Scrooge?"

"Didn't get his last name, but I suppose so, it's not a common name," and turning again to her mother, Rose asked again, more insistently, "So come on mum, Aunty Trish knows him, spill the beans, who is he?"

"Just someone I used to know before I met your father," Bella replied. "Is that coffee percolating yet?" she said, changing the subject. Putting cups and saucers on a tray she added, "Everyone will be wanting coffee and liqueurs soon."

Rose grabbed her own head with her two hands, "Grrrrgg, that's so infuriating Mum! There's got to be more to it than just, someone I knew before I met your father."

Bella didn't answer, but Trish tipped Rose a wink and said, "Don't worry, I'll give you all the gossipy details later if your Mum doesn't want to."

Bella laughed, saying, "I'm sure you will. That's the problem with a life-long best friend, they know all your secrets."

***

The afternoon wore on at Fred's house, and as the others were engaged in a serious game of Monopoly, Ebenezer finally managed to get Fred on his own in a corner of the sitting room. Fred sat down and turned to his Uncle saying that he couldn't express how happy he was that Scrooge had finally come to dinner. Scrooge smiled and took Fred's hand in his own.

"Now then, my boy," he said, his voice filled with emotion, "what would you like to know about your mother?"

Scrooge talked for hours, telling Fred everything he could remember about Fan. Eventually, everyone abandoned the monopoly game and came to listen. Fuelled by endless cups of coffee, cakes, cookies, and turkey sandwiches, Scrooge answered all Fred's questions as best he could. As it grew darker outside and Fred turned up the fire to keep everyone snug and warm, Ebenezer talked about Fan's sweet nature and understanding, but also that she'd had strong determination, and was fiercely loyal to those she loved. He told Fred how much she'd loved Scrooge all her life, and how much he had always loved her, and of her determination not to lose contact with him despite their father's efforts. With tears in his eyes, he laughed when he said how, as a small child, he couldn't pronounce his R's, so he'd always called her Fan, not Fran or Francesca, and it stuck and became his special name for her. He told too, how she always called him Buzz, her special name for him, instead of Ebenezer.

"Hang on," interrupted Kate, "Why did she call you Buzz? You were both too old to be *Toy Story* fans."

Scrooge, not knowing what *Toy Story* was, laughed and said, "When we were little, she used to call me Eb-ee, short for Ebenezer. But when got older, she said it sounded so much like, "a bee" and so she was going to call me Buzz instead." He smiled again, the memory sweet and joyful.

He spoke about her visits to his school, and how the best day of his life was still the day she came to take him home that last time. Fred brought out the photos he'd had since he was a child and his Uncle told him all about the pictures, filling in the story behind each image that Fred had never known.

Finally he showed Fred and Kate his one and only connection to the past that he always kept with him. Inside his wallet was an old picture Fan had taken in an old-fashioned photo-booth, the likes of which used to stand on railway stations and shopping centres back when Ebenezer had been growing up. She'd needed some for her passport and he'd carried this one in his wallet ever since her death. It was easy to see Fred bore a strong resemblance to his mother, right down to the constant smile and the flashing green eyes.

Soon the women were wiping away tears, and Scrooge found himself hugged by several of them in a kind, maternal way. He was, by this time, getting used to receiving hugs, and found that he rather liked it. Not having had any physical contact with anyone, other than a cool business handshake, since Fan's death, he now realised how much he'd missed normal human touch, and the effect that physical isolation had on him and how he'd viewed the world.

Topper objected playfully and asked was that all he himself needed to get girls' attention, a good sob story? Both Fred and Scrooge roared with laughter as the girls threw cushions and started hitting him with them, calling him an insensitive brute and a soulless barbarian.

Scrooge couldn't possibly tell Fred all about Fan in one day he said, there had been so much to share about her. Looking at the clock above the mantle, he'd been talking for over 6 hours and there was still more to tell. But that would wait for another day. He also promised he would look out some old photographs he had of Fan that were kept in a precious album, locked in a drawer, in a desk in his house. (It appeared when it came to his sister, Fan DID have some cash value!)

At last, it was very late. Everyone else had left, and Scrooge too began to make noises about going home. But before he left, he insisted that Fred and Kate both come to dinner with him on New Year's Eve. A celebration to mark the new year and the new Scrooge! They laughed and the dinner date was made. Kate popped outside looking for a taxi and Scrooge took this moment of privacy to put his hand on Fred's shoulder.

"Fred," he said, very quietly, almost afraid. "I need to tell you something, something I did, something very wicked that I must tell you about and ask your forgiveness for. You see I...I...when you were born, I..."

Fred put his hand on the Scrooge's arm, interrupting him, saying, "It's okay, Uncle, I understand."

"No, no you don't understand. What I did was very wrong. What I felt was no excuse. I let you down when you were a baby. I let Fan down. I let your father down. I must tell you...you see I was very angry with your father, for not being there, for leaving her to struggle, then when you were born, God forgive me, but I blamed you for her death. I was so wrong. You were just an innocent baby, but I couldn't see it. I just couldn't...I..."

"I know what you're talking about Uncle, it's okay, don't get upset," said Fred again.

259

"It's just, I loved Fan so much, she was the only one in my family that loved me and then when she died, I said some terrible, awful things…about you, about your father. Awful things, I'm ashamed to say. I just wanted her back you see, just her…I didn't think."

"Ebenezer," said Fred, catching Scrooge's attention by using his first name without the usual "Uncle" appended to it. "Stop now! I know what happened after my mother died. I know how it affected you and I know what you said. It's water under the bridge. Stop thinking about it. I never held it against you."

"But I said some awful things." said Scrooge, before whispering, "How can you possibly forgive me?"

"I forgave you years ago, now you must forgive yourself. My father never held it against you. He always understood how you felt and desperately wanted to tell you. Now you need to let it go. What would Fan say? "Just don't screw it up anymore," right?. "Start as you mean to go on." Wasn't that what she always said? Now you need to let it go."

"How, how did find out about it?" asked Scrooge.

"I asked my father when I was younger, why you didn't want to visit us. He explained it all to me. I've wanted to say something to you for years, but, well…anyway, now you know."

Scrooge and Fred hugged, both with tears in their eyes as Kate came rushing in through the front door saying hurriedly, "Got one, finally! Oh, what's all this? Caught you chaps in some male bonding have I?"

Scrooge pulled on his coat and buttoned it against the cold as Kate held the taxi. Before he got in, he reached out and gave Fred another hug, saying, "Your mother would have been immensely proud of you, you know. She never abandoned anyone she loved either."

Fred smiled, suddenly shy and looked down, shuffling his feet to clear his glassy tear-filled eyes. Then Scrooge turned to Kate, took her hand, and kissed it.

"And with you my love, she would have found a determined ally who loves her son so much."

Kate grinned and gave him a high five to cover her emotions and so smiling at them both he jumped into the cab. As it pulled away, he yelled out of the window to Fred, "Don't forget to call the newspapers about the Christmas miracle!" And he laughed at the look of puzzlement, then the dawning of realisation on Fred's face.

Walking back inside, Kate turned to Fred and asked her husband, "What Christmas miracle?"

Fred, pausing on the doorstep under the mistletoe, kissed his wife, saying "It's a long story."

Chapter 16: Boxing Day

The following day Scrooge had a lighter heart than he'd had for years. His delight in all things Christmas had been so wonderful yesterday he thought he would never have a better day in his life. It was time for so many changes, and he had so much to do he couldn't wait to get started. But today? Today was Boxing Day.

Traditionally, St. Stephen's Day, it was called Boxing Day by the British because, in the past, it was the day those in service received gifts from their employers, their 'Christmas Box' and a day they could return home and visit their own family, taking with them any leftovers from the huge Christmas banquets of those they worked for. Eventually, St Stephen's Day had been almost lost in time and Boxing Day had taken over as a second day of rest and celebration with family.

Boxing Day was another public holiday Scrooge was forced to put up with, but one he complained less about. Even so, he griped, moaned, kvetched and protested up to, during and after the holiday, declaring not only was it not necessary but it was dangerous as it gave, "the great un-washed" too much time to think. He was rude, disagreeable, and downright miserable about it and all holidays, but Boxing Day held less of the sad and desperate memories than Christmas did for him.

Boxing Day was actually filled with some happier memories for Scrooge. Memories of Fan visiting his school with gifts, a huge picnic, with crackers to pull and games to play. It was lying in the snow outside school making snow angels; of building snowmen and snowball fights, then running back to the common room for hot cocoa in front of a warm fire. It was playing cards and charades, singing carols, and opening gifts and telling bad jokes.

Boxing Day was Mr Fezziwig, calling round to take Scrooge to the pub for a pint with Mrs Fezziwig, and Dick stopping to pick up Fan on the way. It was a warm saloon bar, lots of laughter and singing and Guinness. It was Fan drinking Baby Cham, saying the bubbles went up her nose.

Boxing Day was him and Bella in their pj's in front of the fire watching *Jason and the Argonauts* on TV, eating cold turkey sandwiches and Christmas pudding fried in butter with clotted cream. It was swapping gifts and kissing under the mistletoe, cuddling, loving and being so happy. Boxing Day was Bella and him, outside the pub, dancing together in the freezing cold under a full moon, close and warm. Boxing Day was a day he wasn't alone, not until Fan died.

After that, Boxing Day was a day he'd spend in the office, quietly catching up on paperwork, checking contracts, finding errors, correcting mistakes so that he would have a large pile ready for Cratchit to amend on the 27th.

Today he had the entire day to fill and found he couldn't sit still. He'd watched the dawn come up over the city on the second day of his new life. He had still had no sleep but didn't feel tired. He was like the *Energizer Bunny*, full of ideas and ready to get started. He made list after list of what changes he wanted to make, sticking them onto the wall in order of priority. He started by sorting through drawers and files, bundled together old papers and stacks of those hoarded takeaway cups, all ready for the garbage, and chucked out bag after bag of useless rubbish. He spent half an hour going up and down in the service lift to dump the bags into the apartment skips, to the mounting curiosity of his fellow tenants who'd watched his activities with lots of curtain twitching. Their curiosity reached fever pitch when apartment three decided he would take his dog for a walk to get a closer look and received a pleasant, "good morning" from Scrooge as he walked past. This surprised him so much he stumbled over his Scottie who didn't appreciate the foot fumble, growling its disapproval. A phone around on his return set the other neighbours clacking so much that apartment one declared she had to see it for herself and, despite the freezing temperatures, she took out some bacon rind for the robins and almonds for the squirrels. She too was gobsmacked when Scrooge waved and called hello on his way back upstairs for more bags of rubbish.

Then Scrooge went to his local for a pub lunch. It was warm and full of customers; He enjoyed the atmosphere and the company even though he was eating alone. It reminded him of all those times at the pub with Dick after work, popping in for a drink after the movies with Fan, and a quick ploughman's lunch with Bella. Now he leisurely read his newspaper, one he'd actually paid for, and slowly ate a large bowl of Christmas pudding with brandy cream.

Home again, he opened the locked drawer in his desk and took out his photograph albums filled with pictures of Fan. He took them into the sitting room, turned on his fire and made coffee. Then, oblivious to the passing hours, he looked lovingly at all the pictures, remembering those moments that were fixed in time in the photographs before him. He laughed and cried, and he talked out loud to Fan, as if she was there with him, reminding her of this moment and that, and he could hear her laughing too, quite clearly, as she always did. Then he told her about his time with Fred yesterday, about Fred's wife, and said sorry he hadn't kept his promise about being there as Fred grew up. As the day grew darker and colder, Scrooge had finally cried out all his pain and those emotions he hadn't allowed himself to feel when Fan died. In the end he felt so much better that he couldn't describe it. He knew Fan was there, looking at him, just like the Spirit of Tiny Tim had looked at his family when Scrooge had been with the ghost of Christmas Future. He could hear her saying, "It's all okay Buzz, it's all going to be fine from now on. Just don't screw it up any more ok?" He laughed, remembering Fred quoting those exact words yesterday. "I won't Fan, I promise," he said quietly. "I won't this time."

Scrooge's Second Dream

It started as it always did. The school, the car driven by the chauffeur up the magnificent sweeping driveway. The master, matron and Teddy standing by the main doors, waiting to receive him as a little boy. He would arrive in that car with his father, six years old, to that huge, strange house with only Teddy to look after him until the other boys came back from holidays. He watched from the outside, as once again the dream's familiarity threaded through his sleeping mind. The car stopped and the driver got out, went to the rear door to let his younger self and his father out just as he always did...

But then....

The door opened and Fan stepped out. His Fan, beautiful as she was that day she took him away from school. Smiling, she took the drivers hand to steady herself, then walked to the steps where now, *he was waiting*.

264

Not a young Scrooge, not a child, not even the age he was when he left the school that day…but as he was now, older, tired, grey, but with new hope.

He walked down the steps and she smiled. Grabbing her up in a hug, he spun her off her feet, around and around and around.

She laughed with him, then took his hand, saying, "It's time to leave all this behind you now, Buzz. Time to look to the future," and she pulled him into the car. He watched from the outside again as the driver shut the door, dropped into the driver's seat and the car motored off, away from all his sad memories forever.

When he woke up, his face was wet with tears, but his heart was light and free.

Chapter 17: And As For Bob...

The next morning, he was up, listening to the dawn chorus, dressed and down to his office trying to look busy and as much like his old self as he could. He'd been thinking since yesterday about the best way to approach Bob Cratchit and had been practising what to say over and over. He wanted his change of heart to be a complete surprise, so last night he rehearsed what he was going to say, standing in front of the bathroom mirror as he brushed his teeth, and practised it again when he was shaving this morning.

He remembered what Fred had said when he'd been in the company of the ghost of Christmas Present, that Bob had received lots of job offers from other companies but chose to stay where he was. Now, Ebenezer earnestly wanted Bob to see he was sincere, but also to surprise him, so he'd played out the likely scene dozens of times to get just the right effect.

Currently, he was sitting at his desk, bubbling with excitement as he watched the clock move past the time Bob was due to arrive. A little box wrapped with a ribbon was in his desk drawer. This was going to be goo-ood!

It was forty-two minutes past when Bob came puffing through the door, quickly removing his overcoat and gloves, and opening some files on his desk in one fluid, unbroken movement. As soon as his bottom hit the chair behind his desk, Scrooge made his move.

"Well, well, well now," came Scrooge's voice, slowly, snarly and rude as he could make it. "And why are you so LATE this morning, Mister Cratchit? Didn't I specifically ask you to come in early today to make up for those two days you had off? Come in here, Sir! AT ONCE!" (Ooh, could he do this without bursting into laughter too early he wondered?)

"I am sorry, Mr Scrooge," said Bob pushing himself to his feet and walking into the room. "I'm really not that late, but I overslept a little. We had such a lovely celebration you see, someone sent us a wonderful hamper and…" Bob dried up under Scrooges steady gaze. He tried a final attempt at mitigation, "After all, it is only once a year Sir," he finished wearily.

"Indeed," said Scrooge very slowly, "well that is as may be with you, Sir, but I've had it up to here with this inconsiderate behaviour and I've made a decision, Mr Cratchit." Scrooge stood up and thumped his desk in a threatening way. "Yes! Made my decision!

THUMP!

"I'm afraid you have left me no alternative…"

THUMP!

"Mr Scrooge…" interrupted Bob despairingly. Wondering if he really had to go over the whole public holiday thing again. "If you would just understa—"

Scrooge talked over him, ignoring his protest, "NO ALTERNATIVE SIR, THAN FOR ME TO **IMMEDIATELY GIVE YOU THIS!**" he thundered, thrusting a serious looking envelope at Bob with a stern scowl on his face.

Bob took the envelope but made no move to open it, fearing the contents.

"OPEN IT MR CRATCHIT, I INSIST. OPEN IT AT ONCE," bellowed Scrooge.

Bob looked down and, with a sigh at the inevitable, slit open the top of the envelope. Expecting to find his P45 papers indicating he was now unemployed, his only thought was, what would he tell Amy?

Inside the envelope however, he found cash.

Lots of cash.

A great deal of cash.

By his quick count, there had to be at least five thousand quid in the envelope!

Bob was totally confused and looked up at Scrooge in astonishment. Scrooge was watching him with a huge grin almost too big for his face. "And I'm also going to double your salary, starting immediately!" he said, slapping his palm on the desk to emphasise his promise.

Bob hadn't moved, was still standing, holding the cash, when Scrooge bounced from around his desk like Tigger, grabbed his hand and shook it vigorously for a few seconds. Then, unable to confine his joy to a hand-shake, he grabbed Bob in a huge bear hug!

A hug!

From Ebenezer Scrooge!

He looked deeply into Bob's eyes, his own dancing in delight, so much so Bob wondered if he was on something and said, "Yes Bob, it's true. I've not gone bonkers, I can assure you. I will increase your salary, and you can take that Christmas bonus home today to your lovely wife and family. Plus, if you're agreeable, we can go to lunch at the pub and chat about how I can help you with your finances and other commitments, especially any needs for Tim. In fact, we can talk all day. I've closed up, and all we're going to do today is talk about you, Bob Cratchit, and what your family needs."

Bob still hadn't said anything, mainly because he couldn't get a word in, but Scrooge's actions were so out of character, especially giving him such a large amount of money, that Bob was greatly alarmed. He was trying to work out whether Scrooge was sincere or had indeed gone crackers. If the latter, it placed Bob in an awkward position, because he had entered the lion's cage, as it were, without a whip and a chair. Now he slowly stepped back-wards and scanned around for a weapon of some sort, thinking if he needed to, he could at least knock Scrooge down and make a run for it while he was getting to his feet.

Scrooge was looking earnestly at Bob's face and smiled at his confusion. "It's okay Bob," he said, putting his hand on his arm, "you heard me cor-rectly, lunch today at the pub? You pick the place, I'll pay the bill. I'd like to do what I can to help your struggling family, and we can talk about it all day. Yes? But first, I have a gift for you Bob Cratchit!"

Scrooge leaned back over his desk to open the top drawer and retrieved the little white box wrapped with the ribbon. He handed it to Bob. Looking suspiciously at it, wondering what more surprise this could hold after the five thousand pounds, Bob made no move to unwrap it.

"Go on, go on, open it," said Scrooge happily, dancing from foot to foot with excitement.

Bob looked at Scrooge, then slowly removed the ribbon and opened the box.

Inside was the tap wheel for the radiator in his office.

Bob slowly smiled.

"Yes!" laughed Scrooge, delighted. "You go and turn up the heat in that office of yours before you do anything else Bob Cratchit!"

Bob's smile grew larger and he looked up into Scrooge's eyes, seeing the changes there and the layers and layers of Scrooge's thoughts and intentions.

Bob laughed softly. "It was you," he said as he read Scrooges eyes. "The hamper, you sent it didn't you?"

Scrooge laughed again and grabbed Bob in another bear hug as his emotions flooded over him again. This time, although he was slightly winded by Scrooges enthusiasm, Bob hugged him back and smiled, saying, "Ebenezer, I—"

Scrooge interrupted him, saying, "Shush, shush, shush! None of that, off you go Bob, go and get that office warmed up."

So Bob said no more and hurrying into his office, he knelt and quickly fitted the wheel, turning up the heat to a delicious warmth.

When Bob finally stood up, he saw Scrooge was standing in the adjoining doorway, with one hand behind his back, looking quite mischievous. With a huge grin that lit up his whole face, Scrooge produced the Christmas cracker that Fred had dropped on his desk Christmas Eve.

"Go on Bob," he challenged happily, waggling the cracker,

"PULL!"

Chapter 18: Here My Story Ends...

Scrooge was a changed man from then on. He kept his word to the Spirits and did much more besides. His enthusiasm for change was boundless as he tried to make amends for forty years of neglect, indifference, coldness, greed, jealousy, and downright misery.

To Bob, he was as good as his word and better. When Bob arrived home that first evening, after spending the day talking with Scrooge about Amy, Tim's illness and all the children, including Martha and Peter leaving school to help with Tim's expenses, he walked in looking tired, and dazed. Amy, thinking he had seen something dreadful on the way home, made him sit down and poured him a double brandy for shock. However, once Bob told Amy what had really happened, she collapsed onto a kitchen chair, grabbed the glass out of Bob's hand and downed a healthy swig herself. Bob spread the bonus on the kitchen table where he and Amy looked at it for over an hour, trying to figure out this new Scrooge.

From that day on the Cratchits no longer had to scrimp and save or worry about money and bills again, and as anyone who has ever been in that position will tell you, this was a huge weight off their minds. Hand-me-downs and make-do-and-mend became things of the past. Bob and Amy could afford to keep the children at school longer, and even send them to college or university, which meant a successful and rewarding future for everyone. Martha finally accepted the university scholarship she'd deferred, while still working part-time at the shop, and, thanks to Fred, Peter was able to secure an excellent job, which guaranteed him a proper career, excellent prospects and decent wages.

Amy Cratchit herself received an unexpected boost from Scrooge, together with a little collusion from her husband, who'd arranged for her to be out of the house for several hours one day. When she finally arrived home, totally exhausted, she saw, standing in her kitchen, with no indication of how it got there, no boxes, no packaging, no mess at all, a brand new, state of the art, dishwasher. On the front was a large bow and on top, a magnum of champagne, tied with several smiley face balloons and a card that read:

To Amy Cratchit,

Wishing you a belated merry Christmas. I hope you can see your way to forgiving a foolish old Man. Wishing you the joys of the season.

Feliz Navidad.

Ebenezer Scrooge.

Feliz Navidad, from old sourpuss? How was Amy ever going to adjust to this new Ebenezer Scrooge when he came up with surprises like this? The gorgeous dishwasher was surprising enough, but *Feliz Navidad?*

Still, though, she thought, examining the bottle, he had picked out a nice bottle of champers. It would be rude not to drink it...

... By the time Bob got home that evening, bringing a Chinese takeaway to celebrate, Amy had washed every dish in the house, drunk a quarter of the champagne, and was dancing around the kitchen to Queen's Greatest Hits. And she loved every bloody minute of it!

Scrooge completely overhauled the office, buying new equipment, modern computers, printers, a new photocopier and mobile phones for them both, all of which helped Bob's working life enormously. The old computer and printer were finally retired (Bob not in the slightest way sentimental about their demise) and productivity increased with the speed of the new computer hardware. They also connected to the internet and everything opened up for Scrooge, who would often be found, between clients, exploring the world he'd shut out for so long. He discovered social media and was busy trying to trace his old school friends from all those years ago.

For his clients, Scrooge completely changed his business practices too. Out with the old ways, in with the new. He still offered financial services for business deals but at much lower lending rates and better, more reasonable terms than before. No more three strikes and he foreclosed. No more usury interest. Longer lending times and lower rates had the effect of increasing his business and word spread fast. Soon he had all the customers he could manage. He made Bob his partner and hired another two clerks to cope with the flourishing business.

The profits from these deals were used to help everyday people struggling with money problems and debt. Scrooge called it, the New Horizon Debt Reduction Scheme. With the help NHDRS offered, anyone could refinance and restructure their debts, so they didn't have to think about selling up, bankruptcy or bailiffs. Parents no longer sat up all night and worried about losing their homes or dreaded their children having to sleep in cars or hostels. The scheme offered one low fixed interest rate spread over months or years, so people could get back on their feet without having to struggle to make those payments. Families he helped didn't fall apart through arguments and anxiety over money. Marriages didn't crumble, kids weren't caught in the middle. The threat of losing children to family services was gone. Scrooge poured his own money into this venture and was gratified to discover this work was more satisfying than any of his other business deals.

He made a point of giving regularly to lots of charities, but always to the one he had encountered his "first Christmas" He frequently tapped every corporation, organisation, company, group or individual he had business dealings with for donations and soon became very involved. On a personal level, he sold raffle tickets, sponsored fundraisers, gave to flag days, had charity tins on his and Bob's desk, helped at car boot sales and swap meets, cooked sausages at outdoor events, collected for the jumble, made coffee, did a turn at the pub's talent night for the church's outreach program by reciting, *The Highway Man* and once, to his great alarm, held a sleeping baby.

He went out with the night van offering hot soup and warm blankets, told stories to kids while mums and dads spoke to outreach workers, distributed sleeping bags, dispensed condoms and accompanied people to hospital for treatment. He talked and he listened, used his connections to get as many donations as he could for charities when they needed it, and totally flummoxed everyone who had known him with this extraordinary change in character.

Scrooge finally got to know all the neighbours after his Boxing Day clear out. Thankfully, he was not surrounded by strangers anymore, but by friends, who he could call on and chat with. Years of loneliness were swept aside, and he never felt happier. He redecorated his apartment, got rid of the old, broken down furniture, put light globes in each room and laid new carpets, making sure it was more comfortable to live in, not just for himself but for the increasing number of visitors who now came to see him.

To his delight, he also adopted one of Lucky's puppies, who turned out to be a brown and white border collie cross he named, Spirit. When Fred asked him why the name, Scrooge simply said because it meant a great deal to him. Spirit continued to teach him about loving and caring, about wanting to do something for someone rather than having to do it and wanting to do it just because you loved them, not because you wanted something in return. Spirit went everywhere with him, slept on his bed, and on weekends he would take her to parks and commons and let her run and play while he chatted to other dog owners…

…And made friends.

To Fred and Kate, he became a father figure and best friend. Scrooge was determined to repay the debt he owed to his sister, and so his relationship with them grew stronger every day. What began as a friendship became something deeper when, eighteen months later, Fred and Kate had their first child, a little girl. They called her Francesca after her grandmother, and Theresa after her great-grandmother, and said to Scrooge nothing would make them happier than for him to be godfather to their precious little girl. For Ebenezer things had finally come full circle. He was to be a beloved 'grandpa' and as he held little Francesca Theresa at her baptism, he finally felt he was honouring the promise he'd made to his sister all those years ago. He knew Fan would be so happy that he could love and care for the granddaughter of the sister who had loved him so much.

One of the more amusing changes that happened occurred on the first Monday back after New Year's. Everyone who worked at the Corporate and Mutual Fidelity Bank of England was astonished when, during his usual time for checking his account, Ebenezer Scrooge strolled into the bank. Wearing a suave grey suit and a warm, friendly smile, he stood in the queue chatting happily with the other customers. When he approached the wary teller, Scrooge put his little book down on the desk saying, "Good afternoon, how are you today? I wonder, may I have a printout of my current account please?"

The entire staff had stopped what they were doing, and an expectant hush had descended as they all stared at him in open mouthed amazement. The shocked teller serving him smiled the kind of smile one gives when you're trying to keep someone calm until help arrives and hissed to his colleague to quickly get the manager.

Don't worry, despite a few early reservations on behalf of the staff, it all worked out well in the end.

BUT...The BEST NEWS I've saved for last...

All these things were wonderful of course, and a vast improvement in Scrooge's life, outlook, and of benefit to those around him. But none of it would have been as important and none of it would have meant as much if not for the one truly miraculous change that happened.

The greatest change, through the grace of God, was for Tim, whose life was saved.

I could write a long essay about the lengths Scrooge went to helping the Cratchits and Tim in his fight against leukaemia.

I could, for instance, write about how he freed up vast amounts of Bob's time, so he could be with Tim when he needed therapy, outpatient treatment or to attend appointments. Bob no longer sat at his desk worrying about his boy, trying to keep his mind on his work, waiting for Amy to text that everything was okay. Now he went with Tim, could be by his side, hold his hand and carry him home to his mother's loving arms.

Or I could say how he arranged for extra help for Amy. He engaged a laundry service that picked up dirty washing, returning it clean, ironed and folded within 24-hours. Another service took care of the heavy garden work and house maintenance that had been delayed too long. Tidying, clipping, raking, trimming, and pruning, house painting and other long-deferred household improvements. They even put the bins out, a weekly task that drove her nuts because the kids spent so long doing "one potato, two potatoes" to decide whose turn it was, she usually ended up doing it herself. A window cleaner appeared every couple of weeks, and a mobile mechanic every two months. Also Scrooge, who'd never touched a computer himself until recently, insisted on giving Amy an iPad so she could do her weekly grocery shopping online and have it delivered.

Happily waving goodbye to the weekly bunfight at Tesco's, she began to look forward to their delivery van pulling up every Friday. The driver even brought the bags right into the kitchen for her! Oh yes, she purred to Bob, she could get used to this.

Now she had more free time to spend with her other kids who had, admittedly, missed out on a lot of her attention when Tim was ill.

Additionally, she could able stay overnight at the hospital when he was very sick and needed mummy cuddles to get through the long, unhappy hours.

I could mention the holiday Scrooge arranged for all the kids, full of activities like horse riding, windsurfing and abseiling, so that Amy and Bob could get their first break away since they married. Ten days of relaxation and sightseeing in France did them both the world of good. Nonetheless, Amy did ensure she had a full supply of her little pink pills with her. There was no way, she said, that she was coming back from this holiday with anything more than a few bottles of wine and a postcard of the Eiffel Tower.

Then there are the stories that would really make you laugh, about the times Ebenezer stepped in to babysit the rest of the kids when Bob and Amy were going to be late at the hospital. He quickly learned the power of Pizza and Pepsi, and the kids, taking full advantage of their parents' absence, barraged him with questions about himself, especially young Simon, who skewered him with all the mastery of a BBC reporter, asking repeatedly why he wasn't mean anymore.

Or of his struggles trying to get Abigail to sleep, feeling a bit of a fool singing made-up lullabies, hoping she would finally nod off before he did. And when Bob and Amy eventually arrived home in the small hours, they found them both fast asleep, Abigail curled up in his arms, thumb in her mouth, head on his chest, the two of them on the sofa in front of the fire. Amy snapped a picture of that because she couldn't believe her eyes.

Perhaps I could tell you about the money he deposited in a special account, opened in Bob and Amy's name. Money, he told them, that was theirs to use as they saw fit. It didn't matter what they spent it on he said. Games, toys, tickets to the football, a girl's day at the spa, even, when Martha asked jokingly, yes, even a new car if she was tired of getting the bus. No one would question it, Scrooge said, the money was a gift, and he kept it topped up because it made him happy.

But really, all of that isn't important.

What is important is with his help, Tim got what he needed and started on the long journey to recovery. Physically, medically, mentally, holistically, all the bases were covered to give him the strength he needed to get him on the road to wellness.

He eventually beat the cancer and grew into a strong, intelligent man, full of compassion and faith.

He became an apprentice to Bob at the office, finally taking his place, and eventually, he took over running the whole business.

Tim learned everything from Scrooge about finance and always treated him like a second father. And Scrooge learned about faith from Tim and treated him like the son he wished he'd had.

And to Bob's family, he became a good friend.

Soon after that fateful night, he visited Jacobs grave, where he stood for a long time, thinking of his friend. Whispering a thankful prayer, he knew that now, he must do what he could to help his old partner.

Setting up a charity in Jacobs name, Scrooge used Marley's money to buy a recently closed infirmary and turned it into a crisis accommodation and medical centre. A charitable trust was formed, staff were engaged, and **"The Marley"** opened its doors to anyone who needed support, medical attention, a safe place to stay for a few days, or just somewhere to go to get a hot meal, a shower, or clean clothes. With the motto of ***"Non: sed per gratiam Domini"*** it was soon financed by several companies searching for a worthy charity, and ways to reduce their corporate taxes. Whatever their motives, it didn't matter. That they gave was important, nothing else.

Scrooge was known from then on as a good boss, a good friend and good man to know. Certainly, as good as anyone in the entire city. Of course, those who'd known him before laughed and said, don't worry, it was a just a phase the old screw was going through, the real Scrooge would soon be back. Everyone had an idea about what had changed him. Some kept their ideas to themselves, simply happy to see the positive changes in the man. Some gossiped, speculating that perhaps he'd had a stroke that altered his personality, and there were those ill-mannered individuals who flat out questioned him about the sudden change as if it were entitled to an explanation.

I'm sure he'd never admit it, but I think it did make him a teensy weensy bit proud in the face of those backbiters who insisted "the old screw" had knocked a screw loose, maintaining that this was the sole explanation why he was suddenly behaving in a very un-Scrooge-like way! He never gave a response, so people made up all sorts of ridiculous stories, which they had a good laugh about.

He let them all laugh; it made no difference to him. He knew the truth, and he knew that no matter what changes happened to anyone, there were always those gossip mongers and rumour merchants who would inevitably

276

poke fun. He even had a chuckle over a couple of stories himself. The gossip claiming he was abducted by aliens was his favourite.

He never saw any of the three Spirit's again. He remembered them very well and occasionally thought about that night of ghostly visits. He wondered if they could see the changes he'd made and the promises he kept. But perhaps they already knew.

He thought too about his friend in the Spirit world, and while he didn't know for certain if his redemption led to Jacobs release from suffering, for there had been no mention of it, either by Jacob or by any of the Spirits, Scrooge believed the ghosts who had helped him would surely help Marley, and lighten his burden, bringing his penance at last to an end. Ebenezer hoped and prayed his old friend now rested in peace.

Every Christmas Eve, Scrooge would light four candles and put them in his windows, so their brightness shone out into the dark streets. One candle each for the Three Spirits and one for Jacob Marley. He would sit and watch the flames dance in the darkness and think about that night and thank God for the messengers who had vouchsafed his life in this world, and his soul in the next.

So, did Scrooge *ever* talk about his night of Spirit visitors? Honestly, at the time, he thought only Bella would believe him, but he never tried to contact her, other than asking Rose to pass on that message for him. He knew he didn't have the right to invade Bella's happy family to tell his story, but he also knew she'd realise something wonderful had happened and be happy for him.

Later though, as he learned to live in the world again, he may have mentioned it, just once...

From then on Scrooge carried the message of peace and love, fairness and understanding, tolerance and acceptance with him and in his heart all through the year, just as he had promised the ghost of Christmas Future. And between you and me, there wasn't anyone who could say he didn't celebrate Christmas joyously and well, as good as anyone else alive. Wouldn't it be great if that could be said about us all? How different the world would be!

The most surprising outcome of his night of ghostly revelations was given to Scrooge himself by the three Spirits, though it did take a little while to manifest. Scrooge lived on to a ripe old age, celebrating Christmas Day every year with Fred and Kate, Bob and Amy and their growing families, which expanded as the children married and had children of their own. Martha was the first Cratchit to wed. She married Jacob, who'd delivered the hamper on Christmas Day all those years ago.

Peter and Belinda followed a few years later, when they had a dual wedding, the brother and sister marrying a brother and sister, making their children double first cousins. Nothing unusual in the gypsy community. Confusing, yes, but unusual? No.

After the years passed and his hearing grew duller, his hair white, and his eyes closed earlier in the evening, he sat with everyone at Christmas dinner and made his, now traditional, after-dinner speech, where he referred to his other self from all those years ago. The mean, miserable, rude, and rotten Scrooge that only the oldest family members remembered. Many jokes were told about him as he used to be, and they all laughed and chipped in a comment here and there. However, Sally, Ebenezer's nine-year-old "niece" grew more cross with every word and piped up seriously, "I think you're all being horrible! I don't think Uncle Buzz could ever be like that because he's too nice," and picking up her glass of lemonade she determinedly got to her feet and raising her glass in a toast said, "To Uncle Buzz!"

Everyone followed suit, and stood around the table, glasses in hand as they proclaimed in unison, "To Uncle Buzz!" Watching them all, this group of people who'd become so close, he couldn't help remembering the first time he'd seen a Cratchit toast him. That day when he was with the ghost of Christmas Present. He smiled and looked around the room full of people. Yes, he knew he'd been given a wonderful gift and one he'd come so close to never having. The gift of family and friends.

And me? Oh, I'm mentioned in this story, along with many other people who witnessed the changes in Scrooge's life. But I'm not going to tell you who I am. You'll just have to work it out for yourself.

So finally, at the very end of my story, I'll give the last word to Tim. Tim, who lived so much on faith and hope that he had enough left over to help someone he'd never met. Was he also sent to guide Scrooge on his path to redemption? We'll never know. But his faith was strong, and his heart was hopeful, and those are two formidable weapons in the face of bitterness and sorrow. Without even speaking to him, he planted the seed of change in Scrooge's heart, where it grew and blossomed into a new and happier life. So, as he said that day, many years ago...

God bless us all, Every one of us.

The End

Acknowledgements

I'd like to thank Toni Smyth for her extensive efforts in editing my words to bring them to a semblance of sanity and sense that I couldn't have achieved on my own.

Also, to Ian Hooper of The Book Reality Experience for helping me in bringing the finished product to publication.

To my family and friends for all their love and support whilst I pounded away on a keyboard realising my dream and of course, as I mentioned in the dedication, to Charles. Thanks for gifting the world Ebenezer, Marley and all the rest of your wonderful characters. Knowing how much you liked the idea of spirits, I trust you are reading over my shoulder right now and are pleased with my efforts.

Oh, and a huge thank you to Taylor Swift. Yes, the singer, whom my daughter wants to thank for being her harbour of calm and serenity during my difficult creative process.

About the Author

Jacqueline Maylor was born in Wigan, England and, in 1974, at the age of ten, emigrated to Western Australia.

She knew virtually nothing about Australia at the time, other than it was the home of an extremely intelligent marsupial who could communicate the direst state of affairs with just a few clicks, or anything about Australians themselves, except that there were apparently seven of them. In fact she thought she was actually relocating to Scotland when her parents said they were all going to live in Perth.

The youngest of three daughters in a family with gypsy heritage, she consequently grew up as a socialist and is gratified that her extensive list of qualifications begin, and end, with the 400 metres free style, a typing speed of 220 words per minute and a driver's license.

Her greatest achievements in life are her two beautiful daughters, Rosie and Kat

Jacqueline now lives in Bunbury, Western Australia with her four cats, two dogs and a ferret. There she's fulfilling her long held dream of living in a seaside town.

She has a lifetime love of history, especially all things Egyptian and her ambition is to explore the burial sites of the pharaohs. She imagines she'll make a great international traveller and doesn't think her dislike of chilli, coriander or tripe will limit her in anyway.

Jacqueline is also a sculptor, a photographer and is proficient with a Dowsing Pendulum. However, unlike in the story, she says it's not very helpful when forecasting lotto numbers.

A Christmas Carol (The 21st Century Tale) is her debut novel.

www.ingramcontent.com/pod-product-compliance
Lightning Source LLC
Chambersburg PA
CBHW010537100726
47903CB00011B/3031